THE SILVER FALCON

Also by Katia Fox:

The Copper Sign

The Golden Throne (forthcoming)

THE SILVER FALCON

KATIA FOX

Translated by Aubrey Botsford

amazon crossing

Printed in the United States of America

The Silver Falcon by Katia Fox was first published in 2008 by Bastei Lübbe
in Köln, Germany, as *Der silberne Falke*. Translated from the German by
Aubrey Botsford. First published in English in 2013 by AmazonCrossing.

Published by AmazonCrossing
PO Box 400818
Las Vegas, NV 89140

ISBN-13: 9781611090369
ISBN-10: 1611090369
Library of Congress Control Number: 2013900606

For MaPa

Author's Note

Dear Reader,

I am delighted to present my second novel, and with it I invite you to accompany me to the twelfth century. Allow yourself to be transported back to the fascinating world of knights and nobles and their favorite pastime: falconry. If you have read *The Copper Sign*, I'm sure you will be glad to hear more about William, the swordsmith's son. If you don't yet know *The Copper Sign*, I warmly recommend it.

Do you like history? Would you like to peep behind the curtain for a view of the novel from behind the scenes? If so, don't miss the Closing Remarks at the end.

Now, make yourself comfortable and follow me…

With best wishes,

Katia Fox

Prologue

Prologue

In the days when gods still lived on Mount Olympus, Hera gave birth to a boy and named him Hephaestus. When she saw that the child's feet were deformed, she was ashamed of him and tossed him off Olympus. The boy plummeted down toward the sea, but instead of being smashed against the jagged cliffs, he was caught by Thetis and Eurynome. They were the daughters of Oceanus, god of the sea, who had also raised Hera. The two sisters kept the boy with them, hiding him in a grotto for many years.

Hephaestus grew up and learned to be a blacksmith, using the volcano as a natural forge. He fashioned fine jewelry, gorgeous palaces with golden maidservants, and exquisite, sharp swords for Achilles, the brave warrior. And yet Hephaestus was not happy; he desired revenge on his mother. He forged a golden throne and had it brought to her. When Hera sat in it, she was immediately gripped by golden shackles. No one could free her, so the gods decided to summon Hephaestus back to Olympus. He refused. Ares tried to bring him back by force and failed, but Dionysus managed to get him drunk and lead him back to the circle of the gods on Olympus.

And so Hephaestus, the god of blacksmiths, allowed himself to be reconciled, and he released his mother from the shackles of her throne. And it seems he forged some very special arrows for Eros…

Apprenticeship

Near Saint Edmundsbury, October 1184

L ook at it go!" cried William with delight, peering open-mouthed into the radiant blue autumn sky. In high spirits, he set off in pursuit of the bird. Never letting it out of his sight, he ran across the big meadow. Suddenly he tripped over a molehill and fell flat on his belly. He sat up in the grass and examined his palms, wincing. They were scraped raw and burned like fire.

Despite his best efforts, tears welled up in William's eyes. He sniffed noisily, blinked for a moment, and then licked the dirt and droplets of blood off his hands before checking his knees. They hurt, too, but at least they were not bleeding. And his wool chausses remained undamaged, too. William breathed a sigh of relief. Nobody would find out about his clumsiness and tease him for it!

He stood up and rested his weight on his right foot. It hurt more than usual, but he gritted his teeth and took a couple of steps. There was no way he was going to let a sprained ankle get the better of him. Ever since he could walk, he had been doing battle with the malformed foot he had been born with. Determined to pay no further heed to the searing pain, he clapped the dust off his clothes and pulled himself together. Although he did not feel the slightest desire to return to his swordsmith mother's workshop and the chores he loathed, he decided, with a heavy heart, to head home. He looked up again at the place where he had last seen the long, narrow wings and forked tail of the bird he had identified as a red kite.

"Jesus Maria!" he cried.

A falcon had attacked the kite, and the two birds were dropping to earth like stones.

William set off at a run, forgetting the pain in his ankle. His heart was pounding so hard, he could hear the blood rushing through his ears.

The frantic beating of the birds' wings was audible from a distance. William stopped and watched, breathless, as they fought fiercely. The falcon that had attacked the kite was almost completely white and exceptionally large. William had never seen one like it, and yet it was certainly a falcon: he could tell by the shape of its nostrils. He looked more closely and gasped in awe: it was so beautiful. The small golden bell on its foot tinkled brightly every time it moved. Slender leather thongs dangled from its legs. It had been trained and must have escaped from its master.

William sighed thoughtfully. He had been out and about for a good while that day, but he had not seen a single hunting party. William knew the kite's sharp beak could be dangerous for the rare white falcon, and he ran his hand through his hair anxiously. No one else was going to come to the falcon's aid, so it was up to him to save the magnificent beast. He hesitated for a fraction of a second, then started running. The falcon's beak could injure him, too, and even a small scratch could be a death sentence, so he could not simply put himself between the birds. William remembered the knife his mother had made for him a few years before. He was tremendously proud of it. It had brightly colored wavy lines on the blade and was one of the few presents she had ever given him. William always carried it, guarding it like treasure. Just two days ago, he had given it a thorough sharpening. Rapidly drawing it from its sheath, he seized a forked branch and cut it loose. As he hurried toward the two combatants, he stripped off the leaves.

The falcon seemed somewhat weakened now, but it would not release its prey. And the kite fought on, dead tired as it was.

Slowly, William approached the two birds. When he got within reach, he attempted to hold the kite's head to the ground using the forked stick, while trying not to endanger the white falcon. But the kite defended itself fiercely. William sprang back, impressed, and the stick slipped off.

If you want to save the falcon, you can't be such a frightened rabbit, he thought, cursing himself. He screwed up his courage and, with his third attempt, managed to catch the kite's head with the forked stick and hold it to the ground. The falcon saw its chance and delivered the coup de grâce with a powerful bite to the neck.

Once the kite had stopped moving, William threw the stick aside and fell to the ground a short distance away. His hands were damp and shaky, and his heart was racing. He was sorry about the kite, for it, too, was a marvelous bird. But the falcon, with its magnificent off-white plumage, was something quite special and worthy of this intervention. Given the choice, he would have saved both birds. As the falcon stripped the feathers off its prey and filled its crop greedily with the flesh, William examined it more closely. How wonderful it must be to own such a remarkable bird, he thought, falling into a daydream in which he was a falconer training such a specimen.

When the falcon had finally had enough of the carcass, William noticed it was favoring its left leg. It had obviously been hurt in the battle.

"I'll take you with me and take care of you," William whispered tenderly. He felt a deep happiness at this stroke of fate. He stood up slowly. The falcon would not allow itself to be caught just like that, so William took off his cloak, crawled over, and covered the bird with it. He wrapped it up so he could lift it carefully. As he did so, he was careful to keep clear of its razor-sharp talons, which projected from the wool like dangerous weapons. He carried the bird respectfully in his outstretched arms. It seemed to get heavier with every step, but William's joy at his extraordinary catch buoyed him so he felt as if he were walking on air. His decision to keep the falcon was firm, even if his mother would not accept it. She would undoubtedly say the bird would distract him from his work in the smithy, and she would probably be right, for the work there quite simply did not suit him. He would have to find a place for the falcon where his mother would never find it.

William sighed from the bottom of his soul. The falcon was the fulfillment of a dream that had begun three winters before, when he had been permitted to spend an utterly wonderful afternoon with William Marshal and his falcon, Princess.

Marshal was one of the most important knights in England, and he had been young Henry II's tutor until the latter's death. He was not only an exceptionally impressive man but also a favored customer of William's mother. Her swords were famous far beyond the borders of East Anglia, and she counted several powerful barons among her clients. Some were friendly; others less so. Marshal, whose visit to the smithy that day had been his second, had paid considerably more attention to William than on his first visit, when he had hardly paid him any attention at all.

He had been particularly friendly that afternoon, repeatedly placing his hand affectionately on William's shoulder and calling him "my boy." While waiting for the dulled edge of his sword to be made good, he gave William, no doubt out of boredom, an exhaustive account of how to tame falcons—"manning," he called it—and described in some detail how one trained a falcon to hunt. William was even allowed to hold Princess for a while and was praised by Marshal because he showed himself to be so adept. William had been filled with overwhelming pride that day. He had been eight years old at the time, and birds of prey had been his great, albeit secret, passion ever since.

From then on, he had observed the falconers of the area and watched the noble hunting parties that met near the smithy from time to time. William was eleven now, and he knew a good deal about falconry, about as much as it was possible to learn without attracting attention. How could he possibly miss an opportunity to capture and keep such a wonderful bird for himself?

Marshal, whom he had warmly admired since that day, would certainly be impressed, thought William proudly, standing up straight. A smile played on his lips as he imagined what it would be like to own his own falcon. A warm glow of happiness came over him and his pace quickened.

When William reached the smithy a short while later, he looked around anxiously. The yard was deserted. William breathed more easily. The others must be inside the house or in the workshop; there was only Graybeard, lying lazily in the autumn sun, warming his old bones. When the old dog noticed him, he wagged his tail limply but did not even lift his head off the ground.

William crossed the yard swiftly. He must not be spotted! He glanced around quickly. To begin with, he would house the falcon in the woodshed. Since it was his job to replenish the woodpile, hardly anyone else came here. Once in front of the storehouse, William carefully slid the heavy bolt aside with his elbow, opened the door with his foot, slipped through, and closed it behind him, finally feeling relief.

Inside, it was almost dark. The few rays of sunlight that penetrated the chinks in the plank walls bathed the interior in diffuse light. William sat down, straddling a stack of wood.

"Let me have a look at your leg," he murmured, not really knowing what he should do first. The bird was still hidden beneath his cloak, and he was trying to clasp it gently between his thighs when the door opened with a scrape.

"William?"

He recognized his stepfather's warm, deep voice, but William did not answer. His heart was in his mouth, and sweat spread across his forehead. He hardly dared breathe, as if this would render him invisible.

Perhaps he'll go away, he thought hopefully, immediately cursing himself as a fool. He must have missed Isaac outside, and Isaac must have noticed him hurrying across the yard with his strange bundle.

William turned around. The sun streaming in through the door blinded him. He blinked and feared for a moment that he would sneeze.

"What are you doing in there?" asked Isaac in a friendly manner, walking in and closing the door almost noiselessly behind him.

It seemed to William that the blood had frozen in his veins, and his shirt was now like ice frozen to his back. "Nothing," he lied, but he did not feel comfortable doing so. He loved Isaac like a real father, and lying went against his conscience. So he avoided looking into Isaac's eyes. The falcon's feet began to scrabble in William's lap.

"What are you hiding there?" Isaac looked over his stepson's shoulder and pointed at the cloak with his good arm. His voice took on a sharper tone. "You haven't been stealing, have you?"

"No, Father!" William raised his head immediately. "Truly I haven't!" It was too late to keep the falcon a secret from Isaac. Now he could only try to make him an ally.

"I…I found a falcon. Its foot is injured." William was annoyed that his voice sounded a little thin. After all, he hadn't done anything wrong.

"Let me see," Isaac ordered.

"We'd better leave the cover on until I've looked more closely at its foot. If it sees us, it'll struggle even more," William explained eagerly. "But you could help me hold it, so I can look."

Isaac came closer and stroked his stepson's brown hair. "If you think I can…" He held up the stump of his arm, sighing. A few years before, his left hand and half his forearm had been amputated because of an infected wound. It had taken him a long time to come to terms with this mutilation.

"Of course you can." William showed Isaac what he needed to do, then examined the falcon. "Its leg is bleeding!" he said, looking anxiously at Isaac. "We should bind it the way Rose did Marie's arm when she fell off her horse," William went on, thinking about Rose, the house's benevolent angel. She had brought up not only William but also Isaac's daughters by his first marriage, Agnes and Marie, while William's mother, Ellenweore, took care of Isaac's smithy. William took one of the canvas strips his mother used to wrap scabbards and tore it in two. He dabbed at the blood with the first, then wound the second around the bird's leg.

"It would be best if your mother didn't come here just now," Isaac observed while William was doing this. "If you want to keep the bird for a while, you'd better find another hiding place for it. And come to the smithy soon, before Ellenweore misses you," he suggested. "I'm going there now." He nodded conspiratorially and left the shed.

William breathed a sigh of relief. Isaac wouldn't give him away! He put the falcon down on a stack of wood, waited for a moment, and removed the cloak.

The falcon shook itself and protested loudly.

"Shh!" William put his finger to his lips, alarmed. "Be quiet! If anyone hears you and gives us away..." he whispered, warning his new friend. He took a couple of steps back.

"Isaac's right," he murmured sadly. "I have to go to the smithy or she'll scold me. But don't worry. I'll come back soon—you just have to keep quiet in the meantime."

That night, his mother was due to harden off the swords she had made in the past few weeks. This was done by quenching the heated iron in a basin of water. It was important that the preparatory work was blemish-free and that the blade did not become brittle because of the sudden cooling. Like most swordsmiths, William's mother would harden swords only under the total darkness of a new moon. For the whole day leading up to this important task, which determined whether a blade would be good or useless, she was usually tense and irritable. It would be unwise, therefore, to aggravate her ill humor.

William approached the falcon cautiously and stroked its breast with his finger. The bird's plumage tensed, and it spread its wings indignantly.

William knew what this meant, and he lowered his hand. It was afraid. It had to get used to him. Anyone who thought birds of prey hunted with men because they were dependent was mistaken. What falcons saw in a falconer was, to begin with, an enemy; later, at best, they saw a useful companion who provided the best food. But they never really took the falconer into their hearts. And yet William was driven by the desire to become a falconer. The birds' wariness of people made them very difficult to tame, and it was considered a high art to train them to return to their master consistently, despite the freedom they tasted with every flight. Marshal had described it to him so vividly that William's highest dream was to train the finest falcons in England. It was a perfect ambition for the bastard son of a knight, William had decided, ever since he discovered by chance that his father truly was a knight. He had been unable to find out more, try as he might, for his mother remained stubbornly tight-lipped on the subject. William sighed and thought about the wild sparrow hawk he had captured the previous summer, with the aim of manning and training it. Unfortunately, the bird had disappeared forever into the heavens on its first free flight. For this reason, William was determined to spend sufficient time letting this falcon get used to him before he allowed it to fly.

"William?"

He was startled out of his thoughts. Although his mother's voice was muffled, he could hear her impatience. William held his breath.

Ellenweore called out again.

William peered out through a gap in the wall. His mother was standing with her back to the shed, shaking her head. "Where has that boy got to?" he heard her grumble, and then she strode off.

As soon as he could be sure the coast was clear, William slipped out, closing the door carefully and sliding the bolt back into position. He ran to the smithy as fast as he could. His mother would scold him for being late again. In a way, he understood her: she desperately wanted him to love swordcraft as she did. Hoping to avoid an argument with her, he opened the door to the workshop just wide enough for him to squeeze through. I hope she doesn't notice I'm not wearing my cloak…The thought struck him like a thunderbolt, for he had left the garment in the woodshed.

The smoke from the fire left a bitter taste on William's tongue. How could his mother love her work in the smithy so much? He shook his head pensively. Every day in the workshop was like every other: dark, dirty, stifling. William held his breath, closed his eyes, and conjured up the marvelous scents of nature: the wonderful, earthy smell of leaves and moss released from the humid soil by the autumn rains; the clear, clean smell of snow in winter; the fragrance of flowers and dry grass perfumed by the warmth of the summer sun. Outside in the open air, every season was wonderful. William smiled briefly. Summer's heat did not scare him, and strong winds did not freeze him to the bone, though they might try. Icy cold, the kind that numbed one's fingers and toes, held no terrors; rain, though often a nuisance, was not an enemy but mostly a friend, as he well knew, indispensable for survival in nature. To be exposed to the forces of nature meant, for William, to feel alive, though he was always glad for a warm bedchamber at night.

He gasped for air suddenly, like a fish on dry land. He could not keep holding his breath forever! With some difficulty, he suppressed a cough. He tried to reach his place without being noticed, but his mother had already spotted him.

"You're the last one at the anvil again!" she rebuked him.

"I was just…" muttered William, exchanging a quick glance with Isaac. It occurred to him that he had not even prepared a plausible excuse for his tardiness.

"Go to your place," his mother ordered brusquely.

William dawdled on his way to his station and reluctantly began to work.

"Haven't I told you before to oil your tools and tidy them away?" she shouted at his back.

William turned and nodded, but rather than look at her he stared at an oily stain on his shoe. How he hated this work!

"Well? And is one single pair of pincers in its place?" Her voice rose menacingly.

"No, Mother." William shuffled his feet on the beaten dirt floor. When she was in a bad mood, it was better not to offer a flimsy excuse.

"Don't tell me you forgot again!"

"No, Mother."

After his morning's work, he had run to the meadow instead of carrying out his assigned tasks. He simply did not see why he should sit in the workshop alone and take care of the tools while the others could rest or do as they pleased before they commenced the forge work.

"I'll do it now," William said, sighing audibly. After all, he was not allowed to help with the hardening of the swords anyway. Since he was permitted only to watch, he could just as easily oil the tools and put them away while doing so.

"When I give you a job to do, you're to do it at once and not put it off till later, understood? Just like the other apprentices!" His mother stared daggers at him and then took a deep breath, adding in a slightly conciliatory tone, "Now pass me the wolf-jaw tongs. I've lots to do before I can get started with the hardening."

William spun around helplessly, looking for the tool.

"Get on with it," his mother urged him. "The iron's getting too hot!"

William could hear two of the apprentices whispering behind him, and he sensed their gleeful glances like needles in his back. He felt the heat rise to his face as he flushed with shame. He would have found so much pleasure in throttling them. Instead, he grabbed the nearest pincers and handed them to his mother.

"For heaven's sake, child! I said the wolf-jaw tongs, not the round-jaw ones!" she scolded as the iron in the fire overheated and began to throw off sparks. "When I wasn't even half your age, I could already tell all the tools apart."

William drew himself up to his full height, angrily filling his slender chest with air. Because he was small for his age, people often thought he was younger than he was. But he was certainly old enough to know every tool in the smithy, as well as how to use them. But tongs, burins, and hammers—these things did not interest him in the slightest. Round-jaw and wolf-jaw tongs were almost identical, apart from the shallow serrations on the latter. Unless you looked closely, they were easily confused, and he just hadn't looked. William rolled his eyes. He really didn't have the slightest wish to become a smith.

Ellenweore wiped her face with the back of her hand, leaving a broad streak of soot around her mouth. William giggled. The streak looked just like a beard. He struggled with all his might not to laugh.

"You should be ashamed of yourself, instead of grinning," Ellenweore went on, now furious. "You really are good for nothing."

His mother's hurtful words cut him to the quick, but the last thing William wanted was for the other apprentices to notice. He bit his lower lip and stared at the ground, focusing on a small piece of hammer scale. Once he had composed himself, he looked up again, but Ellenweore had turned back to the anvil.

"You poor thing." Adam mouthed the words silently behind Ellenweore's back, his expression mocking. He was the oldest and cheekiest of the three apprentices. Smirking, he poked Brad, the guildmaster's son.

"Luke, give me the wolf-jaw tongs," Ellenweore ordered the youngest apprentice. She raised her eyebrows as Luke, who had been learning the craft only since the beginning of the year, handed her the right tongs. She looked reproachfully at her son.

William knew he had disappointed her yet again, even though she ought to be proud of him.

"I hate the smithy, and the stupid tongs, too. I don't need them because I shall never be a smith!" he blurted out defiantly.

Ellenweore looked at him in astonishment.

William glared at her, turned on his heel, and rushed out of the workshop without another word.

As the door latched shut behind him, he took a deep breath.

October's glorious sunshine and light breezes had stripped the dry leaves from the trees and piled them up in rustling heaps. A gust of wind swept them about the yard in miniature whirlwinds, as if they were dancing a lively round. But even the sight of this was not enough to lift William's spirits. In search of a little affection and security, he went over to Graybeard, who was still lying in the same position in the yard. He knelt down beside his old friend and pressed his cheek against the dog's rough gray fur, stroking behind the animal's ears.

"I can't do anything right as far as she's concerned." William was still upset. He plucked a stray twig from the dog's hairy chops.

Graybeard looked at him with devotion, his left and right eyebrows twitching alternately.

"And it's not even what I want," William growled stubbornly. "I'm going to be a falconer."

The dog whimpered, suddenly uneasy, and rose to his feet despite the obvious pain it caused. William listened, too. He could hear horses' hooves approaching quickly. William stood up as the first rider burst into the yard holding a banner. The bright-red cloth, with its three lions passant in gold, fluttered proudly in the autumn wind. Every child in England knew whose colors these were. The continued clattering of hooves indicated that many horses were approaching the smithy. Before the man could address him, William ran off, the quarrel with his mother immediately forgotten. He rushed to the smithy, tore open the door, and called excitedly into the workshop, "The king! Mother, the king!"

After a few blinks, his eyes adapted to the darkness inside and he saw that his mother's cheeks had turned red—presumably from joy. William knew how deeply she wished that King Henry might order swords from her.

"At last," she gasped, visibly relieved, awkwardly pushing an unruly lock of rust-red hair back beneath her pale linen bonnet. She wiped both hands on her long leather apron before readying herself to go out.

"Wait." Isaac grabbed her arm. "You have a big fat streak of soot around your mouth. It looks like a little beard. No wonder the boy couldn't stop laughing." He licked the corner of his right sleeve and affectionately wiped the black stripe off his wife's face.

As Ellenweore left the smithy, she glanced at her son. Along with happy expectancy, William thought he also saw forgiveness in her expression, and he was relieved.

Isaac put his right arm around William's shoulders in a friendly manner, hiding his left arm to conceal the stump. He nodded to the smiths to indicate that they should follow him outside.

The evening sun hung over the horizon like a glowing ball, as if it, too, had turned red with pleasure at the king's visit. It bathed the yard with its soft light, glittering off the chain mail tunics, weapons, and silver harnesses, making the knights look like figures of legend. This dreamlike sight enchanted William and confirmed that afternoon's intimation that this was a rather special day, one he would never forget.

The king, whom William recognized at once from the insignia on his horsecloth, had broad shoulders, a powerful chest that emphasized the cut of his clothing, and the beginnings of a slight paunch. Despite his decidedly advanced age—he was about fifty—he remained an impressive and stately figure. The tonsure-like bare patch on the top of his head was wreathed with light-red hair whose brilliant hue was increasingly dulled by streaks of gray. His cheeks were clean shaven, and his skin looked leathery and weather beaten. His round eyes looked out at the world severely but above all alertly. The deep vertical clefts etched in his brow revealed an eternal doubter. Over his fairly plain hunting clothes of fine moss-green fabric, Henry wore a short woolen cloak trimmed with ermine. As William knew from stories his mother had told him, Henry's preference for short cloaks as a young man, at a time when cloaks were still worn long, had earned him the nickname Curtmantle.

Ellenweore had often talked at the table about Henry II and his dead son, Henry the so-called Young King. Eleanor of Aquitaine, King Henry's wife, had previously been married to King Louis VII of France. After the annulment of her marriage to Louis, she had brought all her lands with her, making Henry an extremely powerful man, though at the time he was only Duke of Normandy and not yet king. William's mother loved describing how Henry's coronation had ended years of anarchy and war. Stephen, the previous king, and his cousin, the Empress Matilda, had fought each other bitterly for the throne of England. But since Stephen had no heir, he had adopted Matilda's son Henry and named him as his successor. Thirty years had passed since then, and Henry had brought peace and prosperity to England. Although they feared his notorious fits of rage and his severity, the English still loved their king.

As well as daughters, Henry's wife had given him four healthy sons, so the succession was assured. Eleanor was a little older than her husband, but she was blessed with great beauty and exceptional intelligence, and they had been a happy couple for many years. At some point, however, the king had turned to other women. The embittered Eleanor had withdrawn from her husband and skillfully exploited the princes' hunger for power to wreak her revenge. On several occasions, she had spurred on her sons to rebel against their own father, until the king felt he had no choice but to lock up his disobedient wife to keep her from further intrigues.

William could only stare at the king. His mother said the queen must have loved him very much, if she now hated him so. Could that be right?

A large number of lightly armed knights and their squires had gathered close behind the king. The dog handlers waited a little farther off, their lead dogs sniffing curiously and straining at their leashes. The younger hunt assistants put their heads together and giggled. As soon as they thought they were unobserved, they began play fighting. The falconers, by contrast, stood erect and silent on the fringes. They radiated pride and elegance, with the noble birds on their slightly outstretched fists.

When he saw them, William forgot everything else around him.

The smiths, meanwhile, had doffed their leather caps respectfully and were bowing deeply.

Ellenweore, who was standing a little in front of the others, as well as Rose and the housemaids, curtsied, their demurring eyes cast toward the ground.

William alone continued to stare openmouthed at the falconers. How stately and elegant they looked. It was not until Isaac gave him a less-than-gentle shove that he closed his mouth and bowed. He watched the beautifully dressed knights out of the corners of his eyes. Their horses pranced and steamed in the damp air of the autumn evening. For a moment, he wondered whether his father might be among them. Was he in the king's service, or was he long since dead?

"Which one of you is the swordsmith woman?" asked Henry. His powerful voice sounded rather ungracious.

"That's me, sire, at your service." Ellenweore spoke clearly, though her repeated curtsy looked a little awkward.

Henry frowned down at her. "I hear you made a very fine sword for my eldest son—God rest his soul." The king glanced up at the sky briefly and crossed himself.

William knew from his mother that the young Henry had died more than a year before. William thought he saw in the king's eyes not only resolute majesty but also grief for a dead son.

"May he rest in peace," murmured Ellenweore, likewise crossing herself.

"The sword was called Runedur, was it not?"

"Yes, sire." Ellenweore looked up at him. Her small smile showed that she was flattered.

William grew warm with pride beneath his child's smock, though it was by no means hot. Tiny droplets of perspiration trickled down his temples. Ellenweore was surely the most famous swordsmith in all England. Would the king himself have come to her otherwise?

"Good, good," said the king dismissively, "but I have not come here about the sword."

"If not with a sword, how can I be of service, sire?" Her voice did not betray the slightest tremor.

Despite his best efforts, William's face fell. He marveled at his mother's composure. She must be much more disappointed than he was.

"My most precious falcon has escaped," the king growled, so sharply that some of the bystanders started.

William felt faint, and his face began to burn, as if he had been standing too close to the forge. The falcon belonged to the king! The words had an intoxicating effect. As if in a dream, he stood up.

"Is it, perhaps…this big?" he asked hesitantly, demonstrating with his hands the approximate height of the bird he had found.

The king's companions looked at him with astonishment, and so did the smiths, shaking their heads in disbelief at William's impertinence.

"White, with light-brown spots?" William went on, unperturbed.

"Have you seen her?"

The king's horse pranced restively as Henry sat up in the saddle.

William nodded a little diffidently.

"Where? When? Speak up, boy!"

William glanced briefly at the shed. "It's in there, sire."

The king snorted with disbelief and began to dismount. Suddenly there was movement among his retinue. Each of his men wanted to dismount first, as it was impolite to sit on a horse while the king did not. Henry seized the hawking glove that hung from his saddle and went up to William amid angry mutterings.

His legs are as bowed as a Saracen's saber, William thought, still a little intimidated. The king's every step looked as though it brought him pain, and suddenly William felt a strange bond with this royal figure. Henry did not wear gloves when riding, so his powerful hands were covered with calluses, and his fingernails were as black as a charcoal burner's.

"Lead on, boy," he commanded, grabbing William by the shoulder and pushing him toward the door as if expecting an ambush.

When the king entered the shed, the falcon spread its wings.

Henry smiled fondly. "It's all right, Blanchpenny," he said soothingly, approaching the falcon slowly. He stroked its back, cautiously probing its wings and tail feathers to make sure they were undamaged.

William was amazed by how tenderly the king's large, horny hands performed this task.

"His foot was bleeding, sire. I dressed it," William explained, although Henry had not asked him to speak.

"Her," the king corrected him, though without rebuking William for his improper behavior.

William looked at him, puzzled. "I beg your pardon, sire?"

"Not *his* foot but *her* foot," Henry explained, baring his teeth in an attempt at a friendly smile. "This is a lady! A tiercel, which is what we call a male falcon, is about a third smaller than a female," he continued, inspecting the falcon's leg more closely. "This probably happened when you caught her."

William was not sure whether this was a statement or a question, but nevertheless he blurted out, "Oh no," and then hastily added, "sire." He continued. "She attacked a red kite and hurt herself."

"A red kite? Well done, Blanchpenny," said the king, praising his falcon.

"She fought fiercely, sire, but the kite was very strong," William explained hoarsely. "I helped her and then discovered that her leg was hurt. I couldn't leave her to fend for herself. So I brought her here."

"Well, well." The king smiled. "That means you saved her."

William felt the blood rushing to his head with pride and embarrassment. "Believe me, sire, I would have nursed her back to health."

"And then kept her, perhaps?"

Henry sounded a little angry, but William thought it wiser not to respond, so he changed the subject. "I've never seen a falcon like her. Is she a gyrfalcon?"

This time Henry smiled genuinely and pulled on his gauntlet. "Yes, my boy, she is the most valuable gyrfalcon I have ever owned, for gyrfalcons with white plumage are extremely rare and therefore costly. You seem like a clever lad," he complimented William, clapping him on the shoulder. "Out you go now, though. I'll come out soon."

This time, William obeyed without hesitation. Everyone stared at him expectantly, except for Ellenweore, who did not even glance at him. How he would have loved to see the same pride in her eyes that he felt in his heart. But he waited in vain for her to turn toward him.

It was not long before the king emerged from the shed. When the knights spotted the gyrfalcon, they applauded; the muffled sound of their leather gloves did not frighten the bird. They nodded and congratulated the king, while he handed Blanchpenny over to one of the falconers and turned to William.

"You acted calmly and saved my Blanchpenny's life. I'd say you have earned a generous reward, lad." With these words, he brought out a particularly heavy silver piece.

The smiths stared at the shiny coin, speechless.

But William drew himself up and shook his head. "Forgive me, sire, but couldn't I become a falconer instead?"

William's brazenness shocked the crowd. A cry escaped Ellenweore, and she turned white as chalk. Frightened, she looked first at the king, then at her son, then back at the king.

She's worried for my sake, thought William with a rush of disbelief.

Astonished and even, it seemed at first, rather amused, Henry raised his eyebrows and flushed. Before he could express his fury, one of the knights from his retinue stepped forward. William knew him but had not noticed him before. His name was Baudouin de Béthune, and he was both a customer of his mother's and a friend of Marshal's. Ignoring William, de Béthune bowed down before the king, then whispered something in his ear. Henry nodded, apparently wishing to hear more. The king listened carefully, glancing at Ellenweore from time to time and expressing his surprise with a short grunt. Then he smiled understandingly and, with evident pleasure, gave his full attention to the rest of Baudouin's narration.

William was sure Sir Baudouin was telling the king about Ellenweore's feat of heroism many years before. When Sir Baudouin was still a boy, she had saved his life. In pulling him out of a raging torrent, she had put herself in danger. The child's well-being was more important to her than her own life, and she had succeeded in saving the boy from drowning.

William lifted his chin slightly and beamed proudly at the king. Henry nodded graciously and beckoned him to approach.

"Now, lad, I hear your mother is quite a remarkable woman with powerful friends. I shall therefore forgive you your impudence and give your request some consideration. But for the time being, you'll have to make do with the coin and go back to your mother in the smithy. Is that understood?"

Despite the imperious severity in his voice, William thought he detected a conspiratorial glint in the king's eye as he handed over the coin. William was a little disappointed, but he nodded obediently and bowed as he accepted the silver piece. It was so large he could only just enclose it in his fist.

The king turned to Ellenweore, who was still pale with fear. "You will be hearing from me, smith woman." He nodded to her in a friendly manner, then turned around. "It will be dark soon," he called out to his companions.

One of the knights sent his squire for some fire with which to light their torches. Then they all mounted their horses, and the king gave his men the signal to set off. None of the smiths moved until the last of the retinue had left the yard, and even then it took them a while to remember that they had swords to harden.

After the hardening of the blades, shortly before dawn, Ellenweore and Isaac came back into the house. They had sent William to bed long before, but he was still awake. When he heard voices, his ears pricked up.

"You will be hearing from me, smith woman," said his mother, mimicking the king and snorting with rage. "I'll be waiting till the day of judgment. I'll be bound. I always knew he'd come someday. I was prepared, and yet I missed my chance. I should have asked him into the smithy, shown him a few weapons, perhaps I could have persuaded him—" She broke off as her disappointment surfaced. "Why doesn't he want a sword from me?"

"Just wait, Ellen, I'm sure—"

"Well," she broke in, "why is it surprising that the king doesn't want one of my swords when my own son can't bring himself to be enthusiastic about our work? I wanted to be swallowed up by the ground when William said he'd rather be a falconer. He's set his sights on higher things, just like my mother. The smithy wasn't good enough for her, either."

"Ellen, he's good at handling birds. Truly he is."

"Did you know about that falcon?" William could hear the suspicion in her voice.

"Yes, I did," Isaac retorted, lowering his voice instantly. He was probably afraid of waking the children. "I saw how he bound the falcon's leg. And take my word for it, he wasn't the clumsy clod I know from the smithy."

"Fie!" It sounded as though Ellenweore considered her husband a traitor for defending the enemy. "What's to become of him, if not a swordsmith? A farrier, perhaps? I'd die of shame."

"The king said he'd think about William's request," Isaac objected.

"The boy won't hear from the king any more than I will. You should know great men better. The king owes William nothing; he's already rewarded him handsomely. Why should he grant him anything more?"

"I'd say that depends what Sir Baudouin told him."

Ellenweore gasped with fear.

"I'll give William more work. That will drive the nonsense out of him," she said, changing the subject. "When he's a little older and has more experience…"

"He still won't care any more about smithing than he does now. Falcons are his passion—why won't you grasp that? You of all people ought to understand!"

William closed his eyes for a moment. His mother would never understand, never. No matter how long Isaac talked.

"The boy has your stubbornness and the same extraordinary dreams you used to have. And were *you* willing to listen to your mother?"

"That's not the same thing at all," replied Ellenweore indignantly. "After all, I only want what's best for him. My mother hated me. If it had been up to her, the only fire I would ever have tended would have been a hearth. And of course that would have suited you better, too."

"You know very well I stopped thinking like that long ago." Isaac sounded hurt.

Ellenweore must have realized she had gone too far. "Oh, Isaac, try to understand," she pleaded, trying to make up. "The thing with his feet is a sign from God."

Even though he could not see her, William knew her eyes were shining as she said those words. His nostrils flared with fury. First, only one of his feet was malformed, not both, and second, he did not want to be compared with Hephaestus or Wayland or some other blacksmith cripple. Lord, he was so tired of her bringing it up all the time.

"Ellen, you're wrong, believe me," Isaac pleaded afresh. "The boy hates smithing as much as you hate housework. You let the food burn. He lets the iron get too hot. You leave the seasoning off the meat. He forgets to add flux. Where you start soaking the grain too late so the gruel goes hard, he strikes the iron when it's too cold so it develops cracks. You know yourself that you've never been a good housewife, and he, Ellen, will never in his life be a good swordsmith, however much you may wish it."

"Nonsense, he's lazy and contrary, that's all. The men in my family have been smiths for generations."

"His father wasn't," Isaac reminded her sharply.

"Do you hold that against me?"

William was astonished at the bitterness of her retort.

"No, Ellen, you know very well that I love the boy like a son," Isaac replied softly. "But you shouldn't forget that it's not only smiths' blood that flows in his veins."

William listened eagerly, but neither his mother nor Isaac said any more. It was only by chance that William had once learned from Sir Baudouin that his father was a knight. Sir Baudouin, Isaac, and his mother had never provided any more information, so William did not even know his father's name. He closed his eyes, tired. As he'd so often done in recent years, William imagined his noble father riding into the yard, leaping down from a mighty warhorse and commanding Ellenweore to give up her son so that he could take him away. Although the knight in his fantasy was armed to the teeth, William was not afraid of him for one moment. He sat serenely on the huge horse, holding the reins his father had passed to him, and slipped on the glove he was handed. The knight placed a wonderful small falcon on his fist, and William looked his unknown father in the face for the first time. It seemed strangely familiar, and at last William realized that the strange knight was the very image of William Marshal.

A good week had passed since the king's visit, and William was still confident that a messenger would come to fetch him before long. To be as ready for that moment as possible, he took every opportunity that presented itself to flee the workshop and run to the hay meadow where he had found Blanchpenny. He had often seen the abbot's falconers there, but until now he had only watched them. Today, he wanted to change that. This time he would talk to them, for he would soon be one of them.

But when William reached the meadow, there was nobody to be seen. Disappointed, he lay down in the grass, folded his hands over his stomach, and stared up into the sky. Although the ground was damp and the autumn cold crept gradually into his limbs, he remained there for a long while, motionless, staring into the bleak blue-gray void and dreaming of his future as a falconer.

Suddenly, he heard voices and sat up. Not far off, two men were running across the meadow.

William stood up and brushed off his damp behind. "Greetings!" He nodded politely and went up to the men.

"Be off with you—you're making the falcon anxious!" said the younger one pompously, though the bird was not stirring.

"I won't frighten it, I promise." William looked at the older one. "Look, master," he said in a gentle, even tone. "It's not afraid; its feathers are all fluffed up."

The older one raised his eyebrows in surprise. "That's well observed. Is your father a falconer, too?"

"No, but I shall be one myself one day."

"I know you," said the younger one with a sudden frown. "You're that smith woman's son. The lame one." He laughed. "How could a cripple like you, of all people, become a falconer?"

The bird took fright at his loud voice and hopped along the falconer's arm. The falconer glared at his assistant and turned away.

"Last year I had a sparrow hawk," said William stubbornly.

"Did you tame it?" asked the older man, scratching his neck.

"No." William bowed his head sadly. "It flew away."

"I told you, someone like you is better off as a smith. At least iron doesn't fly away." The younger one hooked his thumbs together, grinning, and mimed the flapping of a bird's wings.

"And I found a white gyrfalcon recently," said William triumphantly, though without raising his voice.

"A gyrfalcon? And a white one at that?" The falconer looked at him skeptically. "That I don't believe. They only exist up north, far beyond where England ends."

"Yes, I did. It had flown away from its master. The king himself came and took it from me. That's why I'm going to be a falconer, because I took good care of his Blanchpenny," William boasted, though he knew he was on dangerous ground, since the king had not said that his wish would be granted.

"A cripple for a falconer. Surely you don't believe the king would allow something so ridiculous. If he really did say that, he was taking you for a fool. Wasn't he, master?" The young man looked at the older one, hoping for confirmation.

"He's right. A hunt assistant must be able to run very fast and have stamina besides."

"But I want to be a falconer, not an assistant!" William protested.

"Do you indeed? Who do you think you are?" the falconer went on. "Everyone begins as an assistant. If you can't accept that, forget your dream. And now let us get on with our work."

"May I watch?" asked William contritely.

"As long as you're quiet and don't get in the way, I don't mind." The falconer gave his assistant a few ill-tempered instructions and paid no further attention to William.

He watched the men attentively, but the older one's words would not leave him. If running was so important that it would determine whether he could become a falconer, then he would have to practice as long as it took for his foot not to be a handicap anymore.

Near Sevenoaks,
December 13, 1184

ou're doing exceedingly well, my lady," exclaimed the midwife. "Soon it will be time to push."

Alix de Hauville had just turned seventeen, and this was her first child. The labor pains demanded her attention for a while, but then her fear of the moment of truth returned. It was very possible that her husband was not the father. What if it was obvious right away? Alix groaned at the thought and allowed herself to be overwhelmed by the next powerful contraction.

"You're nearly there." The midwife wiped the sweat from Alix's brow. Several braziers filled with coal heated the lady's chamber so that the newborn would not catch a chill. Despite the damp cold outside, the room was comfortably warm.

"I can already feel its little head. Now push with all your might," the midwife ordered.

Alix could scarcely follow the instructions; she was so afraid of the punishment awaiting her if her sin was found out. She should never have given in to his wooing. She had been weak.

"Good, now once more," the midwife coaxed.

Richard de Hauville was nearly thirty years older than Alix, and not the man of a young woman's dreams. Alix had lived in his household since her seventh year, so he was more like a father to her than a husband. Perhaps this was why she was so afraid of disappointing him. She had been married to Richard for two years when she succumbed to Prince John's youthful charms. He had spent a few days as a guest under their roof earlier that year, and he had exploited the master's absence to turn her head. They were about the same age and could laugh about the same silly little things. Was it so surprising that she had ended up in his arms?

Alix groaned. She should never have given herself to the prince. Although she had always patiently tolerated her husband's exercising of his conjugal rights, she had not fallen pregnant, so he had been particularly glad when he learned she was with child.

Alix could not say why she was so sure the child's father was Prince John, but it was her very certainty that made her so afraid. The prince had not stayed long enough to arouse suspicion. In fact, no one seemed to have noticed anything. Even John had no idea what she was going through now because of him. At the thought of the child resembling the prince, Alix began to sweat even more. John's hair was a little darker than his older brother's and his father's, but as with all the Plantagenets, it had an unmistakable tinge of red. She, on the other hand, had dark-brown hair and her husband's was pure black, though the years had woven in a considerable number of silver strands. Alix let out another sigh as she thought about bringing a red-haired child into the world.

"It will soon be over, my lady."

She felt another spasm coming on. Alix pushed with all her strength, and the child was born.

"It's a girl," said the midwife with a hint of regret. "But don't worry, my lady, you're young and will have many sons yet," she added reassuringly, scooping away the remaining muck from the infant's mouth with her finger. She picked up the little girl by her feet. The newborn gave a full-throated howl. "A robust little girl, just like her father," the midwife cried with satisfaction.

Alix shivered involuntarily at these words.

The midwife cut the cord, washed the infant, cleaned her nose and ears, and checked every inch of her body. When she lay her down on her front, a frown appeared on the midwife's forehead. "Most unusual," she murmured.

Alix sat up a little. "Is there something wrong?"

"All her fingers and toes are there, and her eyes, nose, and ears look as they ought to." The midwife's head rocked from side to side. "It's just her bottom…"

"What is it? Speak up," begged Alix.

"The cleft between her buttocks is strangely crooked," said the midwife, shrugging her shoulders. "I've never seen anything like it."

Alix fell back onto her pillow. It was John's child. A little wistfully, she thought of the handsome prince and his skewed crack, over which they had laughed so heartily. For a brief moment, she was happy the child was his. Then fear took over. God would punish her for her sin. She mouthed an oath.

"Fear not, my lady." The midwife smiled archly. "A crooked nose would be far worse."

Alix giggled with relief. The wise woman had no idea how right she was. An obvious resemblance would have been much harder to hide.

"Here, take your daughter in your arms." The midwife held out the swaddled infant.

Alix looked curiously at the little girl. She had dark downy hair and resembled neither her husband nor John. Would that change? She felt the fear rise up in her again. What if the dense shock of dark hair were to fall out and reddish Plantagenet hair were to grow in its place?

"She has your gentle features, my lady." The midwife bowed. "Her father's strength and her mother's beauty."

Alix sighed. Perhaps fate would be kind to her, and the secret would never be revealed.

"Your husband." The midwife dragged her from her gloomy thoughts.

"My dearest." Richard, who had stepped into the chamber, was obviously rather moved at the sight of his young wife with the infant in her arms.

Alix held her daughter out to him, and he kissed her on the forehead, thus accepting her into the family.

"It's a girl," Alix said softly, looking down, not wanting to see her husband's disappointment in not having a son.

"A girl!" His voice was tender and not even slightly angry. He took the infant uncertainly, inspected her, and then kissed her.

"She's beautiful, just like you, my darling Alix." He stroked her cheek tenderly. "We should call her Marguerite, like my late mother," he suggested, kissing the child's forehead again.

Just outside Saint Edmundsbury, 1185

Sitting in his room, William unwound the filthy bandage, sucking in through his teeth the cold, damp February air. His malformed foot hurt, and the pinky-toe side was bleeding again. The skin on this side was always dry and regularly developed particularly painful cracks. Nevertheless, at night and when he was working in the smithy, William would strap his foot to a narrow wooden board that reached from his heel to his toe. He hoped that this would straighten out his foot over time.

He had been subjecting himself to this torture for weeks, but every step still hurt, for the wooden board chafed against his skin. Standing for hours while he worked was difficult, too. But since he wanted to become a falconer one day, trying to straighten his foot was his only choice. Hopefully one day he would be able to run as fast as other boys his age, perhaps even faster. To prove what he had in him, he would have to last at least as long as other hunt assistants, but that was going to require a bit more effort.

The king's visit lay several months in the past. William had hoped so hard that a messenger would come, but nothing had happened. And yet he clung to his dream. If the king did not help him, he would handle this on his own. One day everyone would marvel when William would step out in front of the king with his head held high and a magnificent falcon on his fist. His mind made up, he dabbed a slightly rancid-smelling mixture of herb-infused fat on the inside of his foot first and then over the wound. William winced, for the ointment stung. Then he kneaded and massaged his foot until the blood was flowing properly and the skin turned pink. He pulled at each toe, wiggled his ankle, and finally wrapped a strip of clean bandage around his foot. This was a delicate process: if the binding was too loose, it would come off as he ran; if it was too tight, his foot would start tingling and then go numb, and then running would hurt even more than it did normally.

William pulled his shoe on over the binding and stood up. Dawn was breaking. Everyone else was asleep. Only Rose, who was always the first one up in the morning, met him in the yard.

"You look a little green about the gills. Are you going running again?" she asked anxiously.

William just nodded and ran off.

"I'll give you a cup of fresh goat milk when you get back—that'll give you strength for the day," Rose called after him, keeping her voice down.

William started off along the narrow path at the edge of the forest and then ran behind the sheep pasture and around the wheat field until he reached the hay meadow, at which point he turned around. He did this circuit three times every morning and three times every evening. At first he had only been able to manage one; soon he would increase it to four. His foot was burning particularly hot today. A searing pain shot up his right leg when he stepped on a sharp stone. But giving up was out of the question. Tears of pain and desperation ran down his cheeks, but he ignored them. He paused briefly to catch his breath after his second circuit.

Running felt much harder than usual today. He had hardly slept and found himself short of breath. Had he caught a chill? His head felt as if it were stuffed with down, and his nose itched. Just one more circuit, he urged himself, and finally fulfilled his expectation.

When he got home, he dropped onto the bench, exhausted, and laid his head on the table. "I feel like death," he groaned.

Rose put the promised cup of warm goat milk down in front of him, as well as some porridge, and looked at him tenderly. "Eat up quickly. You're late. The others are over there already," she warned him, stroking his sweaty head affectionately.

When William entered the smithy, he could tell immediately that his mother was furious. He got down to work in silence, careful to avoid her stern gaze.

The workshop seemed stuffier than usual as William caught shallow breaths through his mouth. His nose was now completely blocked, and his head ached terribly. After only a few blows with the hammer, his strength failed him. His neck, the small of his back, his legs, and his arms—everything hurt. Although he was standing some distance away from the fire, it felt like he was standing in the center of the flames. Suddenly, the room began to spin, and then everything went black.

"William!" Someone was slapping his cheek roughly. "Wake up, lad," Isaac said anxiously.

William tried to get up, but he was too weak to stand.

"I'll carry him," said Jean, Rose's husband, picking him up off the ground.

"I'm sure he's been at that running nonsense again. I don't understand what purpose it's supposed to serve."

She cares about me, thought William, amazed. A tiny smile flickered on his pale lips. "It's all right, Mother. I'll be better soon," he whispered.

When they entered the house, Rose hurried over, leaving the dough she had been kneading untended.

"Has he hurt himself?" Although Rose was used to problems with the smiths, since it was always she who came when they needed help, she sounded worried. William knew she loved him as she loved her own children. She meant almost as much to him, too, as his mother did.

"Fainted," Jean explained, without wasting words.

"For heaven's sake." Rose laid her hand against William's overheated forehead. "He needs to go to bed and get some rest. The poor boy has a fever. I'll make him an infusion and cool some bedclothes. That's bound to help." She turned to reassure Ellenweore. "Don't worry yourself—I'll look after him. He'll be fine in a couple of days."

"This running is going to be the death of him!" muttered Ellenweore grimly.

Once in bed, William sank into a deep sleep. Sweating and groaning, he dreamed of marsh monsters trying to devour him and of a dragon pursuing him with its fiery breath.

When he woke up, Rose was sitting by the bed, cooling his forehead. William felt something wet on his calves. Rose had wrapped damp cloths around them. Although they absorbed the heat of his burning body, they did not reduce the fever. He felt weak, and he looked at Rose dully. Even his eyes hurt.

"Have a drink," she ordered him, holding a cup to his lips. She lifted his head slightly and supported it.

"Thanks," William whispered feebly. He soon slipped back into a feverish sleep.

When he awoke again, it was already dark. William listened. His stepsisters, Agnes and Marie, who were also his cousins, were lying not far away. They slept together in a shared bed. One of them made a tiny sound like the squeaking of a mouse. That was Marie. William was glad not to be alone. He licked his dry, chapped lips with a trembling tongue. Surely Rose must have left the cup with the herbal infusion near his bed. He felt for it laboriously and finally found it. He drank greedily and put the cup back down. The effect lasted until he fell asleep again; he began to feel so cold that his teeth chattered. Even the touch of his blanket hurt his skin.

When he woke up the following morning, he was sweating so profusely that his body was as wet as a rain shower. This time, his mother was kneeling beside the bed and cooling his forehead.

"I know you run because you want to keep up with the hunt assistants. But you're going to be a smith, not a falconer. When will you grasp that?"

To William, her voice sounded almost pleading. Just for a brief moment, he opened his eyes to look at her; then he turned away and closed them again.

He heard a heavy tread and knew Isaac had entered the room.

"When he's better, I'll send him to Arthur at Orford," she said. "He knows William will take over the smithy one day. I'm sure he hopes the boy will take one of his daughters off his hands when that day comes, so I'm certain he'll give him the attention he needs. At Arthur's he'll learn how to forge good tools. In a year or two we can look at it again." His mother seemed to have made her decision. "It's better for him."

She wanted to send him away. William could not take it in. He tried to open his eyes in disbelief, but he couldn't. His eyelids were too heavy. Or perhaps he was only dreaming?

"I'm glad you're better again." Rose beamed at William when he stood up for the first time two days later. He was still weak, of course, but soon he would be able to go back to work.

"Was it just a dream, or does she really want to send me away?" he asked dully, warming his clammy fingers on the cup of hot milk that Rose had put down in front of him.

"Arthur's a nice fellow. I'm sure you'll get on well with each other. It's for the best." Rose tried to convince him.

William looked at her, dismayed. He had hoped she would tell him it all had been a feverish dream; instead she had confirmed his fears. Worried, he blew away the rising steam and took a cautious sip of the milk. "You've sweetened it with honey," he remarked quietly. He liked sweet milk above all things, but right then he could not take pleasure in it. He felt nothing but sadness.

"For strength, so that you can be up and about again soon." Rose stroked his hand affectionately.

"'And be sent away,' you should say, too," William said, bitterly disappointed. He ate his porridge in silence, then went back to bed. Evidently everyone in the house was conspiring against him. William started sweating again and felt dreadful. Wounded to the core, he turned his face to the wall and pulled the blanket up around his ears.

Almost five months had passed since the king's visit. The sun's rays were gaining strength, and the air was no longer as bitingly cold as it had been in February. William had recovered some time ago, and he was working in the smithy as before. He tried hard, but it did not help. His mother was ill-tempered, probably because the king had still not ordered a sword from her. Yet she did not so much as mention Orford again, so William at last put her words behind him and began to run again. He got up from his bed even earlier than before. He took care not to encounter anyone and tried not to attract attention when he returned from his circuits. One day, though, his mother caught him, stepping out in front of him as if molded from the earth itself.

"You've been running, even though I forbade it," she stated tonelessly.

Her anger stood like a wall between them. Though he did not really feel he had done anything wrong, William looked down.

"Tomorrow morning we leave for Orford," said Ellenweore coldly.

William looked up sharply. "No, Mother, not that."

But she had already turned away and was on her way back to the workshop.

William ran after her. "I have to be here when the king's messenger comes."

Ellenweore stopped, turned around, and looked at him almost pityingly. The anger had left her face. "No one's coming—don't you see that? Get that idea out of your head, once and for all."

"I know he'll send someone."

"You're to be a smith, and that's all there is to it. I'm sure Arthur will be happy to take you on if I hand over a share of the tenancy. He'll be a good master."

"But—"

"There's no point arguing about it any longer. My decision is made. You have only yourself to blame: you were warned."

William's shoulders slumped, and he followed her silently into the workshop. He knew her decision was irrevocable. Perhaps it really would be better if he left this place.

Over the evening meal, Ellenweore told the others about their departure, which she had already arranged for the next day.

Rose tried to make it easier for William with a smile and some encouraging words, while Jean gave him a few well-intentioned pieces of advice about the journey and how to behave with his new master.

But William only half listened and said nothing. Confused thoughts whirled about in his head. Was it disappointment, hope, or fear that was making his heart race?

Rose gave them some provisions, a loaf of bread and some cheese, all tied up in a piece of cloth. Then she added two water skins.

The previous evening, Jean had found William's favorite hammer. "If you must go in for smithing…" he whispered in his ear as he gave it to him.

William was touched by the gesture.

"Come and see us at Christmas, and show us what progress you've made," Jean continued with exaggerated heartiness, clapping William on the shoulder kindly. "She won't be on your back all the time, and you'll learn a lot of new things."

Rose took William in her arms, sighing, and pressed him to her breast like a young child, which made him blush. "Make sure you don't catch a chill again when you go running," she whispered in his ear. Then she pinched his chin and looked serious. "We're really going to miss you."

William looked down through tear-filled eyes. "*She* won't miss me." He glanced angrily toward where his mother was standing.

Ellenweore seemed not to have heard him. Gesticulating excitedly, she was talking to Isaac and checking the saddles on the two horses that Peter, the longest-serving and most faithful of her apprentices, had prepared for the journey.

"Nonsense, my lamb. It's hard for her, but she thinks sending you to Orford is the right thing to do. That's why she doesn't show her sorrow. She only wants the best for you, believe me."

"You sound like Isaac," grumbled William. He was disappointed that his stepfather had not done more to change his mother's mind.

"Well, you see, then you know I'm right." Rose winked at him encouragingly and stroked his hair. "Take good care of yourself." Hastily, she wiped away the tiny tears that were running down her cheek. "Now I must get back to my work," she said briskly, then rushed into the house.

This leave-taking only made William's heart heavier. He said good-bye to Agnes and Marie, and to Raymond and Alan, Rose and Jean's two sons. Then he shook hands with Peter, the two hired hands, the new apprentices, and Brad and Luke. He even shook hands with Adam, though he was probably the only one William would not miss.

Isaac took his arm and privately slipped him a figurine he had carved for him. "It's a falcon, cut from a nice smooth piece of ash wood, so you'll never lose sight of your dream," he uttered. "It will protect you on your journey and comfort you when you're alone among strangers." Then, louder, he said, "You will be successful, William. One day your mother will be very proud of you, as will I."

A short-lived smile flitted across William's face at those words as he gripped the little wooden bird in his fist. Isaac was on his side, after all.

"When the king's messenger comes, tell him where I am," he asked his stepfather in a whisper, and Isaac nodded confidently. William was not ready to give up hope.

He went over to Graybeard and embraced him one last time. The dog was already old, older than William. Would he still be alive when next William came home?

"Let's be on our way, son," Ellenweore suggested with surprising gentleness.

William let go of the dog with a heavy heart, stood up without looking at her, and took the reins from Jean. He mounted his horse in silence, trying to remain dignified and not weep. His mother must not think she could break his will.

Orford, May 1185

Arthur, the tenant of the smithy that Ellenweore had inherited from her father, and his wife, Elfreda, welcomed William with open arms. Ellenweore had reached an agreement with Arthur without difficulty and was on her way back to Saint Edmundsbury the following day. Despite his anger, her departure had been hard on William.

More than a month had gone by since then, and William had realized that it was possible to be very happy in Orford, even if he missed Rose's gentle ways and even occasionally longed for his mother's dry directness. For Elfreda was a cheerful, warmhearted woman who could cook almost as well as Rose, and Arthur, the blacksmith, was patient and friendly.

Nevertheless, it seemed to William that every day he spent here took him further away from his dream. One night, he decided it was time to take control of his own happiness. All he had to do was wait for a suitable moment to turn his back on Orford, provided the endless rain stopped one of these days.

At last, the May sun slowly dried out the marshy land. Impatience bubbled in William's stomach, like cider on the palate. To be sure, it took a hefty dose of courage to go off alone into the unknown, but the thought of one day being a falconer helped him put all his fears aside. He had not let the previous weeks go to waste: he had kept his ears open wherever he went, but still he knew far too little about his surroundings. William had also resisted asking too many questions, so as not to arouse Arthur's suspicions. Soon he would simply run away and go from one falconer's establishment to the next, looking for work. Although he did not know where he might find falconers or what he would live on during his wanderings, he refused to believe that his enterprise might be doomed to failure. Every night, he prayed ardently to the Lord for his help.

One day, he decided to set out on Whitsunday, immediately after mass. He had two days to get ready for his clandestine departure. He collected provisions by secretly pilfering them from the table and laid out some tinder and a flint so that he could light a fire, in case he had to spend the hours of darkness alone. He wrapped his few belongings in a bundle and hid it in a hollow tree on the edge of the forest, along with his wool cloak and the knife that his mother had given him.

On the morning of Whitsunday, William was decidedly anxious. He had to take his leave without anyone noticing. Now that he had come to a decision, the thought of going weighed surprisingly heavily. Elfreda and Arthur would worry about him when he did not come to the table at supper time. The thought of disappointing them, when they had been so good to him, sat uneasily. But if he did not want to spend his life as a blacksmith, the sooner he acted the better.

During mass he pulled himself together, praying to the Lord for his blessing and for forgiveness for his disobedience. Just before the end of the service, he slipped out of the church. The sun was already quite warm. Up in the sky, which was almost unnaturally blue, seagulls cawed as they wheeled around in their endless circles. They knew no Sunday and did not understand that the fishermen's boats would remain in the harbor today.

A strong breeze brought with it the sharp scent of the salt water that flowed in the River Ore. With all of his strength, William ran along the western edge of the meadow toward the woods. The bright sunshine coaxed out of the rain-heavy land brightly colored blooms that lined the river. The first buttercups beckoned with their radiant yellow. Lady's-smock and campion flowers, soft pink and bluish violet, stretched up toward the sun. Bumblebees and butterflies flitted to and fro among the flowers.

William ran in a straight line across the colorful meadow. A few of the flowers and grasses reached almost to his hips, so he had to take some care that no bees strayed under his smock. Don't turn around now, he thought as he crossed the meadow, but still he glanced back. A rider was arriving at the church at a full gallop. A riderless horse followed behind.

William hesitated. Who could that be? He turned away abruptly. It didn't matter anymore. Determined to grasp his destiny, he removed his bundle and cloak from their hiding place. He fastened his knife and water skin to his belt.

Had his mother also traveled through Tunstall Wood when she had fled all those years ago? She had never told him exactly why she had fled, or where she had gone. Still, she had achieved her dream, and he would, too. In an optimistic frame of mind, he followed the narrow path into the wood.

The trunks of the tall trees were completely bare until far above his head; only high up did their vigorous branches form a diffusely lit canopy of tender green leaves. Younger saplings, with slender stems and thin branches, sprang up all around. A squirrel ran adroitly from one branch to another. A second one ran head-first down a tree trunk, crossed the path William was on, stood up on its hind legs, and peeked around before disappearing into the undergrowth. It must have been looking for food. Not far from the place where it disappeared, William spotted the first mushrooms among the half-decayed leaves of the previous winter. The pale-green fern that grew like a weed around Orford made the ground seem brightly lit. In the distance, he could hear the call of a cuckoo and the tock-tock-tock of a woodpecker.

William was in good spirits. His stamina had improved, and his foot hurt less. His return to running circuits in the past few months was finally paying off. That morning, as usual, he had rubbed ointment into his foot, and, as he bound it, he had taken particular care to avoid any creases in the bandage, so that he would not get blisters so quickly. He had some clean strips of cloth and a small clay pot with ointment in his bundle. William knew the path would lead him to the road that connected Orford with Ipswich to the south and Norwich to the north. When he got to the fork, he would have to decide which way to go. He had time enough to think about that between now and then.

The sun's rays, filtering down through the thin ceiling of fresh green leaves, bathed the wood in a marvelously gentle and benevolent light. What a fool I was to be afraid of being alone, thought William optimistically.

He did not rest until it was getting dark, and then he spread out his cloak beneath a beech tree and sat down. Because of his work in the smithy, he was accustomed to regular mealtimes, and now he felt a powerful hunger. He got a fish pasty out of his bundle. Biting into it reminded him of Rose. Her pasties were better than Elfreda's by a good margin. They tasted of dill and cloves. William sighed. Was everyone in Saint Edmundsbury well? Something clutched at his heart, and he knew he was homesick. He wondered whether his mother and the others thought of him from time to time.

William was still quite sunk in thought when he heard a rustling in the bushes. He looked in the direction of the sound. Two curious young boars were running toward him. One of the little wild piglets with white stripes along its hairy back snuffled busily at William's bundle. Its expression was so sweet that William broke into a smile. But then he was suddenly struck by a frightening thought: where there were piglets, the mother boar could not be far off. He leaped to his feet. There were few things more dangerous than a wild boar protecting its young.

Sure enough, William heard stamping on the forest floor. It was the little fellows' mother, running toward him in a fury. He had only a brief moment to decide what to do.

He shouted loudly and waved his arms about, but that only seemed to make the boar even angrier. Panting with fear, William started to climb the tree under which he had been sitting only moments ago. He slipped, scraping his forearm and right knee, dangled briefly from a broken branch, tore a hole in his smock, and finally reached safety. Breathless, with heart pounding, he settled himself on the sturdy limb. Instead of retreating into the wood, however, the enraged beast trampled around and about his cloak and bundle, grunting furiously. She rooted through his provisions with her snout and ate every last bit. To make matters worse, the sow decided to rest at the base of the tree and suckle her young. When the little ones were sated, she made no move to leave. On the contrary, she seemed to have settled in for the night. As long as she remained there, he could not possibly climb down.

For better or worse, William decided to climb a little higher, to a stronger branch. Once there, he tried to make himself as comfortable as he could.

As darkness fell, he began to doze off. His head dropped to one side. William started. He had come a whisker away from falling out of the tree. He clung tightly. Whatever happened, he mustn't fall asleep again. If he fell, the sow would trample him to a pulp, perhaps even eat him. Wild boar was delicious, but they were ferocious and fearsome beasts, as William knew from Jean. He shifted about despondently on his uncomfortable seat. His tongue was sticking to the roof of his mouth. The fish pasty had made him thirsty. Unfortunately, his water pouch was on the ground, trampled to pieces.

"If you think I'm going to give up on your account," muttered William angrily, "you've got another think coming." He was determined to leave Orford. As soon as the boar had left and he could climb down, he would be on his way. He would not lose heart so soon.

He reached for the leather pouch on his belt, in which he kept a couple of copper coins and the king's silver piece. He opened it reverently. It also contained the little falcon that Isaac had carved for him.

William took it out. He had looked at the wooden creature often in the days since he had left Saint Edmundsbury. As he admired it now, so comforting and enticing, he got a lump in his throat. He took a deep breath. Better to put it back in the pouch. He wouldn't see Isaac, or any other familiar faces, for quite a while. If he wanted to become a falconer, he had to go out into unfamiliar territory. He had known it wouldn't be easy, and that was why he wouldn't give up at the first hurdle.

William moved his fingers. They were stiff with cold, as were his feet, which he could scarcely feel. "I have to stay awake," he said, half-aloud. How good it felt to hear one's own voice. Loneliness was a poor traveling companion. William looked up toward the crown of the tree. Like an old friend, the moon sent its pale, unexpectedly comforting light down into the dark forest. William admitted to himself that his situation, on closer examination, was almost hopeless. Sooner or later, he would be so tired that he wouldn't be able to hold himself up any longer. What if the boars still hadn't sought out the open spaces in the morning? William began to sob. He so wanted to become a falconer. Fighting his rising desperation with all his might, William closed his eyes and began to sing.

His voice trembled with cold, but it calmed him down. His singing became more enthusiastic with each new song, so he did not hear the horse approach or see the glow from the torch in the rider's hand.

"William? William, is that you? What are you doing up there?" someone shouted.

William froze, holding his breath before he recognized Arthur's voice. The blacksmith did not even seem angry with him, though he had every reason to be. On the contrary, he seemed amused by the situation.

"There's a wild boar with her young sitting under the tree," William called out in warning.

Arthur dismounted and tied his horse to a young oak tree. Only then did he approach.

"Hey! Ho there!" He waved his torch from side to side and charged at the boar. "Be off with you. Make haste," he roared, brandishing the torch in a threatening manner.

Although it looked for a moment as though she was going to attack, the sow decided on flight.

"You can come down now."

William clambered down, scraping his knee a bit more in the process. As quickly as possible, and without saying a word, he checked his cloak and the little that remained of his bundle. Head bowed, he walked toward Arthur.

The smith clapped him on the shoulder amiably. "Elfreda was worried when you weren't home for supper, hungry as you always are." He smiled briefly, then fell serious again. "You should know that I'm not happy about your leaving. I'd have really liked to keep you with me, though it hasn't escaped me that you don't get anything out of the work in the smithy."

William felt the blood rush to his face and hoped Arthur could not see it in the darkness. "But I—" he began, then broke off. Why should he lie to Arthur?

"Well, William, if the king gives an order, we must obey. There's nothing for it." Arthur sighed. "Not even running away."

William did not understand what Arthur meant. "But I..." he said hesitantly.

The smith climbed back onto his horse. He offered William his hand, so that he could swing up behind him.

"Elfreda said I should tell you tactfully, but it looks as though you already know. You must have been eavesdropping, is that it?"

"No," replied William in a thin voice, shaking his head.

"The knight that came to the church today wants to take you to some castle or other. King's orders, he says. I've never heard of the castle before, but that doesn't mean anything."

"The knight, where is he now?" William's heart was beating so hard it hurt. The king had kept his word.

"He's searching for you on the other side of the wood. We agreed to meet at the workshop at dawn. I don't think you need fear him. Who knows what God has in store for you. Perhaps you'll become something really special. The ways of the Lord are mysterious." His efforts to reassure William were well-intentioned, but Arthur could not have suspected how long his charge had been waiting for this day.

William thought of the wild boars with something close to gratitude. But for them, he would not have heard about the king's messenger.

"You must be hungry. There's some porridge left," said Elfreda, relieved, when they returned to the smithy.

"I'm thirsty more than anything else."

Elfreda placed a cup of water and some food in front of him.

"There's still a little time before sunrise. Go and lie down for a while," Arthur suggested. "I suspect the knight will be here at first light. He seemed in a hurry."

William obeyed without protest, curled up in his pallet, wrapped the wool blanket around him, and fell asleep instantly.

It seemed to him that he had hardly closed his eyes before voices and the rattling of spurs woke him. He sprang out of bed immediately and straightened his clothes. Dawn was breaking, so he had had a little sleep, after all. William rubbed his eyes briefly, and then he was wide-awake.

"Sir Baudouin!" Filled with joy, he rushed toward the knight. Just in time, he remembered himself and made a small bow in front of him.

"Well, you little runaway, where were you off to?" de Béthune greeted him with playful severity in his voice.

Arthur was surprised that William knew the strange knight, and he looked from one to the other questioningly.

"May I be a falconer now?" William looked expectantly at Sir Baudouin.

The knight smiled. "Yes, William, you may. That's why I'm taking you to Thorne."

"How on earth did you know I was here? Did my mother...?"

"She would have preferred not to give away where you were. She wasn't even in favor of letting you go," he answered mischievously. "Not even an order for ten knights' swords, which I had brought her from the king, was enough to placate her. Isaac explained that she had placed all her hopes in you and was afraid of losing you. She was always pigheaded, your mother. She never hid her thoughts from me, and yet I like her. Fortunately, Isaac told me where you were. Your headstrong mother actually wanted to stand in our way." He laughed out loud. "The look she gave Isaac when I told her I was going to fetch you away from here was almost as deadly as her swords. But I dare say he'll survive."

"So does she know where you're taking me?"

"Of course, my boy. Don't worry. She'll get used to the idea that you won't become a smith." He turned to Arthur. "I must make up for the time I lost yesterday. We have to leave right away."

William put his bundle, and what the boar had left of his possessions, under his arm and was ready to leave immediately. For a brief moment he had to fight back an attack of homesickness, but then he pulled himself together and stood up straight.

Arthur and Elfreda said good-bye to him with such sincerity that his eyes began to burn despite his best efforts, and suddenly a nameless fear crept over him. For all that's holy, what is there to be afraid of? I'm going to be a falconer at last. He beamed at them both.

"Thank you for everything," he called to them, then followed Sir Baudouin.

"You do know how to ride?" the knight asked, offering him the reins of the horse he had brought with him.

William nodded and mounted the horse. As they leaped into motion, he looked back, just once, and tried to catch a last glimpse of Orford. Then they came to a bend in the road, and from that point on William looked only ahead.

☙❧

"Hey you, boy. Wait!"

Robert turned, frightened. He had recognized the voice immediately, and he tried to weigh up the situation in a flash. Odon looked as though he felt as strong as a bear again, which was not surprising, since he was accompanied by three of his friends. A chill ran down Robert's spine. There was nothing, absolutely nothing, he could do against the four squires, for each of them was at least five years older than he was and two heads taller. They enjoyed picking on those weaker than themselves, and he had walked right into it. Even running away was out of the question.

"Come here," ordered one of them, a lean youth with dark hair and a thin beard.

Since he had no choice, Robert walked toward them with his head bowed.

"Clean my boots," the squire commanded.

Robert knelt down and began to wipe the dust off the boots with his sleeve, gritting his teeth. He bit down on his quivering lip.

"Lick them," the squire ordered arrogantly, and his companions roared with pleasure. "They're supposed to shine."

Robert's eyes grew moist, and his nose began to run. Only cowards sought out the weak in order to humiliate them. But if he did not do as the squire ordered, they would all pounce on him. He bowed down over the boot and dribbled spittle from his mouth.

"I said lick!" roared the squire. He gave Robert such a kick in the shoulder that he fell backward. "What a simpleton."

Robert was rattled. In desperation, he did as the squire commanded. When Robert's tears dropped onto the boot, Odon waded in.

"Look at him, blubbing like a maid," he cried. He grabbed Robert by the arm and hoisted him high. "If you'll lick *his* boot, what will you do for me?"

Odon's face was so close that, for a moment, Robert considered head-butting him. But he quickly rejected the idea. Everyone knew that Odon was a bad loser and a thoroughly vindictive person to boot.

"Whatever you wish, Master Odon."

"So, whatever I wish." Odon looked at his friends with satisfaction. "You heard: he knows who his master is," he said triumphantly, waving him away dismissively. "That's enough—you may go now."

Robert turned away and was about to make his escape when he fell full length to the ground. Odon, the odious fellow, had tripped him.

"Did you hurt yourself?" Odon asked with artificial compassion. "I hope you take a bit more care with our falcons and don't fall on your face when you're carrying them!"

Robert stood up in silence. Just as he was about to leave, a knight rushed up. Robert knew him: it was Reginald de Vere, a cousin of the Earl of Oxford and fencing master to the squires. He had a reputation for being strict but fair. Moreover, he was the only person the arrogant squires respected, for he came down hard on them if they tried to play their games with him.

"Why aren't you in the practice area?" he demanded. "Run around the field five times!" The squires just smirked at each other surreptitiously, showing no sign of making themselves scarce, so he added, "With the big sandbags."

They moved off, groaning.

"Lazy good-for-nothings!" he shouted after them. "They've a long way to go before they become men," he muttered to himself as he turned to Robert. "Go home and give your father a message: Sir Ralph is sending him a new apprentice for a few days. You'll save me a trip to the mews."

"Yes, Sir Reginald. I'll tell him."

The fencing master spun his horse around and dug in his spurs, leaving Robert feeling puzzled.

"An apprentice," he muttered to himself. "What does my father need an apprentice for? He's got me, after all. Aren't I good enough for him? Things could go badly for me if the lord of Thorne is sending some nobleman's spoiled brat into my father's house to compete for my post."

Thorne, June 1185

The weather was mild and dry during their ride, so Sir Baudouin and William reached their destination in three days. The castle at Thorne sat on a gentle rise in the land. To the west, where the sun was already low in the sky, a narrow strip of muddy ground fringed by dense forest abutted the lower bailey. To the east, the cottages of the day laborers and serfs huddled together on the hillside, all the way up to the oak palisades that protected the stone accommodation tower and a few other buildings against intruders.

In William's imagination, the castle had been bigger, and he came close to being a little disappointed. The tower was not half as imposing as the keep of the castle at Orford. Moreover, it was not made of pale, welcoming stone like the latter, but of dark-brown bricks, creating a gloomy, almost eerie atmosphere.

Once they had ridden over the wooden bridge and into the bailey, Sir Baudouin handed over the horses to a stable lad. "Bring your bundle and come with me," he ordered William curtly, hurrying ahead.

William rubbed his aching back and behind, which would probably continue to ache for a few days more, and limped hurriedly after the knight. Whenever he sat in the saddle for such a long time, his foot became stiff, and it took a while before he could walk properly again.

"Sir Ralph." Sir Baudouin walked into the hall and strode toward the lord of the manor.

"Baudouin, what a pleasure!" His host smiled and came toward him. They embraced each other warmly.

"I was expecting you yesterday." Sir Ralph put his hands on Sir Baudouin's shoulders and examined him closely. "You look as though things couldn't be better. A bit dusty, perhaps, but otherwise quite splendid." He turned away and poured some wine into a tin goblet.

"I was delayed," Sir Baudouin said, looking at William and winking conspiratorially.

"Nothing unpleasant, I hope."

"No, no, don't worry. Nothing important. Unfortunately, the king is expecting me back as soon as possible." He took the goblet that Sir Ralph offered him and drank. "Very good wine, as is to be expected in your house."

"Will you stay the night, despite your haste? I'll have something delicious cooked for us."

"Gladly. If I leave Thorne at sunrise, I can still reach the royal encampment before darkness falls."

William was standing by the entrance and did not dare move.

"Your new page?" asked Sir Ralph, nodding in William's direction. "Come closer, my son."

"No, forgive me. This is William." Sir Baudouin held William's shoulder and pulled him closer.

"William Fitz…?"

"FitzEllen, the swordsmith's son." Sir Baudouin finished the word hastily.

"Oh yes, of course." The lord of the manor considered William for a moment. "I remember now. You can't miss a certain resemblance," he said through a grin directed at Sir Baudouin.

"You know my mother?" William asked happily, then immediately bit his lower lip. Sir Baudouin had impressed on him that he should never address a knight without invitation. "Forgive me, my lord," he whispered, looking down in shame.

"That's all right." Sir Ralph smiled expressively. "Odon!" he shouted. A broad-shouldered, straw-blond squire of about fifteen rushed in.

"Welcome to Thorne, Sir Baudouin," he said, bowing as he spoke. Then he turned to his master. "My lord?"

"Take this lad to the master falconer." Sir Ralph turned back to Sir Baudouin. "And between us we'll dispatch a couple of jugs of good red wine. What do you say?"

"Excellent idea!" Sir Baudouin nodded to William. "Good-bye, lad."

"Come on, then." The squire poked his side. "I have to be back when supper is served."

William suppressed a sigh and followed him. He tried not to limp too much, but the squire noticed soon enough.

"Are you hurt?" he asked after they had walked a short way, pointing at William's foot.

"No, it's been like that since I was born," he explained with a shy smile, "but it's not too bad."

Odon snorted in disbelief. "Who is your father, that they take you on as a hunt assistant even though you're a cripple? That is what you're here for, isn't it?"

"Falconer," William corrected him proudly. "The king—" William broke off. Perhaps it would be better if he did not say the king had sent him here. "The king has fantastic falcons," he said, knowing full well that it did not sound right.

Odon merely nodded. "Me, I'm going to be a famous knight one day. The lord of the manor is my uncle. He was a knight-errant, a second son. Until he married my father's sister, he didn't have a title or lands," he explained condescendingly. "I'm better off. I'm the firstborn, and I'll inherit my father's estate. Beside, I'm going to marry a rich lady later, which will make me even more powerful." He looked at the smaller William complacently. "What about your father. Is he a falconer, too?"

"Oh no, he's a famous knight. A friend of Sir Baudouin." He beamed at Odon, full of pride.

"And does he have a name? I know all the famous knights," he boasted self-importantly.

At this, William just shrugged.

"You're probably a bastard, and he doesn't even know you exist." There was a certain note of satisfaction in Odon's voice. "And your mother?"

"Is the best swordsmith in all England," replied William. His green eyes shone with pride.

"A swordsmith's bastard! No wonder your father wants nothing to do with you. What's your name, anyway?"

"William."

"William the Bastard. That's a name to conjure with. Have you ever heard of William the Conqueror?"

"No, who's he?"

"He died long ago. He was a Norman duke who conquered England more than a hundred years ago. My grandfather's grandfather fought for him."

After they had been walking through fields and meadows for a good while, they reached a house with several outbuildings and a wooden tower.

"This is where the head falconer lives. His name is Logan. I reckon he'll be overjoyed to see you," Odon said smugly, then turned away without another word.

The sun was already half-submerged below the horizon. It would be dark soon. William stood in front of the falconry for a while, not daring to knock on the door. There was not a soul to be seen. Was anyone actually expecting him? William gathered his courage and was thinking about how he should introduce himself to the falconer when the door of the main house opened. A boy about William's age, if not younger, stumbled out.

"Three buckets," a man shouted from behind him.

The boy picked up two leather buckets and muttered crossly, "Three buckets with two arms."

"Either you'll have to make two trips, or I can help you—if you've got another bucket," William suggested, managing a timid smile.

"Who are you, now?" A frown passed over the boy's face.

"My name's William." He wiped his hand conscientiously on his smock and held it out. "I'm here because I want to be a falconer. I hope I'm expected."

"Maybe." The boy shrugged and took no notice of William's proffered hand. "We'd better hurry up—he can get pretty angry." With his thumb, he pointed over his shoulder at the house.

Disappointed, William picked up the third bucket the lad pointed at and followed him.

"I'm Robert," said the boy, without looking at William. "The falconer is my father. Why have you come to him of all people?"

William did not know what he should understand by this. Did the boy think his father was a bad master? Or did he just find him too strict?

"To be honest, I'm just happy I can become a falconer. I didn't have any choice about where." William smiled uncomfortably. If Sir Baudouin had brought him here on the king's orders, there must be some reason.

"Hmm," replied Robert dismissively.

Something was not right about this Robert. William decided to watch him and, for the time being, to be careful in his presence.

Once they had filled the buckets with water from a nearby stream, he followed the falconer's son into the house, heart pounding.

The falconer was sitting at the table, drinking from an earthenware tankard. His deeply fissured cheeks, his unusually long, matted gray beard, and his watery blue eyes gave him a wild and forbidding appearance.

"What do you want here?"

"I…er, didn't the lord of the manor…? I'm here to, I can…" William stammered.

"What's your name?"

"His name is William, Father," Robert answered on his behalf.

William looked at him gratefully, but Robert's expression was not exactly friendly.

"So you want to be a falconer?" Logan exclaimed contemptuously. "Why?" His scrutiny was so penetrating that William suddenly felt naked and helpless.

"Because I…er, because I love birds," he answered, then immediately wished he could crawl into a mouse hole. He really couldn't have said anything more foolish, for more birds were killed in a hunt than anything else. "Falcons, I mean. Falcons," he corrected himself hurriedly, blushing.

"I see. I expect you hope you'll be hunting with the knights soon, in expensive clothes and on the back of a noble horse?"

William's eyes began to shine despite his best efforts.

"But there'll be none of that, do you hear?" the falconer barked at him. "As a falconer's boy you'll be on foot, and if you want a cloak with fur trim you'd better hunt down a couple of rats and skin them." Laughter could scarcely sound more hateful.

William had never in his life felt so small and insignificant. Despite his crippled foot, which the falconer had not yet noticed, fortunately, he had on the whole been treated decently up to now, not least out of respect for his mother. Now he found himself standing in this strange room, dusty, hungry, weary, and more than anything else disappointed.

Logan stood up. "I'm going to bed. The boy can sleep with you," he told his son brusquely and turned away to get his pallet ready.

Robert did not seem particularly happy about this, but nonetheless he took him over to his corner, which was separated from the rest of the room by a piece of cloth.

William was painfully hungry but did not dare ask the falconer for food. He had resigned himself to going to sleep with his belly grumbling when someone tapped his arm.

"Here," whispered a girl of about eight, handing him a slice of bread and a piece of ham. The child put a finger to her lips.

William nodded to show he understood.

"Go to sleep now, Bug," Logan called out.

"My name is Nesta, not Bug," she protested quietly.

"Thanks, Nesta," whispered William. "Have you got any water for me?"

"Back there, the bucket with the dipper in it. We can all use it. Whoever takes the last bit has to go fetch more, but you've just done that," she said.

It was obvious that she was Robert's sister. She had the same dark-brown hair, though it was finer. Even her eyes were the same warm hazel color. If they were the falconer's children, they must take after their mother, thought William.

"Will you be quiet now," Logan thundered, yawning loudly. Soon, apparently, he was asleep; his even, sibilant breathing was clearly audible.

William ate his bread and ham and drank a few gulps of water. Only then did he realize how long and tiring his day had been.

He was so tired he could hardly stand, so he lay down on the straw mat beside Robert.

"Hey, you, time to get up!" Robert gave William an ungentle shove. "It's getting light already."

William stretched, yawning. It must still be early. He could make out only indistinct outlines in the little bit of light that penetrated the wooden shutters.

Logan was still snoring.

"We have to get ready before he wakes up. Come on—hurry up," Robert urged William, letting himself out of the house. William had slept in his clothes, so he soon slipped out after him. Nesta followed hot on his heels.

William made his way down to the stream where he had filled the buckets with Robert the previous day; relieved himself in the bushes; and washed his face, neck, and hands, as he was used to doing at home.

"What's wrong with your foot?" asked Nesta curiously.

"Crooked, since I was born," he answered tersely, adjusting the binding. In Saint Edmundsbury, the younger children had occasionally teased him about his foot, but Nesta just nodded.

"Can you run with it?" Robert inquired.

"Of course," growled William.

An expectant glint appeared on Robert's face, and he jumped up. "So much the better. Falconers have to be able to run fast. My father says I'm quick. Let's see if you can keep up with me. Let's have a race around the house and back," he challenged William, drawing a line in the sandy soil with his toe. "Starting here."

William hated this kind of competition. If he lost, Robert would make fun of him. If he won, despite the pain in all his joints from his ride, the falconer's son would probably resent him for it. William sighed. It was out of the question for him to turn down the challenge. So he positioned himself next to Robert, who had already begun to count. On "three," they both started running.

Robert ran like the wind, panting, and quickly left William some distance behind. But William tried his hardest, too, and caught up, so they reached the starting point at the same time.

A draw! William was thoroughly satisfied with this result. He sat down and took off his shoe. The bandage around his foot had shifted and was cutting into his skin.

"It's bleeding!" Robert said, pointing at William's foot.

"I know."

"It looks as if it hurts."

"It's all right." William did not want to let on that he was in severe pain.

"If you want me to help you, it's all right to say so. I don't mind." Robert touched William's foot, as if he wanted to show that he meant it.

William was embarrassed, and he refused his help. He massaged the injured foot with both hands. When Logan's thundering voice suddenly rang out behind him, he jumped.

"What the hell is that?"

William had not noticed the falconer's arrival until Logan's thundering voice boomed out from right behind him.

"So now my lord sends me a cripple who wants to become a falconer." Logan raised his right hand to the almost bald spot on his head and stroked it, as if he could not quite believe it. "They have no idea, these great men, how much work it takes to tame a bird. They just have the trained birds placed on their fists and they think they know something about hunting," he went on, more and more worked up. "And I'm the one who has to deal with it."

"The king is a good falconer," protested William, hurriedly rewrapping his foot. He pulled on his shoe and leaped up.

Robert was already standing.

Logan went to William and poked him in the chest with his forefinger. "I don't know who put you forward, but even if it was the king his majestic self you needn't think you're something special." He sniffed sharply and lowered his hand. "Perhaps you believe that I care who sent you here? Hear this: As long as you do what I tell you and don't become a thorn in my side, you can stay. If you don't work hard, you'll be out quicker than you got here."

William stood there, thunderstruck, but then his defiant spirit reasserted itself. The falconer had greeted him without the slightest show of hospitality; not even the poorest serf would have done that. He drew himself up. "I haven't had anything to eat yet," he protested daringly.

"Sweeping first, then eating. That's how we always do things here. If it doesn't suit you, you can leave whenever you like. I dare say there are plenty of other falconers who can't wait to take you in."

Not yet, but they will, thought William sullenly, looking the falconer bravely in the face.

"Now get on with the sweeping."

Robert gave him a gentle poke in the ribs and pulled him away.

"And you, go in the house and do your work," Logan snarled at his daughter, who had been watching all this from a safe distance.

"The dogs we use when we go hawking are in the barn there. And back there in the little shed we've put a bitch with her litter, so that nothing happens to the puppies. They won't join the others until they're big enough and weaned." Robert's little tour began.

"And what's in the tower?" asked William, determined not to let anything grind him down.

"The falcons! Where did you think they were?" Robert smiled rather contemptuously, but that did not bother William. The thought of the falcons warmed his heart. He examined the tower curiously from top to bottom.

"My father raises nestlings in an aerie he made himself. Up there, see?" Proudly, Robert pointed at the top of the tower, but William could not make anything out. "The other falcons are housed below. That's where we have to clean now. But quietly, mind you. Otherwise they take fright and we get into trouble."

William fought down his rising irritation. Robert seemed to take him for a fool. As if he would have gone into the mews shouting and waving his arms about.

As they entered the tower, he felt the same excited fluttering in his stomach he had felt the day he had found the royal falcon. Specks of dust whirled and glittered in the broad beam of sunlight streaming into the room through the open door, wafted about by the draft. Robert closed the door, and suddenly it was dark. Fortunately, William's eyes were used to adjusting to the dark quickly, thanks to his work in the smithy, and soon he could make out some details. The floor was almost completely covered with sand. In the middle of the room stood a dozen cylindrical wooden posts that had been driven into the ground, each fitted with an iron ring. There was a bird perching on nearly every block, its leash fastened to the ring.

There were falcons of several sizes, colors, and markings. Sir Ralph must be very wealthy, for he owned—William counted lightning fast—nine falcons.

With the ease of habit, Robert took a glove from a hook by the door and approached the first bird. It was only slightly smaller than Blanchpenny, and its plumage was completely different. So it couldn't be a gyrfalcon. Robert knelt down beside it, released the leash from the ring, and took the falcon onto his fist. With his free fingers, he gripped the leather strips attached to the falcon's feet. Robert carried the bird toward a wooden frame, explaining to William that the strips were called jesses, as if William didn't know such a thing.

William frowned at the sight of the falcon's closed eyes, which looked as if they had been sewn shut. Robert raised the falcon to the wooden perch, lowered his hand until the bird's feet touched it, then opened his fist to release the jesses. He wound the leash around the perch and carefully moved his hand away. Unable to see anything, the falcon stepped backward onto the perch. Robert wound the leash around the frame one more time so that the bird could not escape.

"They all have to be on the high perch, so that we can replace the sand," he explained quietly as he picked up the next falcon in the same way and put it beside the first.

The high perch. William nodded, taking note of the new phrase so that he could master the language of falconry. Fascinated, he watched how easily the falconer's son handled the birds.

"Can I try?" William asked after a while.

Robert shrugged and fetched another glove. "Of course, that's what you're here for."

William slipped on the gauntlet. In silence, he knelt down beside the falcon, imitating Robert, and took the creature onto his fist. Feeling the raptor's talons through the thick leather of the glove set off an extraordinary feeling of happiness. He stood up cautiously and lifted up the falcon to the high perch. Although he had carefully noted each separate hand movement, something he had never managed when he was smithing, he was trembling inwardly with the fear of making a mistake. Only when he had carried the falcon to its perch without difficulty and fastened the leash did he relax.

"Good." Robert's enthusiasm was muted, whereas William was almost bursting with pride. He lifted the next two birds onto the high perch without difficulty and fastened them, too.

"Now we have to clear up the mutes and castings," explained Robert as he handed William a small shovel and broom.

"Mutes and castings?" William had never heard these words.

Robert sullenly pointed at the birds' excrement, which was embedded with small pellets that appeared to consist of undigested remains. "That stuff."

The boys began to clean the blocks, one by one, removing the mess from the sand around them.

"The mutes should be white with a black spot. If they're green or reddish, it means the falcon may be ill and we must call my father," Robert explained, pointing at the droppings around the first block. "That's what they should look like—do you see?"

When they had finished, they put the birds back onto their blocks.

"Now we'll get something to eat," whispered Robert. "Come on, I'm hungry."

At the door to the tower, William pointed to a ladder that led up. "Can I see the aerie?"

Robert hesitated for a moment, then nodded his consent and started going up. William climbed close behind him. After a few rungs, the falconer's son stopped. "We're not really supposed to be up here."

William could only just see into the room. The wind whistled through the three open sides; the fourth side was closed off with planks, making for a space that was considerably smaller than the lower room. An aerie made of brushwood and twigs stood in the middle of the room, and in it sat two nestling falcons. They immediately started screeching.

"Those are eyasses taken from the wild," explained Robert. "They're calling for food."

William grinned as his stomach growled loudly at the word.

"As soon as they can fly properly, we'll take them down to be with the others." Robert seemed nervous. "Let's get out of here."

They had only just reached the foot of the ladder when the door opened and Logan stepped in.

"Are you *still* not ready?" he demanded harshly.

☜✦☞

"Nana, look what we've..." Enid's words stuck in her throat upon discovering Nana lying on the ground, groaning quietly.

"David!" The shrill sound of her own voice frightened Enid.

Grinning foolishly as always, David approached, stopped in the doorway, and looked questioningly at his sister. "Wha?" He brought it out laboriously, tilting his head to one side and pressing his clenched hands to his cheek.

"She's sick. Help me. Onto her pallet." She pointed to Nana's feet and grabbed the old woman under the armpits.

As usual, it took a moment for David to understand Enid's instructions.

Nana came to as they moved her to a straw mattress. "It's nearly...over for me," she breathed.

Enid shook her head. There were tears in her eyes. She stroked a strand of white hair away from the old woman's face and kissed her lovingly on the forehead. "Please, no," she whispered.

"You must...be strong. David needs you." Nana coughed. "When I'm dead, you must dig a deep hole and bury me. You mustn't let me lie here more than a day. Do you understand?" Groaning, the old woman lifted her upper body toward Enid. When she fell back onto her mattress, she looked as if a hundred years of sleeping would not help her recover.

"Sit with her," Enid ordered her brother as she searched through her stores of herbs. She scooped water into a pot from a half-filled bucket under the table, stoked the fire, and hung the pot over it. "I'll make her an infusion. It's bound to help." She looked anxiously at the old woman. Her pale face was wrinkled like newly washed linen. Fear clutched Enid's heart. They still needed Nana.

Although they had been strangers to her, Nana had raised the siblings with infinite love and goodness. Enid had long since learned the story by heart, but Nana had to tell it again and again anyway. Only a few days before, they had sat by the fire and listened to her.

It was thirteen winters ago that the Lord showed me his great favor by placing the two of you in my path. The snow was waist deep, and I was looking for something to eat when I heard a soft whimpering. Beneath a mighty oak tree not far off, a young woman sat cowering, an infant in her arms. She was bleeding heavily and sat still as if her child's crying had no effect on her. I went up to her cautiously and saw that she was with child. She seemed utterly exhausted. So, speaking soothingly to her, I took the starving child, helped her to her feet, and supported her emaciated body all the way back here to the hut.

I was glad to have a little company, for by then I had been living alone for years. I fed the tiny infant gruel, and when I wrapped it up in a fresh cloth I saw that it was a little girl.

"Enid," the strange woman croaked in her distress. She said no more. I wrapped the girl in a warm blanket and thought sadly of my own daughters, whom the Lord had taken to him much too soon.

That night, the woman gave birth to a tiny boy with a head that was much too big. I knew there and then that he would never be like other children, and yet I loved him immediately.

His mother never saw him. She was unconscious when he was born and died two days later. There was nothing I could do for her.

The Lord sent you to me, and I accepted his gift with great gratitude, for to me you are the dearest things in the world.

Enid felt as if she could still hear Nana's loving voice telling the story. But the old woman was motionless on her mattress. Enid glanced affectionately at her brother, drained the infusion, and poured it into a small clay cup to cool it down more quickly. She tried to get the old woman, weak as she was, to drink some.

Nana's tiny sips took great effort, but she looked at Enid gratefully. "Tastes of sweet woodruff. Did you add speedwell…?"

"And cowslips and mistletoe, too, yes, Nana," Enid broke in gently. "Drink, it will do you good."

Everything she knew about herbs, roots, trees, fruits, mushrooms, and the animals of the forest she had learned from Nana. For her, the forest was not just an herb garden but also an abundant larder, a place where you never had to go hungry as long as you knew it well enough.

"I'll cook you something nice. That will bring your strength back." Enid smiled confidently.

"It's all right, child." Nana sighed dully. "I'm old and weary. The Lord is calling me, and I'm ready."

"But you *can't* leave us alone." Enid felt the fear of death rising in her, even though it was Nana who should have been afraid of death.

The old woman looked at her with infinite peace and goodness. "Enid, you know the forest better than anyone else." Nana wheezed breathlessly. "From now on you'll have to look out for the both of you. Just be sure to watch out for strangers, won't you," she warned before the cottage fell completely silent.

Enid pressed her ear to the old woman's chest. The heart had stopped beating. "No, Nana, no!" A wave of pain broke over Enid, and she began to weep bitterly. After a while she looked over at David. Obviously distressed, he was crouching on the ground and rocking back and forth. Even he understood that Nana was dead.

Enid gripped the ever-colder hand like a frightened child. She did not even notice how long she sat there weeping. She did not come to her senses until it was dark and her brother's voice reached her indistinctly.

"Foo," he whined, pointing at his belly and rubbing it.

"Nana's dead, and all you can think of is food," she scolded him, sobbing without tears.

David looked at her contritely, hugged himself, and started rocking back and forth again.

All of a sudden, Enid felt guilty. David must be just as sad as she was, but he could not express himself. "It's all right," she said gently to reassure him. She stroked his matted blond hair. "I'm not going to let you starve. You're all I've got now." Tears came into her eyes again, but she wiped them away bravely and started to prepare a meal for him.

July 1185

The amount of work falconry required exceeded William's imagination. Including Logan's other assistant, Alfred, the four of them always had their hands full and never seemed to finish. William diligently carried out every task he was given, trying to complete them to Logan's satisfaction. Mostly he helped Alfred take care of the hounds, clean their kennels, and feed them. Sir Ralph's hunters would bring them scraps and bones from the hunt, or else Logan would go hunting with the boys.

Only the best meat would do for the falcons, and it could come not only from chickens and pigeons but also from hare and deer. Logan had a marked preference for wild birds. He thought wood pigeons, turtledoves, thrushes, sparrows, and larks were the most suitable feed for falcons, so he had built a large wooden shed beside the house, where he kept a considerable number of small birds. Every month, bird catchers would come from far and wide, bringing him their catches. William and Robert nonetheless had to set and check traps every day and go hunting with nets and catapults in order to keep the shed adequately stocked.

Robert was allowed to help his father with the falcons, while William, who had been with the falconry for a good month now, had hardly been allowed to work with them.

"The puppies are old enough now. Bring them to join the pack, William," Logan ordered one morning after breakfast before setting off toward the tower to join Robert.

Once again, William was not allowed to go with them. Suddenly he missed his mother. She was strict and had high expectations, but she had never held him back the way Logan was doing. Disillusioned and near tears, he went after Logan. "Please, master, wait," he cried to his back.

Logan stopped and turned. "What is it?"

"Master, listen to me, I beg you. I was so happy I could learn about falconry from you, but you pay me no attention." William took a deep breath and plucked up his courage. "My greatest wish is to learn everything, every detail, about falcons. Not because I dream of fame and honor and fine clothes, as you seem to think, but because falcons fill my heart with joy. If my mother had her way, I would have become a swordsmith, like her. But all I want is to raise falcons. The best, the bravest, good hunters—healthy, beautiful creatures." William, out of breath, paused for a moment. It was the first time he had spoken his mind, and he looked deep into Logan's watery blue eyes as he did so.

"So you were supposed to be a swordsmith?" said Logan, stroking his bushy beard.

"I'm the eldest son, and I was supposed to take over the smithy eventually, but I want to be a falconer, nothing else. Please, master, teach me the most beautiful of all the arts. I will do everything the way you tell me to, and I'll do it willingly. I will work, work hard, whenever and whatever you want, just as long as you teach me everything there is to know about falcons."

William's earnest words appeared to placate Logan, for he nodded pensively. "Good, now go and take care of the hounds," he said at last, not unkindly, and turned away.

William's heart beat faster with rage. "Hounds are wonderful, but I want to be a falconer, not a dog handler!"

"Do you think I'm so dense I didn't understand you?"

William held the master falconer's gaze and did not move.

"Falcons and hounds must work together in the hunt, else they won't catch anything. Besides, many's the hound that has saved a falcon's life."

William was reminded of Blanchpenny and nodded.

"You want to train good falcons? Then mark this: a successful falconer has to have an excellent eye for dogs, with the ability to pick from the pack the right one for hunting, get it used to the falcons, and train it to hunt alongside them. So when I send you to the hounds, you'll go, without complaint, and you'll do your best. Understood?"

"Yes, master," William answered, looking down in shame.

For the rest of the day, he stayed out of the falconer's way as best he could. Even when they were eating, he remained silent and avoided looking at Logan.

"Tomorrow we can remove half the blinding from the female peregrine. I've already brought the passagers down from the aerie. They'll need seeling. Since Alfred won't be there tomorrow, you can both help me," Logan announced before going to bed without further explanation.

William had not the slightest idea what to expect. He asked Robert to explain the meaning of blinding and seeling but received only a curt reply. William was sure that Robert was not exactly happy about his presence. He was never unfair, admittedly, but he was often quite dismissive. William, therefore, decided not to ask him about anything in the future unless it was unavoidable. Besides, he told himself, it would be no bad thing for him to learn certain things over time.

Very early the following morning, William and Robert followed their master to the tower. Without a word, Logan pointed to a peregrine that was standing on one of the previously unoccupied blocks.

"The leftmost passager first, Robert," he told his son, pointing.

The boy picked up the bird with both hands, enclosing its breast and back with his fingers. William admired Robert's relaxed manner. Whenever Logan was in the vicinity, William trembled with anxiety.

"This is a merlin. Why do I call it a passager, do you know?" Logan asked, looking at William.

"Because it hasn't molted yet," replied William confidently. He knew from Marshal that every falcon, regardless of its type, was given this name until its first molt, when it grew new feathers.

"Good. Do you know what seeling is?"

"No, master."

"To get the bird accustomed to the hand, we must prevent it from seeing people. So we stitch its eyes shut. This is called 'seeling' or 'blinding.' When it has grown used to being handled by people, we first half and then fully 'unseel' it."

William nodded, though the thought of having to help with this operation made him feel uneasy inside.

"Here, take a gauntlet and hold its feet firmly, but watch out for the talons."

William obeyed, gripping the passager's legs with trembling hands.

"If there are only two of you doing the seeling, it's best to wrap the bird in a damp cloth that covers its feet, too. Watch out—you'll see how strong its legs are when it defends itself." Logan took the needle and horsehair from his quilted jerkin and pushed it through the falcon's lower eyelid from the inside to the outside. Then he tugged on the needle until he had pulled most of the thread through.

William's knees felt weak.

The falcon struggled. William felt the little bird's strength and felt sorry for it, but he continued to hold its feet tightly.

"You have to be careful not to stick the needle in too close to the edge of the lid, else the stitches tear easily," Logan explained without looking up.

William felt sick, and his mouth was filling with saliva; he gulped it down desperately, fearing that the falcon must be suffering.

Logan drew the thread over the falcon's head and pierced the eyelid on the other side. Then he pulled the lower lids up toward the brow until both eyes were completely closed. He brought the ends of the thread together at the back of the bird's head, tied them in a knot, and trimmed the ends using the knife he carried in his belt.

"You have to hide the horsehair among the feathers as best you can, so the bird doesn't get caught in it when it scratches. And it will scratch, because the stitches will make it feel unwell."

William nodded apprehensively.

"Some birds try harder than others to get rid of the thread, using their talons. If a bird struggles too much, you can tie the forward talons together with a strip of leather. That way it can't lift its foot to scratch its head."

Watching a falcon be exposed to such indignity, William felt an ungovernable rage. Tears sprang into his eyes, and, for the first time since leaving Saint Edmundsbury, he asked himself whether his wish to be a falconer was right, after all.

Logan seemed to guess what he was thinking. "Seeling is not a pleasant task. At that moment the falcon hates men, because they are holding it tight and bending it to their will."

"It must hurt, too."

Logan shook his head. "I don't think it hurts much. When you stitch the eyelids shut, the falcon barely twitches. I think it only struggles because it wants to escape. But seeling is absolutely essential. If you want to tame a falcon properly, you have to get it used to being handled by people. And that goes best when it can't

see. Even birds that have been captured as nestlings, like these passagers, are better off being seeled so they stay calm, even if they're
already used to the sight of people."

William understood Logan's explanation, but he still could
not conceive how anyone could do anything so humiliating to a
falcon.

Logan trimmed the merlin's talons, and Robert returned it to
the block.

Once the same operation had been carried out on the second
merlin, it was the one-year-old passager's turn. It already had
stitches, and it was time to half-unseel it so that it could become
accustomed to seeing again. Robert went to fetch it, but Logan took
his arm and held him back. "You fetch it," he ordered William.
"You've seen how Robert holds the birds."

William hesitated for a moment, then picked up the passager
in both hands, as he had seen Robert do it. His fingers encircled the
falcon's breast and back with a gentle firmness. Robert took its feet.

"First you have to check whether the eyelids have been
harmed," Logan explained. "If the holes have torn, and you think
they won't hold, you have to remove the thread and seel the eyes
all over again. But this time you only pull the lids halfway up. The
lids on this one are still perfect." He undid the knot at the top of
the bird's head and loosened the threads so that the eyes were only
half-covered. Then he did up the ends in a knot again.

William felt sick again.

Logan told him to put the bird back and patted him reassuringly on the shoulder. "You get used to it."

William could not bring himself to nod.

"Come, we've still got things to do." Robert elbowed William in
the ribs and dragged him away from his dark imaginings. "Let's go."

"I think it's horrible, too," said Robert once they were no longer near Logan. "But my father's right. The more often you see it,
the more bearable it becomes."

"Have you ever done it yourself?" William asked shyly.

"No, God forbid. And I'm not keen to start. Look, I've grown up with hawks. I love them, and I'll be a falconer one day, like all the men in my family, but to be honest I prefer working with the hounds. Unlike falcons, they love their masters and become their most faithful friends. And the best thing is that you don't have to inflict pain on them to train them."

If Robert prefers dogs, why doesn't Logan let him take over that side of things and leave the falcons to me? William wondered. Perhaps it was Robert's love of the hounds that made him treat William so contemptuously? William came to the conclusion that Logan demanded the most from each of them in precisely the area they were least willing.

William took a deep breath. He would be the best one day. A falconer with the most superbly trained hounds and the most magnificent falcons that England's nobles had ever seen. And if seeling was among the unavoidable tasks that fell to a successful falconer, he would do his best to carry out this disgusting job as well as it could possibly be done and to inflict no more pain on the birds than was necessary. And he would devise other ways to train falcons. Perhaps, one day, he would succeed in finding a better solution than seeling.

Once both young merlins had been successfully seeled, Logan assigned a bird to each of the boys.

"You will man them, following my instructions to the letter. In order to get them used to your hand, you will have to carry them on your fist for a couple of days. They can perceive daylight even through sewn-up eyelids, so you'll have to start in the dark. You will feed them twice a day. That way they will get used to you. You must learn to judge their mutes and castings correctly. That's the only way you can tell whether they are digesting their food properly and are in good health. If falcons are to be good hunters later, they must have frequent opportunities to bathe, for that makes them courageous. And once they're manned, I'll show you how to train them to a lure—which first you'll have to make, using feathers from the birds you want them to hunt. It's only after a falcon has hunted a lure many times, earning the choicest tidbits, that it will love it and come back to its master whenever he uses the lure. Alfred and I will be watching you at every step. But you will have to do most of the work, because you can gain a full understanding of falcons only by working with them over time. When the merlins are trained, we'll introduce them to the hunt and see which of the two is better. Sir Ralph wants to give the stronger one to his nephew."

"Oh no, not Odon of all people," Robert groaned quietly.

William looked at him in surprise. Odon was the squire who had brought him to the mews when he had arrived. He had appeared to be exactly what a young nobleman should be. What could Robert have against him?

Logan rebuked his son with a glance, then continued. "The other merlin is to go to Sir Ralph's daughter, so she can get used to keeping falcons."

William was overjoyed. At last he would learn to be a proper falconer. Taking on Robert, who already had much more experience with birds, was a challenge very much to William's taste. He hung on every word of praise from Logan, soaking it up as the dry earth soaks up the summer rain. Since friendly words were not exactly the falconer's strong point, William and Robert courted them all the more assiduously, fanning a healthy rivalry between the two boys.

Using an elderly falcon, Logan showed them how to hold their arms and hands in various situations. The falcon must always be able to stand safely and to tolerate long periods on the fist. They also practiced mounting and dismounting horses to the point of exhaustion. After a while, in fact, Robert and William felt that they could have done it in their sleep.

When they had mastered holding the older falcon and could do it with confidence, Logan ordered them to carry the two merlins around in the dark tower, in silence, for three days and nights. The boys, and the birds, were allowed only a few breaks. But these breaks did not give them time to rest, for they still had to carry out most of their normal tasks. Though the merlins weighed very little, the boys' arms quickly felt like lead because of the awkward posture. They would change hands, carrying the birds first on their right fist and then on their left.

The pain in his upper arms and shoulders, as well as the darkness, reminded William of his mother's smithy. But instead of the resentment he had always felt when working in her workshop, carrying the falcon filled him with pride.

Although he was now sure he had chosen the right path, from time to time he still thought sadly of Ellenweore, Isaac, and the others. Had they forgotten him?

Logan had taught them that they should speak soothingly when feeding the falcons, so that the birds would learn to recognize their voices and lose their fear. Each of them had a particular way of calling his merlin, and the boys would never feed the birds together, so that they could gorge, or feed, in peace.

While William and Robert were occupied with the merlins, Logan and Alfred were training the newly unseeled falcons. Robert and William watched them as often as they could, in order to get ready for their next task. This meant that they were busy from the first glimmering of dawn well into the night, gulping their meals down hastily and hardly getting any sleep, but William was happier than he had ever been in his life.

Robert had gone off on his own to capture a special treat for his falcon. Pleased with himself, he held up the thrush he had brought down with his slingshot. His merlin would find it very tasty indeed. He stuffed the dead bird into his falconer's bag.

That morning's hazy, pale-gray sky had given way to a slate color that promised rain. Robert made haste, knowing a heavy downpour could break out any moment. Late August had been unusually hot, and the nights had been so muggy they had brought little relief. They had been waiting for a thunderstorm for almost a week, hoping it would deliver the cool weather they craved. The birds were flying low, which was an almost certain sign that it would rain soon. The little forest that covered the hill was not far from the falconry, but when the first fat drop of rain fell, Robert feared he would be soaked through in a few steps.

Cautiously, he slithered down the slope. He had started his climb at a different point, where it was not as steep and stony. Before he reached the path, though, he tripped on a root and fell the last part of the way.

He landed, heart pounding, against the trunk of a magnificent hornbeam. His sleeve was torn and his elbow was bleeding. Tears burned in his eyes. He did not notice the gash on his face until he wiped the tear away with his sleeve. His father must not see him crying. Logan would not mind a torn sleeve half as much as weeping.

As he stood up, Robert heard horses approaching. He stayed close to the hornbeam to let the riders pass, since the path was narrow. It was not until they got closer that Robert recognized Odon and the young de Aston. It was already too late to get out of their way. Odon reined in his horse and leaped down.

"What is it, Odon?" asked de Aston as he, too, came to a halt.

"Well, if it isn't our little friend." Odon pointed at Robert, sneering with malice. "All alone in the woods?"

Robert knew Odon well enough to know what would happen next. The villagers held their breaths with fear when Sir Ralph's nephew rode through the streets in the company of his friends. He did not hesitate to humiliate anyone he could, with mockery or even blows. Although this time he was accompanied by only the young de Aston, the most harmless of his friends, Robert guessed that Odon would think up something degrading, and he felt his knees go weak.

છ્ઉ

William ran across the meadow toward the little forest. Although he scarcely had the time, he had started running again, and his stamina and form had both improved.

The clouds building up to the north looked very threatening. Logan had sent him off to find Robert before the storm broke. They had had an argument about the hounds a few days before and had not spoken since, but that did not matter now. William heard the first rumblings of thunder. He had no desire to be struck by lightning. He ran up the slope and took a short-cut over a bank. He heard voices and laughter, and he ducked down. You couldn't be too careful. All manner of villainy lurked in the woods.

The voices were coming from the path, so he crept closer. Hidden behind a bush, he could see Odon and another squire. They were walking toward a third whom William could not see because his view was blocked by a horse's hindquarters. William moved in order to see who was standing between Odon and the other squire. Robert! William was about to show himself and call him, when he saw Odon give Robert a shove.

"Go on then—show us your little pizzle," he taunted Robert.

"Yes, out with it," cried the other one, laughing.

Robert, his face flushed, refused.

"Ah, he doesn't want to, the poor little fellow." Odon grabbed a bare branch off the ground. "Do it. Or do you need help?" He poked Robert with the stick and laughed loudly.

William reached for his belt. Fortunately, he had his slingshot with him. He looked for a suitable stone. It would not be difficult to hit him. Odon was no farther away than the songbirds he brought down almost every day. William found a stone, placed it in the strap fastened between the stubby forks, pulled the strap taut, aimed, and fired.

Odon collapsed to the ground without a word.

His rosy-cheeked friend held his sides with laughter when he realized that Odon had been laid out by a simple stone.

Robert, meanwhile, did not spot William until he emerged from his hiding place, crossed the path, and gave one of the horses a hefty slap on the rump, making it gallop away as if the devil were in pursuit.

"Hey," shouted the squire as the second horse panicked and followed hard on the heels of the first. He threw up his hands and ran after them.

"Come," said William to his friend. He had already placed a second stone in the strap, but the apple-cheeked squire was far too busy trying to catch the horses to notice the danger he was in.

Odon groaned quietly.

"We'd better get away from here." William grabbed Robert's sleeve and pulled him away.

William preferred not to think about the consequences of felling Odon, and he simply ran as fast as he could. Robert stayed close behind and only stopped, panting, shortly before they reached the mews.

"It's better if we don't tell my father about this. He thinks the squires are honorable men and wouldn't believe us. He doesn't know that everyone in the village lives in fear and worry because these men vent their arrogance on the old, the sick, and the weak.

The lord of the manor himself has no idea. Odon's aunt conceals his outrages. Reginald de Vere, the fencing master, is the only one who knows the squires well enough to see through them. He punishes them when he catches them, but unfortunately that's all too seldom. You challenged Odon today. He'll never forgive you for it," Robert warned him. "But though you were a fool to stand up against him on my account—thank you, Will. Friends?"

"Friends!"

They shook hands.

"Where have you been?" Logan addressed his son, striding toward him.

"I shot down a thrush."

"And you?" Logan asked of William.

"Father, didn't you send William to look for me, because of the storm?"

"Of course I did. But couldn't he have shot a bird while he was about it? To miss an opportunity like that, when you're already in the woods," he scolded them. "Now go and feed the dogs."

"And what a bird you shot down, Will!" Robert burst out as soon as Logan was far enough away. "As a thank-you, you're getting the best bits of my thrush for your merlin."

"Well, in that case it's been worth making an enemy." William winked, giving Robert a friendly poke in the ribs. "From now on we'd better go to the woods together. It won't be entirely safe for the next few days."

"He'll find a way, believe me," Robert predicted darkly. "The only question is what and when."

❧❧

A stormy wind was rushing through the leaves, still warm with summer heat, as William and Robert made their way to the tower. August had been hot and dry, and September was scarcely better.

The dirt in the yard spun about in whirlwinds. William was putting the two water buckets down to rub the dust out of his eyes when he heard the stamp of horses' hooves on the path toward the mews.

"My lord, Sir Reginald." Robert greeted the two leading riders first, bowing politely.

William remembered Sir Ralph, the lord of the manor, though he had not seen him at all since his arrival at Thorne. The other man, whom Robert had called Sir Reginald, was the fencing master he'd been told about. William groaned quietly when he noticed Odon riding behind them.

"My lord, Sir Reginald," said William, imitating Robert. He bowed before the two barons. "I'll go and fetch Logan."

"You stay here. Robert can go," said Sir Ralph firmly.

Odon grinned broadly.

William tried to control the trembling of his knees. Had Odon told his uncle about the incident in the woods? If so, he could be sure the lord of the manor knew only half the truth and would punish him severely.

"Odon says you've been boasting about your skill and claim your falcon flies better than Robert's."

William's mouth was dry, and his head felt drained of blood. He had not said a word to Odon about the merlins.

"I've promised the better bird to Odon," Sir Ralph went on. "Logan and I will decide when to make them hunt, so that I can judge for myself which one is better. Then we'll see." He kept his eyes on William, observing him as though he hoped to find from his face whether William was a braggart or not.

"I haven't been boasting." William found the courage to protest. He did not deign to look at Odon, but he could almost feel the squire's grin. "Both merlins are good birds. When they hunt, you will be able to see for yourself that it makes no difference which one you choose."

Odon grinned even more. He seemed all too sure of his approaching triumph.

"Look, Father, here comes Logan," said a young girl who was sitting on a pony not far from Odon. William had not noticed her before.

"Welcome, my lord! Sir Reginald." Logan managed to bow without looking subservient.

"Have you got any more puppies, Logan? May I see them? Please?" the girl pleaded softly, adroitly slipping down from her pony.

Logan glanced at Sir Ralph to seek his approval. "Of course, mistress. William, go with her. Go on, make haste."

Happy not to have to put up with Odon's grinning any longer, William ran after the girl, who had already hurried ahead, caught up with her, and threw open the door of the stables. Then he followed her in. The wooden shutters were wide-open to let in the air, and it was hardly any darker inside than outside.

"You can call me Sibylle when my father's not there," the girl said in a soft voice, smiling charmingly. "Oh, isn't he sweet," she cried, trying to pick up one of the puppies.

"Wait, I'll show you how to hold them without hurting them." William put his hand on her soft arm, and Sibylle let go of the puppy. "Put one hand under its tummy, just behind its front paws, and the other under its behind." He scooped up the little dog and handed it to Sibylle.

"How old are you?" she asked, folding the fidgeting dog in her arm. "What a fine little dog you are," she cooed to the little bundle of brown fur.

"I was twelve at Eastertide." William felt as though he had grown a little there and then, so proud was he. He towered over Sibylle, whom he reckoned to be nine or perhaps ten years old, whereas Robert—though almost two years younger—already stood eye to eye with him, much to William's chagrin.

"Are you friends, you and Robert?"

William felt as though he had been caught thinking about Robert. Two tiny dimples appeared on the child's cheeks when she smiled. William blushed, then nodded. "Of course we are." He leaned down to a puppy that was snuffling around his leg, whimpering quietly for attention, and stroked it. "You're to have the other merlin, aren't you?"

Sibylle nodded. "But I'd much rather have a dog. You can play better games with them."

"You can't play games with a falcon at all," William corrected her. What a waste, he thought, giving a young girl like Sibylle a falcon!

"I know," she said slowly. "Perhaps I should get to know falcons properly. Maybe I would like them better. I should come here more often. Then I could play with the dogs, too."

William nodded, still disconcerted by her clear, bell-like voice. "If your father doesn't mind."

"He lets me do more or less as I wish." She waved her hand confidently. Her eyes sparkled mischievously. "But as for my mother"—she shook her head indignantly—"only my beloved cousin Odon can wrap her around his little finger."

When the stable door creaked open, William jumped.

"Will? We're to show them the merlins. She's to come, too." Without so much as glancing at the girl, Robert went out again.

"I don't think he likes me." In place of the dimples, there were now two sad little creases.

"Stuff and nonsense," William reassured her. "We had a little problem with Odon a while ago, so he's in a bad temper."

Sibylle smiled with relief. "I can well understand. I don't like him, either, although he's my cousin and I'm supposed to love him like a brother. He's just too cruel and deceitful. My maid complains about him almost every day. Odon pinches her bottom," she added in a whisper. "My mother says she shouldn't make such a fuss. An ugly creature like her should be proud to be noticed by a squire like him. But she isn't ugly at all. And Odon isn't exactly handsome himself. Although all the girls do have an eye for him... Sometimes I kick him in the shin. He can't hit me, you see. That would be against his code of honor. But when there's no one looking, he pulls my hair."

Picking on little girls, that's typical of a coward like him, thought William angrily.

Robert opened the door again. "Are you coming or not?"

"Yes." William hastily took the dog from Sibylle, put it on the ground, and pushed her out through the door. "We don't want Robert to get into trouble on our account."

"No!" Frightened, Sibylle shook her head.

That evening, once the lord of the manor and his retinue had left, Logan scolded the boys. "You must work harder. Young Odon is impatient. He wants his falcon as soon as possible. Sir Ralph is far too indulgent with the fellow. Not that the lord is a bad master, but he doesn't pay enough attention to what goes on at Thorne when he's away," Logan growled angrily. William and Robert were surprised and hung spellbound on every word. "What are you staring at? Don't you have things to do? Go on, fetch some water and then make up your pallets. Plenty of work waiting for you tomorrow." To add force to his words, he gave them each a light cuff on the back of the head. "And you, go scrub the table," he told Nesta. "I'm going to cut some wood before it gets dark." He stormed out of the house, slamming the door behind him.

The next day, when the sun was already high in the sky, Sibylle came to the mews alone. She was wearing simple clothes, like a servant, and arrived on foot. When she asked to be allowed to help the boys, William refused indignantly. She was the lord of the manor's daughter!

Robert had a different view. "If she wants to learn how to handle falcons—which is advisable, because she's to have the merlin, after all—then it's only right and proper that she should help with the occasional task," he declared firmly. He pressed a water bucket into her hand and gave her the task of filling the falcons' baths.

Sibylle beamed at him and followed Robert around for the rest of the day. As it turned out, she was not proud and did not behave like a spoiled little brat when faced with dirty or difficult tasks. After only a few days, she felt confident enough to hold a falcon on her gloved fist and offer it the bony scraps of dead birds.

Sibylle was always cheerful and often made the boys laugh. She kept her eyes open and helped wherever she could. Whenever Robert did not assign some work to her, she would frolic with the hounds, which she still preferred over the falcons. But she did begin to see the worth of the birds.

"She's completely different from her cousin, helpful and always good-tempered," William said to Robert one evening after they had walked Sibylle back to the castle and, afterward, had a race. He threw himself down on the grass, panting, and looked up into the softly tinted evening sky. "She doesn't seem to take after her mother, either. She doesn't even look like her, except perhaps for the color of her hair."

"Hmm, perhaps," Robert replied, resting his head in his hand and drawing wavy lines in the packed dirt with a twig. "She's all right."

"Has she gone, finally?" a little voice said from out of nowhere.

"Nesta, you nosy little toad," Robert growled at his sister.

"She's always allowed to run around with you. You never take me," she cried petulantly. "I always have to make the meals, feed the chickens, sweep the house, do the laundry. She can do whatever she wants, all day long, or have it done for her." Nesta's eyes were black with resentment.

"She is the lord's daughter, after all," Robert replied with a shrug.

"It's still not fair." Nesta stamped her foot.

"Come, don't be angry with her." William smiled reassuringly at Nesta. "Sibylle can't help it that she's Sir Ralph's daughter. In fact, you might even feel sorry for her. It can't be easy to have Odon for a cousin and the lady of the manor for a mother."

Nesta shrugged and thrust out her chin. "If I catch you, I'll tickle you," William threatened, leaping to his feet.

"Catch me if you can!" she taunted William, waiting until he had almost caught her before running away again, laughing joyfully. When she looked round to see if he was following, he realized she was making eyes at him, even though she was still only a child. William decided he would not tickle her so often anymore, so as not to raise her hopes. One day, the young men of the village would line up before her father, but she would marry the son of a falconer. That was the custom, for it was a privilege to be a falconer, a privilege that was handed down within the family.

The sun was as warm as in summer, though autumn had begun, and the October sky was brilliantly blue and clear. William moistened his right forefinger and held it up in the air. The wind was easterly, but fortunately not so strong that it would spoil the forthcoming hunt with the young merlins. Sir Ralph and the fencing master had come to the mews with two other squires and were waiting.

"I haven't forgotten the thing with the stone," Odon hissed at William when no one was looking. "Sometime I'll catch you alone, and then you'll be in trouble." Odon spat on the ground near William and went over to his friends to show off in front of them, for he was the first of them to get his own falcon. But when one of them observed that the merlins were the smallest birds in the mews, Odon took a more critical look. Once he had established that his companion was right, his anticipation was somewhat dampened.

William could not resist a smirk, but he turned away when he saw that Odon was looking at him menacingly.

When everyone had gathered, the little hunting party set off for the flat terrain merlins preferred for hunting.

William and Robert bore their birds safely and proudly. They kept a careful but discreet eye on Logan, so that they would not miss any of the instructions he kept issuing by means of small gestures. Their first hunt with the merlins, Logan had told William and Robert, would remain in their memories forever. Like first love.

The two boys were apprehensive. At last they would see whether they had trained their falcons to be bold hunters.

Before a falconer could give a suitable name to a bird he had trained, the falcon had to show what it had in it. Despite their friendship, each of the boys naturally hoped his merlin would prove to be the best. They took up their designated positions with their birds. The two squires who had accompanied Odon moved through the grass and flushed out the songbirds.

The moment the first birds rose, William cast off his merlin. Biting his lip with tension, he watched every beat of her wings. As though she had been hunting all her life, the merlin picked out a lark that had become separated from the flock, flew low and swift after it, pursuing it single-mindedly, and struck after a thrilling chase.

Sir Ralph was delighted, and even Logan seemed thoroughly satisfied.

William ran over to the little falcon as she crouched over her prey and covered it with her wings. Logan called this "mantling"; it was how she protected her prey from the prying eyes of envious rivals. The merlin began to tear greedily at the lark.

A falcon was allowed to gorge on her first catch for as long as she wanted. Earlier, Logan had emphasized to William that it was important to pay close attention to the falcon during this time, because it would take a good while for her to eat her fill. Some falcons ended up almost unable to stand upright, let alone reach their prey with their beaks, they were so gluttonous. And in the early evening hours, like now, they became particularly easy pickings for eagles and eagle owls, who viewed falcons as competitors.

Later, on other hunts, the falconer would have to rush to lure the falcon away from her prey with a bit of prepared food—a heart or a liver—so that the kill would not be shredded and devoured. The more experienced a falcon became, the easier it was to distract her from her kill and back onto her master's fist.

Next it was time for Robert's merlin to prove herself. More birds were flushed out, and the merlin took off. But she could not immediately single out one bird from the fleeing mass. At first, in her bewilderment, she chased the whole flock, then changed course and went after a young thrush that was straying from the other birds. Flying as low and swift as William's merlin, Robert's falcon pursued her prey. Both boys watched the scene tensely and were relieved when she struck successfully.

Both boys could be proud of their merlins, though William's had emerged as the clear winner of the competition, because she had selected her prey more decisively.

"You've trained very good hunters there," Sir Ralph praised them, shaking their hands. "They're a delight to behold. What are you going to call them?" He looked at Robert first, questioningly.

"Will—" Robert cleared his throat. "Willowy."

"And Grace," William added with a smile. He had been racking his brain for two days trying to think of a name, and he suspected it had been no different for Robert. But they had not breathed a word about it to each other. William thought Grace was just right for his little merlin because of her particularly elegant flight, so he had chosen that name even though it would not be quite so suitable for a bird that would belong to Odon.

"Splendid." Sir Ralph laughed out loud.

The birds' names showed not only how similar the falcons were but also how close the young falconers were.

"So Grace shall go to Odon and Willowy to my daughter. Come here, Sibylle," he called to the girl. And while Odon was busy showing off in front of his friends, Sibylle hurried happily over to the lord of the manor and curtsied before him.

"Father." She kept her eyes down demurely.

"The falcon I promised you." He nodded to Robert.

Robert stepped forward and held out the merlin to Sibylle. He bowed to the lord's daughter as if she were unknown to him and they had not spent the previous day roaming about together. "This is Willowy, mistress, your merlin," he said respectfully.

With flushed cheeks, Sibylle held out her fist, which was already clad in a deerskin glove. Her father had had it made for her specially.

"Willowy," she repeated gently, skillfully holding out her hand to Robert so the merlin stepped onto it without hesitation. She supported the diminutive falcon exactly as Robert and William had taught her. "You've eaten—no, gorged—too much." She laughed softly. "You're far too heavy for such a pretty little bird." She looked at Robert with the same amount of affection that she had bestowed on the falcon.

Robert turned away in embarrassment. William smirked, having realized long ago that Sibylle had a soft spot for Robert. When William had teased him about it once, Robert had flown into a rage and stayed away from him for half a day, offended.

When Odon saw that his cousin was holding her bird on her fist, he strode up to William. He held his gloved fist a little too high and a long way in front of his body.

He hates not being the center of attention, thought William contemptuously, deliberately ignoring him.

Grace remained on William's fist, even though Odon had approached far too quickly, with spurs jangling.

William felt extremely proud that he had trained the merlin so well, but at the same time he felt a surge of helpless anger. Odon had no idea about falcons and didn't deserve Grace. Giving her away was worse than William had imagined. But he wanted to be a falconer, and he knew he would not be able to keep all the falcons he trained. With a little good fortune, he would not lose Grace forever, though. When she was molting, she would stay at the mews, and she would need to be trained again before the following hunting season. Nonetheless, it felt dreadfully hard to surrender her now, especially to Odon of all people.

And here he was, stepping up without a single word of praise for the falcon or the hunt, looking haughtily at William and waiting for him to place the falcon on his outstretched hand.

"You think you're something special, but you're just a servant, and don't you forget it," Odon growled quietly.

"This is Grace," William said as calmly as he could, although he felt an urge to scream. The bird stepped onto Odon's fist, surprising him and sending him stumbling a few steps back. The merlin adjusted her grip before finding a reasonably comfortable position. But Odon lacked experience. His hand position was insecure and unskilled, something Grace could feel. In her anxiety, she bated off his fist and ended up dangling upside down from her leash.

"Look at this, Logan, your bird is worthless. It's not well," Odon shouted like a spoiled child. "I don't want it."

"Nonsense, that falcon is perfectly healthy. You just have to help her back into position. Go to it," retorted Sir Ralph angrily.

William fought back the tears welling up in his eyes. Normally, Grace was the definition of calmness. How could she get so agitated? Anguish weighed on his chest like a heavy stone. Then he remembered where he was, quickly gripped her securely under her breast, and helped her back onto Odon's fist.

"She doesn't know you well enough yet, Master Odon," he said, apologizing for the merlin in a raw voice.

When it had come to Odon's attention that Sibylle was visiting the mews almost every day, he had mocked her and boasted that he would soon master a bird like that himself, without the help of "some falconer's underlings." But this humiliation with Grace had exposed him as a braggart, even to his friends.

He looked at William with hatred. "It's your fault. You've brought it on badly," said Odon, now on the offensive.

"She has been exceedingly well trained, master," he declared firmly. "You just need to become more confident in handling her. Grace feels it when you are hesitant, and that's why she becomes anxious." He knew full well that his words were bound to stoke Odon's fury, but he found it impossible not to defend the merlin.

"The boy is right, Master Odon," Logan observed.

Even Sir Ralph agreed. "I reckon you have a lot to learn yet, Odon." Turning to Logan, he went on. "I suggest you take the lad under your wing for a few days."

"I'll only stay with the falconer. I want nothing to do with those two," roared Odon, gesturing with his head toward William and Robert. "I won't have them telling me what to do."

Sir Ralph took a deep breath.

"That's what we'll do," Logan agreed. "Leave the falcon here for now, and come to me first thing after sunrise tomorrow morning. Then I'll show you all about feed and mutes, and tell you what you need to pay attention to, Master Odon."

When William heard that Grace would stay a while longer, he smiled with a sigh of relief and decided to give her a particularly delicious treat that evening.

"Have an eye for yourself, cripple, for I'll be near you more often now, and I'll soon wipe that damnable grin off your face," Odon hissed at him before departing.

Spring 1186

nid leaned over her brother, happy to have found him at last. "David." He was lying under a bush, sleeping like a log. She gripped his shoulders and shook him gently.

The boy rubbed his eyes and groaned.

"You mustn't run away again, understood?"

David shook his head and made a few signs with his hands. Apparently he had seen a pretty girl. Enid looked around, but there was nobody nearby.

"Strangers can be dangerous," she warned. "How many times have I told you?"

David wiped his face with the back of his hand. His features contorted themselves into something like a smile.

"I don't care how beautiful she was. If you frightened her, she may set her people on us."

Her brother shook his head again and hid his face in his hands.

"I hope she didn't notice you," replied Enid. It was a long time since she had spoken so many words at a time. The sound of her voice sometimes felt oddly hollow, strange somehow. The solitude was not always easy to bear, even if she did have David, and so she feared losing him all the more. Once, after eating berries that poisoned him, he nearly died. Then he had cut himself with a knife and bled terribly. Another time he caught a fever, and once he even ran into a troop of soldiers. Enid had managed to rescue him at the last moment.

Her fear of losing him, and ending up alone, was great. Alone in the forest, without her brother, she was sure to go mad. She understood, of course, that David wanted to meet other people; she felt the same way, after all. But she could always hear Nana's words: "Be sure not to let anyone find you."

Enid was at home in the forest. The animals, the plants—she knew them all. But people were a puzzle to her. Just like David this afternoon, she sometimes secretly watched travelers as they came through the forest. Most of them stayed on the path for fear of losing their way. They told each other gruesome stories about the fairies and goblins that lived in the forest and the mischief they got up to, but Enid knew none of those things existed. The forest was big, and it seemed dark and impenetrable, but only to those who did not know their way around. She knew exactly where flowers grew in small clearings and where to find nuts, berries, and all the other good things the forest had to offer. She set traps to catch small animals, made warm clothing from their skins, and used their meat to keep up her strength when it grew cold and the forest no longer brought forth fruit.

Enid stroked David's tangled mop of hair. "Let's go back to the hut."

Her brother looked at her with his child's eyes and nodded.

April 1186

Spring had arrived unusually early and been particularly
mild, bringing forth thousands of marvelously fragrant
yellow, white, and pink flowers. Now, after the recent
heavy rain, everything was sprouting lovely plump green buds.
A few birds were still building their nests; others were already
laying their first eggs.

In the mews one day, as they were preparing to train the peregrines for heron hawking, William ran up to Logan with rage-induc-
ing news. "Imagine, master. Odon doesn't want Grace anymore. He
says he's too old for a child's falcon. He wants a peregrine."

"Disagreeable lout," Logan muttered. "No idea about hunting
but gives himself airs. Well, if the lord's nephew wants a peregrine,
then he'll have one. But either the lady of the manor or her husband will have to order it. Tell him that."

William nodded with satisfaction. Odon's wish was not
enough on its own. Grace was a magnificent falcon. Though merlins were small, hunting with them was wonderful. Odon really
had no idea. William went back to Odon and passed on the falcon
master's message.

During the past few months, Odon had lost no opportunity
to take revenge on William. He had tried to make him look bad in
front of Logan, and twice he had ambushed him from behind. But
he had not really succeeded in making William afraid of him.

"My aunt will be damnably angry that Logan won't obey my
orders," Odon fumed, heading back to the castle.

It took two days for the mistress's order to arrive: a peregrine for her nephew was to be selected as soon as possible. But this did not annoy William half as much as the fact that Odon returned the little merlin to the mews without a word. On the other hand, he was overjoyed to have Grace back with him again.

"My goodness, look how badly he's taken care of her," said Logan when he saw Grace on the high perch. "Her wings are drooping, and her back and tail don't form a line. Just look how she's holding her tail feathers, all spread out like that. And her eyes. It's pitiful, this dull expression. Always pay attention to the eyes, do you hear? You can always see in its eyes how a falcon feels. Whether it's starving or sick. Whatever's bothering it—you'll see it in its eyes."

William nodded obediently. It was not the first time Logan had emphasized paying attention to a falcon's eyes, and it would certainly not be the last.

"Let her rest in here for a few days, William," Logan continued. "But give her some tirings every now and again so she doesn't go back to being wild in the dark of the tower. Whenever you feed her, bring her among people, so that she stays tame and we can get a good price when we sell her."

William nodded, taking her onto his fist since it was time to feed her.

"You carry well. One can see that she feels safe on your fist," Logan observed. William blushed with pride at this praise. If only my mother had heard that, he thought, and for a moment he was overcome with terrible homesickness. Someday he would go home again, and Jean, Rose, and Isaac, but especially his mother, would greet him with great joy and pride.

"Are you all right?" asked Logan, frowning.

"Of course, master." William left hastily to put Grace down in the tower.

A few days later, when Sir Ralph came to the mews, Logan complained about Odon.

"Before the boy gets the peregrine, he must learn to look after it properly and hold it correctly. He still doesn't know how. The merlin was fearful and weak, but your lordship's nephew will not accept that the fault is his." Logan did not conceal his anger well.

"Handling swords and lances is closer to the lad's heart, that and his equally sharp tongue," answered Sir Ralph, understanding's Logan's ire. "Believe me, I know this all too well. You'll never make a decent falconer out of Odon."

"As long as he does no harm to the birds," Logan growled, insisting that Odon come back to the mews to learn how to carry a falcon.

William and Robert did their best to stay out of Odon's way, but their eyes sparkled with satisfaction whenever Logan criticized him.

Odon noticed. He was boiling with rage and swore bitter revenge on them if he ever had the chance. His oaths and dire threats increased their fear of him. So they cast their eyes downward whenever he came past, so as not to challenge him.

A few days later, William discovered that Grace's tail feathers had been snapped. He had not expected Odon to avenge himself on the merlin, but William knew at once who was to blame. What was worse, Odon had the impudence to accuse William of having done it himself. Fortunately, Logan saw through the young squire and did not unjustly punish William.

Odon had wanted to hurt William, but since Grace had already molted, all the broken tail feathers meant was that she could not be sold that year. For Logan, this was a financial loss, but one that Sir Ralph, rather than William, would have to bear.

Thus, Odon had unwittingly done William a favor, for now Grace had to stay in the mews until the next time she molted, and it fell to William to care for her.

Winter 1186

William's first winter at Thorne had been exceptionally mild, but the next came in far too early, with bitterly cold weather. December felt more like January, and two weeks before Christmas a hostile freeze made the ground rock hard.

When Robert and William awoke in the gray dawn light, their limbs were stiff with cold. And yet they jumped out of bed eagerly.

"Come on, lazybones, get up," cried Robert playfully. When his sister just stayed there, wrapped up in her blankets, he gave her a friendly thump.

"My head," Nesta whined, fluttering her eyelids.

William knelt down beside her and felt her forehead. "Good heavens, she's burning up." He rushed to Logan's bedside and shook him awake. "Nesta's ill."

Logan got up grudgingly and dressed. He did not really seem to believe that Nesta was unwell. But after feeling the tremendous heat of her body he was worried, too.

"Cold water, get some cold water," he told William and Robert while he looked for a piece of cloth.

William grabbed a bucket and ran out to the river, dressed in only his smock. He had not even put on his shoes. He hardly felt the frosty ground underfoot, but the icy river water burned his skin. As fast as he could, he ran back to the house with the full bucket. A sharp stone wounded his malformed foot, but he paid no more attention to the pain than he did to the blood oozing from the wound.

He handed Logan the bucket. Logan dipped the cloth in the water, wrung it out, and laid it on Nesta's forehead.

"Go and take care of the animals. I'll stay with her." Logan's order sounded uncharacteristically gentle. Obviously, he was worried about Nesta.

William and Robert made themselves scarce. They carried out their duties even more conscientiously than usual, fed both hounds and falcons, and explained to Alfred why Logan had not left the house. They did not return until long after midday. Logan was still sitting at Nesta's bedside. The stench of sickness and vomit filled the house.

William opened the wooden shutters to let in some fresh air. Robert, without a word, took out and emptied the pan into which Nesta had thrown up.

"She says her head hurts, as if it's going to burst." Logan stroked her hair anxiously.

"And the fever?" William asked.

The falconer shook his head. "Go fetch old Cwen," he told his son. Robert ran off immediately.

"We could try wrapping damp cloths around her calves. They swear by it at home. It's supposed to draw the heat from the rest of the body."

Logan agreed, and William wet two cloths and wrapped them around Nesta's lower legs. He then wrapped dry cloths around the wet ones.

"Please, Lord, don't let anything happen to her. Don't take her from me," Logan murmured. He folded his hands and prayed devoutly.

William watched uncomfortably. Not even at Eastertide, when Logan marked the anniversary of his wife's death, did he show this kind of despair—drink, curse, rant, and rage though he might. Here, beside his daughter's sickbed, helplessness was etched into his features.

When Robert came back with the herbalist Cwen, Nesta was no better. She lay on her side, groaning, with her legs pulled up and her spine taut as a bow.

The old woman placed a hand on the girl's forehead, turned her over onto her back, and carefully prized open her eyelids. Nesta whimpered when Cwen tried to raise her head.

"Completely rigid," she said, concerned. She boiled up a broth of medicinal plants and tried in vain to get Nesta to drink some. Then she burned some fragrant herbs and muttered a few unintelligible words, continually probing Nesta's head with her fingers.

"What's wrong with her?" asked Robert. Although he normally took every opportunity to tease his sister, he was extremely anxious.

"Worms in the head, that's what's paining her," the herbalist whispered mysteriously. "The stiff neck is a bad omen. It looks bad for her, right bad. I don't know anyone with signs of future misfortune like these who has survived the fever. Pray for her. I can say no more. It's dusk. I don't know whether the child will live through the night. You should call for a priest."

Though her voice was gentle, Logan quaked, as if each word were the lash of a whip. He sagged and fell to the floor; tears disappeared into his gray beard. "Please, Lord, forgive me, whatever I may have done. I'll do penance. Desire of me what you will, but don't take away my child."

Logan's suffering moved William. He knelt down beside the man and gave him a comforting hug.

"I'll go and fetch the priest," said Robert, who had been pacing up and down in agitation. He asked Cwen to stay until he got back, and he took a torch so that he could run back to the village. When he hurried out through the door, a blast of icy air blew in a fine dusting of snow. The sun, on the point of setting, stood in the gray sky like a silver coin, ready to hand over dominion of the firmament to the moon.

The fire had gone out at some point, and no one had thought to build a new one. The house was bitterly cold. Old Cwen lit a couple of slender twigs and sent William to the shed to fetch a few logs so that they would have enough wood to replenish the fire during the night.

"Have you eaten anything?" she asked.

William shook his head. The thought of food had not occurred to any of them.

Old Cwen rummaged through Logan's provisions and prepared a broth, which she pressed on William with a certain firmness. His stomach ached with hunger, and the broth smelled delicious, but he could not bring himself to swallow more than a few spoonfuls.

Wrinkled old Cwen, however, having tried in vain to get Logan to eat something, ate a good-size dish herself, smacking her lips.

"Why isn't Robert back yet?" In contrast to his habitual anger, Logan sounded worried.

William looked at him compassionately. Logan was moody and demanding, but he had never been unjust. He knew how fond of Nesta his master was, though Logan certainly never showed it. He must feel the same about Robert, William thought. He loves him, too, for sure, without letting it show. William's thoughts suddenly turned to his mother. Did she hide her love for him behind her often-harsh manner?

It was late at night when Robert finally returned. He was frozen through and fearfully angry.

"He won't come!" Robert stamped his feet on the threshold to shake off the snow.

Logan, who had just dozed off, awoke in fright. "What?" he asked, confused.

"The priest, he won't come. It's too cold out for him. Nesta is young and strong, he says. We should wait till morning." Robert tore the woolen hood from his head and beat the fine snow out of his clothes.

"A sinful man who will not walk among us on this earth for much longer," muttered Cwen, her head swaying from side to side, but no one heeded her.

Robert's hands were red, his fingers rigid with cold. He held them out over the fire and rubbed them together fiercely. "How is she?" he asked, looking anxiously at Nesta.

"She hasn't come to, poor little thing. He should have administered the last rites, that worthless sot," old Cwen grumbled angrily.

"The villagers are right: the Lord's shepherd is more comfortable in bed with that maid of his," exclaimed Robert. "I begged, pleaded, threatened, but he just slammed the door in my face and slipped back under the blankets with his sweetheart. I spent half the night waiting outside his cottage for absolutely nothing."

Nesta was getting worse rapidly. She was pale; her skin was sallow and waxy. Did the Lord want to take her to him because she was such a lovely little girl? William sat on the edge of her bed and held her hand. He took the damp cloth and dabbed at her glowing-hot forehead. He knew Nesta liked him. She had even admitted to her brother that she thought she loved him and longed for nothing more than to be William's wife when she was old enough to marry. Although she was still a child in William's eyes, and the thought of marrying her had never even occurred to him, he would have made whatever pact was necessary, with God or the devil, if it would save Nesta.

"When you're well again, I'll take you dancing when there's a feast day at the village," he whispered in her ear, hoping the prospect might give her strength.

And Nesta did move her head slightly, and her feverishly bright eyes opened for a brief moment. Then she closed them for the last time. On her lips there remained only a tender smile.

Logan sobbed uncontrollably. "Please, Lord, let me keep her for tonight. Tomorrow, when the priest has anointed her, I'll give her into your hands."

But it was too late. God had already taken the child to him.

March 1188

W illiam, Robert, are you ready?" Up since the crack of dawn, Logan was getting more and more agitated, standing there with one of his favorite hunting peregrines on his fist. "We must set off. I'm sure Sir Ralph is wondering where we are. What are you waiting for, William? Go fetch the gyr."

William, who had turned fifteen at Easter and was at last taller than Robert, had become his master's right hand. He had been at the mews for nearly three years. He now knew everything about falcons that he could learn from Logan. Robert's early jealousy had turned into respect, and even Logan had long since understood that William had emerged from the cradle with a special talent for handling falcons. He valued his prudence, his expertise, and the feel he had for each individual falcon.

On this particular day, Logan had especially high hopes for William. Sir Ralph had organized a duck and heron hunt in honor of the Earl of Chester and other important barons. It was the first time William had been permitted to join a hunt with such powerful men and fly a falcon he had trained.

William entered the tower's dark room quietly, greeted his favorite falcon with a cooing sound, and stroked her head and back. On her very first hunt, this two-year-old gyrfalcon had struck her prey with such ease that William had named her Easy. Deftly, he took her down from her perch and prepared her jesses.

"You're going to catch a fine heron today, aren't you?" he murmured to Easy, carrying her outside, her head covered so that she would not become agitated during their ride.

"At last," grumbled Logan, visibly anxious.

Most of the trees were still bare; only the willows and alders were starting to bud. William inhaled the invigorating cold air. It had a tangy scent of dew-moist earth. A few yellow cowslips stood out among the still-withered grass around the mews, their bell-shaped flowers swaying gracefully in the spring breeze. William glanced up at the slightly overcast sky and held up his free hand. The wind was neither too weak nor too strong, ideal for hunting.

Robert looked on encouragingly. He was still too young to take his falcon on this hunt.

If he's envious, he hides it well, thought William, digging his spurs into the horse's flanks in order to catch up with Logan, who had gone on ahead.

As Sir Ralph climbed down the wooden stairs on the outer wall of the keep to welcome his falconer and the falconer's men, the tower guard's horn announced the arrival of the expected guests.

Presently, the clattering of horses' hooves could be heard on the wooden bridge. Into the bailey rode Ranulf de Blondeville, the young Earl of Chester; Peter de Sandicare; Walter de Hauville and his nephew Richard, who was scarcely younger than his uncle; and William de Vere, who was not only bishop of Hereford but also a relative of the fencing master's. Their retinue included three ladies and several hunt assistants, pages, and squires.

Sir Ralph's hounds sensed that a hunt was in the offing. They yapped loudly with excitement, pulling so hard on their leashes that the dog handlers struggled to hold them back.

When William saw the richly dressed lords and ladies and the magnificent horses and superb birds they brought with them, he felt thoroughly out of place. How was it possible that he, the son of a smith, could think for one moment that he might belong in such exalted company? Most falconers came from families steeped in the rich tradition of falconry; many of them had lands, frequently even titles. He, on the other hand, was nothing, a bastard whose father didn't even acknowledge him as his son. In other words, William was a nobody, as Odon had recently reminded him in no uncertain terms. William twisted the reins between his fingers. He had never been this nervous before, not even on the day King Henry had come to the smithy, looking for Blanchpenny. Observing the guests, he saw that one of them was staring at him particularly intently. William could not remember meeting him before, and he turned away uneasily.

Sir Ralph greeted his guests most warmly. He clapped shoulders, kissed hands, offered refreshing wine and must, and at length, with great excitement, announced the opening of the hunt. He invited the ladies to join the hunt, too, but neither the lady of the manor, who was obviously glad of the change provided by some female guests, nor the other ladies, who had been on the road since morning, felt it necessary to join the men. They chose instead to spend their time eating dainty morsels of food, embroidering, sewing, and exchanging news. Sibylle had decided to stay with the ladies, and she waved at William and Robert from a distance.

They both indicated, with discreet nods, that they had seen her.

Odon was as frisky as a rooster in a henhouse. Craving attention, he continually sought out the earl's company.

William knew from Sibylle that Chester had only recently received his knighthood, so he must be slightly older than Odon. Was he as stupid and conceited as the young squires and Odon? William decided to watch the fine lords carefully, to learn what they were like.

"I hear you are to wed Constance of Brittany, Prince Geoffrey's widow, next year," said Odon so loudly that everyone heard it. He bared his teeth in a broad grin.

William wondered whether Odon was forcing himself on the earl to flatter him or was just using his uncle's distinguished guest to impress his friends. If Chester was marrying into the royal family soon, it could be very useful to Odon to cultivate a friendship with him.

William could not stomach the thought of judging people by their social status; the thought was utterly alien to him, even repellent. But he knew, from both his mother and Sibylle, that the rich and powerful were accustomed to thinking this way, and he behaved accordingly.

"Quite right, my young friend," replied Sir Ranulf, with a touch of arrogance, as he mounted his horse. He was neither particularly tall nor imposing, nor could he be called handsome, but he had a certain youthful charm, and he was obviously aware of its effect on women. "Not an attractive lady, like the ones I prefer to have around me, and a few years too old for my taste, but a truly excellent match. Prince John himself arranged it with his sister-in-law, which means, I fear, that I shall be in his debt forever and a day." He gave Odon a theatrical look. "You're not married yet, my friend, so enjoy your freedom while you still have it."

Odon grinned lewdly. "Well, if you want some company tonight, let me know. You're still a free man!"

Sir Ralph frowned at his nephew. Although marriage had never yet prevented a man from having a lover, he found the subject disagreeable. The bishop was within earshot. He would certainly not be pleased by the young men's banter.

"That's a magnificent falcon you've brought with you," he said to the earl to distract his attention, referring to the bird Sir Ranulf's squire was carrying on his fist.

"A superb creature, is it not? A gift upon my knighthood. My favorite tiercel, agile and a remarkably effective hunter," he began enthusiastically, going on to describe the bird's breathtaking flights during their most recent hunt. He looked at one of his men and nodded toward him complacently. "Richard de Hauville is an excellent falconer. He trained him. As it happens, Prince John has a female from the same clutch," he said with unconcealed pride, stroking his little mustache.

As the hunting party set off, William had to get in line behind them, so he could not follow the conversation as it continued. He rode beside Logan and asked a great many questions about the barons.

The guests, meanwhile, passed the time with the exchange of important news, gossip, and laughter.

When they reached the open, expansive area that Logan and Sir Ralph had chosen for the hunt, the hounds were unleashed. The flat land, with its small ponds, watercourses, and marshy meadows, was a perfect habitat for waterfowl and an ideal hunting arena for the falcons. As the party split up, the hounds began to sniff about, flushing out wildfowl, ducks, and songbirds. The smaller falcons of the older squires were let loose on the prey first, and a frenzied hunt began.

When a few gray herons rose as well, it was the turn of the first peregrines and saker falcons. Falcons were cast off at the herons one by one so they would not attack each other. When a lone gray heron rose, the falconer who had looked at William so suspiciously earlier cast off his peregrine at it.

William now knew that this was Walter de Hauville, and that he was in charge of one of the royal mews at Winchester. He watched the peregrine's flight tensely. After a while, he noticed that she was on the point of abandoning her prey and flying away. William held his breath, spellbound, but de Hauville showed no reaction; he did not even appear to notice the signs of imminent loss. It was not until the peregrine let the heron go and started pursuing a duck, which she must have hoped she could strike down more easily, that de Hauville started riding after her, cursing. He tried to attract her with a lure, spinning it in circles above his head and calling her. But she seemed uninterested in either the lure or the falconer's voice.

He's probably made it hunt too soon, thought William. After all the things Logan had told him about Walter de Hauville, he was very disappointed. A man with such a reputation as a falconer should have known that to prevent peregrines from flying away they needed to be "made" to the lure more often than other falcons. Logan had told him so many times. William caught his master's eye and read the same disappointment.

Shortly afterward, when a gray heron rose from the reeds and climbed into the sky with dizzying speed, it was William's turn. He removed Easy's hood, spoke to her quietly, then cast her off into the air.

Again and again, the heron swerved skillfully to escape the falcon's pursuit, but Easy did not let herself be discouraged. As she spiraled up above the heron and then stooped, someone cried out in horror, "Look at that."

All eyes were on the heron's sharp beak, which threatened to spear Easy.

William, too, looked up breathlessly. His heart pounded. He was afraid for Easy. A falcon needed to be hungry in order to hunt successfully. On the other hand, overpowering hunger could cause it to forget its natural instincts and could lead to recklessness and uncharacteristic boldness. William had tried to find the middle way. He had obviously succeeded, for Easy was in excellent condition, saw the danger in time, and knew what she had to do. She plunged elegantly past the heron.

Gasps of relief could be heard all around.

When the heron tried to come back to earth, where the falcon would not be able to strike, Easy spiraled up into the heavens again. The hounds kept flushing the heron out, not leaving it in peace. Distracted by their baying, it flew up and did not notice Easy overhead until it was too late. She stooped toward the oblivious creature and landed a powerful, wounding stab with her hallux, the claw of her backward-facing talon.

The onlookers murmured with admiration as the gray heron fell out of the sky, spinning and flailing. Easy followed the mortally wounded bird and seized it in midair.

William and Robert knew that the risk from the heron's sharp beak had not disappeared. The injured bird could still defend itself. So they hastened, one from each side, toward the spot where the falcon and her prey would land.

Their horses' hooves squelched across the damp ground, sending up a fine spray. William was gazing skyward, keeping Easy in view, when he was suddenly catapulted off his horse. Before he knew what was happening, he was flying through the air. He landed on his back in the mud with a bone-shaking impact.

"Can't you watch where you're going?" Walter de Hauville shouted at him. "Are you blind?"

William struggled to his feet. His foot was injured, and his backside hurt like hell. "I have to get to my falcon," he growled, glaring resentfully at the falconer. De Hauville had cut him off, and William felt sure he had done it on purpose, though he did not understand why. Grimacing with pain, he limped toward Easy as quickly as he could. The little bell on her foot led him to the place where she stood over her prey.

To prevent the heron's beak from hurting her at this late stage, Robert had drilled it into the ground.

William found a particularly good piece of meat in his satchel and gave it to Easy, who was still perched on the heron, to gorge on as a reward. Deftly, he got her to step onto his fist and finish her meal there. The amount of meat was so meager that Easy would remain hungry enough to be let loose on another heron later.

William carried the falcon away from her prey so that Robert could pick up the heron and take it to Sir Ralph.

Since Easy had struck the first gray heron of the day in such a spectacular fashion, both bird and falconer were greeted with delighted applause. But as William limped past de Hauville, the latter glared at him sullenly.

If only I knew what he has against me, thought William furiously.

After Easy's success, the hunt was resumed with even greater enthusiasm, and both horses and riders were soon covered with mud. As always, many a hunter fell from his horse and landed in the filth. Most of them, like William, came away with sore buttocks, a few bruises, and minor sprains. Fortunately, there were no more serious injuries.

By the end of the hunt, they had all worn themselves out to the point of exhaustion. Ecstatic at the plentiful catch and the happy outcome of the hunt, the party headed back.

Walter de Hauville, who had recaptured his peregrine, kept shooting spine-chilling glances at William. Had de Hauville seen his critical expression when his falcon flew off? Was that why he was angry? But why had he looked at him in such a strange way before that? William was still puzzled by this when someone tapped him on the shoulder.

"Congratulations, William! Easy flew superbly today. The earl is delighted with her, and Sir Ralph would like to give her to him as a wedding present," Logan said, looking very pleased. "You've done us proud with her."

Easy at the Earl of Chester's court. William nodded proudly, though it would be hard for him to give up this marvelous creature. The king would certainly be pleased with him, if he knew how well he was doing. With gladness in his heart, he thought back to the day when Henry had visited them at the smithy, and suddenly he knew where he had seen Walter de Hauville before. He was the falconer with no falcon, the one to whom the king had handed Blanchpenny.

April 14, 1188
Three Days before Easter

illiam folded his cloak more tightly around his shoulders, but he was freezing cold even so. Spring had begun very promisingly, but shortly after the great hunt the weather had become distinctly unpleasant again. Sometimes the air was cold enough to turn raindrops into heavy, wet snowflakes that melted as soon as they touched the sodden earth. The sky had been the same uniform, brooding gray for more than two weeks. The damp cold gnawed at William's joints and his spirits.

"Only fifteen, and already sensitive to the weather," he grumbled. These were the remnants of the fever that had struck him without warning two weeks after the hunt and forced him to stay in bed for several days. His nose was still red and sore, and he continued to cough. Today was the first time he had been on his feet for any length of time. He wheezed breathlessly, and his whole body felt too heavy. Every step was an effort. This is what it must feel like to wear a tunic of chain mail, he thought as he ran toward the small pond. He urgently needed some more ducks in order to fashion a lure for the magnificent peregrine that was soon to be unseeled fully.

William would have loved a dish of Rose's chicken soup. She fed it to anyone who was ill, and it made them stronger and put them back on their feet. William missed Saint Edmundsbury and his family.

The pond was still some way off. William stopped to catch his breath for a moment and sat down on a tree stump, exhausted.

Several dozen trees had been blown over like straws during the previous year's ferocious autumn storms. The serfs had chopped up the splintered trunks and used them for firewood. Only the many stumps remained.

William stared into the distance, lost in thought. A bit of sunlight would do me good, he thought.

From where he was sitting, he could barely make out the pond. The reeds, which grew taller than the grass, gave away the water's location. William glimpsed a group of riders in the distance, and he shaded his eyes with his hand. If he was not mistaken, it was Odon and his friends. William sat stock-still so they would not see him. He could hear their braying laughter from afar. They were obviously pursuing something. William squinted. It couldn't be an animal; it was too big. He stared so long and so intently that his eyes began to smart. The quarry was a human being, but they were hunting him like an animal. Judging by the brown clothing, it was one of the peasant boys. William shook his head with disgust. Four on horseback against one on foot. Only cowards did that sort of thing. Had he been stronger, he would have gone to the aid of the quarry, but, wobbly on his feet as he was, he would not have been able to achieve anything. William lowered his head in shame.

When he looked up again, the hunted person was no longer visible. The squires rode round and round a few times and finally lost interest. The victim must have found a hiding place, thought William, relieved, as the young men galloped off, laughing uproariously.

William stood up and staggered, admitting to himself, much to his chagrin, that he was still too weak to go duck hunting. With a heavy heart, he decided to turn back with his task uncompleted. Even Logan had advised against this undertaking, but his obstinacy would not let him yield.

With an uneasy feeling in the pit of his stomach, William headed back to the mews.

When the new village priest did not appear for Easter Sunday mass, there was an uproar. He had been missing for a while, it was true, and there were rumors he had been summoned to the castle. Some said he had gone to the forest to hear confession and administer last rites to the father of the pretty charcoal-burner. Others sniped that the old charcoal-burner must have had a good many sins to confess if the young priest had to stay away so long. Some even thought he must have succumbed to the daughter's charms, so accustomed were they to his predecessor's excesses. When the priest did not come to church on Easter Sunday, though, the villagers were furious. He had done nothing blameworthy since he had arrived a few months before, but they all weighed in with their complaints.

At first, he had seemed quite different from his recently deceased predecessor. The old priest had taken more than one lover, and he had collapsed and died in the last one's bed after being with her. A fitting punishment, the villagers had murmured, but nobody said anything publicly.

Now, though, since the young cleric had disappeared so unexpectedly, people suspected him of straying, too, and whispered behind their hands. But nobody was worried. Their only concern was the Easter blessing, which they did not want to miss. When the priest did not appear, the villagers decided to go up to the castle and ask old Pater John, who had been in the lord's service since time immemorial, for his Easter blessing.

They walked up to the castle like a flock of pilgrims, only more boisterous and chattering loudly. William and Robert were among them. Logan, who had not set foot in the village church since Nesta's death, had stayed at the mews.

The village elder went ahead to present the villagers' request to the lady of the manor in her husband's absence.

As the first serfs and laborers entered the upper bailey, they were driven forward by those behind them, until a sudden cry of horror ran through the crowd and people on all sides started crossing themselves.

William and Robert pushed forward to see what had happened.

They were greeted by the gruesome sight of the village priest on his back in a wheelbarrow. He was dripping wet; his head dangled to one side, like a wilted flower. His face was white and bloated, his eyes wide with fear, his expression pleading. His cowl was smeared all over with mud. His right foot was missing its sandal, and a few lengths of weed were wound around his ankle. A dark snail with a pointed, horn-colored shell was smearing a slimy trail across his naked calf.

William shuddered.

A few women started wailing, and children began to howl.

One of the two servants who had probably brought him into the bailey, and who were now standing beside the barrow, realized what was happening, took pity, and made the small gesture of closing the dead man's accusing eyes.

But the excited whispering and murmuring continued to swell until Pater John appeared in the yard with another servant. With a crucifix and a rosary in one hand and the staff he used to support himself while walking in the other, for he was afflicted with gout, he shuffled toward the dead priest.

"Who among you saw what happened?" he asked the assembled company. When no one answered, he walked around the barrow, looking at the dead man.

"He drowned, that much is obvious," someone mocked from the crowd. It was one of Odon's friends, grinning as if he thought the common folk around him were too dense to arrive at this simple conclusion for themselves.

Pater John said nothing in response, but he examined the priest's hands intently. They were balled up in fists. There were a few blades of grass between the fingers, as if the poor man had tried to save himself by clutching at the bank. He also had cuts on his hands, of the kind caused by reeds.

"Had he been drinking?" said Pater John, probably thinking of the young priest's predecessor. He looked questioningly at the villagers.

"No, Pater," the village elder declared. "He was a decent, God-fearing man. He didn't go whoring, either."

"We'll bury him in the graveyard tomorrow," Pater John announced. Then he said a few words about Jesus and the cross they all had to bear and gave the dismayed villagers his Easter blessing. When his comforting homily came to an end, the crowd dispersed. Whispering quietly, the serfs and laborers went back to the village in small groups with their families.

"By our lady, you're pale!" Robert gave William a friendly nudge in the ribs with his elbow. "Bad thing that. I suppose it's upset you?"

"I need to speak to you. Alone," hissed William, dragging his friend away without turning toward Odon and his companions. He had been watching them the whole time. At first they had seemed frightened, but soon they had started cracking coarse jokes. Neither angry comments from the villagers about their disrespectful behavior nor several reproachful looks from Pater John had any effect on them. But they knew exactly what had happened. They obviously felt completely safe, untouchable. None of them could have an inkling of what William had seen.

When he was alone with Robert, he looked around cautiously.

"It was Odon and his friends."

"What was?"

"They've got him on their conscience."

"The priest? Come on, William—he drowned. Not everyone can swim."

"And what was the priest doing by the water? Swimming, in this weather? With his cowl on? Everyone knows how heavy a thing like that is when it's full of water."

Robert tugged at the sparse beard that had just begun to sprout on his chin and shrugged. "He must have fallen in."

"Fallen in?" William grimaced. "The path is far enough from the pond, why should he leave it, unless…"

"Unless?"

"Unless someone was after him?"

Robert raised his eyebrows in disbelief, creating small furrows in his forehead.

"I saw it with my own eyes, Rob."

"Odon?"

"Him and his charming friends, yes." William sat down on the ground, uneasy. "I didn't know it was the priest they were chasing. I thought it was one of the village lads. They're nimble and wily, so I didn't worry too much. But it was the priest, I'm sure. I know it now. Suddenly he wasn't there. I assumed he had escaped. But now I think they pushed him into the water and let him drown like a rat. They just rode off, the swine."

Robert was at a loss for words.

"What should I do, Robert?"

"You're better off forgetting what happened."

"And let them get away with it?"

"It would be your word against theirs."

"But…"

"William, trust me, you'll find yourself in a hell of your own making."

"But I can't just…"

"You must, William. Now come, before they all start wondering where we've got to."

For the next two weeks, William carried around with him what he knew, but the death of the priest would not leave him in peace. The image of the corpse kept appearing before him. On Sunday, after mass, his guilty conscience could not bear it any longer. He asked Pater John, who was now conducting the services in the village, to hear his confession.

"Forgive me, Father, for I have sinned."

"Speak, my son."

"I know what happened."

"Explain yourself more clearly, my son."

William told him what he had seen that afternoon before Easter, and Pater John listened to his words without interrupting. "When the sheriff comes to Thorne, I shall have to tell him. Otherwise my soul will not rest. I feel guilty. If I had only suspected what was happening, I'm sure I could have saved him."

"You have committed no sin, my son. God knows your heart is pure. You did right to come to me." Pater John gave him absolution and two Our Fathers to pray. Then he blessed him and sent him on his way.

May 1188

I t's going to rain," muttered Robert, looking up with annoyance. Wet weather for days, just when he wanted to train the falcons in the open. It was enough to put anyone in a bad mood. An early drop fell near his nose. Sighing, he picked up both buckets, quickly filled them, and returned to the tower. Through the trees he saw Sibylle running toward the mews. She stopped in the yard, breathless.

"William! Robert!" Her voice sounded shriller than usual. "Where are you?"

"Here I am," answered Robert. "What's the matter? Why are you shouting so?"

"William! Where is he?" Sibylle looked around anxiously.

"You must have passed him on the path. He wanted to go to the village to buy some chicks." Robert showed her William's knife. "He forgot this. I thought about running after him, but I'm sure he can do without."

"Good God, no."

"Don't you think you're exaggerating?" Robert looked at Sibylle, frowning. Why did girls always have to overreact so dreadfully?

"I don't mean the knife. I'm scared because he's not here. He's running straight into his arms."

"Will you please tell me what you're talking about?"

"My mother, Pater John," Sibylle stammered. When she saw that Robert was still looking at her questioningly, she made an effort to collect herself and started from the beginning.

"Pater John was with my mother this morning. He pretended to be apologetic and took a long time to get to the point. 'I'm violating the sanctity of the confessional and risking my salvation, but I have no choice'—that sort of thing. He kept whining and beating about the bush until my mother lost her patience. 'I act out of a sense of duty,' he said, then told her that William had accused Odon of being responsible for the priest's death."

"Merciful heavens. I told him he should keep his mouth shut."

"Pater John told my mother the whole story. A foolish prank that unfortunately cost a man his life. That's what he called it. Then he talked about his brother, who doesn't have enough money to send his daughter to a good convent. My mother promised to consider helping the child and told him to go on with his story. When she found out that William had talked about going to the sheriff to bear witness when next he came to Thorne, she promised to use her influence on behalf of Pater John's niece, as long as he promised to keep silent about what he had heard and, if necessary, testified that William had confessed to murdering the priest himself." Sibylle sighed deeply. Her shoulders, normally erect, slumped. "I know how my mother idolizes Odon, so I'm not surprised. But Pater John, he's a man of the cloth. I would never have thought it possible that he would agree to such a thing!"

"Indeed." Robert's resentment of priests was rekindled.

"My mother spoke to Odon as soon as Pater John had gone and gave him leave to capture William. She wants to accuse him of murder and throw him in the dungeon. He won't survive that for long. You should have seen Odon's face. He couldn't wait to see William locked up." Sibylle sobbed with anguish. "She didn't have a bad word for Odon. No rebuke. She didn't even ask him what he was thinking of when he let the priest drown. And do you know the worst thing? As long as my father isn't here, I can't do anything for William." She clasped her hands together and looked up at the sky. "Our Father in heaven, help him, I beg you."

The ground seemed to sway under Robert's feet. "How do you know all this anyway?"

"I eavesdropped. I know it's unforgivable, but Pater John seemed so agitated when he arrived that I couldn't help it." Sibylle looked down in shame.

"Nonsense. The main thing is that you weren't caught. Now you have to go on keeping your ears open. That's all you can do for William at the moment. Meanwhile, I'll do some thinking."

Sibylle nodded and wiped away her tears. She kissed Robert on the cheek and left.

Robert stroked his cheek in surprise, touching the spot on his skin where her kiss burned like a branding iron.

⊗⊗

When William came to, his head was throbbing. He was lying on damp straw that stank of urine and feces. It was a while before he could think clearly. How had he come to be here? The last thing he remembered was being on the path to the village. William touched his head and started with pain.

Anxiously, he felt the spot again. It was warm and sticky with blood where a huge lump cushioned a gaping wound on the back of his head. William tried to remember what had happened. On his way into the village he had met Odon. William tried to sit up, but his skull ached whenever he moved. So he reclined back on the moldy-smelling ground and closed his eyes in despair. The memory was coming back to him gradually.

"I told you the day would come when you would regret taking me on," Odon had said with his sneering smirk. Then he'd dismounted his horse and punched William in the midriff. William had crumpled but had not fallen to the ground until he'd taken another blow and everything went black. Odon, or one of his companions, must have hit him over the head.

William noticed that his left arm hurt, too, and checked to see whether it was broken.

"Is anyone there?" he called out, suddenly afraid. But there was no answer. "Where am I?"

"Nobody there," came a strange, snickering voice. "Never. Always alone."

A shiver ran down William's back. Mad Leonard. So he was still alive. Everyone in the village had heard of this unfortunate man. He had been locked up in the dungeon for years. Nobody really knew what crime he had committed or what had become of him. Some said he had become too familiar with the lady of the manor; others, that he had rejected her advances so she'd had him locked away. William had heard that his years in a cell had driven him mad with anguish and loneliness. Perhaps also with despair, he thought.

"Who are you?" William tried to start a conversation.

"Nobody there. Always alone."

"My name is William. Leonard, is that you?" he asked as if they had known each other for years.

"Alone, so alone," the voice wailed.

"No, you're not alone anymore." William felt the resentment rising in him. No, he thought bitterly, now I'm in here, too, and I don't even know why.

"You won't catch me, Satan," the madman hissed suddenly, rattling his chains loudly. Then he thrust out his fist. "Get thee hence! Nobody there."

William gave up trying to speak to him. Although he was not in irons, like the unfortunate madman, William felt very sorry for himself. At some point he fell asleep.

When he awoke, he felt an urgent need to relieve himself. He stood up slowly, swaying for a short while, and looked for some kind of vessel. A small window set high in the wall of the cell let in just enough light to reveal a feces-encrusted wooden bucket in a corner. The penetrating smell of excrement emanating from the bucket so revolted William that he decided to wait. He withdrew to the corner where he had woken up, sat down with his knees to his chest, and fell to brooding over what could have brought him to this evil place. He had committed no crime. What was he accused of? It was a bit late to take revenge for the stone he had flung at Odon's head so long ago. Was it something to do with the death of the priest?

The intense pain in his head did not make thinking easier. Only Robert and Pater John knew what he had seen. How could Odon have found out? The father was bound by the sanctity of the confessional. William groaned. Robert hated Odon. Perhaps he had forgotten himself and threatened Odon with what William knew? No, he couldn't have been such a fool.

"Stand up!"

William started with alarm when a kick landed on his ribs. He must have fallen asleep again. Doing his best to look confident, he gritted his teeth and got up.

"You are a vile piece of dirt, William."

The light of a flaming torch entered the filthy dungeon through the open oak door, amply revealing its neglected state.

"I know you can't stand me, Master Odon. But don't you think you're going too far? When your uncle—"

"My uncle?" Odon laughed mockingly. "Do you think he's going to come here and rescue you? Who knows if he'll even come back safe and sound?"

Sir Ralph had been traveling with the king for months. It was said that he had stopped in Normandy. Nobody knew for how long. Perhaps Odon was right, and he was not even alive. Gripped by despair, William shuffled his feet in the rotting straw.

"It wasn't my decision to throw you in the dungeon," said Odon with a shrug. "My aunt insisted. She thinks it's a fitting punishment for the death of the young priest." Odon made a face, as if he felt sorry for William.

"But I had nothing to do with it," William retorted angrily. "As you well know."

"Do I? The last time I saw the priest, he was alive. I have three witnesses who can confirm it. Besides, Pater John says you confessed to it."

"No, that's not true. He can't do that! *You* pushed the priest into the pond and left him to drown."

"He fell in, an unfortunate accident. He was wet, that's true, but he was very much alive when we rode away. My aunt says *you* drowned him. He fought back, apparently."

William gasped, helpless as a fish out of water. "I didn't touch him."

"Who cares about that now? Have you noticed that one there?" He pointed toward Leonard, who was humming quietly. "You'll die here, slowly, just like him. No one will ask after you, and if they do, well, then you just…died of a fever. How sad for poor William."

Driven by raging panic, William threw himself at Odon. But Odon, a practiced fighter, stepped lightly to one side, grabbed him by the collar of his tunic, and drew him close.

He looks as if he's been licked clean, thought William, staring at Odon's pink, carefully shaven face.

"Maybe I should have you put in irons, too?" Odon said.

William did not doubt that he would carry out this threat, so he lowered his eyes.

Odon thrust him back to the ground. "You'd be better off saving your strength. I think you're going to need it. Truly grim in here. I don't think I'll be coming back anytime soon."

As the heavy oak door with its tiny eye-level grating creaked shut behind Odon, William felt lonelier than he had ever felt before. God, where are you? he wanted to scream, but his voice failed him. Trembling with fear, he cowered in the corner and stared gloomily ahead.

The time passed with dreadful slowness. When at last the jailer came by, William saw Mad Leonard for the first time in the flickering torchlight. His filthy, emaciated body was covered with bluish-brown bruises, his long hair was matted, and his eyes were troubled. Sallow skin, thin as parchment, lay in folds over his bony knees and hung from his arms and legs as if it no longer fit him. William's fear increased. Absent a miracle, he would end up just as pitiful.

For two days, William sat there hoping that help would arrive soon, fearing that he would never be released, and hoping again. But nothing happened.

When the hopelessness of his position began to sink in, he was gripped by cold fear. Frantically, he ran up and down in his cell. Searching every corner for an escape route, he scratched at the joints of the walls to see if he could scrape away some of the mortar and loosen a stone. With his bare hands, he tried to dig up the solid clay floor; he tried to climb up to the tiny grated opening that gleamed at the two prisoners like a cyclopean eye. All in vain.

Mad Leonard rattled his chains and laughed hoarsely. He shook his head, as if he knew from personal experience that all these efforts were futile. Had he lain in chains all this time? Or had they been put on him because he had tried to escape?

Eventually, William dragged himself back to his corner, exhausted and discouraged, his hands and knees raw and bleeding.

The jailer, an old man with a curly reddish-blond beard and matted shoulder-length hair, came twice a day. He brought them bread or meal; occasionally an overripe pear, a worm-eaten apple, or some wilted cabbage; and a bucket of water. He was escorted by two armed men. William could see that there was no point in taking them on.

"Please give me a pot to relieve myself in," he begged on the very first day, looking down humbly. And in fact he had been heard. The jailer, whose ashen pallor spoke of his long presence among these dimly lit corridors and dark cellars, emptied the bucket every other day.

The bread was dry and often moldy, the fruit was putrid, and the meal must have had more stones than grain ground into it, for it grated terribly on William's teeth. The worst, though, was that there was never nearly enough to satisfy his hunger. The days were long, and sometimes William did not know when one ended and the next began, because he was constantly dozing off. Sundays were the only days he recognized. On that day they were given an extra piece of bread soaked in gravy, taken from the lord's table, and William would dig in eagerly. He would bolt the moistened bread without hesitation, even after the young soldiers escorting the jailer spat on it once. He had learned that hunger and thirst were the worst enemies of self-respect.

Three Sundays had gone by when, instead of the jailer, a young man brought the prisoners their food. Judging by his stubby, robust nose and the reddish color of his hair, he was the jailer's son. He fussed about in William's corner for some time. The two soldiers paid no attention; they were too busy making fun of poor Leonard.

"From Mistress Sibylle," the young man whispered, pushing a large piece of roast meat, a small cheese, and a fresh red apple toward him. "She's very worried about you."

"What about the falconer? Has he asked after me at the castle? Will he ask the lady for clemency?" A spark of hope kindled William's heart.

"I don't know," whispered the young man, shrugging. "But I don't think so. No one even half in his right mind mentions your name. Nobody dares."

The laughter from the soldiers in Leonard's corner grew louder.

"She said she would speak to her father when he returns. I'll try to come again soon," said the young man, winking at William conspiratorially. "That stinks," he said loudly, turning toward the soldiers. "The bucket's full."

"Then empty it, little one. It's your old man's job. It'll give you a taste of what's waiting for you when you take over his work." They laughed unkindly and showed him the way to the door.

The young man dragged the bucket out and soon came back.

"Thanks," whispered William, lowering his eyes in shame.

Though tormented by hunger, William gave the emaciated Leonard some of the meat. Weeping with gratitude, the old man fell to his knees and gnawed at the meat with his toothless gums until the sun went down.

"You won't lead me astray twice, Satan," he hissed when William tried to share his meat again after the young man's next visit. Outraged, he held out two crossed fingers.

Although the sight of this poor man distressed William, and brought home to him the fate that awaited him, his company was certainly better than complete solitude. William had cursed Mad Leonard several times during his first few days, but after a while he started telling him about his life in the mews and the training of falcons. The confused old man was probably not even listening, but the sound of his own voice comforted William, as it had on that night in the forest when he had run away from Orford. Sadly, he thought of Arthur and Sir Baudouin, but most of all he thought of his mother, Isaac, Jean, and Rose. If he died there, he would never see them again. None of them knew he was rotting in this wretched hole, so they couldn't come to his aid. Perhaps Sibylle would talk to her father when he came back from Normandy. But how long would it be before he returned?

Early July 1188

obert sat on a large stone in the lower bailey, his shoulders slumped and his chin resting on his knee. "My father behaves as if William never existed. He never talks about him, but he can't fool me. I know he's worried. Even though he's never shown it—he likes William, but he's afraid, like everyone here." Robert tossed a stone into the small puddle in front of him and looked at Sibylle. "What's it like for William in that dungeon?"

"The jailer's son Eadric brings him food every now and again. I get it from the castle kitchens. He's a little bit in love with me." Sibylle made her confession with a small, embarrassed smile. "Believe me, I would never take advantage of that under normal circumstances, but William needs our help. Look, here he comes." She pointed at a red-haired young man, who was almost a head taller than she. He was carrying his father's basket and was escorted by the two soldiers who normally went to the dungeons with the jailer.

Robert and Sibylle waited quite a long time, but it did not seem as though the young man was coming back. Sibylle fidgeted nervously on the rampart where she had settled herself. "I can't understand what's taking so long."

"Look, the door's opening." Robert pointed at the entrance Eadric and the men had disappeared through earlier.

Sibylle leaped joyfully down from the wall, but when she saw that not only the young man but also his father were coming out, she became frightened. The jailer had grabbed his son by the ear. Eadric's face was contorted with pain.

"Come, let's creep a little closer. Maybe we can hear what happened," whispered Robert.

The jailer stopped by the door with his son, then gripped him by the shoulders and shook him. "Who put you up to it?"

Sibylle put her hand to her mouth, terrified. "Please don't let him give me away!" she whispered to Robert. "My mother will beat me black and blue if she finds out."

But Eadric kept his peace, and when his father struck him again and repeated the question, he just shook his head defiantly. After yet another blow to the ear, the jailer gave up and rained further blows on his son all the way home.

"If he doesn't betray you, you should reward him with a kiss later on," Robert teased her, raising his eyebrows. "For if he's kept his mouth shut, we still have a chance of saving William eventually. As for me, I'm not going to stop thinking it over. First, we have to hope that William won't starve without his extra food. Next, we have to find a way to get him out of there as soon as we can."

ᐒᙋᐭ

Every day, William hoped the jailer's son would come back, but he came no more. Had he been caught? Or was William no longer important to Sibylle? He was tormented by hunger, and when, a week later, Mad Leonard stopped rattling his chains, William felt abandoned by everyone, God and men.

The soldiers dragged the dead man out, and William stayed behind, utterly bereft.

At night, when no sounds penetrated from outside, the darkness and solitude became pure intolerable agony, and the constant dripping somewhere in the distance roared so loud in his head that William thought he would go mad. He scratched at the fleabites on his bony rib cage and fingered his raw and sagging skin with disgust. The itching did not stop until the bloodred spots that covered him all the way down to his belly had been scratched raw.

William slept restlessly, occasionally waking in terror and screaming when mice or rats rustled through the straw. At those times he would comfort himself with thoughts of the smithy. He imagined how it would feel to be there instead of in this dungeon; he longed for Rose's pasties and her loving care and saw before him the smiling faces of Isaac and his mother.

One night, when loneliness was threatening to drive him to despair, he thought he heard Nesta whispering. She enticed him with her gentle voice. "Come to me," she seemed to whisper. "For where I am there is light and peace."

But William's will to live was stronger, and he withstood the temptation to give up. His mother would be proud of him one day yet.

He stood up, took the sharp stone he had loosened from the wall days before, and sharpened it some more by scraping it against the wall of his prison cell.

☙❧

"It's time we got him out of there." Robert wiped his nose with the back of his hand and sniffed loudly. "We can't just leave him to rot in that hole. It's already been a week since Eadric was caught. We have to think of something, or else William will be too weak to escape."

"But how, Robert? How are we supposed to rescue him?" Sibylle sounded as though she had given up hope.

"For heaven's sake! If I knew that, he'd have been out long ago," Robert rebuked her.

"You're right. I know it's not your fault," said Sibylle gently, resting her hand on his arm.

Robert pulled away, stood up, and paced about. "We can't sneak into the dungeon; we'd never get out again. What if we bribed Eadric's father?"

Sibylle shook her head. "I can't think what with. I have neither money nor jewels. Besides, he knows full well what would happen to him if he was caught, and I don't think he's keen on ending up in his own dungeon. If we went to him, he would betray us to my mother."

"What about force?" As he made this suggestion, Robert himself did not seem to believe it was a possibility.

"When the prisoners get their food, two soldiers always escort the jailer. We can't do anything against three, but for the rest of the day, and at night, there are only two men in the guardroom," said Sibylle thoughtfully. "I know that much from Eadric."

The dungeon that held William was one of several cellars beneath one of the castle's outbuildings where food and weapons were also stored. Sibylle had not been able to find out more from the castle servants without arousing suspicion. But neither she nor Robert had yet set foot in the cellars.

"Eadric could draw me a map. But how would we get in and then out again?"

The mere thought of entering the dungeon voluntarily was so awful that Robert shuddered. "Whom do the castle's men fear most?"

"My mother. What are you thinking?"

Robert stroked his chin. His beard was still soft and fluffy, like a young bird's down, but soon he would be able to risk shaving it with a sharp blade. He remembered that William had started shaving the previous autumn. Beards did not grow very fast at his age, so William shaved only every few weeks and had cut himself on the throat the first time. The sight of the blood dripping out had caused a very strange sensation in Robert's knees. William was his best, his only, friend. That was probably it, for the sight of blood from the animals they hunted had never caused him any discomfort.

"Robert, what are you thinking about?" Sibylle interrupted his reflections.

"Does your mother ever demand unusual things? Is she occasionally unpredictable?"

"Occasionally? She's as hard to predict as the weather in April." Sibylle snorted.

"In that case we may have him out soon, after all."

"You've thought of something. How? Tell me." Sibylle rushed toward Robert until she was standing so close to him that their noses were almost touching. "Out with it."

Robert did not like her being so close. Something about it felt wrong, probably because she was the lord's daughter. He took a step back and explained what he was thinking.

"That's wonderful! I shall pray for our success, for it's not without danger." Sibylle glowed with righteousness. "I just hope you're right, and that I can be convincing enough."

"If the jailer doesn't believe you straightaway, you'll have to stay calm."

"But the guard is bound to send the soldier, too," Sibylle fretted.

"Don't worry, I'll take care of him. Just get hold of some food without anyone noticing and I'll bring a filled water pouch. If we do free William, he'll have to flee immediately. Maybe he should take a horse from the stables?"

"Odon would be able to follow the hoof marks easily. He'd soon catch him. William will travel more slowly on foot, but he'll be harder to find. So far he hasn't actually committed any crime, but if he becomes a horse thief, he'll get no mercy. If they caught him, they'd string him up on the spot, and we wouldn't be able to do a thing about it."

"You're right. No horse, then." He looked at Sibylle intently. "You'll get into a lot of trouble with your mother if she finds out you had a hand in this."

"What can she do? Shout, rant, beat me? It's a small price to pay for William's life, isn't it? And maybe nothing of the sort will happen. She's not going to throw *me* in the dungeon. It's you who has more to fear if they catch you."

"I don't mind."

They discussed every detail of their plan again. Then Robert said, with a conspiratorial look, "So we meet here tomorrow morning and take our chances."

෨෬

William did not know how many days had passed since Leonard's death; time seemed even longer, hope of rescue even slimmer than before. At some point he would be old and mad; lonely and alone he would die, like Leonard. And nobody would care, just as no one seemed interested in the fact that he was sitting in this wretched dungeon. William sharpened his stone. He had torn a strip of cloth from the hem of his tunic and wrapped it around his hand to protect it against injury. His arm ached, and he decided to take a break.

He heard a muffled voice in the corridor outside his cell, and his ears pricked up. If he was not mistaken, the jailer had already been around twice. It was almost dark, and nobody else came at this hour. Was there another prisoner soon to join him? What else could the jailer want? William's heart began to beat faster in a panic. Perhaps they were coming for him. At the thought that his last moment might be upon him, he realized how fond of this miserable life he still was. He did not want to die; he was still young and wanted to live, wanted to be a falconer, wanted to feel the wind and rain on his skin again. William curled up in his corner, frightened. If only he could be as tiny as a mouse. Then he could scurry through the guards' legs, race up the stairs, and escape.

෨෬

It was dusk by the time Robert slipped across the upper bailey. The setting sun painted a sea of colors on the western horizon— orange, violet, and soft pink. Anxiously, he directed his gaze at the dark clouds sweeping in from the east. William would need the light of the moon on his flight. On no account could he risk a torch; its flame would betray him from afar. Robert tried to put aside his fear for his friend. There was no going back now anyway. The situation had become dangerously critical.

Sibylle had eavesdropped on her mother again and had learned that she wanted to be rid of William once and for all. Sibylle had come to Robert in the mews during the afternoon and insisted that they, come what may, free William that very day.

Robert crossed the courtyard unseen and hid in the agreed-upon place. He found the food that Sibylle had hidden in a hole in the wall as planned, and he put the water skin on top. It would not be long before she came into the courtyard, too.

Looking bored, she strolled casually to the entrance to the cellar and knocked on the heavy wooden door. Robert crept a little closer to the corner of the wall so that he could hear what she said.

"The boy is to come to my mother," she told the guard disdain-fully when he opened the door. "Immediately!" She made as if to turn on her heel and leave. Robert held his breath.

"What?" asked the jailer suspiciously. "Now?"

"Well, I don't think she means Christmas," retorted Sibylle haughtily.

Robert had to smile. She was playing her part well.

"And why does she send you and not one of her men?"

"How should I know? Ask her yourself. Do you think I was keen to come?"

The guard scratched his head.

Sybille persisted. "If it's not too much trouble?"

"I don't know," muttered the jailer. "I don't like it."

"Very well. I'll go and tell her you don't like her order." Sibylle really did turn away now.

"No, mistress, I'll go and fetch him. Unless you want to come with me." The guard gestured invitingly and, to Robert's surprise, Sibylle accepted. The door closed behind her, and then there was silence.

Robert grew anxious. Even if she was the lord's daughter, the thought of her going down to the cells with the jailer and the soldier made him feel weak.

❧❧

William huddled in his corner as his emotions swung from fear to a glimmer of hope and back again. When the footsteps stopped outside the door, his heart almost did a somersault. Perhaps they weren't going to kill him; perhaps they finally were going to release him?

He heard the rattle of the heavy bunch of keys. In case this late visit had a less joyful purpose, he gripped the egg-size stone he had sharpened, doing his best to hide it in his fist. He had waited too long for justice to be done. If he had to hold out any longer, there wouldn't be enough of him left to emerge from the dungeon alive. If it was not that the lord of the manor had come back and was having him released, he would make use of the opportunity and try to escape, for that was perhaps his only chance of survival. Quite soon he would be too weak to run away.

As the iron key turned in the lock, William closed his eyes and pretended to sleep.

The jailer and a soldier stepped into the dungeon.

William opened his eyes briefly to see what was happening.

Each of the men carried a torch. When one was thrust toward him, William shut his eyes tightly.

"There he is, see?"

"My mother won't wait forever. Let us go now. The stench is unbearable."

A shiver went down William's spine. Sibylle! He had recognized her voice immediately, and yet she sounded alarmingly strange. He opened his eyes in disbelief. Yes, it was the lord of the manor's daughter. How coldhearted she could sound, thought William resignedly. He felt sick with disappointment. He had trusted her. But blood was thicker than water, after all. The lady of the manor had probably convinced her that William had killed the priest.

"Stand up. The lady wishes to see you." The jailer kicked him in the side.

William stood up carefully, not letting the pain show.

The young soldier was eyeing Sibylle like a hungry wolf.

Serves her right, thought William bitterly, not rewarding her with a look.

"Go on ahead, mistress." The soldier showed her the way with a suggestive gesture, then followed her.

William's anger at Sibylle broke over him like a hot wave. His mother had always said you couldn't trust noble folk.

While the guard was locking up, Sibylle nudged William swiftly and winked. Suddenly, William doubted his judgment and clutched the stone in his fist as though his life depended on it. Had she come to help him? Yes, all things considered, there could be no doubt about it. Gratitude flooded through him. The stairs were steep. William's heart was beating so hard, it was fit to leap from his chest. After only a few steps, his throat was burning as if he had been sprinting. How was he supposed to run away? He was far too weak from his imprisonment. He would collapse, exhausted, after a few paces.

"You will have to take him to the lady by yourself. I'll stay here. We're not allowed to leave the guardroom unattended," the jailer murmured to the soldier, stroking his dirty red beard.

"With the greatest pleasure, given such charming company." The young man's eyes rested on Sibylle longer than appropriate.

William could hardly restrain himself, but a look from Sibylle told him to remain calm.

"Better tie him up," the guard ordered.

William held his crossed hands out in front of his chest, trying to keep the stone hidden between them. Fortunately, the light was so dim that nobody noticed the stone. The man wound the cord around William's wrists and pulled it particularly tight. "Is that how you like it?" He grinned mockingly. Though the cord was cutting into his skin, William made no reply.

"Let's go." The guard opened the door and gave William a push.

He stumbled on the threshold and nearly fell over.

"Weakling," the guard snarled contemptuously.

The soldier took a torch from the wall, let Sibylle lead the way, and followed her.

William breathed in the balmy summer air. Could there be anything more wonderful? A hot meal, a jug of fresh ale, a pallet with a straw mattress, a hot bath, and clean clothes.

"Make haste. Over to the tower," the soldier ordered, pushing him forward.

William staggered for a moment, but he stumbled on so that he would not be shoved again. He saw a shadow out of the corner of his eye. When he saw the hand signal, he understood. It was Robert. So it was true: Sibylle had come to rescue him. She had played her part outstandingly well; even he had been taken in. William pretended to stagger again, then fell to the ground.

"You'd better get up, or I'll help you." The soldier kicked him. He never saw the stick whistling down on the back of his head. He just let out a muffled groan as he collapsed.

Robert's shadow emerged from the darkness. With Sibylle's help he grabbed the soldier by his feet and bundled him into the dark corner. Once there, he tied him up with a cord and stuffed a rag into his mouth. It would be a while before the soldier could call for help, even if he came to quickly. "And now let's be off!"

"The rope! Can you get it off me?" William held out his hands and dropped the stone he had been hiding between his palms.

"You came prepared, eh?" He cut the cord. "It's your knife, by the way. You left it behind. I blamed myself for not coming after you. Maybe it would have helped."

"I wouldn't have stood a chance against Odon, even with the knife. He would have just taken it off me, and I never would have seen it again. Thank you, my friend." He smiled at Robert to cheer him up.

"Your purse and some food are in there." Robert indicated a small bundle. "I'll come with you for a while. Say good-bye to Sibylle quickly—we need to go."

William embraced the girl warmly. "Take care of Robert while I'm gone. Odon must never find out that he helped you, or he will fare badly. I don't even want to think about what your mother will do to you when she hears what you've done." He gave her a friendly kiss on the cheek. "Thank you. Between you you've saved me from madness and certain death. I hope I can make it up to you someday."

"You'll probably have to make it up to someone else. I'm not sure we'll ever see each other again." A pained smile crossed Sibylle's face before she ran past him toward the tower and went in without looking back.

"We need to leave," Robert urged him, looking apprehensively at the soldier lying in the corner, still unconscious.

"I hope you didn't kill him," said William, quite out of breath. They had left the castle far behind and were out of view at last. "Though he deserved it, the way he was staring at Sibylle."

William stopped. The fast walk had used up an enormous amount of his strength, far more than he had thought possible after his imprisonment in the dungeon. Exhausted, he sank to the ground.

"I'm less worried about the soldier than I am about you." Robert untied the bundle and offered William a hunk of soft white bread from the lord's table. "Here, you need to get your strength back." He opened the water pouch and held it in front of William's nose. "Drink."

After a few eager bites and a couple gulps of water, William felt a little better. "You must tell Logan how sorry I am. I would have loved to stay with you all."

"I'd prefer it if I just came with you." Robert's voice sounded pleading.

"No, that won't work." William spoke from the heart, with the voice of conviction. "Your future is here at Thorne, in the falconry you'll take over one day. Logan needs you. He would never get over it if he lost you as well as your mother and Nesta. We'll see each other again someday. Trust me, I know."

Robert kept quiet.

William ignored his friend's tears so as not to embarrass him. "Go home now. Be thankful for everything."

William's newly won freedom gave him fresh courage. When Odon found out about his flight, he would come after him. Of that William was certain.

By sunrise he was exhausted. Over the last few miles he had fallen several times, struggled to his feet, and trudged on. After a piece of bread and a few sips of water, he had thought he might be able to last a little longer, but finally he had been forced to accept that he was too grievously weakened. With his last ounce of strength, he sought out a hiding place.

He found a soft, mossy hollow beneath the massive root of a tree. Using his knife he cut two leaf-heavy branches from a shrub, curled up in the hollow, and spread them over him as camouflage.

By the time he woke up, it was broad daylight. He had slept deeply and dreamlessly. As he stood up and stretched, William felt surprisingly well. Judging by the position of the sun, it was already after noon. He ate the last piece of cheese in his bundle and drained the water pouch. He would need to fill it up again at the earliest opportunity. He checked his remaining provisions. He had been so hungry that he had eaten more than half his food on the first evening. Nonetheless, he ate another slice of ham and an apple. He needed strength to continue his journey.

It was a waste of time to wait for the sun to go down. If he stayed away from the forest paths during daylight, there was no chance he would meet anyone.

By the time dusk began to fall, not a single person had crossed his path. Suddenly he heard the pounding of heavy hooves on the forest floor.

"There he is!" someone shouted. William turned fearfully. Three riders, one of them pointing in his direction, were hard on his heels. Odon and his men.

He started running like a hare trying to shake off his pursuers. But still he could hear them close behind. William was gasping, and his foot hurt. He ran toward a row of trees and suddenly found himself on the edge of a steep bank. He hesitated for only the briefest of moments, then leaped over the edge, rolled over several times, and ended up on a broad path through the forest. He crossed it and slid down another bank until he reached a section overgrown with bushes. He could scarcely keep his footing, and he was in danger of falling back down the slope. William clung tightly to the bushes, tried to steady his breathing, and waited to see what would happen.

Nothing happened for some time, and he was beginning to feel safe when he heard the stamping of horses' hooves again. William pressed himself to the bushes, hardly daring to breathe.

"Hey, you there," an overbearing voice rang out.

Odon!

"We're looking for an outlaw who broke out of the dungeon at Thorne. Have you seen him?"

William closed his eyes. Apparently there were some travelers on the path above him. In his haste he had not noticed them, but if they had seen him and now betrayed him, he was lost.

"No, my lord. I'm afraid we've seen nobody since dawn," a man's voice replied deferentially.

"Leave it alone. Come here," a peevish woman's voice cried.

A shrill, anxious child's voice answered, "But my doll's fallen down."

Now William could see it, too. The rag doll had fallen into the very thicket where he was hiding. He ducked down, but it was no use. The dirty face of a girl no older than five suddenly appeared before him. The child looked at him wide-eyed.

William's heart was beating so loudly he thought it might leap out of his chest at any moment. He put his finger to his lips, hoping the girl would understand his gesture and not give him away.

"Mama!" the child said loudly over her shoulder.

William closed his eyes and held his breath. He thought he was lost for sure.

"I'll reach her in a moment," the girl called to her mother.

William breathed again, relieved, and opened his eyes.

The child reached out her hand toward the battered doll and tugged at it, but the doll's raw wool hair was tangled in the branches.

William untangled it carefully and held out the doll, smiling. To be safe, he put his finger to his lips again and pulled even farther back into the bushes.

The girl stood up and disappeared from view.

"Look, my lord, isn't she beautiful?"

Despite the seriousness of the situation, William had to smile. The girl was probably holding out the doll to Odon and aggravating his fury.

"Let's go. On," Odon ordered, evidently annoyed, without addressing the girl.

"A goblin gave her back to me," the girl said in her high voice.

"Yes, of course," her mother replied. "Come, we need to go."

William watched them go, peering out through the bushes. The mother, a young peasant with the waddling gait of a pregnant woman, pulled the little girl behind her. The man who had spoken to Odon carried a large sack over his shoulder. They were probably on their way to the next market. The child looked back a few times and smiled at him shyly, then disappeared among the trees.

William decided not to go any farther for the moment. It was safer to wait for nightfall, even if that meant he would make slower progress, for hardly any moonlight would shine into the woods through the thick canopy of branches. In order to avoid going round in circles or walking in the wrong direction, he would have to follow the path. Odon and his men had ridden northward, so he would head south. William took the last provisions from his bundle and began to eat.

Although he chewed slowly and deliberately, to make the most of his frugal meal, it was not enough to satisfy him. After his privations in the dungeon and the opportunity to fill up since escaping, his hunger felt worse than before. It was as if he had grown out of the habit of hunger and had to get used to it all over again.

Weak and despairing, William continued on his way as soon as the pale light of the moon permitted. He kept thinking he could hear Odon and his men. He would hide hurriedly and not creep out of his hiding place until he was sure he had been mistaken. His pursuers had probably been sitting in front of a cheerful fire for some time, filling their bellies and discussing how they would continue the search for William tomorrow. They'll give up eventually, he thought. I just have to hold out for long enough without getting caught.

❧❧

Enid crept closer cautiously. There was a young stranger over by the stream, shivering by the knee-deep water that gurgled over some large stones. He retched on his own feet and stumbled a few steps. Then he fell to his knees, bent double. He was in great pain.

Enid flitted to another bush closer to him so she could watch him better without being seen. The dirty, threadbare shirt the man wore over his dark chausses had certainly seen better days. He looked like a vagrant, but Enid did not feel afraid of him.

The young stranger, visibly distressed, ran his hand through his lank, almost shoulder-length dark hair. He was wheezing, his lungs rattling as if they were getting no air. His eyes brimmed with tears, and slender threads of saliva dripped from his mouth.

Enid was certain she was seeing the signs of poisoning, but she could not think of any poisonous berries nearby.

The man writhed in agony on the ground, groaning loudly and holding his belly.

Colic, thought Enid sympathetically. It occurred to her that perhaps he had eaten some fiber cap mushrooms. They were very poisonous and grew in huge quantities beneath the trees around there. More than once David had tried to make a meal of them, for some varieties smelled deceptively like pears. They could easily attract an ignorant, starving traveler.

"Beware of strangers," said her inner voice.

"I can't just leave him here suffering," she replied in a whisper. The stranger did not look as though he was in any condition to do her harm. Since he was likely to die if he did not get help, Enid went to him, examined the vomit, and found her suspicions confirmed. He had not really chewed the mushrooms; some he had bolted almost whole.

"Come," she said briskly, raising him up and putting his arm around her shoulders for support. She hauled him toward her hut. He stumbled along beside her in a daze, meekly allowing himself to be led by her.

"Oh God, my stomach," he groaned, and Enid wondered whether all men were as inept as David, for her brother was the only man she knew. She had always steered clear of the few strangers that came through this part of the forest, just as Nana had taught her.

Fat beads of sweat stood on the young man's forehead and dripped down his temples. His shirt was also damp with sweat. Enid's nose wrinkled. Even if his face was nice to look at, he stank horribly.

The stranger must have come into the forest on foot, she thought. She had not seen a horse or a mule anywhere in the area. His torn shirt, stiff with dirt, and the weakened body she could feel through his shirt, led her to the conclusion that he was on the run. Enid shrugged despite herself. It didn't matter to her. After all, her mother had once fled into the woods, too. She would help the stranger and ask no questions. He probably had good reasons for his flight. And if he made trouble, David and she would get rid of him as soon as he recovered. First, though, she had to make sure he survived. Then, perhaps, he would tell her why he was on the run.

As they approached the hut, David came running up. "En?" He looked at her questioningly.

"We must bring him inside." She pointed first at the stranger, then in the direction of the hut.

David nodded, grinned awkwardly, and took the man by the hand.

Enid laid down the stranger on her pallet and searched her provisions for the right ingredients. She possessed more than three dozen small clay pots, which she had fashioned herself out of earth and baked in a small oven. They were filled with herbal extracts, essences, and tinctures, including juice from the deadly nightshade plant. It had to be carefully administered, for it could be deadly. Taken in the right dose, however, it was the only remedy for fiber cap poisoning.

Cautiously, Enid let a few drops of the liquid trickle into a half-filled cup of water.

In the meantime, the stranger had become unresponsive. Enid raised his head carefully and poured the mixture into his mouth. Then she took off the poor fellow's dirty clothes. She gave his emaciated body a cursory wash and covered him with a wool blanket when he began to shiver with cold. Compassion filled her as she watched over him. His muscles relaxed gradually, and the expression on his face softened. The antidote was starting to work.

Relieved, Enid took his things, went to the stream, and washed them with the stale urine she kept in a clay tub for this purpose. She scrubbed his clothes until the stains were completely gone and rinsed them thoroughly. Her hands raw and red, she wrung out the wet garments and hung them from a tree. The balmy air and the wind would dry them quickly, despite the overcast sky.

When Enid entered the hut again, the young stranger was just recovering his senses.

"Where am I?" he whispered. His cheeks were sunken with hunger and, like his thin lips, still pale with fatigue.

"Shh." Gently but firmly, Enid pressed him down. She turned away and started preparing a meal. Out of the corner of her eye, she watched him following every movement of her hands. She offered him a full wooden bowl, and he eyed its contents suspiciously.

"Eat!" Enid raised her right hand to her mouth, made a lip-smacking sound, and smiled encouragingly.

At first hesitantly, and then more and more eagerly, the young man ate.

Enid watched him with unconcealed curiosity. Now that he was a bit cleaner, he looked handsome. His arched eyebrows emphasized his green eyes, which were all the more expressive for not being particularly large. They sparkled like small gemstones when he looked at her. Enid looked down uncomfortably and found herself looking at his slender, powerful hands. Would it be pleasant to be touched by them?

"Thank you very much."

Startled, Enid looked at him in dismay. It took her a moment to realize that he was holding out the empty bowl. When she went to take it, his hand brushed against hers. She smiled at him shyly. When he returned her look, she felt strangely weak.

"Where are my clothes?" He pulled up the blanket to his chin, as if suddenly ashamed at his nakedness.

"Still drying." As usual, Enid illustrated her words with a gesture and pointed outside. Except for David, who did not understand very much, she had not spoken to anyone since Nana's death. They had been alone for so long!

"You undressed me? Did you wash them?" The young man cleared his throat with embarrassment.

Enid nodded without looking him in the eye.

"Thank you. They were in sore need." He rubbed his eyes the way small children do when tired and then closed them. Shortly afterward, he fell asleep.

Enid gave her brother some food and then sat by the stranger's bedside for a long time, watching him. She relished the wonderful new sensation of physical longing until she too fell asleep.

The next day, she mended his now-dry clothes and then made food for them all. The stranger slept almost the whole day and then the whole night, waking only in order to have a drink, take some nourishment, or relieve himself in the pot she had put out for him.

The sun was almost at its zenith when the young man awoke a few days later. After a hearty meal, he announced that he now felt strong enough to get up and go on his way.

Enid tried to convince him to stay on his pallet and not leave, but his mind was made up.

Disappointed, she handed him his clothes and went outside so that he could get dressed.

"You saved my life and gave me shelter. I feel ashamed, for I cannot return your kindness," said the stranger regretfully once he had dressed and joined her outside. "I have nothing to give you. But I will include you and your husband in my prayers from now on."

"David is my brother," Enid replied, shaking her head as a diffident smile flickered on her lips.

"Your brother?" He nodded his understanding and looked curiously at David.

Was he happy that she had no husband? For a moment, Enid thought she saw something on his face akin to relief.

"Forgive me, I haven't even introduced myself. My name is William, William FitzEllen."

"Enid." She could not manage to say more. As she looked into his green eyes, it was as if her brain was incapable of forming a single sensible thought.

"Enid. A lovely name. Thank you, Enid, for letting me use your pallet. It was yours, wasn't it?"

Enid nodded and blushed. Unchaste thoughts rushed into her mind and then filled her with shame. Some time before, she had watched a couple of lovers in the forest, and since then she had longed to lie with a man. They had done it like animals and enjoyed it. Why shouldn't she try it with this stranger? He had gentle eyes and beautiful, strong hands. He seemed like the right one.

When William walked past her without another word, she was gripped by naked fear. She couldn't let him go. Unlike the other men she had seen in the forest up to now, she really liked this one.

That morning, he had asked for a bucket of water and washed thoroughly. She had turned away to prepare some food, but she had watched him out of the corner of her eye. Although he must have been starving for some time, it was clear from his body that he had known better times.

He was young, probably younger than she was herself, and no older than David. He would recover quickly and would certainly make a good companion. He represented no danger to her; on the contrary, he represented a temptation.

Enid was lonely and no longer wanted to be alone with David all the time. She wanted to hear William talk and hoped, if he stayed, that he would tell her stories about the world beyond the forest, about which she knew next to nothing. Yes, he would talk to her and make her laugh. She was sure he liked laughing; she had seen it in his eyes.

Now that he was leaving, she feared it might really be forever. So she followed him secretly to the stream. Not far from the place where she had found him, he stopped. She hid in the undergrowth and watched William remove his clothes, spread them carefully on a stone on the bank, and then wade into the glittering water, stark naked. His behind was round like a little apple, and she found it exquisitely attractive. The stream was so deep here that William was soon standing hip deep in rushing water. Warmth flooded through Enid in a wave, and a pleasant tingling sensation ran from her belly down between her legs.

ഌ

The refreshing water felt extraordinarily good. Cleansing for body and soul, thought William, stroking his cheeks pensively. He did shave his beard from time to time, but its growth was rather weak. Still, it would do him good to get rid of the stubble that had grown during his imprisonment. But first he would have to sharpen his knife.

His time in the castle dungeon had damaged more than his body. William was well aware that his confidence had suffered, too, and that it was important to regain it. Robert had told him that he'd spent only two months in that noisome hole, but that had been enough to drive him to the edge of despair. How long a few weeks could feel when the situation felt hopeless.

His flight had cost him a great deal of strength. William still felt weak and would have been all too glad to stay with the kind young woman and her simpleminded brother. But the two of them probably had barely enough to eat themselves. He had certainly been unable to find much that was nourishing on his way through the forest. His body rose up in goose bumps as he thought of the mushrooms and the cramps they had caused.

William waded a little farther into the stream, scooped water over his upper body with his right hand, and opened up his left fist. He had taken a handful of ash from the hearth in the hut, for he knew that it cleaned well. He rubbed his body and hair thoroughly with it. Once finished, he ducked under the water to rinse off both dirt and ash. He was still not clean, so he picked up some sand from the bottom of the stream and scrubbed himself with that.

The filth of his cell had eaten its way into his skin; on his hands, in particular, it was dreadfully stubborn. This dirt will persist till Judgment Day, thought William, scouring his hands until his fingers were red and raw but at least somewhat clean. He waded toward the bank and felt for the herb he had picked along the way and left there. He didn't know its name but liked how it smelled. He rubbed the small, fragrant leaves hard into his skin and hair and ducked under the water again to get rid of the crumbled remains of the plant. Now he felt better.

How swiftly a dark, stinking cell, with its dank and pitiless cold, hunger, and despair, could transform a human being into an animal that craved only nourishment and freedom, he thought.

Suddenly, William was startled out of his dark thoughts. What was that he heard in the bushes? He was gripped by panic. Were Odon and his companions still after him? Five days had passed, at a guess, no more than six, since he had escaped them in the forest. William looked over at the bank, and his mouth fell open with astonishment upon seeing Enid standing there.

He had already noticed her soft, pale skin in the hut. Now, as she slowly lifted her shift and pulled it over her head, her remarkable complexion, which seemed almost to speak of high birth, dazzled him. Enid untied her long blonde hair from its knot on the top of her head and shook it loose until it tumbled down over her back and bare breasts. It glowed like gold in the sun, lending her an elfin air.

William rubbed his eyes, but it was no mirage. She was actually naked, as God had made her, on the bank. His breath caught in his throat at the sight of her lovely body, and his manhood stirred, despite the cold water. He had had no experience of love, so he stood stock-still, waiting to see what would happen. As she slowly entered the water, Enid behaved as though she could not see him. She rinsed her hands with water, washed her face, then stroked her neck and down toward her breasts. She did not even glance in William's direction. She ducked under the water and reemerged with wet hair, which half covered her delightful rear. Her appearance and catlike movements were almost enough to make William faint. Still, though, he was incapable of movement.

As if she were alone, she laid herself on the grassy bank, face down, drying herself in the sun. And when she turned over, William's longing increased. His desire hurt him physically, and yet it felt like a gift from heaven. Although he was starting to freeze in the cold water, William stood still, as if nailed to the spot, until Enid had dressed and gone away again.

Only then did William dare to step out of the stream and get dressed.

Suddenly, Enid stepped out from behind a big bush. "Stay with us," she begged with an innocent, pleading expression in her eyes.

William was startled. He thought she had gone back to the hut long since. She must have watched him getting dressed.

Her breathing was quick, as if she had been running, and her cheeks glowed pink. He nodded without a word, took the hand she silently held out to him, and followed her back to the cottage.

From then on, in a sort of ritual, he would go to the stream every day, alone, and she would follow him a short while later. Sometimes she would get undressed more quickly, sometimes more slowly, and always he would be close to bursting with desire for her. He suspected that she enjoyed his admiring looks, yet he did not dare to get closer to her, for she had not so far given him a single word of encouragement. William was all the more astonished when, on the sixth day, Enid waded over toward him. He could scarcely grasp what she was doing. Every sinew in his body was taut.

Enid walked around him wordlessly, slowly coming closer and closer, until he thought he was going to faint with desire. She clung to him from behind, wrapping her arms around him and pressing her firm breasts against his back. William closed his eyes. His breathing grew heavier as she silently began to caress his chest. With agonizing slowness, her hands slipped over his belly and down into the depths. William gasped with arousal as she touched him coyly between the legs.

She let go of him abruptly, took him by the hand, and led him back to the bank.

Once there, she knelt down, offered up her pleasingly rounded behind, and made it plain that she was ready to accept him.

William approached her, full of desire but not really knowing how to go about it. But his hope of assistance from Enid was in vain. She seemed to be just as inexperienced, so they tried together to find a way toward union.

As he pushed cautiously into her, Enid replied with a soft moan, which frightened and aroused him in equal measure. William pulled out almost completely and thought he might faint with pleasure. He moved only timidly, and yet it was not long before a powerful spasm released the pressure within him and he sank, exhausted, into the grass beside Enid.

"Don't leave me alone," she whispered after a long period of silence. Her lips touched his ear gently as she spoke. William shivered despite the summer heat. He wanted her again, already. He would not be able to leave the hut in the forest as quickly as he had first thought. Revived, he held Enid's neck, pulled her toward him, and kissed her passionately.

From that day on they lay with each other regularly. They laughed and played like children, living with David like a real family and passing a carefree summer. William no longer thought about his original plan to leave the forest.

He fashioned himself a slingshot so that he could go hunting with Enid; he gathered herbs with her and got to know all the roots, berries, and mushrooms of the forest. En, as he now called her more and more, taught him which plants were poisonous and which were edible, and showed him how to prepare them to create a delicious meal or mix a healing potion.

David, though tall as a man, was as clumsy and awkward as a child, but he loved William and was glad to receive attention from someone other than his sister. The two of them would often sit in front of the hut, and William would give him small tasks that the boy could carry out despite his clumsy fingers. At first, William had looked at him discreetly and wondered how two people who were so different could be brother and sister. Where Enid was tender and beautiful, David's legs were far too thin for his massive body. He had the protruding barrel-like belly of a child, and he behaved like one, too. His hair was the color of dirty sand, instead of golden and glossy like his sister's. But David was lovable, open, and always cheerful and in a good mood, so William and he soon became friends.

As for Enid, there was something wonderfully mysterious, wild, and untamed about her that was extraordinarily attractive to William. She was insatiable in love and burned with desire like a flame licking hungrily at a log. Thus it was that they coupled almost every day, sometimes twice or even three times, licentiously, flagrantly, uninhibitedly, passionately. They did it in the forest, in a clearing, or down by the stream, their favorite place. And at night, when David was asleep, they lay with each other in the hut, on their shared pallet.

Thus winter came, and William stayed in the forest with Enid and David.

April 1189

Teeth chattering, Marguerite stood beside the open grave in which they had just laid her father to rest. A fine rain moistened the earth, seeped through her clothing, and ran down her face like miniature tears.

A few days before, her mother, Alix de Hauville, had said through sobs, "He's dead." But Marguerite had not really understood what it meant. She had seen animals die when they were slaughtered for food, and she had seen people weep because they had lost someone like a husband or a child. But she found it difficult to understand what it meant to be dead.

"We shall never see him again," her mother whispered, and Marguerite felt a sudden urge to suck her thumb, as she had done every day until quite recently. Sucking one's thumb felt good, her father had said, but it was unsuitable for a big girl like her. But Marguerite was still small.

She clamped her thumb in her fist and stared at the hole in the ground. It must be cold down there. Freezing cold herself, she pulled her robe tighter, but it did no good. She had often heard that the dead went to heaven, but whenever she looked upward she could see only blue sky or clouds. She searched the unending gray overhead, but in vain: her father was not in the sky—he was down here, in the damp, dark earth.

He must be getting cold, thought Marguerite. He needs a cover. She let go of her nurse's hand and ran off.

"Let her go," said her mother as Marguerite ran across the big green meadow and into the house. The soft hide one would be best, the one on her bed.

"He'll never go hunting again," her mother had said the night before, weeping and clasping Marguerite in her arms. So her father would never be able to make another bedcover for himself. Never again.

As usual, she had to throw the entire weight of her slight body against the heavy oak door before it creaked open. The room was dark and cool and smelled of sleep. She was used to feeling her way to her bed when she had no light. She gathered up the thick, soft cover. Why did it have to be so heavy? Too heavy for a little girl like her, she thought despondently. She sniffed. She was freezing cold and felt very alone. It was comforting to lay her cheek against the hide bedcover and close her eyes for a moment. Why couldn't she even remember her father's face? He was gone, simply extinguished.

Warm tears ran down her cheeks. Reluctantly, she wiped them away with the bedcover. It was marvelously soft and familiar, and yet it was only a small comfort. She had not slept alone the past few nights; she had joined her mother, climbing into the high bed with the heavy curtains. They had snuggled up close to each other, and she had not needed her bedcover. So she would be quite able to do without it.

Marguerite's eyes had adjusted to the diffuse light in the room, and her gaze fell on the small golden bell hanging from a strip of leather beside her bed. Her father had given it to her a few days before. It was a falcon's bell. Its ring was loud, but for her father the sound had been like music, for falconry fascinated him more than anything else. She took the strip of leather and hung it around her neck. Then, heartened, she reached for the heavy hide cover and dragged it behind her out of the room, down the stairs, and to the door. Not until she was there did she try to gather the thick and unwieldy cover into her arms. One corner dropped to the ground, dragged through the soft mud of the courtyard, and almost tripped her up when she stepped on it. Crossing the meadow, she kept stumbling because the bulky blanket prevented her from seeing the ground in front of her.

"What are you doing?" cried her mother in astonishment, hurrying toward her.

"Father must be warm," said Marguerite. "Will you help me cover him up? It's so big."

With tears in her eyes, Alix agreed. "Of course, darling."

"I shall keep the bell until I'm grown up. Then I shall have falcons, too," she explained in an almost defiant tone.

"Yes, you will, my little one." Alix stayed by her husband's grave for quite a while longer. Marguerite remained at her side, clinging to her mother's soft, warm hand with her clammy fingers. It had stopped raining, but it was still bitterly cold. Marguerite could hardly feel her feet anymore, and the goose bumps all over her body were beginning to hurt. It was not until one of the servants, on her mother's signal, began shoveling earth into her father's grave that she looked up in fright and ran away sobbing.

She ran as fast as she could, though her breath was burning in her chest, and did not stop until she reached her favorite tree. To her it seemed tall, but she had learned by experience that it was easy to climb, for it branched not far from the ground. She had often climbed it, but never very high because her nurse usually warned her off. This time, though, she was alone and she wanted to go to the very top. She wanted to touch the sky, to be closer to her father. He must be there by now, not in that dark, damp grave.

Tears ran down her face. She would never sit in his lap again, listening to his stories, and never again be kissed on the nose by him. She understood that now. Why had he left her alone?

"You're cruel," she cried up at the sky, first muted and then louder. "I hate you for going away."

There was a clap of thunder. Marguerite started with fear, lost her balance, and fell out of the tree.

"Marguerite," cried her mother, rushing to her. "Are you hurt?"

Marguerite felt a burning pain on her forehead and right knee, but she shook her head bravely. Blood flowed down over her eyebrows, mingling with the tears. "I'm sorry," she howled. "I didn't mean it!"

Alix knelt down on the muddy ground, cradled her child in her arms, and rocked her. She was weeping, too, and kissed Marguerite. "It's not too bad, just a scrape on your forehead," she told her comfortingly.

"Did you hear the thunder?" Marguerite sobbed. "I'm sure father is angry with me because I cursed him."

"No, darling, but he doesn't want you to be sad. Trust me, all is well with him, for he is with God," she replied gently, rocking Marguerite until she calmed down.

June 1189

Enid did not weep or shout when William told her he wanted to turn his back on the forest forever. She just looked helplessly at David and shook her head sadly. No rebuke passed her lips, as she was overcome with anguish and fear.

"Come with me," William begged her, as he had countless times before. Enid was expecting a child. His child. But she refused to leave the forest.

William knew she feared people and was afraid for David, but his longing for the falcons was too great, and he was wasting away in the solitude of the forest. "But I *have* to go," he shouted at Enid, louder than he meant to, and stormed out of the hut in a burning rage.

He left the tiny clearing behind him and ran as fast as he could. Just get away, he thought bitterly. He had already been here too long; he had spent a whole year with Enid. Yet his fury gradually subsided as he marched through the forest with his long strides. Once he had left the densest part of the forest behind him, he walked noticeably more slowly. Soon he was just strolling; he went uphill for a while and then climbed the chalk outcrop. From here there was a wonderful view far down the valley.

He had been up here many times in recent months, fondly remembering his falconry dreams. How he missed the proud birds!

William sat down on the moss-covered rock, placed his hand on the warm stone, and stared down. Whenever he observed hunts from up here, he imagined what it would be like to be part of them. The world of falconers was so much more colorful and attractive than his lonely life in the forest. Every fiber of his body longed for it. He had never intended to spend so long in the forest. If fate had not put Enid in his path, he would have returned to people, and especially falcons, long since.

At first it was Enid's eager and passionate ways that persuaded him to stay in the forest with her. Later, he realized that she was more to him than just a lover. She was the most unusual person he knew: wild and at the same time shy, like an untamed animal. Mysterious and beautiful, wise and innocent, good-hearted and sometimes ice-cold. Enid was strong willed and yet hungry for affection. Her almost childlike devotion made him feel needed, and her selfless love of David moved him profoundly. She knew so much about the plants and animals of the forest but so little about people's sensitivities. She simply didn't understand how sorely he missed falconry.

He sniffed bitterly. Perhaps it really was time to leave. He looked down into the valley and saw a falconer and his assistant. The men were training a bird to a lure.

William thought of Isaac, who, with everything he did, felt physical pain at the loss of his severed hand. He felt a similar anguish himself whenever he thought about the mews. He missed it so badly that it caused him bodily pain. It pierced his chest like a mighty thorn had been embedded there. He didn't want to—no, he *couldn't* give up his dreams!

At first he had convinced himself that he could live without hawking, but over time the sense of loss had become simply unbearable.

As dusk fell, William gathered a few dry twigs together and lit a fire. One warm summer evening shortly after his recovery, Enid had shown him how this could be achieved without tinder or flint. Afterward, they had lain with each other, passionately, by the light of the fire.

William groaned out loud. What should he do? How should he decide? He put another branch on the fire and stared into the bright flames. No, he couldn't just leave Enid and the child behind. If she didn't come with him, he would have to stay, for better or worse.

Perhaps he could train some more goshawks and then sell them, if nothing else. Even the king owned several of those birds, for one could hunt with falcons only in open terrain; for hunting in the forest, one used goshawks. William had caught and trained a young goshawk that spring.

Hawking with that bird had made him feel a little better, but he did not consider this kind of hunting an art. It served principally to put food on the table. Hunting with falcons, food was secondary; what mattered was the beauty of the high flight.

But he could make money selling goshawks, thus obtaining clothing and food for his family, thought William. Enid's dress was so old and worn that her naked skin peeped out almost indecently in places. Although he frequently found this arousing, it could not go on. William knew Enid needed him. And the child needed his help, too.

"I'm going to be a father," he murmured, suddenly moved, and he felt as though he had not understood the full implications until that moment.

For no reason he could fathom, he was sure Enid would bear him a son. Smiling ruefully, he tried to imagine how he would teach the boy everything he knew about birds of prey and hunting. William shook his head. Leave Enid? It was absurd.

"I won't let you down, Enid," he murmured decisively.

☾☾

Enid slammed the door in fury. "Come with me," William had said and then, when she had refused, he had simply left. She pounded her fists against the shiny, silver-hued oak in a fit of helpless rage. He couldn't expect that of her.

Enid's head felt as if it were going to explode. She hit herself on the forehead with her hand. Sometimes that stubborn skull of hers was crowded with too many things. Words she didn't say, thoughts she never confided to anyone, and feelings she couldn't express.

"I…love…you," she said out loud. *That* was what she had wanted to say to William for a long time. But even if she loved him, she couldn't just leave the forest. The very thought sent an icy shiver down her spine. The forest was her home. Out of love for William, she might have been able to overcome her fear of people, but she had to think of David, too. He would never be comfortable beyond the forest. People would push him around and say cruel things. Nana had warned her about people often enough. Leaving with David was impossible. Enid let out a long sigh, put her hands together in front of her chest, and closed her eyes. "Please, God, let William come back to me," she whispered.

The unborn child stirred below her heart. Quickly, she laid her hand on the taut skin of her belly, tapped her fingers lightly, and waited for the child to reply with a kick or two. A wonderful surge of joy flowed through her. Perhaps William was right and the forest wasn't the best place for her child?

Enid opened the door and looked out. The oppressive heat of the summer's day hit her. The air smelled of dusty earth and blossom; the sky was gray and overcast. David was crouching in the sparse and withered grass in front of the hut, playing with pebbles like a five-year-old. Enid shook her head sadly. He had the body of a man but the mind of a child, and that would never change.

No, she thought, considering the peaceful scene, it can't be wrong to want to live here. It's been good for David and me, and it will be good for our child.

Enid went over to her brother, affectionately stroked his mop of blond hair, and breathed in the heavy air. While the child was little, she would be as careful as she had been with David to make sure it didn't put anything poisonous in its mouth. And when it was older, she would teach it to understand animals and plants, for when you were at one with the forest it was akin to paradise. Full of hope, Enid looked out for William, but he did not come.

By evening, a nameless fear was creeping up on her. Had she lost him forever? It wasn't the first night William had spent in the forest, but he had never left in the middle of a quarrel. She glanced longingly outside again. "Will," she sighed quietly.

She prepared supper as she did every evening. Whatever happened, David was constantly hungry. He could eat at any time and gobbled down whatever she put in front of him. Enid, on the other hand, was too downcast to feel hungry. She had to force herself to take a couple of spoonfuls of food. The unborn child in her womb shouldn't have to starve because she had argued with William. She set his dish and cup at his usual place and filled them in the hope that he might yet return.

When David had spooned up his broth, he pointed at William's food and looked at her questioningly.

Enid frowned with annoyance, but then she nodded.

David fell on the second helping like a starving animal. Once he had wiped that plate clean, too, he leaned down toward Enid, sated and happy, waiting for her to kiss him good night on the forehead as she did every evening. Then he crawled onto his pallet, wrapped himself up in his blanket, and huddled up close to the wall. That was the only way he liked to sleep.

Enid remained seated awhile longer at the big wooden table that Nana's husband had made. In truth, it was too big for the little hut, but it was of great service to Enid when she had to sort large heaps of herbs. For a while she watched David as he slept the sleep of the innocent; then she stared into the tiny flickering flame of the tallow candle, brooding. It shed very little light on the room and cast agitated shadows on the walls.

The longer Enid sat, the heavier her head grew. At length it slumped forward and she started. Weren't there noises outside, as if someone was up to something outside the hut?

"Will, at last." Overjoyed, she leaped up, lifted the wooden latch, and threw the door open. Then she stood there, thunderstruck.

It was not William she had heard. Three young knights stood by their horses. One of them thrust a torch in her direction; another, the leader, to judge by his self-important manner, approached her.

Enid shrank back involuntarily. The man's broad shoulders almost filled the doorway. His beardless face was fresh and smooth. His straw-blond hair was shaved behind the ears in the Norman manner. He glanced briefly past her into the hut and nodded with satisfaction. He turned to one of his companions, and the flame of the torch made his blue eyes shine.

"Have Bevis tie up the horses—we'll stay here tonight," he ordered, grinning broadly at Enid. "If you've no objection, dear lady," he added with a small bow.

Enid suspected he was mocking her, but she was not afraid of the blond knight. He's too good-looking to be wicked, she thought, taking a step back and letting him in.

The man with the torch extinguished the flame and followed him. The one called Bevis came in, too. In contrast to the blond one, neither of his companions looked very trustworthy. Like their leader, they wore swords and hunting knives on their belts. Not only did they look as though they knew how to handle them; they looked as though they were actually eager to get to work with them.

Enid immediately regretted letting in the men. But had she really had any choice? She closed the door and indicated, with a curt gesture, that they should sit at the table.

The spurs on their boots jangled at every step. The strong smell of horse sweat, leather, iron, and ale emanating from the three of them caught in Enid's throat. Bravely she fought back the urge to retch, swallowed a few times, and then silently withdrew into the most distant corner of the room. She glanced swiftly at the corner where David was sleeping. He was not moving and still lay close to the wall, so that he was almost invisible. The men had not noticed him yet. Enid prayed to God that it might stay so.

"We're thirsty," cried Bevis, who was shorter and fatter than the others, pounding his fist on the table so hard that Enid jumped. His plump cheeks glowed as red as raspberries. "Bring us drink, and be quick about it."

Enid stood up as quickly as her condition allowed and placed the water bucket on the table, along with its wooden dipper.

"Water?" Bevis looked into the bucket with disgust. "Have you no ale or wine?"

Enid shook her head, looking down at the floor.

"Can't you speak? Or don't you want to?" the second knight intervened. He was somewhat bigger than the blond one with the friendly look, but he was leaner and his face was angular. He wore his shoulder-length black hair in a ponytail, tied up at the neck.

When Enid did not answer, he grabbed her by the arm and drew her close to him. She looked at him, frightened. His left eyebrow was disfigured by an ugly, bulging red scar that resembled a glowing worm. Enid looked down. The muscles in his sinewy forearm twitched as he clasped his fingers more tightly around her wrist.

"No," she cried, trying to escape his grip.

"Come now, don't be shy." The lean one came even closer. Since his head was tilted slightly upward, Enid could not help looking right up his long, slightly hooked nose. Hairs sprouted from it. They were as dark as the hair on his head and the bristles on his chin. His breath smelled terrible.

"If you haven't anything decent for us to drink, at least let us have a bit of fun with you instead."

Enid felt sick.

The knight grinned, grabbed at her breasts, and started kneading them roughly.

Without hesitation, Enid slapped him in the face. The blond knight with the clear blue eyes and fat Bevis laughed and clapped their thighs with mirth.

The lean one, however, grabbed the hand that had struck him. "Who do you think you are? Mistress Touch-Me-Not?"

"Leave her alone." The blond one stood up with exaggerated slowness and looked threateningly at the lean one. "You shall not touch her."

He won't allow him to do anything to me, thought Enid with relief, looking at him gratefully.

The lean one stared at him with hostility; he seemed to be toying with the idea of rebelling. "But I want her." He turned to face Enid, lewdly licking his lips and repulsive yellow teeth.

Enid inched closer to the blond one.

"Tomorrow. You'll have to wait till tomorrow, my friend," he answered condescendingly. The icy tone of his voice was chilling, but Enid did not believe he really meant what he said. She was sure he only wanted to protect her and would not think of leaving her to his companions.

"Why wait?" growled the lean one impatiently. The red scar on his brow was even more prominent now.

Raspberry-cheeked Bevis nodded in agreement, wiping the sweat from his forehead.

The blond knight laid his hand on Enid's hip as if it were his. "You shall wait till tomorrow. Tonight she belongs to me. Now leave me in peace." Almost tenderly, he pulled Enid toward her bed.

Since she still thought of him as her protector, someone who clearly was just trying to get her beyond his companions' reach, she thought mainly of David. He mustn't on any account wake up. It didn't bear thinking about, how the two coarse youths would treat him. So Enid was even relieved when the blond one told his companions to extinguish the light and lie down to sleep. But when he began pressing himself against her eagerly she understood, bewildered, that it was not her virtue he had been defending but his right to be the first to have his way with her.

Crippled by fear, she allowed him to lift her shift. If she wanted to protect her brother, she realized with horror, she could not put up a fight. Mute with desperation, she offered up her rear end to the blond man, holding her hand protectively against her belly. God in heaven, don't let him notice that I'm with child, she prayed silently, else he'd ask where the father was. She buried her face for shame in the wool blanket she used when she slept. It smelled of William. God, don't let him come back now, Enid prayed fervently. The knights outnumbered him, and they were armed. William wouldn't stand the slightest chance against them and would be killed if he tried to rescue her.

Hot tears poured down her cheeks, seeping into the blanket.

When he had finished with her, he embraced her from behind, like a lover, holding her firmly between his arms.

Enid could hardly bear his breath against her neck. It was only her desire to protect David that gave her strength.

"Just wait till tomorrow. Truly, it'll be incredible. Nothing else will matter." It was a voice in the dark. It must have been the lean one.

She began to tremble at the thought that her martyrdom was not yet at an end. Bravely she fought back the urge to vomit. She did not want to wait until the other two fell on her, too, and cudgeled her brain to think of a way to escape further humiliation.

Meanwhile, the blond one had fallen asleep and was making small smacking sounds.

Enid did not dare move, though she found it intolerable to feel his arm across her breasts.

After a while, he began snoring softly.

Enid kept her eyes wide-open and listened in the darkness. Nothing but regular breathing could be heard. The other two men must have fallen asleep, too. Enid did not know what she should do. If she tried to flee, she would be leaving David at the mercy of these brutal men.

At the thought of what shameful acts they might still be capable of, her ire rose. But she had to think not only of David but also of her unborn child.

Just before dawn, Enid decided to creep out. The men were fast asleep. If they were still in the hut at daybreak and David woke up, he was in danger anyway. But if she managed to lure the men from the hut by fleeing, she might even be able to shake them off. Certainly no one knew the forest better than she did.

Enid sent a quick prayer up to heaven. She had to try, and hope that God and all the saints were with her.

Holding her breath, she slowly removed the arm that now lay on her hip and crawled toward the door on all fours. She stopped repeatedly to check that the men had not stirred. Carefully, she picked up the poker in case she needed to defend herself. Then she quietly lifted the wooden latch and stood up, heart pounding. She felt sure she had managed to leave the hut unnoticed, but then she felt her shift being grabbed from behind.

"Where are you off to in such haste?"

Enid turned, startled.

It was the lean one. Grinning cruelly, he was holding on to her and pulling her toward him.

Enid's hand twitched. She wanted to lunge at him and hit him over the head with the poker, but he saw through her, gripped her arm, and twisted it with lightning speed. All she could do was drop it.

"What's happening?" The blond one's voice sounded sleepy. He stretched pleasurably.

"The little thing tried to leave us," guessed Bevis, who had woken up, too.

When the lean one turned toward them, Enid was able to free herself. She flung herself out through the door, but her adversary was swift as a ferret. Enid had run only a few steps when he grabbed her by the hair and held tight. Enid flailed about in desperation.

Unfortunately, David chose this moment to come out of the hut. "En?" He rubbed his eyes and looked at her questioningly.

The blond one looked him up and down disdainfully. He grabbed David's chin. "Now who have we here?"

Enid tried to escape once more, but the lean one held her back by the hair and shoved her to the ground.

David cried out with shock and tried to rush to her aid, but the blond one punched him right on the nose. David fell to the ground.

Enid froze and stopped struggling. The lean one removed his sword belt and started fiddling with his clothing. As the lean one undressed, Enid's eyes were wide with terror and shock. The blond one had been modestly equipped and had caused her hardly any pain, but the lean one was built quite otherwise. God protect my child, she begged mutely, starting to weep, which seemed to excite her tormentor even more. Egged on by Bevis, who could obviously hardly wait for his own turn, he put his hand under her shift and lifted it up to her chin. When he saw her rounded belly, he hesitated for a moment.

"You can't be very particular if you carry on with this booby. It's high time you had a real man." He grabbed her crotch contemptuously and thrust more than one finger into her womanhood.

Enid's whole body shuddered. She turned her head aside and locked her gaze on David. The poor fellow was desperately trying to protect his head with his hands, but he could not fend off his attacker's repeated punches. He tried again and again to escape and reach Enid.

"Straw in his head, but fire in his loins," sneered the blond one. "We'll soon beat that out of him." He continued to punch David, kicking him in the belly and sides until he was on the ground weeping like a child.

Instinctively, Enid started singing the lullaby that Nana had always sung for her when she needed comfort. David's whimpering subsided gradually. Enid could not tell whether this was the effect of her song or the kicks, but she was relieved nonetheless, for even the blond one stood silent for a moment, as if spellbound.

"Silence," the lean one roared in a fury, grabbing her by the throat and squeezing until she could only croak. She nearly fainted. He let her breathe again and forced his way into her.

A fierce burning sensation between her legs made Enid cry out. Tears ran down her cheeks. She feared for the life of her unborn child and began to sing quietly again.

But her song so enraged her tormentor that the veins in his neck filled with blood, bulging and pulsing visibly. He shut her mouth with the flat of his hand and then, not long afterward, arched back with pleasure.

"Let her breathe! You're suffocating her! I still want her," Bevis told him, his face bright red with arousal. He started undoing his chausses.

When the lean one pulled out of her and released her mouth, Enid gasped for air, spluttering. In desperation, she started singing again.

Fat Bevis lay down on her, but her singing made him lose his temper, too. "Shut your mouth," he cried furiously, punching her in the face.

But the lullaby brought Enid comforting memories of affection and warmth, and this time she did not fall silent. Suddenly, it was as if Nana, through this song, were watching over her, David, and the unborn child.

"I can't do it with this howling," snorted Bevis in annoyance, but he did finally manage to take his pleasure. It did not take long, and she sang with even more desperation all the while.

"Just wait and see what happens if you don't stop singing this moment," the lean one threatened. When she went on singing, he came closer.

Bevis had finished with her and was adjusting his clothing.

There was a rushing sound in Enid's ears. Wavy lines and tiny dots obstructed her vision. The lean one's face was right in front of hers now, and in disbelief she examined the scar on his eyebrow. It was glowing bloodred with fury, and it made his sallow skin look even grayer.

Hands trembling, he took his hunting knife and sliced at the loose cloth she wore wrapped twice around her waist in place of a belt. He cut it into two halves and used them to tie her to a tree.

Enid was still singing; it was as if she had to. She clung to the familiar words of the lullaby and fervently hoped David would remain calm so that he would not be beaten again.

Bevis hurried to help his scrawny companion. "Why don't you stop her mouth? I can't stand this howling," he cried, blocking his ears. "She's driving me mad."

Enid twitched under the blows of the men, but she did not stop singing. In some mysterious way it gave her strength; it was her only weapon in this unequal fight.

The child began to kick powerfully. It needs comfort, thought Enid, just like me and David. So I mustn't stop singing.

"We've had our fun. Now let her go," the blond one ordered, visibly uneasy. He did not seem comfortable with what the other two were doing to her.

The lean one glared at him, as if sensing an opportunity to become the new leader of their little pack. "Perhaps you're too soft-hearted?" he asked challengingly, stroking the scar on his brow with his middle finger. "She's defying us and mocking us with her singing."

Enid looked pleadingly at the blond one. Despite the brutality with which he had first punched and then kicked David, his face looked pink and innocent. As if freshly scrubbed. Enid thought she could see doubt in his blue eyes, perhaps even sympathy, and quiet hope rose in her. He was the only one who could help her. She stopped singing for a moment. One word, just one word from him would be enough to make the others stop.

But the blond one hesitated, avoiding her eyes, and turned away. "Oh, do what you will with her!" he growled over his shoulder. He kicked David in the guts again, then leaned down and started polishing his boots with the boy's shirt.

"God in heaven, please be merciful," whispered Enid. The cloth was biting painfully into her flesh.

"Someone like you can't rely on succor from God." The lean one laughed cruelly, took his knife, and slit her shift open all the way up. He approached her face and licked it.

Enid threw her head aside in disgust. Her terror made her start singing again.

"I'll stop her mouth once and for all," she heard. Then a terrible pain stabbed through her. It took her breath away, shocked her, horrified her; it caused her song to fall silent. The child, she thought, panic-stricken. Then everything went black.

❦❦

William awoke, startled, and looked about. He had meant to go back to Enid, but he must have fallen asleep. Dawn was well advanced. Before long it would be broad daylight. It looked like a clear summer day. He stood up. Going back to Enid was the right decision.

He kicked some earth over the ashes of his fire so that the wind would not catch some of the embers and ignite a forest fire. He would learn to love the forest as much as Enid did, and he would try to use the goshawks to drive out once and for all his longing for falcons. After all, he would be responsible for a family soon. He swore he would never utter the slightest word of reproach to Enid. It was his decision, and he would never regret it.

Thus decided, he set off. All of a sudden he was impatient to see her. He ran across the big meadow and stopped abruptly when he noticed the red flowers that covered it. Poppies! A smile flickered on his face as he bent and picked a large bunch of the fragile flowers. Enid loved their fleeting beauty. When the petals dropped, after less than a day, she would use them to brew a marvelously delicate tea, sweetening it with wild honey. William felt infinitely glad that he had decided in favor of Enid and their child. When he came back with the poppies, Enid would know immediately that he intended to stay and would forgive him.

Once he had almost filled his whole fist with the hairy stems, he looked up at the sky. The mackerel sky had turned into a dense gray mass that blocked out the sun. But the change in the weather could not dampen his euphoria. He ran off, leaping over bushes and ferns, tree roots, and stands of flowers, until he reached the tiny clearing in which their hut stood. It seemed marvelously quiet and peaceful.

"Enid," he called out when he was still some distance away.

But neither she nor David came to meet him. Surprised, William ran up to the hut. Not a sound was to be heard. The door stood wide-open. Blackness yawned at him from the interior. He noticed tracks in the earth, kneeled down, and examined them closely. There was no doubt: hoofprints from three horses.

A sense of unease flowed into his bowels. Something was wrong. He sprang up and ran around the hut.

The sight of Enid's lifeless body hit him like a blow. Dumbstruck, he stood staring at the gruesome sight. His hand went limp, and the poppies fell to the ground.

"Enid," he screamed like a madman, running over to her. "No, please no! Oh God!"

Enid lay crumpled at the base of the tree, naked and smeared with blood. Her belly had been slit open, and her eyes were vacant. William staggered over to a nearby bush and vomited. He gasped, thinking he was going to suffocate, and vomited again.

A loud sob escaped him as he freed his beloved from her bonds and clasped her mutilated body in his arms. He brushed her hair out of her face and kissed her forehead as he wept.

"Why did I ever go?" he lamented, choking, pressing her to him, and rocking her in his arms. After a brief time, he laid her out on the grass, straightened her disheveled golden hair, and covered her nakedness with the slit-open shift. The wind plucked some petals from the poppy stems and blew them across the clearing. A few landed on Enid's chest and others on her hair.

He did not find the infant child until later; it had been carelessly tossed aside in the grass. William groaned. The tiny little boy's thin limbs seemed strangely dislocated.

"My son." He sank to his knees, despairing, but could not bring himself to touch the child. He covered his face with his hands and wept. Why, Lord? he protested, beside himself with grief. But no sound emerged from his throat. Why?

A little while later, he heard a quiet groan. William looked around. "David?" He found the boy under a bush. His face was in a bad way. His nose looked broken; his chin and right cheekbone were black and blue. But he was alive.

Why didn't you let *her* live instead of *him*? thought William bitterly, looking reproachfully up at the sky as if he could glimpse God's face and receive an answer.

David whimpered with pain.

"It's all right," William said as he sat beside the injured boy and stroked his tousled hair. "I'm here with you."

After a while he stood up and helped David into the hut and onto his bed. "Get some rest," he said gently, stroking his head, just as Enid had always done. Tears were still running down the poor boy's face long after he fell asleep.

William dragged himself outdoors. His chest felt excessively tight, as if an icy fist were crushing his heart. How would he find the courage and strength to bury Enid and their child?

William sat motionless for a long time, staring into the void. He reproached himself for not having come home to Enid and David sooner. Since he hadn't been able to defend them, he certainly owed them a decent burial.

He stood up like a sleepwalker and, with leaden arms, dug a grave big enough for both Enid and the child. He had never had to carry out a more difficult task. Although he poured all his anger into the work, William felt his own death come closer with every inch that the grave grew deeper.

When the hole was big enough, he was so exhausted he could hardly stand upright. He staggered over to Enid, poured water from his pouch onto his shirt, and used it to wash her face, then lovingly combed her hair with his fingers. Using her linen shift, which was drenched in her blood, he bound up her belly, covering the wound as best he could. When he went to fetch her blanket from the hut, in order to wrap her in it, a small enamel plaque fell to the ground. William picked it up and put it on the table without looking at it.

With the last of his remaining strength, he picked up Enid, carried her to the grave, and laid her in the dark earth.

He knelt beside her for a long time, looking at her with his face soaked with tears. At length he fetched the child and, with trembling hands, placed it in Enid's arms. Then he collapsed beside the two of them. They looked so peaceful, as if they were only sleeping. He hadn't been there when they needed him most. How could he go on living with this guilt? And what was the point?

William joined them in the grave, took Enid in his arms, and closed his eyes. The damp earth felt cold. Cold as death, he thought.

And eternity. Why not just remain there until he died? He opened his eyes, stared up into the leaden gray of the sky, and remembered his childhood dreams about his father, the noble knight, arriving on his tall horse to fetch him, and about the mews, and the fame of his falcons. These dreams were far away now, trivial and unreal as if they belonged in a different life. William closed his eyes.

"Wii," came piteously from the hut.

William started. How long had he been lying there?

"Wii-wii." This time it was more shrill. David clearly feared being left alone. He was not capable of caring for himself. Now that Enid was no longer with them, William would have to take care of him. With a heavy heart, he pulled himself together, climbed out of the grave, and went into the hut.

David rubbed his stomach and looked at him imploringly. "Wii."

William nodded and gave him food and drink, but he did not eat a bite himself.

"En?" asked David with an anxious look.

"She's dead," said William flatly.

"En," cried David, bursting into tears, having grasped the awful truth. His eyes were wide with fear. Perhaps the boy, tongue-tied as he was, was less simpleminded than he seemed. He tried to get up, but he could not do it on his own. So William helped him and they went outside together. For half an eternity they stood beside each other by her grave and wept.

William had to close the grave before night fell so the wild animals would not feed on the bodies. He climbed down to Enid and kissed her on the forehead one last time. She felt cold and strange, as cold and strange as his little son's cheek when William stroked it with his trembling fingers.

David stood at the side of the grave, remaining on his feet only by dint of some effort. When William heaved himself out and started to shovel the earth back onto the mutilated bodies, the boy clapped his hands over his eyes and sobbed out loud.

The infant child disappeared first under the dark clods of earth; then Enid's face and body were covered, too. Burying her was an act of love, but at the same time it was so unbearable that it drove William to even deeper despair.

"Don't worry, my darling. I'll take care of David," he promised, as if by doing so he could comfort Enid. Then, using the remains of her waistcloth, he tied two sticks together to make a cross and, with a quiet prayer, placed it in the earth by her final resting place.

Wandering

July 1189

William stumbled along the dusty road in a daze. He had buried Enid and the child and had taken care of David; he had done what had to be done, and in that way he had tried to drive away the searing pain that ate away at him from inside. Looking after David was something he owed Enid. And yet, for him, the forest and the hut were too connected with her for him to be able to stay there without her. So much so that he kept thinking she would appear from behind a bush or open the door for him. He had hunted for food for David, made him meals and herbal teas, and tended his wounds just as Enid would have done. But in the past few days he had taken hardly any nourishment for himself and had slept little. He had not even managed to lie on Enid's pallet. Instead, he had sat at the table and stared into the darkness of the night.

As soon as David had recovered a little, William, anxious to set off, had tied everything he thought he needed in a cloth from Enid's oak chest. While doing this, he came across the little enamel plaque again. With the vague idea that he might be glad one day to have this last souvenir of her, he slipped it into his purse without looking at it more closely. Any thought of her was still too painful. At first he had wanted to release the goshawk to which he had pinned his family's future that fateful night, but in the end he didn't have the heart.

Now that he had finally left the hut, William was glad. The feel of the hawk's claws was comforting, even through the thin cloth he had wound around his fist in the absence of a falconer's glove.

His shoulders bowed with grief, he plodded onward, mile after mile. Not knowing where they should go, he wandered on, losing himself in waking dreams that tore him violently back and forth between deep sorrow and destructive self-reproach.

David trotted alongside him silently, complaining only when he felt hungry or thirsty. Then he would get William's attention with vehement gestures. His face was still bluish green, keeping alive William's memory of the awful events that had come to pass.

It had been two days since they had left the woods, heading south. They just walked away. "Always follow your nose," Jean would have said. Miserably, William recalled the people he had left behind in Saint Edmundsbury years before. He could see them clearly and felt he could almost hear their voices and taste Rose's delicious fish pasties. How good it would feel now to let them pamper him, to sit at a table with the others and laugh, and to go for a walk with Isaac after their meal, not talking, but in understanding and companionable silence.

A short while later, William considered returning to his mother's house. But then he remembered her constant carping at his inability to master smithing, and he thrust out his chest. He was a falconer and would never again work as an odd-jobs man in a workshop. Never! He knew enough about falcons to find work elsewhere. He was not a failure, and he refused to be seen as one at home with his mother. For a brief moment, William was determined not to allow himself to be downcast, but with every step oppression, fatigue, and despair returned.

The air shimmered with heat. William struggled for breath and wiped the sweat from his forehead. The ground was dusty and dried out; the grass was shriveled. William looked anxiously at David as he shuffled along half a step behind him. The giant child was so thickly covered with dust that he looked like an old man with gray hair. I probably look just as pitiful to him, it occurred to William, and he stopped abruptly. He was not capable of a single coherent thought. The blazing sun was burning up his head, and his tongue stuck to the roof of his mouth with thirst.

Stunned by the heat, he took the water skin from his belt, gave David some, and then slaked his own thirst. He drained the pouch, even though the water was warm and tasted stale. Then he listened for a while in the vain hope of hearing the babbling of a nearby brook. But even if such a water source existed, it could not be heard over the scraping sound of many feet, the clattering of horses' hooves, and the creaking of passing carts.

As if waking from a deep sleep, William looked around in amazement. Where had all these people come from? Buried so deep in his distressing thoughts, he had stopped paying attention to his surroundings.

"Hey, you two! Move aside," someone roared from behind him, putting two fingers to his lips and whistling piercingly.

William started, grabbed David's hand, and pulled the boy to one side. David wanted to break loose, but William managed to hold him back just before a massive oxcart rumbled past. The goshawk took fright at this unaccustomed noise and tried to bate off. But since she was still fastened to her leash, she dangled upside down from William's fist, flapping her wings helplessly. David stood beside William, trembling with fright and clutching him anxiously.

William tried to remain composed. First he helped the goshawk back into position. Then, with reassuring words, he alternately stroked both David and the bird on their backs.

They stood by the side of the road for some time. Many people passed them, but no one paid them any heed. You must pull yourself together now, William told himself as despair threatened to overwhelm him again. David needs you, and so does the goshawk. William took a deep breath. First of all, he had to decide which way they should go; then he had to let the bird hunt.

When a motherly old woman with a wrinkled face and hunched back appeared near them and nodded in a friendly manner, William plucked up his courage.

"Excuse me, mother, where are all these people going?"

"Why, they're heading for London, dearie. London. Why not go there and seek your fortune? Who knows, perhaps it's waiting for you there." The toothless old crone laughed at him, mockery glinting in her eyes, and walked by with surprising speed.

London, what are we to do in London? thought William peevishly, tapping David on the shoulder. "Come, let's find some water before we go any farther."

But David did not move. A traveling peddler had stopped near them to reattach some of his wares, which had worked themselves loose on the bumpy road. Mesmerized, the boy was staring at the brightly colored things on the heavily laden wooden cart.

"You can search high and low around here and not find a drop of water," said the peddler, who had obviously heard William's words. "Trust me, this isn't the first time I've traveled this way." He pulled the ropes tight with a grunt and smiled encouragingly. "But don't you worry! There's a spring in a couple of miles, and you can fill up with water there. You'll have to line up for a long time, though." The peddler pointed at the other travelers. "Most of these people will spend the night by the spring. You'd better hurry, rather than standing around here, else you won't find a decent spot." He raised his hand in farewell, merged into the throng, and went on past them.

William sighed and looked at all the farmers and merchants and their various wares in baskets and sacks loaded on donkeys and carts. "All right, we'll go to London." He took David by the arm and pulled him on.

There were also laborers, pilgrims, and simple clerics walking alongside them. The more well-to-do among the travelers, prosperous merchants and princes of the church, overtook them on horseback, demanding most of the road for themselves. If one did not wish to be trampled to death, it was better to yield willingly.

When William and David finally reached the spring, a long line of people had already formed. They were arguing among themselves, cursing, and shoving, and many a lout was threatened with a beating. For better or worse, William and David joined the line.

At first they waited patiently, but after a while David began to complain. He was thirsty and was not accustomed to having to wait for water. But it made no difference. They had to wait like all the others. None of them were willing to give up their place for a simpleminded boy. Why should they? After all, everyone was thirsty.

Dusk was falling by the time their turn came, after they had been standing there with their containers for half an eternity. William lowered the bucket into the spring and pulled it up again, filled with fresh, cool water. He gave it to David, let him drink, and then filled both water skins before taking some refreshment himself.

"Hurry up. We want some, too!" shouted an impatient man from the back of the line.

William paid no attention, took another few gulps, and then passed the bucket to the young woman who had been waiting patiently behind him.

"Do you know how far it is to London?" he asked her shyly as she lowered the bucket into the depths.

"A good half day's walk, I'd say. The people on horses are hoping to get there tonight, before the city gates close."

William nodded his thanks and led David away from the spring.

"Let's look for a place to sleep." He put his hand to his cheek as an illustration for David.

But the boy's eyes opened wide as he rubbed his belly resentfully.

"Yes, yes, don't worry, I'll find you something to eat," William reassured him. For David's sake, William was taking only a tiny morsel every now and again—not to drive away the pangs of hunger, for in view of his guilt he felt they were thoroughly deserved.

Travelers were bedding down all around the spring. A few women were selling food, and buyers thronged around them. William could have taken the goshawk hunting in the woods on either side of the path, but he felt too weak. He had fed the bird generously that morning, so it could wait. With trembling hands, exhausted and hopeless, he took a marten's pelt from his bundle and offered it to a trader in exchange for some fragrant pies. William was offered two large pies filled with plenty of cabbage but not much meat and no more. He stepped back, hesitating. This pelt is worth more than that, he thought. On the other hand, he had the goshawk. With her it would be easy to get more skins from small animals like martens and weasels, as soon as he could take her hunting again. So he accepted the pies. While David was greedily devouring his meal, despite his injured jaw, William chewed listlessly on his food and finally gave half of it to the boy.

That night they tried to sleep side by side on the hard, dusty ground. David fell asleep after only a few breaths. But since Enid's death his nights were not as calm and peaceful as they had been. He would moan and whimper, and then a deep crease would appear on his brow, as if he was making an effort to think. William watched him without moving. He was afraid of falling asleep, too, and tried strenuously to keep his eyes open. Whenever they closed, he saw Enid and the infant child in their damp, dark grave. He would shudder, and his gut would tense in spasms. To escape the pain, William tried to stay awake as long as he possibly could, but his eyes closed with fatigue from time to time anyway.

The outlines of the trees were scarcely discernible in the early dawn light, but the first travelers were already getting up and waking the others with their bustling. None of them had slept deeply, for fear of being robbed. Well before the sun rose, almost all of them were on their feet, preparing for their onward journeys. Many were silent this morning. Some scowled sullenly; others were bad tempered and argumentative.

William had been among the first to rise in the early dawn, but neither the departure noises around him nor the rising sun had awakened David. It was not until William shook him vigorously that he stood up laboriously and rubbed his sleep-filled eyes.

William had hardly noticed the landscape they had walked through the previous day. Now, though, he paid attention to every change. The nearer they came to London, the closer together stood the small settlements through which their road snaked. They were well tended; things seemed to be going well for the people here. Pretty houses with large gardens and trees with children playing in their shade lined the road and gave off a peaceful air.

Late that morning, William finally caught his first glimpse of London from a hilltop. He stood rooted to the spot. Surrounded by thick stone walls topped by massive watchtowers, the city radiated dignity and safety. Probably as good as unassailable, he thought, impressed by this breathtaking vision.

Suddenly, though, other travelers pushed him forward.

"Hey, move along," someone shouted behind him.

William succumbed to the ever-increasing pressure of the crowds heading into the city. Swarms of people and animals forced their way in and out through the gates. He had heard that London possessed seven double-span gates like these. Was there a similar crush at all of them? He reached for David's hand and held it tightly, so the crowd would not separate them.

As they struggled through the city gate, William worried most about David and protected the goshawk against blows. But he could not prevent people from jabbing him in the ribs with their elbows or stepping on his toes. Once inside the gates, the crush of humanity at last spread out a little, for many streets were wide enough to allow two oxcarts to pass side by side and still leave room for those on foot. Where the majority went, William and David followed.

William was astonished to see many expensively dressed women everywhere and men parading through the city with falcons on their fists. Only a few carried their birds with due care. For most of them, it seemed, the raptor was just an accessory intended to demonstrate their prosperity.

William noticed how skeptically these well-dressed people looked at him, and some of the fine men even smirked complacently. William knew his humble clothes did not match his elegant handling or the noble goshawk on his fist. More than once, people looked at him suspiciously and shook their heads, whispering.

William spoke to some of these men, asking for work. But in vain. He had no sponsor and could not even give his apprenticeship at Thorne as a reference, since he had fled there as a criminal. The merchants he spoke to greeted him with disdain and exaggerated suspicion. They seemed to fear he was going to rob them or hurt their birds.

Despair flared up within William again: Was not his desire to be a falconer at the root of all his troubles and the cause of Enid's and the child's deaths? His head sank. His eyes burned with tears. No, he had no right to happiness. He had to atone. But what about David? Hadn't the boy suffered enough? William had to look after him; he couldn't allow David to suffer from want, along with all his other woes.

He had no idea where it led, but William turned onto Bread Street, where one baker after another was selling his fragrant wares. He immediately cursed his choice, for David promptly plucked at his arm and put his hand to his mouth, his eyes glittering with intense hunger.

Truly the boy always had an appetite, but the price of the loaves was horrifying.

"Later, David, later," William said quickly to put him off, then pulled him onward so that they could escape the seductive scent of baking.

How could they survive in London? In a city like this one needed money, a lot of it. Those who had no money or work sat in the street and begged. He had only to look around. There were men and women loitering everywhere, dressed in rags, holding out a pleading hand to the people hurrying by and promising to pray for the donor's soul in recompense. One-legged men leaned on wooden crutches; others had to go through life without any arms or legs at all, whining loudly for alms. People with scalds and burns showed off their scarred flesh; the blind, the mute, the sick, the simple, like David—they all begged and pleaded for donations.

The ones who seemed to have it worst, however, were the lepers. They tried to hide their lesions with bandages, but whenever they rang their bells to signal their approach, as required by law, people fled in panic.

William pulled along the astonished David. He needed all his strength, for the boy was utterly fascinated by this unfamiliar world. His childlike eyes wide-open, he stared fearlessly at people, buildings, and animals. He laughed when he saw children playing and frowned when he saw a girl driving a pig along by beating its back with a crop.

The people were thronging toward an impressive cathedral that towered over the street. From a woman walking alongside him, William learned that it was dedicated to Saint Paul.

Amazed, he stopped in front of the dark and imposing stone facade, looking up into its heights. He had never seen such a big building. Someone threw a coin to David, who was standing just behind him, and a beggar hobbled up to the boy, gesticulating furiously and trying to chase him away from what he considered his place.

David began whimpering and rubbing his belly. This moved the gentle heart of a nobly dressed lady who had apparently come to evening prayer at Saint Paul's. Smiling kindly, she walked up to him and presented him with two copper coins. But no sooner had she turned her back than other angry beggars hurried over. This time, they threatened to beat David up if he did not make himself scarce, and William pulled him away quickly.

The coins were enough for a big loaf of the bread. They ate on the steps of a small and shabby church. There were no beggars here, for it was clear that the people who came to this house of God lived from hand to mouth themselves and could not afford acts of generosity.

William did not touch the bread himself, whereas David ate with gusto and devoured every last crumb. It did not bother him that it was dry and hard.

William noticed that the priest from the small church had been watching them from the doorway. He was about to leave when the simply dressed man of God approached and offered them a place to sleep. They accepted gratefully, and a short time later they were settling down for the night on the church's beaten-earth floor. Before David lay down to sleep, the priest brought them two hand-fuls of cherries and insisted that William eat at least half of the offering. William obediently ate his share of the sweet, juicy fruit and realized for the first time that he was indeed hungry.

Once David had finally curled up and fallen asleep, and the gos-hawk was resting, too, William got up again and asked the priest to take his confession. Perhaps the sacrament would lighten his heart.

At first it was hard to find the right words to express all the painful things for which he blamed himself, but after a while it all came pouring out. How Enid must have gone through hell because he had not been there for her. How she must have suffered, fearing for her life and that of her unborn child. William's sense of guilt came close to stifling him. He struggled for breath, reproached himself, sobbed. What sort of sense did it make for God to put him to such a test?

"I swear by almighty God that I will avenge your deaths," he cried angrily, shaking his fist, before collapsing in helpless tears.

William's anguished confession lasted half the night. The priest sat before him quietly. He tried to encourage him, gave him a mild penance, and absolved him of his guilt, but William did not feel the relief he had hoped for. At last, desperate and having no idea how to take control of his future, he asked the priest for advice on what he could do to ensure that David did not suffer in London.

The man of God thought for a while before saying, "Take him to the church of Saint Bartholomew. He has worked many miracles. Sometimes he heals the sick and the simple. Rahere, the man who founded the church, the priory, and the hospital there, receives the prayers of believers. Have the boy kneel down in front of Rahere's tomb and humbly ask to be cured. It certainly won't do any harm if you pray for him, too. You're young and you're bound to find work, but not with him by your side. Go, and ask Saint Bartholomew for his help."

William nodded gratefully, although he secretly feared that no one could do anything to alter David's destiny. Not even a saint. He wiped the tears from his face and joined David on the floor. William closed his eyes and, for the first time since Enid's death, fell asleep instantly.

When he woke up the next day, the priest was not in the church. They could not bid him farewell, so they set off on their way. William asked directions to the church of Saint Bartholomew and learned that it was outside the city walls, not far from Smithfield. He did not dare to hope for a miracle, but what else could he do for David?

Once out in Smithfield, he let the goshawk hunt before they entered the church. Seeing her fly brought him happiness but also bitter pain. Every beat of her wings made him think of Enid and their quarrel. Despite his harsh words, did she know he would never have let her down? William had a lump in his throat. If only he had been able to tell her.

When the bird had eaten her fill and was perched on William's fist once more, they entered the church. David was already rubbing his belly to show how hungry he was, but this time William did not take the hint. The darkness inside the church would do the goshawk good, and he too longed to pause for rest and reflection.

There was construction work going on. It looked as though the church was being enlarged and, as William could tell as soon as he stepped inside, embellished. High up in the nave, artists and their apprentices were busy decorating the whitewashed walls with colorful biblical scenes. The men sat on wooden scaffolding, chattering, with their legs dangling down over the throngs of the faithful below.

If William had been expecting quiet and time for introspection, Saint Bartholomew's was a disappointment. Among all the builders, stonemasons, painters, and laborers, there were also swarms of pilgrims and clerics. Those who could enter the church on two feet, or at least on all fours, did so. Only the wealthy and those too sorely afflicted by disease allowed themselves to be carried in on stretchers or litters. How much money an individual possessed did not matter—all visitors to the church had one thing in common: hope in God's mercy and a cure.

There was not enough space on the ground in front of Rahere's tomb for all the supplicants, so David had to wait a while before he could prostrate himself there. He looked questioningly at his friend. He obviously did not quite understand what he was supposed to do, but he obeyed because William asked him to.

"Ask the Lord for a cure," William whispered to him, knowing very well that David would not know what to do. So he knelt down on the hard stone floor close by, rested the fist that was holding the goshawk on a raised knee, and prayed awkwardly but with great sincerity.

"Lord, Sir Rahere, Saint Bartholomew, I beg you from the bottom of my heart, help my David. He is soft in his head but rich in his heart. He has suffered great pain. Lift him up through your gracious mercy."

William was deep in prayer when someone tapped him on the shoulder. Who would disturb his worship? A man of the church, wearing a dark cowl, was standing close behind him and indicated with his finger that he should follow.

"I can't leave him alone," William objected in a whisper, pointing at David.

"Don't worry—we won't go far," the monk reassured him quietly. He waited for William to rise and then led him away from the crowd of supplicants toward a quiet corner.

"A beautiful creature." The monk pointed at the goshawk.

William smiled shyly. Was this cleric hinting that the presence of the bird in the church was unwelcome? Nobles frequently entered churches on horseback, and many peasants sought God's blessing for their animals by bringing them into church.

"Is the boy your brother?" the monk asked in a friendly manner.

William answered no and explained in few words how he came to care for David.

The man of God nodded approvingly and sighed audibly. "Saint Bartholomew's help is sought by so many sick people every day, but when the sin for which a person is being punished with his affliction is great, help is often impossible." He raised his eyebrows and glanced at David. "Does he pray regularly?"

"I'm not even sure he knows what praying means. He can't speak, and nobody knows what he thinks. David knows hunger, thirst, fear, and happiness and shows them. But does he know who the Lord God is?" William shrugged helplessly.

The monk shook his head regretfully. "Saint Bartholomew frequently makes the blind see and the lame walk. But it is hard for the simpleminded to ask for forgiveness. It is charitable of you to pray for him, but I fear the prayers of one person will not be enough."

"But what more can I do?" William whispered pleadingly. "How can I look after him? I have no work, and with him it will be difficult for me to find any. Should we beg for the rest of our lives, even though I'm strong and could work?"

"No, that would not be pleasing to God." After a short pause, he continued. "Now, I may perhaps have a solution. If the boy stayed here for longer and prayers were said for him every day—it would certainly take months, perhaps longer and yet, maybe…" The monk sighed resignedly and shook his head doubtfully.

"Please tell me. How could it be done?"

"There are so many in need of help, and the hospital hasn't enough room…" He raised his shoulders and then let them drop again, discouraged. He looked into the distance for a while. Then a smile flickered over his face.

The monk cleared his throat and lowered his voice. "Our father prior saw your hawk hunting earlier. He is a keen hunting enthusiast. I know he longs for nothing more than to own such a bird. Unfortunately, the priory's coffers are empty. Perhaps it would be possible to reach an agreement?" His gaze shifted briefly to David, who was still lying obediently on the floor.

"What sort of agreement?" asked William anxiously.

"Well, I could try to persuade the prior to take in the boy so that my brothers and I could pray for a cure every day."

William was now all ears.

"Perhaps the poor creature will receive the Lord's mercy and be healed. If not, I would make sure he could at least spend the winter with us. That would give you the chance to look for work and lead a life that is pleasing to God. You would have to pay for David's food and lodging, though."

William, who had listened to the proposal with shining eyes, puffed all the air out of his chest in disappointment. "But I have nothing."

"Yes, you have. You have the bird." He lowered his voice. "Perhaps I can convince the prior to accept it as payment. If I put in a good word for you, it's possible he won't demand any more from you than the bird."

William thought. David was sure to be raised well. Perhaps the Lord was in fact showing him mercy. At least he wouldn't have to freeze or starve, and he wouldn't be pushed around in the street. As far as the goshawk was concerned, it would probably be better housed with the prior than in the streets of London, where sooner or later someone was bound to suspect William of having stolen it. The thought that he was giving away the bird for David's benefit felt like a penance he could bear.

"But David must have three meals a day and warm clothes in the winter. And I'll visit him regularly, to be sure he's all right," William demanded, almost defiantly.

The monk smiled thinly. "Don't you trust mother church?"

"I do, I do, forgive me! But David could fall ill or stop eating because he's troubled, though he's always hungry. And if he didn't get enough to eat, he might think I'd forgotten him and die of grief," said William in a small voice.

"I understand your concern for the boy, and it does you honor." The monk laid a reassuring hand on William's arm. "I shall speak to the prior right away. Wait here for me."

It was a while before the monk came back. William suspected the prior did not want to appear too bent on this bargain. To obtain such a magnificent goshawk without paying a penny for it was a real stroke of luck, even for a man of God. Surely, so many hungry mouths were fed at the priory that one more would make no difference.

William paced up and down, thinking. Monks took vows to do good. It couldn't be wrong to trust them and house David here. Perhaps this is the first miracle and a cure is still to come, he tried to tell himself. But Pater John's shameful behavior gnawed at him.

"The prior agrees," the monk reported finally. "You can visit the boy on Sundays, after mass. For the next three weeks, though, you must stay away so that he can settle in."

"Thank you. Before I leave, I shall explain to David that he's in good hands and mustn't be afraid. Is the prior experienced with hawks, or might he need my help at first?"

"Don't worry, young man, the prior used to look after the bishop of York's falcons. He knows what he's doing."

"In that case, would you be so good as to take the bird from me?"

The monk looked at him in shock, but he slipped the sleeve of his cowl down over his hand and held out his fist as William instructed him. Walking deliberately and looking uncertainly at the beautiful bird, he carried the goshawk out of the church.

William went over to David. How could he explain this arrangement? And how could he make him understand that he wasn't abandoning him but would fetch him back at some point in the future? For William, that point was foreseeable, but for David it would seem like an eternity. How much of his explanation would David even understand? William led him out of the crowd of supplicants and took him to a quiet corner. In few words, with the help of hand gestures, William explained that David would have to stay with the monks for a while.

David looked at him in disbelief. Tears sprang to his eyes. They rolled down his cheeks, leaving a dirty gray trail.

William felt terrible. He threw his arms around David and held him tightly for a long time. The boy did not want to let him leave, but at length, with a heavy heart, he let go.

"I'll come back, I promise," he said hoarsely. I sound like a liar, he thought to himself. Since his quarrel with Enid and everything that happened thereafter, his guilty conscience tormented him without respite.

The monk, who had now returned without the goshawk, placed his hand on David's back with a kindly smile and pushed him gently toward a wooden door in the aisle. David followed him, repeatedly glancing back at his only friend. With a heavy heart, William watched them go. Now he too was all alone. No one was demanding or expecting anything from him anymore. William listened inwardly. Was it relief that he felt? No. Although David had been a burden, always reminding him of Enid and the child, he did not feel liberated but empty, as if burned out.

As if in a dream, he stumbled out of the church. The sunlight was blinding, and William wiped a tear from the corner of his eye.

He wandered through the streets of the unfamiliar city until dark, his thoughts constantly with David. Would the monks take care of him properly? William felt like a traitor.

He spent his first night alone in London half sitting, half lying on the ground in a narrow alleyway. Several times he awoke from confused dreams. His legs began to tingle. The longer he sat there, the number they became. In the morning he did not feel refreshed.

He shuffled down to the river, his stomach empty. The Thames was broad and filthy with roiling mud. It stank of putrefaction, sewage, and dead fish.

William heard two men talking about how strong hands were always needed at the port. But when he arrived at the docks and asked the harbormaster for work, the man just shook his head.

"Scrawny, you're far too scrawny," he jeered. "You'll collapse under the weight you have to carry here. No, no, a miserable sprat like you brings nothing but trouble. Move along now."

It was impossible to find work with a growling stomach and trembling hands. There were swarms of strong young men everywhere, offering their services. Nobody needed someone who, like William, staggered like a drunkard on account of his twisted foot. In the end—hungry, weary, and desperate—William gave up the search.

Bowed down with sorrow and utterly discouraged, he shuffled back to Saint Paul's and, for the first time in his life, held out his hand in the hope of a kindhearted donation from some devout person.

He did not allow himself to be driven away by the other beggars. At first he accepted their blows and kicks without defending himself, apparently indifferent. He accepted them as fitting punishment, an opportunity for atonement, and did not complain. In his eyes he had earned any humiliation the world could offer and had nothing left to lose.

One day, however, when he was pushed down the steps again, he fought back, furiously defending his place. From that day on he joined the beggars loitering around Saint Paul's with a quite specific position on the steps of the cathedral.

Sometimes, the coins of the devout were enough to buy food and keep him satisfied till the following day, but most of the time William had to suffer hunger. He could not wash anywhere; he slept on the cathedral steps or in filthy alleyways and was soon stiff with grime. He noted his accelerating decline with grim satisfaction. If he had not thought only of himself that time in the forest, and had stayed with Enid instead, perhaps he could have prevented that grisly deed.

For days at a time, William sat and stared ahead of him, and when the news of King Henry's death spread through the city one day, the abyss appeared to open up in front of him. This was the end of the world, the apocalypse he had heard about in church. His despair and hopelessness could not have been worse. Henry had been well-disposed toward him, and William had been determined to show him that he was right to believe in him. But now it was too late. The king lived no more, and William was a beggar and would remain one forever.

With the few coins people had tossed to him that day, William bought a large tankard of cheap ale. The tavern that served him was crowded with pitiful drunkards. Here, even in the midst of the multitude, one was utterly alone.

On top of a stomach that had been empty for days, the sour brew soon made William drunk, and after a second tankard his tormented soul was at peace for the first time. What a relief! He tumbled from his bench in a stupor, noticed vaguely when he was dragged into a corner, and slept his intoxication off among the other drunkards.

But the pain, self-reproach, and despair were back again the next day. And William longed for the dull sense of indifference the ale had provided. While he was drunk, he had been able to forget his sufferings, at least for a while. So the next day, as soon as he had begged a couple of coins, he made his way there and again numbed himself with the cheap ale.

William rubbed his eyes and blinked up at the lightly clouded summer sky. It was already broad daylight. He scratched his louse-infested scalp. The bites of these tiny bloodsuckers itched terribly, and it was getting worse with every day he spent on the street. William groaned. His head throbbed. He tried to remember how many tankards of ale he had drained the previous night, but he was not up to completing the thought. He closed his eyes with a grunt. His stomach growled. He tried laboriously to get up. His clothes felt suspiciously damp in places. William grimaced with disgust. He opened his eyes again, just a crack this time, for the harsh light was painful.

When at last he could see, he was surprised that there were more people than usual passing along the street and that a sort of path of honor had opened up through them. William raised himself, groaning, and stood up. Important ceremonies often took place at Saint Paul's. What was the occasion this time?

"She must be the richest heiress in the land! A ward of the king's, an excellent match without a doubt."

With undisguised curiosity, William watched a magnificently dressed lady speaking to a young girl who was obviously her daughter. Their strikingly long noses stuck out at the same angle.

"She's not much older than you." The mother sounded almost reproachful. Judging by her clothing, she must have been the wife of a very prosperous merchant.

"And the groom? What does he look like? What kind of a dress do you think she will wear?" asked the girl, fidgeting beside her mother.

William nodded with satisfaction. He would try to approach the betrothed in front of the church. People on their way toward the holy bond of matrimony were in a particularly generous mood, as he now knew from experience. This was as true for rich barons as it was for the sons and daughters of wealthy merchants who could afford to be wed at Saint Paul's. The heat made William feel faint. He swayed and closed his eyes for a moment so as not to collapse. His tongue felt furry, and his mouth tasted disgustingly sour.

Curious onlookers crowded all sides of the procession, whispering and gossiping. The wedding party was led by a large group of knights wearing colorful surcoats and armed with swords and lances, followed by several powerful barons William recognized by their colors. The crowd looked on admiringly, enviously sniping at the costly finery of the wedding procession as it passed. Then came the bride, escorted by fourteen maidens. Two rode ahead of her, four alongside her, and eight behind

her in two groups of four. The manes of their milk-white pal-
freys were braided with ribbons of many colors. The bride's
horse was likewise white. Its mane was decorated with golden
ribbons, and its back with a breathtaking saddlecloth embroidered with layer after layer of gold thread that must have cost
a fortune.

William had once dreamed of being rich and famous for his
birds, but his ambition seemed to have receded far beyond his
reach. The man who was to have this lady as his bride must be one
of those people who inherited good fortune in the cradle.

Erect as a queen, with an enigmatic smile on her lips and a
glow that appeared to emanate from deep inside, the young bride
sat in the saddle. Her delicate face, with its pale, almost translucent
skin and slender nose, radiated calm and nobility without appearing haughty. The costly wedding gown, made from the finest purple silk and embroidered with priceless pearls, made her position
in the upper nobility instantly apparent.

"Purple," Rose had told him once, admiringly, "is the most
expensive color in the world." It existed in various hues, from dark
mauve through violet to strong pink. Its vivid, glowing tones were
predominant in the exquisite young bride's gown, attracting excla-
mations of admiration from the delighted onlookers.

The merchant's daughter, who was still standing near William,
started talking to her mother again. "Look, Mother, what beautiful sleeves her gown has. And the cloth. How it shines. What finery. And those colors. I'd give anything to have a gown like that."

"Nonsense! You'll make a beautiful bride, even without a purple gown. I'll make sure of that," said the merchant's wife before
pointing excitedly at the tail end of the procession. "Oh, look there,
the groom. Doesn't he look handsome? He lodges with Richard
FitzReiner. Your father supplied him quite recently. A fine man,
that FitzReiner, and a truly valuable contract. Probably for the
wedding celebrations."

William could now see the groom. He gasped. In order to be sure he was not mistaken, he rubbed his eyes and looked again. Indeed, it was William Marshal. Beaming with pride, he was sitting on a magnificent black horse that was prancing about with excitement. Marshal looked exactly as he had looked in William's earlier daydreams. William took a deep breath. The morning air was warm and heavy. It promised to be one of those pitilessly hot summer days. He swayed. Too much ale, he thought disgustedly. Then he belched. Spellbound, he gazed at Marshal, as if his eyes alone could cause the groom to turn and look at him. But the man on the splendid black horse continued to face the other way.

Suddenly, William's heart skipped a beat. Baudouin de Béthune, who was riding close behind Marshal, was looking William right in the eye. There was something questioning in his expression, as if he was trying to think where he had seen the ragged beggar before. For a moment, William hoped Sir Baudouin would recognize him. His hand twitched, ready to leap up and wave. Did he remember? William was not a child anymore. He had grown since the last time they had met. And since Enid's death, he had even grown a beard, though it was not thick enough to look good. Sir Baudouin had given him his position at the falconry: no doubt he thought William was safely housed there. Why should it occur to him that William was living in London?

When Sir Baudouin spurred his horse to catch up and unexpectedly turned his attention to Marshal, William quivered with humble anticipation. He must have recognized him, and now he was telling his friend about his discovery.

After a short conversation, Sir Baudouin went back to peering straight ahead and paid no further attention to William.

The realization that Sir Baudouin had obviously not mentioned him cut William to the quick. He must have come to the conclusion that the miserable stranger was just another wretched beggar. William staggered. His head felt hollow and empty, like an exhausted barrel of ale. Cold and clammy sweat broke out on his emaciated body. How could he have let himself go so badly since Enid's death? For the first time, William felt deeply ashamed. Blood and heat shot through his head. Impulsively, he turned away, struggling through the crowd, which was greeting the betrothed couple with ever-louder cheers. Shamefully, he had even neglected his twisted foot of late; it had been an open and suppurating sore for days. William had not had any shoes for some time.

He glanced over his shoulder one more time. The young bride had dismounted and was offering her hand to Marshal so that he could escort her into the church. She looked happy. Why shouldn't she be? After all, she was marrying the bravest, most famous knight in England, the one favored by all the kings.

William turned away once and for all. As long as he could remember, Marshal had been the model for the father he'd always wanted. With all his heart, William wished him well with his beautiful young bride. He would have given anything to be part of the wedding procession, riding with a handsome falcon on his fist—as Sir Baudouin's falconer, or even Marshal's—instead of a mendicant bystander.

William plodded away with his head down. He now knew that he didn't belong in the world of the nobles. He had already suspected as much at Thorne. How had he fallen into the delusion that he could belong one day? Just because he knew how to handle falcons?

As the ale wore off and he became sober, William's neglected body hurt more and more, but even more painful was the sense of guilt he still felt. Down at heart, he limped along the alleys of London until dusk. It was not until he was standing in front of the tavern he had visited far too often during the past few weeks that he half came to his senses. He pushed open the door and was about to cross the threshold when the repulsive smell of rancid ale hit him, making his empty stomach heave.

"No," he muttered. "Never will I set foot in this house again." He stepped backward and came within an inch of tripping over a pig that was rooting about in the dirt behind him.

William began to run like a madman. His foot hurt, and his stomach was rebelling. That's enough, he thought. I must restore order to my life and bring some sense back to it.

Although there were about a hundred churches in London, his feet led him, almost of their own accord, to the little church where he had made his confession shortly after his arrival. Humbly throwing himself to the beaten-earth floor, he spread his arms as if on a crucifix, pressed his forehead to the ground, and prayed fervently. He had so many things to put right. First of all poor David, whom he had so shamefully neglected. The three weeks during which he was not allowed to visit him had long since passed, but he had not yet gone to see him. William knew the monks would not let him near David except on the Lord's day, so he swore by all the saints to go and see him the next Sunday.

This time, his discussion with God lasted the whole night. And unlike after his last confession there, he emerged stronger than he'd been when he had entered the church.

Though he had not slept a wink during the night, he set out with renewed courage and—for the first time in a long while—fresh hope about his search for work. He was even thinner now, and dirty and shabby besides, but he got work with the third artisan he asked. To William it seemed a miracle, but more likely it was because no one else wanted to work at a tannery. But William was glad to earn a few coins doing honest work. Pushing a handcart that held a large clay pot, he went out collecting urine for his master, Tanner. Most of the dwellers of the narrow alleyways were grateful not to have to tip their night soil into the street, and they willingly filled up the pot.

Tanner was satisfied, because his new servant was back before the midday bell, and he gave him further tasks. William had to turn the hides in the bath of tanbark, rinse them out, and hang them up to dry. Then he had to shave half a dozen hides until there was not a single hair to be found on them. His day was hard, and the leather and tanbark gave off a foul, penetrating reek of oak and urine, but the work distracted him from his troubles, and with time it would likely strengthen his body, for the wet hides were heavy.

He was on his feet from daybreak till sunset. In the evening, as he used to before, he rubbed his foot with some herbal ointment he bought with his first few coins and bandaged it so that it would heal quickly. Once in the tanner's outhouse, he sank into a deep and dreamless sleep.

The next morning, his master's wife imposed one of her husband's discarded shirts on William and kept a half-day's wages for it. William was pleased though. He fetched a large bucket of water from the spring and washed discreetly in a corner. Using an old brush he found in the tanner's outhouse, he scrubbed his hands and arms until they were red and raw, but it was hard work to get rid of the urine-yellow stains the tanning mixture left on his skin. Then he slipped on his new shirt. The clean cloth, though threadbare and stained in several places, felt good.

So now he was wearing Tanner's old shirt and was his servant. *Servant.* It was a harsh word that spoke of hard work and poverty, not the freedom, renown, and successful hunting that William had known as a falconer. But he had no intention of being dissatisfied with his lot. First he wanted to save as much as he could. Then he would see.

Mrs. Tanner was not a particularly good cook, but she was generous—so he soon had more flesh on his ribs. William scarcely touched ale anymore, and there was little else on which for him to spend his meager wage. In winter, to be sure, he would need new shoes and warm clothes, but that was a long way off. At present it was warm and his shirt was sufficient. So he saved every penny.

On the very first Sunday of his new life he walked to Saint Bartholomew's to visit David. The poor fellow looked downcast, but then he saw William and threw himself into his arms, weeping with joy. He would not have had the words to discuss William's long absence, but William could find no reproach in his eyes, just happiness at seeing him again. He even accepted with a smile William's explanation that he could not take him back just yet. He seemed to know now that William would never let him down. Although the separation hurt him no less than it hurt David, William left feeling good. He was on the right path. One day, somehow, he would manage to take care of Enid's brother on his own.

The opening of the annual fair at Smithfield came a week later, on the twenty-fourth day of the eighth month, the feast of Saint Bartholomew. Vast numbers of people streamed in for the occasion. In particular, breeders of thoroughbred horses, both for riding and for war, came from far and wide. Cattle and calves, sheep and lambs, pigs and piglets would also be bought and sold, as well as geese, ducks, and other poultry for household use; all manner of ceramics, basketwork, leather goods, and metalware were available, too. The variety was so wide that a trip to the fair was worthwhile not only for knights and nobles but also for farmers and even monks and other clerics. For two solid weeks, traders from all over the country would offer their wares alongside London's merchants.

Tanner had earned an excellent reputation for his wares, and this year he planned to set up his own stall to sell a wide range of animal hides.

William had his hands full the day before. Using a cart, he helped Tanner carry the wooden frame for the stall to Smithfield, and then they set it up. It took them until well past midnight, for William had to make the long journey from Tanner's to the market and back three times in order to move the hides and all the parts of the stand. When the stall was finally ready, Tanner ordered him to keep watch during the night.

"And don't you dare fall asleep. Woe betide you if a single piece of leather goes missing," he warned him before leaving him alone in the Smithfield marketplace.

William was not the only servant keeping watch. The market watchman did his rounds regularly, of course, but he could not see everything. None of the traders could afford to leave their stands unguarded. And since the first customers would arrive early in the morning, none of them wanted to risk losing a good deal by setting up their stalls the following day.

William sprawled out across the evil-smelling hides and stared up into the sky. This being London, the stand's roof was also made of leather to protect the valuable hides against the rain that might fall on any day and in any season, even in August. William peered out at the night sky from under the roof. It was deep black. Probably overcast, he thought, since there were no stars visible.

Just as well, he said to himself, for stars reminded him of Enid. He had known her often out in the open on warm summer nights; afterward, embracing one another, they would look at the sky with its thousands and thousands of twinkling points of light. William felt his eyes begin to burn. He was weary. Carefully, he opened the little leather purse he carried on his belt. The purse had belonged to Enid once; she had been given it by Nana. William stroked the waxy leather and, for the first time since he had left the forest, took out the little enamel plaque. He tried to remember whether he had ever seen a piece of jewelry on Enid, but he could not think of one. So where did it come from?

William held it up close to his face and squinted, but it was too dark to make out anything. He touched the enamel gently with his finger, then put it back in the purse. Where had she gotten it from?

William's head fell forward. He must have nodded off briefly. He leaped up guiltily, shook out his legs to keep awake, then perched himself on the hides again to keep watch.

By dawn, all the traders had arrived at the fair, bringing further wares and issuing final instructions to their servants. A long day awaited them all.

The sun was scarcely high enough for daylight to appear, and yet the first curious customers started arriving. Many just wanted to look and marvel; they could not afford to buy anything. Others hoped to scoop up the finest, rarest, most beautiful items, and that was why they were up and about so early. Only those who compared all the wares and prices, weighed everything up carefully, and haggled skillfully could be sure of a good bargain.

"Here, go and buy yourself something to eat," said Tanner a little before midday, smiling indulgently and pulling a couple of coins from his purse. He had already secured two substantial contracts, with the prospect of further orders, and was more than satisfied with the first day of the fair. "Don't dawdle about, mind," he called to William's back.

William had heard from some visitors at the tanner's stand that there were falcons on sale, too, and since that moment he'd wanted to go and look at them. First, however, he bought a large onion pie. It was cheap, but it satisfied his hunger just as well as a much more expensive meat pie, and it meant he could save a penny from the tanner's food money. William bit hungrily into the still-warm dough and promptly burned his tongue on the steaming, roughly chopped onions. He wandered through the market and looked at the various stands. But none of them interested him, for there were no falcons to be seen.

He stopped suddenly and listened. There it was again—the loud keening of a falcon demanding food. William's heart beat faster, and he forgot the fatigue that had resulted from his sleepless night. He jumped up in the air to see over the many heads, heard the grating cry again, and followed the sound until at last he found a stand selling falcons. A large number of expensively dressed men, nobles, and wealthy merchants crowded around the birds. Within a stone's throw of this stand, several other falconers were selling their birds. Some had only a few, while others had just one. William glanced at the birds on the large stand. They were of good to very good quality; that much was immediately obvious. The prices being called out took William's breath away. And the other falconers were demanding similar sums for their birds. If his goshawk was worth only half as much, the prior had struck a good bargain because of William's inexperience.

A female saker falcon caught William's eye. He approached the falconer and examined her more closely.

"She's been made to ducks, a splendid beast," the falconer was saying to an elderly merchant, who scratched his chin pensively.

A younger, conspicuously richly dressed merchant suddenly pushed his way through the crowd and interrupted the older one as he requested further details.

"How much do you want for the bird?" he asked the falconer, acknowledging the older merchant with a casual nod and then paying him no further attention.

The falconer now had eyes only for the younger merchant and named his price. It seemed fair for a saker falcon of that size, but William, who had examined the bird, shook his head.

"This bird is sick," he said, almost to himself. "Every penny this man pays is a penny too much. She'll be dead within five days."

The falconer started berating him, and even the merchant who had asked the question looked at William with a disdainful shake of the head.

"What does a pauper like him know about such noble beasts?" snorted the falconer.

William simply shrugged and went on to the next stand. Out of the corner of his eye, he could see that the falconer and the young merchant quickly agreed on a price, despite his comments, and the bird changed hands. Fools will learn only by experience, thought William. His mother had used the expression more often than he had really liked, but she'd always been proved right.

It occurred to William that Tanner was probably waiting impatiently for him. He headed back at a run. He felt someone's eyes boring into his back, and when he turned he saw the older merchant looking at him curiously.

When he got back to the stall, William received a sharp clip on the ear.

"I told you not to dawdle, and you've kept me waiting forever. You've three deliveries to make." He thrust the handle of the cart into William's hand. "The first hide—I've put it on top, so you won't get them mixed up—goes to Hagan, in Wood Street. Then take the rough goatskins to Alvin the shoemaker. He sent his boy because he needs the skins urgently. Last, take the fine goatskins to Jacob the tailor in Threadneedle Street. With so many highborn visitors in town, they're all hoping to do some good trade. If they can't deliver because they've run out of leather, it's bad for trade. So look sharp." Tanner patted his chest with satisfaction, and his sweaty hand left a mark on his new shirt. "Now be on your way."

William wiped his brow and lifted the cart. Threadneedle Street was almost as far away as the street where Tanner and his wife lived, and the shoemaker's workshop was on the other side of the city, so William girded himself for a long walk.

"Mind your backs," he called out, loud and clear, so that he could get through the mass of people. Again and again, the crowd almost ran under his cart or stood in the way. If they were people of high rank, William had to go around them; careless peasants he addressed with a loud "Would you mind?" and on the whole they let him pass.

William had almost left the market behind him when he came within an inch of running over an elegantly dressed man.

"You're in a rush, lad. At least let an old man live out his life in peace," laughed the man, leaping to one side and nearly tripping over a low wall.

"Oh my heavens, forgive me. Are you hurt?" William dropped the handle of the cart and turned to face the gray-haired man.

"Don't worry, my boy. No harm done." The man sat on the low wall and looked at William. "What makes you think the falcon is going to die?"

William now recognized the older of the two merchants he had seen at the falconer's stand. "You remember me?"

"A boy who claims a magnificent falcon is going to die? I certainly should remember that, even if I'm no longer young."

"The falcon's plumage may have looked magnificent at first sight, but there were two tail feathers missing. They'll never grow back." William felt his face flush and cleared his throat, embarrassed. "On its own that wouldn't be a reason to say the bird is doomed. But one look in her eyes told me she was sick and couldn't be saved. If I may, sir, either the falconer knows this, and he's trying to sell her before she gives up the ghost in his hands and he has to bear the loss, or the man has about as much idea of falconry as I have of pig rearing."

The merchant burst out laughing, highly amused, and glanced appraisingly at the pile of hides. "You look like a tanner's apprentice, but you sound like a falconer."

"I used to be a falconer. In another life, or so it seems to me. But though my heart is still with falconry, I no longer have a master to serve."

"Tell me your name, my boy, and where you learned your falconry."

"My name is William FitzEllen. I'm from Saint Edmundsbury, and I'm the son of Ellenweore the swordsmith. I once found our late king's escaped gyrfalcon—" William broke off and crossed himself. "God rest his soul. I found his falcon, and as a reward for taking good care of her, I was allowed to learn the art of falconry at Thorne Castle."

"So, William FitzEllen, what brought you to London, and to a tanner at that?"

"Forgive me, I would like to tell you everything, but it's a long story and I find it painful, and I have to deliver these goods for my master. He beats me if I take too long about it."

The merchant nodded. "My falconer could do with a hard-working assistant. Someone who can knuckle down to it properly and help with the dogs in the stables from time to time. How would that be?" He told him the wage he was prepared to pay and the other terms.

William could hardly believe his ears. The merchant was offering three times as much as he was getting from the tanner, plus winter clothing and, on Sundays, a piece of the roast from the master's table.

"There's nothing I would rather do, for tanning work doesn't exactly gladden my heart," William answered incredulously. "But do you really mean it?"

"Well, I certainly enjoy a good joke, but to give someone hope and then not fulfill it? That wouldn't be amusing in the least, don't you agree? Come to my house after mass this Sunday, so that my falconer can meet you. He'll have the final word, since he's the one that needs to be satisfied with your assistance." The merchant introduced himself as FitzEldred and told William where he lived.

Uplifted by the unexpected prospect of getting his life back on the right track, William lifted the cart again and heartily pushed it toward the city gates. The work now seemed easier, and even the muggy, overcast day now seemed fragrant and agreeable.

The days dragged by until Sunday finally arrived. William fetched water from the spring and washed thoroughly, scrubbing his hands especially hard, for they were stained from the tanning mixture. He had washed his shirt the night before and hung it up to dry, so it was now more or less clean. Most important, it did not smell quite so nauseatingly of tanbark. He combed his now-long hair with Enid's wooden comb and tied it into a ponytail with a slender leather band. On his way to the merchant's, he picked a bit of lavender from the tiny churchyard of Saint Helen's and rubbed it between his hands. Now they smelled wonderful.

William noticed that his tension had eased slightly. It really looked as if he was getting a second chance. Perhaps the last in his life. It didn't matter what kind of man the merchant's falconer was—he had to convince him. He would have to tread carefully. In particular, he mustn't show off his knowledge, so that the falconer wouldn't see him as someone who would be after his job. On the other hand, he had to demonstrate that he could relieve the man's burden and work without supervision.

When William reached FitzEldred's house, he knew he was in the right place because the merchant had given good directions and described the building accurately. He took a deep breath and knocked on the door.

It was not long before a servant opened up. Even before William could explain who he was, the well-scrubbed servant let him in.

"My master is expecting you," he said pompously, looking down his nose.

William wondered whether the merchant would be annoyed. FitzEldred had told him to come after mass, but William had chosen to wait a little, for most merchants, whether rich or poor, used their time after church to have a chat with their present or future customers. It was a good opportunity to talk to possible clients or competitors of their own rank, to discuss prices, or resolve minor disputes. Now, though, he wondered whether the merchant would consider him lazy because he had arrived late.

He walked uncertainly behind the servant and tripped over the threshold. Lord, that's a good start, he thought to himself, and felt like sinking into the earth. Out of habit he ducked his head as he went through the door, but it was not necessary here as it was at the tanner's house.

The merchant welcomed William amiably and introduced him to his daughter, Robena, who was thirteen at most and greeted him with a coquettish smile. He led William to the stalls at the back of the courtyard, where his falcon was kept with the horses.

Garth, the falconer, was waiting for them. He showed a certain reserve, but William could understand that all too well. What had the merchant told him? That he had come across a tanner's day man who claimed to know something about falconry? William's heart sank. The saker at the fair had certainly made a good first impression, but how long it would really live was something they would probably never know.

After the first few words he exchanged with the falconer, however, the latter's initial reservations were visibly dispelled. They discussed the details of training and manning, and soon agreed that they held the same opinions on many points. Garth fetched the merchant's tiercel, gave William a glove, and let him take the bird. When he saw how William handled the bird, how well he held him, and how carefully he observed, he nodded to FitzEldred and laughed with pleasure.

William would have preferred never to leave, he felt so comfortable in FitzEldred's house from the first. But decency required him to go to Tanner and ask to be released. If Tanner needed William for the remaining days of the fair, he would remain in his service, provided the merchant agreed. FitzEldred seemed impressed by William's honorable behavior and agreed without hesitation.

William promised to tell him as soon as possible when he could start work, and he took his leave. His heart rejoiced. At last he would be able to work with falcons again!

Tanner, who had found a reliable assistant in William, was reluctant to let him go so easily. He offered to increase his wages or take William on as an apprentice and train him. When William refused, he became angry. He berated him, and his wife joined in vociferously. So William packed up his meager belongings and set off back to FitzEldred's the same day.

The merchant welcomed him happily and sent him straight to the falconer so that he could give him the good news himself: he would be able to take up his duties the next day.

William was given a place in the hayloft in the stables, where the house servant and the stable boy also slept. Garth had his own room, right next to the falcon's enclosure. He was a conscientious falconer who was not exactly open to new ideas but had enough experience to recognize that there was more to William than met the eye. He was a tranquil man who spoke little, and never loudly; did not drink; never went out; and led an ascetic life. William did not find it particularly difficult to work with him or be subservient to him.

He carried out his duties conscientiously, did not complain, and kept his opinions to himself when he saw that they differed from Garth's. In this way he avoided arguments, and everyone was content.

London, September 3, 1189

illiam hurried north through the streets of Cheapside. He was late, and FitzEldred was sure to be waiting for him. William clutched the little packet of leather strips. He was to make them into new jesses for the falcon.

The tang of burning wood entered his nostrils, reminding him of smoked food or a well-heated room in winter. Thoughts of comfortable warmth and simmering broth filled William's mind. Soon, though, the clouds of smoke became denser. His eyes and chest burned. William ran as fast as he could. More and more men armed with torches, pitchforks, and cudgels were arriving from all sides, forming a clamorous mob.

"Kill the greedy Jews. The king orders it," roared some of the men, beside themselves with rage. "Long live King Richard." William heard someone else shout from far behind, "Milk Street is already on fire. Now burn the other Jews' houses to ashes."

Pure horror gripped him as he turned the corner. The Jews had barricaded their doors, hoping to evade the enraged citizens of London, but the latter were not to be diverted from their gruesome intention. They set light to the houses with their torches. The screams of women and children rang through the crackling of the first flames, and the air began to reek of burning flesh.

William looked around in shock. Day laborers, artisans, and traders—both men and women—were venting their fury on the Jews. While a few men with long locks of hair at their temples tried to save their families from the flames and the angry mob, the madding crowd started looting homes and shops. The Jews had no choice but to leave their houses and belongings behind in order to save their skins, but only a few managed even that. The raging hordes struck down the defenseless, skewered them, and trampled them underfoot.

Distressed, William struggled through the tumultuous rabble. Suddenly, he recognized Moses ben Chaim, an elderly Jew he had met at FitzEldred's home a few days before. The old man was bleeding from a gaping wound in his head. He was trying to shield a young woman and a small boy from the blows of a screaming matron in elegant clothes. William saw the wide, terror-stricken eyes of the young mother, who clutched her child, sobbing and half-dead with fear. The scene made him think of Enid. Suddenly, another thought raced across his mind: if he managed to save the two of them, perhaps God would forgive him for not being there when Enid needed him.

He rushed at their assailant, snatched away the plank of wood she was holding before she could use it to strike the old man again, and shoved her into the dirt. He grabbed Moses ben Chaim by the sleeve, took the woman protectively under his arm, and encouraged her to flee. They managed only a few steps before William felt a blow on his shoulder and heard a loud crack. He pushed the old man and the woman into the next alleyway.

"Run to FitzEldred," he told them as he fell to the ground. Before the next blow landed, he rolled over. It was the woman he had just prevented from striking old Moses. She had brought the plank down on his back and split it, though without really hurting him.

"Look, Mother, see how much money, housewares, and jewelry the others have got," cried a young girl with greedy eyes, grabbing the woman by the sleeve. "Come, I want something for my dowry, too."

"You miserable traitor!" hissed the matron at William before allowing herself to be led away by her daughter.

William stood up hastily to avoid being trampled to death by the fleeing Jews or their pursuers. He glanced into the alleyway; Moses ben Chaim and the woman with the child had disappeared. Would they escape the mindlessly baying mob? William looked around to see if there was anyone else he could help, but there did not seem to be any Jews left on the street. The normally decent citizens of London were tearing the loot from each other's hands like drunkards and had even begun to fight over it. And since the wealth of the Jews could not satisfy everyone in the crowd, some were now setting fire to the homes of wealthy Christians, too.

William struggled through the crowd, beseeching God that nothing had happened to FitzEldred. He was jostled so roughly that his shoulder ached. He was knocked over twice and came within a hair's breadth of being crushed by a collapsing roof beam. Eventually, he found his way to a relatively quiet alleyway and ran away, as fast as he could, toward his master's house.

"William, are you all right?" said FitzEldred worriedly as he rushed in through the door.

"They're killing Jews and setting fire to the houses of rich Christians," William reported breathlessly. "We must close all the shutters and hope the mob doesn't force its way here. Did Moses ben Chaim get here? I couldn't think of anything else to do but send him and the woman and child here."

"Don't worry, William. They're back in the stables, hiding. You did right to send them here. His daughter is about to have her third child."

"Her third child?"

FitzEldred nodded distractedly. "She has to be careful. The strain of the fire and the worry about her eldest son—she couldn't find him when the attacks began—haven't done her any good," FitzEldred explained, shaking his head. "Get yourself something to eat from the kitchen. And then go and wash—you're covered with soot and dirt."

William nodded, but instead of the kitchen he went straight to the stables. While FitzEldred sat tensely in his countinghouse tidying up parchments, William and Garth stayed with the animals and tried to calm the three frightened human beings huddled together in the straw, white as chalk.

Garth sat the child in his lap. "Rickety, rockety horse," he sang with the little boy, who went by his grandfather's name, Moses.

William looked at the young woman out of the corner of his eye. She seemed to be about his age, perhaps slightly older. Shyly he looked at her round belly. She did not have long to go before she gave birth, so he made sure she was comfortable. He stood up, fetched blankets for her to sleep in, and brought a hearty meal from the kitchen for the three of them, as well as a jug of refreshing black currant juice.

The roar of the mob was audible for a good while longer. At first it seemed to be coming closer, and once again William feared that FitzEldred's house might be in danger, but then the tumult ebbed, and the city was finally peaceful again.

After there had been no noise for long enough, FitzEldred gave his servant the task of getting the three Jews discreetly out of the town, for they could not be sure they were not still in danger. A wagon was harnessed up and loaded with a few chests; a tarpaulin was stretched over them, and the Jews hid underneath.

William helped the woman get as comfortable as she could, then lifted the child into the wagon.

At first light, the king's men started combing the streets of London in search of those responsible for the massacre. King Richard had forbidden Jews to attend his coronation at Westminster, it was true, but he had never called for them to be killed. So he had given Ranulf de Glanville the task of punishing the culprits. But when it emerged that too many prominent citizens had joined the attacks, it was decided that it was not in the king's interest to bring them all to justice. To keep up appearances, three less important participants were selected and sentenced to death by hanging.

All of London seemed to be up early to attend the execution.

Even FitzEldred, Robena, Garth, the servant who had taken Moses ben Chaim and his family out of the city, the cook, and, of course, William set out to join them. Failing to attend the execution would have seemed like an endorsement of the previous night's atrocities. Thus, even those who had taken part in the uproar found themselves in attendance, too. Several still bore the unmistakable marks of their nocturnal tussles on their faces and on their blood-soaked, soot-blackened dresses. The well-to-do had changed their clothes, tended their wounds, and washed up, and now behaved as though everyone else had been responsible.

William recognized the matron and her daughter. They even dared to show themselves dripping with jewelry—jewelry they had probably stolen in the looting. Disgusted, he sought a different place in the crowd of eager onlookers.

Considering how many people were gathered together, it was remarkably peaceful. The jesters and jugglers received only subdued applause, and the laughter was muted. Even the hucksters selling eel pies and other treats did not hawk their wares as loudly as usual. Did people feel guilty? Were they ashamed? Or did they consider the execution of the condemned men no more than a conciliatory sacrifice that had to be made, so that no more of them need be punished? William tried to read their faces, and he saw not only fear and shock but also satisfaction and defiance.

When Ranulf de Glanville read out the sentence, the people rejoiced but in a restrained manner. In the eyes of many of the onlookers, it was not the condemned men who deserved to die, but the Jews. Rotten eggs, putrid fruit, and stinking cabbages were still thrown at the scaffold and the condemned men, but it was done with less vituperation and enthusiasm than usual. As the executioner put the nooses around the men's necks, a few shouts of protest and an angry muttering could be heard. The city was not of one mind about the events. Executions were a popular diversion for the people, who normally made quite a party out of them, but on this day the onlookers dispersed more quickly than on other occasions.

As soon as the condemned men were dangling from the gibbet, FitzEldred and his attendants went home, too.

The scent of charred wood still hung in some alleys; it stung the eyes and nose and caught in the throat. The ruins were still smoldering here and there, though attempts had been made to put out the fires so that they would not spread to neighboring buildings and side streets. Those who lived in the affected alleyways still must have feared a resurgence of the anger and fire, even if they were not Jewish. With fright in their eyes, the few survivors were trying to tidy up their looted homes and salvage from the mud anything that was still usable.

Whereas FitzEldred was deeply distressed, Robena wandered through the alleyways as if nothing had happened. On several occasions she looked at William enticingly, and when her father could not see them at one point she even put her hand in his and left it there for a while.

William was confused and annoyed at the same time. Was she unaware of the seriousness of the situation, or did she not care that so many innocent people had lost their lives?

FitzEldred was very popular; he was influential and had many friends, and he therefore had to entertain guests frequently. Henry FitzAilwyn, who owned a large house on Candlewick Street, was in and out of FitzEldred's house all the time. Shortly after King Richard's coronation and the night of the fires, he was elected as London's first mayor. Garth had told William that Robena was promised to FitzAilwyn's eldest son. The rumors about the size of the dowry seemed, to both William and the falconer, to be the product of fantasy. Even FitzEldred couldn't have as much money as that!

Robena seemed completely indifferent. She was not particularly friendly to FitzAilwyn, and she didn't give the impression that she was preparing herself for life as a married woman. She quarreled constantly with her father, who was much too indulgent with her because Robena's mother, his great love, had died young.

One day, William was busy rubbing FitzEldred's overheated horse dry when he suddenly found Robena standing beside him.

"Mistress," William greeted her with a bow of the head and continued with his work.

Her expression often suggested a timid doe, for her eyes were large and questioning, but this was deceptive. Robena was not timid in the least, as William had found out on the day of the executions more than three weeks before. She was after him like the very devil, always ambushing him in the stables or lurking in the courtyard and making unwelcome advances.

"Such strong arms," she purred, stroking his upper arm covetously.

"I have to rub the horse dry, so he doesn't catch a chill," William replied tersely, rubbing with even more vigor. He tried to be polite at all times, but he spoke to Robena only when necessary and avoided saying anything that she might take as encouragement to seek him out more. But the girl remained remarkably persistent.

"Sometimes I wish I was a horse," she breathed in his ear, pressing herself against him, closing her eyes, and pursing her lips.

William ducked under the horse's belly and fled to the other side of its body. It was not the first time she had tried to tempt him to a kiss. William's heart pounded. She was lovely to look at and smelled wonderful, but the memory of Enid was still too fresh, and Robena was his master's daughter. Besides, it was indecent the way she pestered him so shamelessly. And if her father ever found out, he was sure to blame William, not her, and would doubtless throw him out of the house. There was no reason to succumb.

But William knew he had to be careful. Robena would not allow herself to be rejected forever. If he continued to spurn her for much longer, he would just antagonize her. How easily she could go to her father and claim that William had become too intimate with her. FitzEldred would take his daughter's word for it and throw William out of the house, or even bring him before a judge. William was well aware of how awkward his position had become and the likelihood that it would end badly. So what should he do?

Robena stroked the horse's nose and looked at him crossly. "I almost think you don't like me," she said sulkily.

"I do, mistress," William stammered.

She beamed at him and tried to press herself against him once more, but then they heard her father's voice.

"Robena," he shouted. "Robena, where are you?"

"I have to go," she whispered, smiling at him flirtatiously again and blowing him a kiss.

He breathed again, escaping this time. But what did the future hold?

A few days later, when Robena murmured to him that she had to go and visit her aunt in the country and wasn't happy about it, William was delighted and set off in high spirits to visit David. His way took him through one of the alleyways that had been in flames on the day of the coronation. Where the houses had borne the brunt of the fire, there were now yawning gaps in the rows of buildings. The houses that had suffered less damage were being repaired; those that had been demolished were being rebuilt. Work was going on everywhere, and children played among the ruins. The sound of carpenters' hammers rang in William's ears, reviving terrible memories of that awful day when the mob had persecuted the Jews.

A cold shiver ran down William's back. He began to run, turning into the next alley as fast as he could, trying to shake off these dark thoughts. He collided with a man, who swore at him. It was the merchant who had bought the dubious saker at the market. William recognized him immediately.

"Aren't you the young man who claimed the falcon I bought at Smithfield would die within five days?" asked the man harshly, gripping him by the shoulders.

"I hope I was wrong and the bird is in good health," William replied cautiously, looking questioningly at the merchant.

"No," he replied, sounding slightly contemptuous. "She's dead. She died four days after I acquired her. So you were right, unfortunately. But I was impressed. I've made some inquiries about you. I haven't learned much, but no matter. I should like to take you into my service. After all, your advice could have saved me a fortune."

"I'm sorry, but I'm already a falconer's assistant," William replied, making a tiny bow.

"Well, it goes without saying that I know that, and I was planning to see FitzEldred. He has but one falcon, whereas I have three: two lanners and a goshawk. My falconer is a drunken sot, and it's high time I got a new one. It seems to me you're capable of better than an assistant's work. How would you like to be head falconer, with an assistant of your own?"

"I, er...I'm too young," William stammered. The merchant didn't even know him. How could he make such an offer?

"I'm surprised, William—that is your name, isn't it? I wouldn't have expected you to be afraid of work as an independent falconer."

"No, I'm not afraid of it, but…"

"I know the good FitzEldred took you in, though he doesn't need a second falconer. Garth is a good man with a spotless reputation. Incidentally, he has nothing but good things to say about you. That and your prediction about my falcon are quite enough recommendation for me."

William did not feel right about the situation. The offer sounded like a once-in-a-lifetime opportunity, but he hesitated. FitzEldred had welcomed him into his home so kindly that he felt obliged to him.

"Think it over. I haven't dismissed my falconer yet. You can come to me whenever you want. By the way, my name is Brian FitzOwen. But don't wait too long. I don't think it will do my falcons any good to be neglected by that drunkard for much longer." FitzOwen told William where he lived, then went on his way.

It took William a moment to collect himself before going to visit David. He spent the day with him, all the time trying hard not to think about FitzOwen's offer.

He carried out his duties as usual for the next two days. On the morning of the third day—he was feeding the falcons and inwardly complimenting himself for his decision to stay with FitzEldred—Robena confronted him. William had not expected her back so soon and looked at her in surprise.

"I complained and said I wanted to go home. I couldn't bear being so far away from you," she whispered longingly, throwing her arms around his neck and drawing him to her. Before William could prepare himself, she pressed her lips to his.

"No," he protested, frightened, disentangling himself from her. "Your father wouldn't permit it. You're promised to FitzAilwyn's son."

"No one will find out. Once I'm married, I'll just ask my father to give you to me and my husband as our falconer. Then you won't have to listen to Garth anymore," she reassured him, stroking his lips with her index finger. "Merchants travel a lot, you know. God willing, my husband will be away for months at a time. And then you can provide comfort for my lonely heart."

William shuddered. He would not have thought the girl capable of such deviousness. He realized he would have to weigh his words even more carefully in the future, so as not to turn her against him. "What if your father notices?"

"He won't." She waved her hand airily.

"Still, it would be better if we weren't alone together for too long, so he doesn't get suspicious," said William.

"You're right, dearest." Robena landed another kiss on his mouth and hurried away.

He had managed to get her away from him again this time, but if he stayed in the house any longer he would have to become her lover sooner or later or risk her wrath. Doubtless, either way, he would be thrown out by her father.

William now knew that he had to accept FitzOwen's offer. It was the only way out, even if he felt extremely uncomfortable about it. FitzEldred would scarcely understand why he wanted to leave and would probably be disappointed, but the sooner William left the house, the better. He knew Robena would stop at nothing, and the last thing he wanted was to lead FitzEldred to believe he had abused his trust by trying to debauch his daughter. Determined to forestall any more of her scheming, he asked to see the merchant that very evening.

When FitzEldred asked him what was on his mind, William plucked up his courage and began to speak. "FitzOwen has offered me a position as head falconer. Three falcons and an assistant. It's an opportunity I can't afford to miss, but I feel bad about it. You've shown me so much goodness and friendship by taking me in that it pains me to let you down. That is why I beg your understanding and indulgence."

"May both be granted, my boy," FitzEldred replied gently. "I've been watching you, and I know the duties you have in my house are beneath your knowledge and talent. I already have one falconer, and I won't need more than one or perhaps two falcons in the future. I can't offer you any more than I already have, and I understand that a young man with your skills wants to advance. FitzOwen has high ambitions. He wants to go further than I do, and if he is successful in rallying good men around him, he will probably succeed. You are free, my boy, and you may go where you wish. Be sure that I bear you no ill will for it, even if I am sorry to lose you."

William gulped, moved by his master's kind words.

"Farewell, William. Seize the chance that fate has placed in your path. Have no regrets. You've earned it." FitzEldred smiled at him wisely, patted William on the head, and released him.

William left with tears in his eyes. He felt like a traitor, like the time he had left David with the monks. He would almost have preferred it if the merchant had cursed and ranted, like Tanner, for then it would have been easier to leave.

Garth warmly shook William's hand and wished him luck. "I'm sure we'll meet again on a hunt. You're a fine lad. You'll do well."

As a precaution, William chose to keep out of Robena's way. He packed up his bundle and stole away without bidding her farewell.

FitzOwen greeted William with a triumphant grin and welcomed him into his house. The walls were lined with costly tapestries, and the room was appointed with heavy, decoratively carved oak furniture and chests with iron fittings. There was a slight smell of beeswax, which FitzOwen's maidservant used to polish the valuable furniture. Intricately decorated silver tableware was set ostentatiously on the large, dark wood table, and there was a heap of coins in a small open chest. FitzOwen obviously enjoyed flaunting his wealth.

For a moment, William doubted whether his decision to leave FitzEldred had been wise.

"Follow me. I'll show you the mews and my falcons," FitzOwen commanded, leading him across the courtyard.

William was shocked when he saw how this part of FitzOwen's property had been neglected. The birds were as magnificent as the merchant had claimed, but their accommodation was filthy. Several days' worth of mutes, as well as food scraps and castings, were scattered across the sand-covered floor.

The falconer shuffled reluctantly out to meet them. He smelled of rank stale beer, and his bloodshot eyes were dull and empty. William felt a chill though London had been blessed with a beautiful and warm late autumn day, complete with colorful leaves and sunshine. William knew what fate awaited the falconer, and it made him feel uneasy.

At the sight of the falconer, one of the birds began begging for food.

"Shut your trap," the man shouted at the hungry creature.

William was horrified. This was not how one behaved with falcons. How could a creature treated like this ever really gain trust? Why should anyone be surprised if the falcon flew away?

"Pack your things and go. You've been falconer in my house long enough," FitzOwen shouted at the man.

"But you can't do that, master," the old man whined, grabbing the young merchant's arm.

"Can't I, you pathetic old sot? Here are your wages till the end of the week. Now get out," declared FitzOwen, shaking him off like some annoying parasite and tossing him a couple of coins. "William," he called as he went. It sounded like someone calling a dog to heel.

William followed him, feeling profoundly uneasy. Had he made the right decision?

"He has abused my generosity for far too long. I hope you won't disappoint me."

November 1190

FitzOwen was as excited as a virgin on her wedding night when he burst into the stables one fine November day. "William, the falcons. We've been invited on a very special hunt."

William looked at his master with puzzlement. It would be dark soon, not exactly the right moment to be setting off on a hunt.

FitzOwen laughed at his young falconer's bewildered expression. "Not now, William. In a week's time. The richest merchants in London will be there, along with one of the highest barons in the land."

"The falcons are in their best form, master, there's no doubt about it. The female, especially, has developed superbly."

"Then starve them just enough that they're hungry and eager for prey. I belong. Finally," he murmured with satisfaction.

To fly well, as William knew, falcons must be neither too fat nor too thin, and he said nothing in reply to his master's advice. He would simply do what he thought was right. FitzOwen might be a good merchant, but about hunting and falcons he knew relatively little. If his birds were to be successful in the hunt, it would be best if he gave William free rein.

A few days before the hunt, William was making his way through the crowded market. He had run an errand and was on his way back to FitzOwen's house. Since he was still saving up for a better future, he was satisfied just to watch the jugglers and musicians entertaining people in a corner of the market square. He wandered on, paying no heed to the colorful displays. One day he would find a very special falcon, train it to hunt, and then present it to the king. He wouldn't handle things like his mother and wait for somebody to put in a word for him with the king. No, he would muster his courage and take the initiative himself.

William did not know much about King Richard, only that he was on a crusade, driving the unbelievers out of the holy city of Jerusalem, and that he had taken several falcons with him because he was as besotted with falconry as his father had been before him. William smiled involuntarily at the memory of the dead king and his Blanchpenny. The two falconers who had mocked him at Saint Edmundsbury had been wrong, and Henry had kept his word.

"The cripple has become a falconer, after all," he murmured to himself proudly. He headed toward a juggler whose jokes were so outrageous that people clutched their bellies and howled with delight. A woman on the other side of the crowd caught William's attention. That blonde, wavy hair, that slightly bowed back, that gliding walk. William's heart skipped a beat. Enid! A feeling of incredible happiness poured through him, and the jester was forgotten. Like a man possessed, he forced his way through the people in an effort to reach her. He shoved aside anyone who did not get out of his way fast enough, afraid that he might lose sight of her.

"Enid," he called. But the woman—who was carrying an infant—seemed not to hear him. She did not even turn around. William deliberately plowed his way through the mass of people. Soon she would disappear into a side street. He raised his hand and called out to her. When he had almost caught up with her, he reached out and grabbed her arm. "Oh, Enid," he cried with relief.

But when the woman turned around, it was not Enid. "What do you think you're doing?" The young woman tore loose, put her hand protectively on the child's head, and hurried away.

William stood there, thunderstruck, and watched her go. She looked back one more time, shook her head as if she thought he was mad, and disappeared into the throng.

"Enid," he whispered to himself. He felt as if he were falling into a deep, dark hole again. He couldn't think straight. He must have known it couldn't be Enid, and yet the feeling had been so strong, the hope so great.

The crowd in the market pushed him on. He allowed himself to be driven along until he was standing in front of a small tavern. Here it smelled of ale and oblivion.

"Come on, open the door! What are you waiting for? We're thirsty, too," a man called out, and his friends pushed William into the inn.

Before he knew what was happening, he was sitting at a long table, with the sleeves of his coat in the pool of ale left by an over-turned jug. For an eternity, he stared at the tankard the serving wench had placed in front of him when he caught her eye. The dark ale smelled bitter and made him salivate. He found it difficult to raise his hand. He moved each finger carefully. The fingers belonged to him, so the hand must, too. Slowly, he reached out his right hand to pick up the tankard, but the man beside him leaned under the table and threw up on William's left foot. William woke up instantly, as if from a deep sleep. He sprang up, disgusted, and rushed out into the street.

The cool, fresh air that greeted him cleared his head. You should drink ale because you're thirsty, he said to himself, not to forget. Enid is dead. Gone forever. You buried her and the child with your own hands.

How could he have mistaken that woman for Enid, even if she did look like her? He knew Enid was with God. Tears ran down his cheeks, and he let out a sob of anguish.

Suddenly, he felt a child's hand slip into his, and a small voice, full of compassion, asked, "Are you hungry, too?"

William looked down and found a little boy gazing up at him with wide eyes. The clothes on his back were no more than rags, his belly was distended, and the spindly bones of his chest and back were clearly visible through his thin skin. William sniffed and shook his head. He wiped his eyes with his sleeve, reached for his purse, fished out a few coins, and pressed them into the child's hand.

He found the little enamel plaque in his right hand and fell to musing. He had known for a long time that it was not a piece of Enid's jewelry. Did that not leave only one conclusion? Did the plaque belong to her murderer? The thought made William shudder, arousing a feeling of physical illness that almost made him choke. The more he thought about it, the more his certainty grew.

William felt life gradually flowing back into him. He opened his fist and examined the plaque more closely. It was round, made of silver with blue enamel, and it depicted a shiny silver leaf with a finely serrated edge.

William wondered where it could have come from. Decorations of this kind were sometimes found on horses' tack, but they also appeared on sword scabbards, knife sheaths, and pommels. Everything suggested that more than one man had been present when Enid was murdered. Most likely they had been soldiers, mercenaries perhaps, or else men who called themselves knights but did not behave like them. The plaque could prove their guilt. William's heart was in his mouth. He would find these men and avenge Enid if it was the last thing he did. His decision made, he put the plaque back in his purse and returned to FitzOwen's house.

The few days leading up to the hunt passed quickly. William did his best to suppress his dark thoughts about Enid, which filled his mind even more since his encounter with the woman at the market. He had enough to do to prepare the birds for the hunt.

His assistant, Jack, had taken a while to understand that William expected much more of him than FitzOwen's previous falconer. William insisted that he clean the falcons' accommodation daily and that the birds be bathed every day, since it calmed them down and was a good way to make them comfortable around human beings. William had spent a good deal of time getting the birds used to him and had then trained them afresh in the manner Logan had taught him. In this way he'd gained valuable experience. Even if he was exceptionally gifted, he still had a lot to learn, and he knew it. "You learn your whole life long," his mother used to say.

To be a good falconer, you had to know each bird intimately, its strengths as well as its weaknesses. The secret was to encourage its good instincts and, with great patience, eradicate its bad habits. Almost every day, he and Jack would ride out of the city with the two lanners to train them to the wing lure and figure out which birds they should hunt. Jack learned soon enough what William wanted. He listened carefully and without argument to all his instructions and hurried to carry them out.

On the day before the hunt, FitzOwen came to William to discuss when they should set out.

"May I make a suggestion?" William asked at the end of their conversation.

FitzOwen frowned. "Namely?"

"What you are most looking forward to is the people you will meet, isn't that right?" William waited until FitzOwen nodded. "If you arrange things skillfully, you are likely to meet influential lords and make some important connections. I think that is more important to you than how your birds fly. Is it not so?"

"You've seen through me, William." FitzOwen laughed encouragingly. "So what do you propose?"

"You are of most interest to the lords when your falcons can impress them, so let me make all the decisions about the hunt. I shall treat you as if you were a baron: I will place the right falcon on your fist at the right moment and give you a sign when it is time to cast it off. That way you will be admired for your falcons and at the same time you will be able to concentrate on the other merchants."

"You're very sure of yourself," said FitzOwen sharply, without immediately reacting to the suggestion.

William did not flinch. "I don't have the faintest hint of an idea about the kind of trade you do, but when it comes to hawking"—he cleared his throat—"I reckon I'm as skilled as you are as a merchant."

"I think you're a cunning little devil more than anything else. You've got guts, my boy. So I accept your proposal, but woe betide you if my falcons don't fly better than all the rest!"

By sunrise the following morning, William and Jack were waiting for their master at the gate, as agreed. The horses were saddled and the falcons ready. William could feel the birds' agitation; it was as if they could sense that everything depended on this hunt. To calm them, he decided to keep them covered for the moment. Jack carried the tiercel on his fist, and William the more powerful female. As soon as FitzOwen was mounted on his horse, Jack would hand over the tiercel. He was more reliable than the female, which was more easily controlled by William.

The two dogs barked excitedly, and when FitzOwen came out of the house it was obvious that he was just as agitated as the animals. He hurried along the two servants who were to accompany them, for a larger retinue would make him seem more important, and gave the order to leave in an unusually harsh tone. The little group set off, heading west down Watling Street. At every crossroad, more of London's merchants joined them. They rode past Saint Paul's and left London by the Ludgate. They were all gorgeously dressed and in high spirits. Even their falconers looked like noblemen. William ignored them disdainfully. Not even King Henry's falconers had dressed themselves up like that.

"They'll take me for a poor man or a miser. It looks as though you're the only falconer who has insisted on wearing his oldest clothes," FitzOwen growled reproachfully.

William's dress was appropriate for the hunt. The cloth was clean and of good quality; the color was a plain brown with narrow green trim. William found the other merchants' falconers, clad as they were in eye-catching red, particularly ridiculous.

The number of riders kept increasing. FitzAilwyn, the mayor of London, had attached himself to them, as had FitzEldred, who was accompanied by Garth and a boy William did not recognize. They nodded to each other amiably and joined the line of riders a short distance away. Outside the city gates, yet more riders joined them: the Earl of Essex, Geoffrey FitzPeter, was accompanied by more than a dozen men on horseback, several ladies, and five falconers, as well as squires, pages, and a pack of ravening hounds and their handlers. Essex, a scion of the lesser nobility, whose family had served the kings of England for more than a generation, had recently become one of the king's four justices. Richard trusted him and had given him titles and power; he had also given him the task, along with William Briwerre, Hugh Bardolf, and William Marshal, of keeping an eye on his chancellor, William Longchamp, while he was away in the Holy Land.

FitzOwen could hardly believe what a noble company had assembled when William went through the list of those he could see on the site of the hunt. Logan had insisted that William learn which colors belonged to which noblemen and which families were related by marriage. He was a little out of touch—new lords had been created and new marriages made, and alliances and titles had changed—but at least William knew of the most important earls and counts.

Marshal was one of those William recognized from afar. He looked stately and proud on his elegant hunter. He had grown older and richer, and both suited him very well. When William first saw him, that time in the smithy, he had been the young king's tutor, with no other means to his name. Now, however, he was one of the wealthiest and most influential barons in the land, and that was evident even from a distance. He wore hunting clothes of the finest cloth, rode a valuable horse, and was surrounded by young knights striving to be noticed by him. Ladies smiled at him graciously, though it was known that his young wife had already presented him with an heir and was with child again. Marshal's charm, his astonishing rise, his courtly manners, and his skill in the arts of war made him irresistible to all.

William watched him, fascinated, and took fright when Marshal looked over at him. For a moment, they gazed into each other's eyes until a pair of squires rode by and blocked their view. By the time they had passed, Marshal had turned away and was deep in conversation with one of his attendants.

"You see, not a single baron has decked out his falconers like the London merchants," William told FitzOwen with quiet triumph in his voice. "People will admire this modesty on your part, believe me."

But the merchant was awed by the splendor of the nobles and just nodded absently.

William had been nervous since he found out that Marshal was taking part in the hunt, too, and glanced in his direction again. His retinue had several falconers with marvelous birds. But it was not only the barons who could count magnificent beasts among their holdings; the London merchants could as well.

Although FitzOwen's two lanner falcons were thoroughly acceptable birds, William feared they would be no match for the others. It didn't bear thinking about how FitzOwen would react if they didn't catch any prey. He was not one of those men for whom the beauty of the bird's flight was more important than a successful hunt. Briefly, William wondered whether he should have kept the falcons hungry for a little longer, in order to make them more courageous, but then he put the thought aside. It was not recklessness alone that turned a falcon into a good hunter. A thinner falcon might become more daring but would also tire more quickly and become careless.

FitzOwen was soon absorbed in conversation with various lords and merchants, discussing his commercial intentions and successes and making jokes. William watched the opening forays carefully. Every now and again, he scanned the crowd in search of Marshal.

The ladies who had joined the hunting party took up positions on blankets at the edge of the large field, where pages served them wine and morsels of food as they chatted animatedly. From time to time they would look up, point at a bird, and admire its flight.

William stayed close to his master but did not pay any further attention to him. He had taken the tiercel away from his master after the first round of greetings, so that he would not become tired. William had immediately noticed that FitzOwen did not hold the raptor securely, which fatigued the bird unnecessarily. Since then he had been watching the hunt, and when the right moment approached he went over to his master, noticing with surprise that he was deep in conversation with Marshal. William went weak at the knees. He had to get a grip on himself and greet the baron without the slightest hope of being recognized. It must have been almost ten years since they'd spent the afternoon with Princess, Marshal's lanner falcon. For William it had been a special day, but Marshal was bound to have forgotten about it long ago; besides, the boy had become a man in the meantime.

"Sir William," William bowed.

"William, what a pleasure to see you." Marshal looked at his face searchingly. "You've changed, and yet you're still the same. When I caught your eye earlier, I wasn't sure, but you have your mother's eyes and look just like her. How is she?" he asked, with a serious, almost anxious expression. "The last time I saw her, she was expecting."

"My brother must be about seven by now. I've been gone from Saint Edmundsbury for a long time and I don't know how my mother is, sir. I hope she is well."

"You should go and visit her," Marshal murmured.

FitzOwen remained silent, quite unlike his usual self, and looked questioningly from one to the other.

William glanced up. He was filled with pride and happiness, for Marshal had recognized him and spoken to him with such warmth. But if they did not want to miss the chance for their falcons to shine, they couldn't wait any longer. He could not allow himself to be distracted by Marshal's presence.

William took his master's arm unobtrusively but firmly and bowed. "You ordered me to bring your bird to you." He placed the tiercel on FitzOwen's fist, casually straightened his arm, and looked up again. With a tiny nudge at the merchant's elbow, he gave him to understand that he should cast off the bird.

The tiercel climbed swiftly into the sky.

William did not let much time pass before he cast off the female, too. During the breeding season, lanner falcons often hunted together, and recently William had repeatedly set the two birds after the same prey.

FitzOwen gave William a brief, slightly irritated glance, but William did not heed it. He knew his master thought he was trying to compete with him, but he would understand William's intention as soon as the lords around them fell silent and watched the birds.

The two falcons were an ideal pair for hunting. They combined spectacular flying ability with unerring precision. The agile tiercel pursued his prey with powerful beats of his wings, tiring it out; he wounded the creature with its talons, and it began to drop. With the speed of an arrow, the female pounced on it as it plummeted downward, administering the coup de grâce with a bite to the head.

William waved to Jack to follow and set off at a run. He hurried to separate the birds from their prey before they could begin to gorge on it, and he rewarded them with some savory treats.

He was on his way back to FitzOwen when Marshal approached him again. "Did you train the falcons yourself?"

"They were already in my master's household when I began working there. I had to train them afresh, though, because they were timid and unreliable, my lord." William tried to sound modest, but he did not quite manage it.

"I already noticed how skillful you are with the birds when you held Princess for the first time." Carefully, he stroked the breast of the bird on William's fist. "Your mother must be very proud of you."

"With respect, sir, I hardly think so. She wanted me to become a swordsmith."

"Because of Hephaestus, Wayland, and your foot, I know. But I'm sure she knew, despite everything, that it wouldn't suit you, even if she did try everything to get her way." Marshal smiled.

"You seem to know my mother better than I thought," he said, intrigued.

Marshal just smiled knowingly, leaving his comment unanswered.

"Forgive me, I must return to my master." William bowed.

"Tell him I shall invite him on a hunt in the spring. We'll see each other again then," he said with an amiable nod.

His thoughts in turmoil after this encounter, William returned to FitzOwen.

"How does someone like you know one of the most important men in the kingdom?" the merchant immediately inquired. "I'm quite sure he only engaged me in conversation so that he could ask me about you." FitzOwen seemed to be hovering between envy and admiration.

"Sir William requires me to inform you that you will be invited on a hunt in the spring." William feigned indifference, but he was agitated to the core as he fiddled with the falcon's jesses on his fist.

"I'd very much like to know what's behind all this," FitzOwen muttered, shaking his head, as William went off to see to Jack and the tiercel.

FitzOwen's falcons showed their capabilities with two more splendid flights, and by the end of the day, FitzOwen was being greeted affably by merchants who had previously ignored him because they were too refined to have dealings with an upstart like him.

"I don't mind whether they bid me good day because my falcons have flown so well or because Sir William was so good as to speak to me. I am thoroughly satisfied—with you, too, William," the merchant said at the end of the day, thrusting a few coins in William's hand.

It was more than twice his normal weekly wage.

"You have truly earned it." FitzOwen laughed. "Even FitzAilwyn the mayor exchanged a few words with me. He will do me the honor of visiting me in my shop as soon as he can. This has been a thoroughly worthwhile day."

April 1191

Barely six months had passed since the great hunt, which had been an outstanding success. Since then, FitzOwen had been able to consolidate his contacts and use them to great advantage.

Over and over again, he told William how advantageous it would be to know Marshal better, and how keen he was to meet him again. He tried to learn from William how he knew the baron and what he knew about him. William answered tersely that Marshal was a customer of his mother's, but he otherwise avoided the subject.

William said next to nothing about his life, concentrating silently on the falcons instead, but this loosened FitzOwen's tongue like a swiftly drained jug of wine. Almost every day, he paid William a visit and chattered tirelessly.

In this way, William learned that his master had entered the service of an elderly merchant at the age of sixteen. While working as an errand boy and assistant at the counter, he kept his eyes and ears open and learned to read and count; over time, he acquired more and more duties. Thanks to brains and hard work, he had made himself indispensable before he was twenty, and the old merchant, whose only son had died, left the shop to FitzOwen. This inheritance did not make him rich right away— the old man was not that rash—but he did at least become a member of the merchants' guild, and that was the foundation of his future success. FitzOwen, who could be utterly charming when it was worth his while, managed to find backers for his ventures despite being unable to offer any sureties to speak of. He took great risks, showed skill, and had a fair amount of luck. In this way, the son of a simple servant had become a successful merchant.

Until the recent hunt, though, he had been made to feel unworthy by merchants whose fathers and grandfathers had grown rich by trading expensive goods. No one had ever asked his opinion when important decisions were being made within the guild; only his money contributions were welcome.

Now all that had changed. Suddenly, even the worthiest merchants greeted him on the street; some of them even invited him to their homes or asked his advice. FitzOwen was still obsessed with the idea of one day rising even higher than FitzEldred, whom he envied as much for his success as for his high standing, and so got it in his head that he should wed Robena. By marrying her, he would finally join the circle of the most influential merchant families, the very people who had so long despised him for his humble origins.

William sometimes wondered whether FitzOwen had made him his falconer mainly in order to take him away from FitzEldred. And since he had no desire to continue to be a mere pawn in the merchant's game, he did not tell him that Robena was already promised to FitzAilwyn's son.

When FitzOwen found out for himself, he just laughed bitterly. "We'll see if FitzAilwyn still approves the wedding to sweet Robena when it comes out that her father can't pay the dowry. I shall bring FitzEldred to his knees. He'll beg me to marry his daughter yet," he predicted confidently.

When FitzOwen received Marshal's invitation to the next hunt, he immediately ordered new clothes and started parading about like a peacock. It was customary for successful men to demonstrate their riches with thoroughbred horses, splendid falcons, costly clothes, the company of a beautiful wife, and a large number of servants.

Fascinated, FitzOwen watched the barons who had been invited and eyed the merchants critically as they joined the assembled hunt one by one. It was obvious that he did not yet belong among the noblest men in London. They stood together in a small group in the center, clad in even more magnificent clothes, leading the costliest horses, and radiating invincible self-confidence. Several of them, it was said, were trying to rise to the lesser nobility by marrying a daughter of an impoverished noble-man who needed a generous dowry.

William knew that FitzOwen admired these men and wanted nothing more than to belong among them. He was therefore particularly pleased when Marshal, after greeting the most important barons, came first to him rather than to the other merchants. FitzOwen looked around, craning his neck, as if convincing himself that the other merchants had noticed the honor that was being accorded him.

Marshal greeted him courteously, exchanged a few pleasantries, praised his falcons, and then turned to William with an amiable smile. "I've brought Princess with me. She's an old lady now, but she's still a good hunter. Would you like to come see her?"

William bowed briefly. "Princess is a female lanner, too," he told his master and asked for permission to leave. FitzOwen gave his consent—he had little choice—but he had to make a visible effort not to show how much he envied the attention Marshal paid his young falconer. William handed the falcon to Jack and followed Marshal.

"How old is she now?" William asked when he saw how magnificent Princess looked. He gently stroked her back.

"She was still young when I brought her to the smithy. It was her second autumn."

"Twelve, then," William murmured, impressed. "A grand old age for a falcon."

Marshal nodded his agreement and looked into William's green eyes. "I'll be watching you today. Come and see me again later."

"Yes, my lord, as you wish." William bade him farewell with a small bow and then stood still for a moment, inexpressibly happy. It took him a while to come to himself, but then he made his way over to a group of young falconers standing not far away from his master. They were talking over one another, boasting of their birds' daring exploits and daredevil flights during previous hunts. William stood silently among them for a long time, but he soon found their conversation boring. They belonged to the merchants and were telling tall tales that made William self-conscious. Perhaps it was because the barons' falconers were staring at them disdainfully from a distance, occasionally pointing at them and laughing mockingly.

William knew that there were men of the lowest sort among the barons' falconers. Right at the bottom of the hierarchy stood the falconers' assistants, most of whom came from simple peasant families. Then came the apprentices, who would be falconers themselves one day. They, too, began their working lives as simple assistants, but they were gradually entrusted with more important duties and were allowed to learn to man and train birds, as he had been. Many came from families in which falconry had been the tradition for generations; some were the bastard sons of barons. The older, experienced men who trained the others were called falconers or master falconers.

Good falconers were sought after. The best served the mightiest barons, owned several horses, and earned a good living. A royal falconer was more than a keeper of valuable birds. He enjoyed the particular trust of his king, was permitted to eat at his table, and was closer to him than many other courtiers. Most of these men came from noble families, had owned falcons since childhood, and kept their own falconers, assistants, and dog handlers. They were men like the de Hauvilles, Richard de Ystlape, Gilbert de Merk, Henry de la Wade, Roger de Cauz, and others. And yet the talk everywhere was of one Henry Falconarius, whose father was a commoner. It was certainly difficult for a lowborn to keep up with the others but obviously not impossible. If a falconer caught the king's eye, he could go far. Once accepted into the king's service, he could be granted lands and could even rise to the lesser nobility, for a falconer's skill and talent for handling birds were more important than his origins. For this reason, William despised the barons' falconers, who considered themselves superior simply on account of their birthright.

He was about to join FitzOwen again when he noticed a young man in the distance. There was something familiar about him that caught William's attention. He reminded him of someone, but who? William approached the young falconer, and when he turned around William's jaw dropped.

"Robert," he called, hurrying over to him.

"William?" Robert's eyes were sparkling, and his voice sounded oddly tight. "I can hardly believe it, William."

They looked at each other wordlessly for a moment, grinned, and then pushed one another gently as they used to.

"How are you?" asked Robert, looking at him searchingly.

Robert, Logan, Sibylle—that was all before Enid. William sighed quietly. "I'm alive. I…it's…" he stammered. There was so much to tell, and he could not find the words.

"Later, you can tell me everything later, in your own time."

"Are your father and Sir Ralph here, too?" asked William, keeping his voice low and looking around anxiously.

"No. My father's dead. I was too young to take over the mews. Sir Ralph found himself a new falconer and I found a new master."

Before William could express his sorrow or say anything else, the hunting party came to life and they had to part in order to go back to their masters.

"I'll see you later." William waved at Robert.

ᘒᘓ

Robert waved back, his knees weak. William was back! Robert found it difficult to concentrate on the hunt. He kept looking anxiously for William, and he could not calm down until he found him. He watched him out of the corner of his eye. A smile played on his lips. William's gait, a bit wooden with its slight limp, was so familiar he was overcome with wistfulness. Robert remembered the day they had first met.

He had not been pleased that another boy was to be trained alongside him by his father, so he had immediately decided that he would never like the intruder.

Three years had passed since Robert had helped William escape, and in that time William had become a man—not a particularly tall one, but powerful. He probably still ran a lot and built up the strength in his arms by regularly hanging off tree branches and lifting himself up thirty or forty times, as he had done at Thorne. Robert took a deep breath. Thinking about William made his stomach feel strangely unsettled. It was so good to see him unharmed, though terrible things must have befallen him after his escape. The new look on his face was proof of that. The thought that someone might have done harm to his friend was almost unbearable.

Robert's thoughts strayed from the hunt, and he hoped his young master, Hugh de Ferrers, did not notice. Nothing had been the same since William's flight from Thorne. Scarcely a month later, Sibylle had been sent to stay with relatives, and Logan had died in his sleep the following winter.

Robert approached his master and bowed. "My lord, may I draw your attention to something other than the falcons and the ladies for a moment?"

The young de Ferrers smiled and bowed graciously. "By all means."

"Do you see that young man over there?" Robert pointed at William. "He is an excellent falconer—he would be perfect for Oakham."

"What manner of nonsense is this, Robert? Never mind that he's a nobody, the boy's scarcely older than you. We're looking for a *master falconer*," he said testily.

"Forgive me, my lord, but you are mistaken. He is exceptionally gifted. I know him well, for he learned with my father," Robert insisted.

"It honors you that you speak up for him, but I'll say it again. He's too young. Forget it." De Ferrers sniffed with annoyance.

Robert struggled to hold back. Hugh was himself a little too young to keep Oakham, and yet his father had entrusted him with the task while he and his older son sallied forth to accompany Richard on the Crusade. Robert was prepared to get down on bended knee before his master, but he knew it would be utterly futile. But surely there was something he could do. "Please, at least watch him," he said, agonizing at the thought of losing his friend again.

Although the birds of a few other barons flew spectacularly and caught plenty of prey, William and FitzOwen's falcons made an impression. People talked in admiring tones about the skill of the young falconer, wondered where he came from, and congratulated his master on a successful hunt.

Robert went to find William, who was busy with the female lanner, and after a short time it was as if they had never been apart.

"Heavens above, how I've missed you," snorted Robert when William mimicked a couple of conceited young falconers stalking across the field, looking around to make sure they were being admired. "Come, I want to introduce you to my master."

De Ferrers was still deep in conversation with some other barons, so they stood aside and talked about hunting, their masters, and above all about the fabulous birds on display.

"You act with the skill of an experienced falconer. You radiate calm and security," said a voice from behind them. It was Marshal. "The falcons obviously feel it, too; they are so relaxed on your fist."

William blushed in response, and Robert's heart missed three beats. He was all the more glad when Hugh de Ferrers, visibly surprised that Marshal was standing with the two boys, joined them.

"A wonderful hunt, Sir William!"

"Hugh! Well, I agree and was just praising this young man's extraordinary talent," Marshal said with a laugh, clapping William on the shoulder. "And his master doesn't seem to have the slightest idea how good he is."

William cleared his throat in embarrassment.

Robert was full of admiration for his friend.

The young de Ferrers glanced from William to Marshal and then at Robert. After a short pause, he bowed to Marshal and said, almost inaudibly, "I was planning to entice him away."

Robert could hardly believe his ears. Moments before, de Ferrers had dismissed this idea as nonsense.

"Oh, you're doing the right thing, my dear Hugh. He's something special, this young man. Your father will like him."

De Ferrers nodded, pushing Robert forward. "My young falconer here knows him from before. They were trained together."

"Ah, so you must be Logan's son. That definitely speaks in your favor," Marshal said to Robert, as if it went without saying that he would know where William had learned his craft.

Robert nodded, astonished, and looked over at his friend, who seemed just as surprised. How did he know all this?

"Hugh's father, Sir Walkelin, and Hugh's older brother, Henry, are by our king's side in his battle with the unbelievers," Marshal explained to William. "Walkelin was always a good friend to me. If you become falconer at Oakham Castle, we're sure to see each other again soon." He smiled at de Ferrers, bade him farewell with a nod, and left.

"I need a master falconer, and although you seem a little young to me, I'd like to take you into my service in that capacity," said de Ferrers, scratching his still-downy beard.

"It would be a great honor, and it is truly generous of you. Believe me, I would enter into your service with the greatest pleasure. Yes, I would like nothing better. It would be a dream come true," he stammered. "But I promised to take care of a friend named David. He is only a little younger than I am; he has lost his family and can't look after himself because he can't speak. I have put him up at Saint Bartholomew's until I can bring him to live with me. I can't let him down. He needs me. I'm sorry."

Robert looked at his master, his eyes wide with panic. "Couldn't we take this David back to Oakham with us? Perhaps he could make himself useful there? And when we're out hunting or traveling with you, Melva could look after him."

Hugh de Ferrers stroked his almost hairless chin thoughtfully. He was probably weighing up whether it would be more difficult to take the mute boy back to Oakham with him or to explain to Marshal why William had not become his falconer.

"Very well, as long as the boy's no trouble," he said to William. "If you feed and clothe him out of your wages, it's all right with me. Let's shake on it. Then I'll speak to your master about when he can release you."

William shook hands with de Ferrers to seal the agreement. "FitzOwen won't be happy unless some trade comes his way as a result," he blurted out.

De Ferrers grinned mischievously. "Well, in that case he's going to be disappointed."

The two boys watched him as he made his way over to FitzOwen. Despite the distance, they could see the merchant's joyful demeanor when the young lord approached him. First, FitzOwen went red, probably with rage, then white, as if he was afraid; finally he nodded, apparently somewhat mollified, and shook de Ferrers's hand.

"I wouldn't have believed it, but you were right," said Robert happily, fighting back the emotion that suddenly overcame him. "Remember? When you left Thorne, you promised we would see each other again. And now it looks as if we're going to be working together again, too."

Elmswick Castle, Winter 1191–92

The trees stretched out their bare branches at Odon like bony fingers. It was mostly elms that grew around Elmswick Castle, hence the name. Their supple wood made excellent bows, wheels, and chairs.

Odon looked up at the dense slate-gray sky. When Dale, his father's most faithful knight, had come to fetch him, he knew what was about to happen, though he found it difficult to believe. As long as Odon could remember, his father had been a bear of a man—powerful, brutal, ungovernable. But now he was on his deathbed. Odon had always idolized his father, though he never lived up to his father's expectations. He had never been good enough, strong enough, or brave enough. Now, the demanding old man soon would depart this world. Odon could not bring himself to feel genuine grief, but this much at least was true: his life would change profoundly.

His body tingled with excitement. Odon's mother had passed away long ago; when his father died he would inherit everything. Gold and silver, the title, the lands—and therefore the power over several villages and their dwellers, eight knights without lands who were obliged to serve him, and thirteen smaller manors whose knightly lords also owed him fealty.

When they reached the dilapidated wooden fortification his father had neglected in recent years, Odon pondered what improvements he would make first. He would build a stone wall, then an accommodation tower; the kitchen had recently been renovated after a fire and, apart from the stables, everything else needed repair.

The damp weather of the past few days had worked its way into every joint in Odon's body. He rubbed his hands to warm them up. It was high time for him to get down from his horse and allow himself to be pampered by his father's maidservants.

When they reached the upper bailey, he dismounted and tossed the reins to one of the stable lads. Servants and maids ran up eagerly to greet their lord's son. Odon nodded at some of them. He had known the older ones since childhood. As a boy, he had feared some of them. Now, though, it was they who did not know whether they should be afraid of him. Odon grinned broadly when they all bowed deeply before him.

"Have a hot bath drawn for me, my little dove," he ordered one of the younger maids, grabbing her chin and looking hungrily into her eyes. She obviously knew exactly what this meant, for she ran away with a bright-red face, gathering her skirts about her.

Odon roared with laughter and ran his hand through his blond hair complacently. Very few women could resist him. He would soon show the little thing who was the master in this house.

"Take me to my father," he ordered Dale, who had dismounted in the meantime.

"Yes, my lord," the knight replied with a marked lack of enthusiasm.

Odon strode after the knight, satisfied that Dale had nonetheless called him "my lord" and not "Master Odon." Everyone at Elmswick Castle seemed to expect the old man to die soon and his son to inherit.

Once in front of his father's chamber, he thrust out his chest, flung open the door, and entered. The smell of sickness and death that greeted him made him retch powerfully. The room was dark and filled with smoke. Herbs burned in a charcoal brazier in a corner, but the air, pregnant with death, was not going to be cleansed by them.

Odon tried to breathe as shallowly as he could so that he did not have to inhale his father's poisonous breath. He found weakness and sickness profoundly repellent; they frightened him to the core, though he would never have admitted it openly. The thought that he might be ill and in pain one day made him shudder. He approached his father's bed hesitantly, his legs heavier with every step.

Sir Rotrou of Elmswick held out a scrawny, trembling hand to his son. His fingers look like the gnarled branches outside, Odon observed. He stood there as if unable to walk and could not take even one step closer to his father. He could not even bring himself to take the dying man's hand to comfort him. Instead, he looked despairingly at Dale.

The old man was racked by a fit of coughing.

"How long has he been like this?" asked Odon, turning his face away with disgust. He rubbed his nose on his sleeve, breathed in his own odor, and felt a little better. This was what life should smell like: sweat, horses, leather, iron, and dirt.

"He's been near the end for some weeks," Dale replied, distressed. He seemed more upset by his friend's illness than Odon. "He can't even get up to pass water. He doesn't eat much either. It's all over for your father. I'll call for the priest so that he can receive the last rites." The knight went over to the sick man, took his hand, and held it tightly.

Sir Rotrou's eyelids fluttered and opened. He tried to say something but failed.

"Your father knows he will die soon. That's why he wanted me to fetch you. He has some instructions to give you before he commends his soul to the Lord."

Instructions? Pah! As soon as the old man was dead, Odon would do what he thought best. He needed no instructions. He looked defiantly at his father, who was breathing stertorously. His gray cheeks had sunken, and his dull eyes had disappeared into their deep and shadowy sockets. His pale, cracked lips were moving feebly. Was he trying to say something, or was he just groaning? Odon wondered dispassionately why the old man didn't simply give up. Why in God's name did he torment himself by clinging to his piteous life?

"My son," the dying man croaked.

"Father." Odon made a slight bow and with some effort forced a smile. He would have preferred to run away that very moment, out into the woods, where the air was clear and pure instead of stinking of death and suffering.

"Come a little closer," his father ordered, and Odon obeyed, albeit reluctantly. "De Tracey, stay close to de Tracey. He has a daughter, Maud. The child is an excellent match—she will get lands, the ones bordering on ours. The marriage is as good as agreed, as soon as the girl is old enough." He broke off, coughing uncontrollably.

At last, some good news, thought Odon, nodding obediently. He still could not bring himself to hold his father's hand. "You should rest a little," he said at last. It would probably be a while before the pretty maid would have his bath ready, but Odon was suddenly in a hurry to leave the room.

"I'll have time enough to rest soon," Sir Rotrou wheezed, grabbing Odon's tunic. "Listen to me, while I can still speak." The old man kept pausing for breath, but he did not let go of Odon's clothes. "When you are the lord, you must keep a firm grip and have eyes everywhere. Be just, but never show weakness." After he had told his son in no uncertain terms whom he could trust and whom he should beware, he released him and went limp.

Like letting the air out of an inflated pig's bladder, thought Odon contemptuously. He stood up and left the exhausted old man alone in his gloomy chamber.

In the kitchen he gave orders for bread and cheese and cold meats to be cut and brought to him, accompanied by a jug of ale, so that he could refresh himself during his bath. Then he ordered all the other maids to leave: only the young one was to stay with him.

A little later, when Odon was standing naked in the half-filled tub, he thought he caught a relieved, even mocking smile on the girl's face. With a nasty look in his eye, he slid into the water and ordered her to come near.

Once she was standing in front of him, he grabbed her neck, pulled her to him, and pressed a kiss on her lips. She should know right away whom she was dealing with. She would soon forget that smile.

First he ordered her to scrub his back and feet with a brush. When they were hot and red, he got out of the tub, dried himself, and told her to lift up her skirt and lean over the table. It was his right to take her. When she went back to the hall, everyone would know what had happened. Her expression would give it away. Perhaps he would single her out more often in the coming days so that she would find herself expecting his bastard.

Odon closed his eyes, relishing the wonderful sensation of power. As soon as his father was dead, it would accompany him at all times, for then he would be lord of Elmswick.

To Odon's dismay, his father survived nearly two more weeks. On the day of his death, he even seemed to revive a little. Odon was frustrated. All he could do was sit around waiting, condemned to inactivity, hoping his father would at last be called to his maker. One day it finally happened.

The old man felt that the end was near, so he gathered every-one around him, divided up his possessions, and died. That he left some gold coins and one of his best swords to the faithful Dale enraged Odon, as did the generous gifts he doled out to the other members of the household. Why the old man's fur-lined coat should go to the dim-witted steward, of all people, was a mystery to Odon. He would be sent packing first. But he had to carry out the dying man's wishes. Everyone had heard his last will, so not even the new lord could ignore it.

As soon as the old man had breathed his last, Odon hurried to the cellar and checked the provisions, silverware, and weapons. Then he had his horse saddled and ordered the steward to show him all his lands.

"Shouldn't you first bury your father and mourn him properly?" the man asked, looking at Odon like a mannerless oaf.

"So that the peasants can cheat me from the very first day?" roared Odon.

"Forgive me, my lord," the steward replied sheepishly. He bowed and accompanied his new master without another word of disapproval.

Oakham, September 1192

William had been head falconer at Oakham for more than a year. It had not been easy to establish himself, even though he had Robert's full support. The older assistants, in particular, refused to accept any instructions from the "youngster," as they called him behind his back, and flouted his orders, thinking they would soon be rid of him. They knew he would not go to Lord Oakham to complain, since that would be an admission that he was not master of his mews. But they were mistaken in their belief that they could simply wear him down.

William and Robert worked like men possessed, carried out the assistants' duties as well as their own, paying only half their wages in return, and trained de Ferrers's falcons as if there were no problems in the mews. Although they were on their feet from early in the morning until late at night, hardly sleeping at all, they never complained. William gave every order only once. If it was not followed, he did the work himself. In this way he demonstrated to the assistants that he could manage without them. When at last he threw out the laziest of them, without making much of a fuss about it, and replaced him with an inexperienced but hardworking lad, the others considered their position. From then on, they carried out their duties without complaint.

Melva, who took care of the mews when the falconers were traveling, looked after David as promised. She soon took a shine to him, thanks to his childlike spirit, and David felt as happy at Oakham as if he had never lived anywhere else. He roamed about with the children and did small jobs for Melva. Most of all, though, he did justice to her cooking.

One morning, Walkelin de Ferrers and his son Henry finally returned after their long absence in the East. Dusty and exhausted from their journey, their clothes ragged and filthy, they rode into the courtyard without prior warning.

News of their arrival spread like wildfire, and soon every member of the family and all the servants had come running.

Sir Walkelin was an imposing man. His small gray eyes gazed out steadily from among many folds. The long scar on his left cheek gave him a certain roughness, in contrast to his otherwise rather dignified appearance, which was heightened by the silver streaks in his dark hair and the embroidered linen robe he wore for the occasion. Sun, wind, and privation had etched deep furrows across his face and neck. One could see from Henry, who took after his father, how good-looking he must have been in his youth. Hugh and Isabella, Henry's siblings, more closely resembled their late mother.

In both castle and village, the people were joyfully tumultuous thanks to the safe return of father and son and the men in their retinue. It was late summer, but it felt as if spring had arrived again for everyone. The girls made eyes at the best-looking young men even more than usual, laughed even more charmingly, and blushed even more quickly, as if gladness had warmed not only their cheeks but also their hearts.

William and Robert were running across the field back to the mews.

"The head groom's daughter is making eyes at me," cried William happily, leaping over a molehill.

"She does it to everyone," laughed Robert, dropping down onto the grass.

William sat beside him. Robert, saying nothing, chewed on a dry stalk of grass, and William lay on his back and stared into the sky. The clouds rushed across it like a flock of fat, woolly sheep. They were becoming visibly thicker and darker. Suddenly, a strong wind blew up.

"We should go back. There's going to be a storm soon," Robert said as he stood and helped up William.

Instead of pulling himself up, William pulled Robert down. Laughing, they rolled across the field, wrestling as they used to when they were boys. Eventually, Robert was straddling William and holding his arms down so that he was almost defenseless. William squirmed and begged dramatically for mercy.

Robert's laughter died. He blushed deeply and jumped up as if he had been sitting on burning coals. "Can we go now?" he muttered, his eyes glued to the ground. He clapped the dust from his clothes and loped off.

William ran after him. What could have made his friend so angry?

The wind blew through his hair, making him shiver. William looked up. There was an unpleasant yellow tone to the dark, menacing gray of the sky.

"Wait, Robert, we won't get back early enough. What about that hut over there?" he suggested amid the tumult of the rising wind. Robert paid him no mind. By the time William caught up with him, the first fat raindrops were falling. The rumbling of the thunderstorm was approaching faster and faster.

"It used to be a charcoal-burner's hut," said Robert, who knew the area very well. "It's been empty for ages."

"Let's seek shelter there." William overtook him and reached the hut first. He was about to open the door when he heard the high peal of a woman's laughter.

"Let's go there instead," he murmured to Robert, grinning suggestively, and pointed at a woodshed that had been built against the hut's wall. They opened the rotting door carefully and crept inside.

The roof had a leak, and a thin layer of straw covered the floor. Using their feet, they pushed the straw into two little heaps where the roof seemed sound and silently settled in to wait out the storm. Whenever the wind let up a little, they could hear murmurs and giggles coming from the hut.

Robert's eyes narrowed. He stood up, pressed his face to the silvery-gray planks, and peered through a gap in the wall. When he did not move for a while, William became curious, too, and crouched down beside him. The rain was falling harder. Water began to drip through the wood, and a puddle formed under the hole in the roof. William hesitated for a moment, then found a narrow crack in the wooden wall and peered through it himself.

There was a small wooden tub in the middle of the hut, and in it, naked as the day she was born, stood a young woman. A man, also naked, was approaching her. His skin was dark, his muscular shoulders broad, his hips narrow, and his buttocks unusually rounded. William had never seen a body like it. It must be the Saracen, one of the infidels who had invaded the Holy Land. Melva had told them about him. Apparently Sir Walkelin had vanquished him in battle and spared his life. Shaking her head with indignation, Melva had made clear to them that he was treated not like a slave but like a guest.

William shared her outrage; he had heard too much about the vileness of the unbelievers, and what he was seeing now confirmed it. He would rush to the girl's aid immediately. He pressed his eye to the chink in the wall again. But when the girl turned around, he saw that her face showed no fear, only desire.

The Saracen gently washed her naked body with a wet linen cloth, dipping it into the bathtub and letting the water run over her back, her breasts, and her light, downy sex. A heady fragrance of flowers drifted through the crack in the wall, mingling with the scent of rain-soaked earth.

The girl giggled with embarrassment. But the longer the foreigner spent cleaning off the dirt that resulted from her lowly work—his movements gentle, almost reverent—the more relaxed she became. She began to squirm in response to his touch, leaning against him and closing her eyes with pleasure. Tenderly, the dark-skinned man stroked her pale-blonde hair away from her face and kissed her eyelids.

William's heart was hammering like mad. Robert was also fascinated by the sight. They remained motionless and just continued to stare.

The girl was well nourished, with generous breasts and magnificent broad haunches. As if she were as light as a feather, the Saracen lifted her out of the bathtub and carried her to a mattress covered with a clean cloth. The girl's pale skin looked like marble next to the man's oaken hue. He took a small bottle and poured glistening golden oil into his right hand. He spread the liquid between both his hands and then rubbed it into her naked body. Under the Saracen's gentle caresses, a simple young girl turned into a desirable woman. She glowed with passion as he stroked every inch of her body, writhing sensuously beneath his hands.

Through the cracks in the wall, a heavy, unbelievably arousing fragrance wafted toward them. William inhaled it deeply, closing his eyes appreciatively, and felt an agreeable tugging sensation between his legs. A wave of warmth flooded through him, burning throughout his body like a long-forgotten, pleasurable pain, leaving in its wake a yearning for physical relief.

With Enid he had been wild and frenzied. What he was seeing here, by contrast, was so full of tenderness and reverence that it moved him to the bottom of his soul. The Saracen's caresses spoke of respect for and homage to not only this woman but all women. Spellbound, William watched the Saracen lie down on top of the girl, embrace her, and then enter her, slowly and cautiously. His movements were gentle and filled with devotion, though he did not lack passion. This was not a struggle for power, such as William had seen elsewhere, but seemingly an almost sacred union of two people.

William turned away, unable to breathe. The Saracen and the girl could not have known each other for even a day. Yet they behaved as though they trusted each other completely. Like lovers. Like Adam and Eve before the Fall, thought William, suddenly ashamed that he had intruded on their intimacy. Nobody had the right to watch lovers in secret. He stood up, sat down in a different corner, pulled his knees up to his chin, and closed his eyes, but he was too shaken to drive away those inflaming images. They were etched in his memory. He heard Robert stand up, too, then sit on the ground with his back to him. He was breathing heavily. The sight of the naked girl and the physical act of love must have aroused him, too.

For the first time, William realized that they had never spoken about Robert's love life. Not even when William told him about his life with Enid and her grisly death.

A brilliant light illuminated the shed, followed by a deafening clap of thunder. A voluptuous moan filled the silence that followed.

William jumped up, rushed to the door, and flung it open. He couldn't stay there another moment.

"Looks as if the rain has slowed down," he whispered, looking out wildly. "Shall we go?"

Robert nodded vigorously, confusion and excitement written across his face as well.

In silence, and without looking at each other, they ran back to Oakham through the weakening rain.

That evening, William and Robert ate in Sir Walkelin's hall alongside his guests—neighbors and friends who wanted to welcome the de Ferrerses—for as falconers they were entitled to a place at the lord's table. When the Saracen took his seat on the bench opposite William, he was embarrassed and could not bring him-self to make eye contact. He only dared to watch the foreigner out of the corner of his eye, and he was surprised to observe the friendly courtesy he showed not only to the nobles but also to the maids, servants, and pages. When the maid who had submitted to him that afternoon placed a large piece of meat and a slice of bread before him, he showed no sign of knowing her. Most men would have slapped her on the buttocks, like a horse, and made a ribald remark. But he nodded to her with faultless politeness and thanked her as if she were a lady, smiling agreeably and revealing white teeth that sparkled like mother-of-pearl.

William was speechless. Had everything he'd heard about Saracens been lies? The dark-skinned man turned to him and introduced himself as Abdul Mustafa Eftaha Mohamedi, from Persia. In slightly halting language, but with carefully chosen words, he asked about William's and Robert's duties. He was delighted to hear that they were both falconers, and he questioned them more, explaining that his former master, a Persian prince, had been a keen falconer, too.

At first, William spoke only hesitantly and quietly. The images from the afternoon were still too fresh in his mind, and he felt as if he was blushing with shame the whole time. He was astonished to see Robert's animation and receptiveness when conversing with the man. He laughed more than usual and listened to the exotic-sounding words with shining eyes. Robert, normally so reserved, was openly delighted by the foreigner's colorful way of telling sto-ries and his modest, cultivated manner.

The Saracen lavishly praised the beauty of de Ferrers's newly built hall, though it was clear from his tales of Persia that his master must have lived in a much more magnificent palace. In the East, William learned, the walls of the rich were decorated with gold and enamel rather than the lime wash and paintings of wealthy Englishmen. The Saracen described his homeland in a way that made it seem comparable in beauty to paradise; he spoke of incredible riches, a wealth of fruits and spices, fabrics laced with gold, the finest medical care, great inventions, and famous thinkers. And yet the foreigner seemed completely comfortable in his new, much colder home. He radiated happiness and contentment, as well as gratitude and common sense.

In no time at all, everyone around him was listening to his words, taking pleasure in his exemplary manners, and admiring the way he spoke of the deeds of Jesus Christ, his new master, to whom he had turned when a crusader had spared his life. William had never heard tales about the Son of God embellished with such inspiration and love, not even in church. Deeply moved by this fascinating personality, not to mention what they had witnessed that afternoon, William and Robert went back to the mews after their meal.

"Isn't he an extraordinary man?" Robert gushed. "He knows so much, and when he tells a story it's as if you're there."

"Hmm," replied William absently. In passing, the Saracen had mentioned that in the East, people put leather hoods on falcons to deprive them of their sight while they were being manned. William had sensed that the foreigner, too, found the practice of seeling barbaric, though he had not gone into the matter in any depth.

"Oh, William," cried Robert, punching him on the arm. "You must admit he's—"

"I'm going to ask if we can invite him to the mews," William broke in pensively.

"I thought you couldn't stand the man. You hardly said a word at the table."

"There are a couple of things I'd like to ask him."

"Don't keep me on the rack, William," Robert replied impatiently. "What do you want to ask him?"

"I can't get the hood out of my head."

"The hood?"

"Didn't you hear what he said? In the Orient they use hoods for falcons. I want to know how it's done and what a hood looks like."

৩⊙ও

On the day they expected the Saracen in the mews, Robert was very excited indeed. He scurried back and forth, straightened his clothes, ran his hands through his hair constantly, chattered unceasingly, and, finally, without saying a word to William, disappeared into the forest so as not to encounter the man.

He could not get the images from the charcoal-burner's hut out of his head. The black man's powerful thighs and his well-rounded buttocks had had more effect on Robert than the girl's pale and low-slung bottom. The play of muscles beneath the dark, glistening skin had got Robert's blood up and aroused him in ways that were forbidden and frightening. Why was it not the breasts and sex of a woman that brought lustful thoughts into his head, but the muscular chest and potent member of the Saracen? The priest had once spoken of such aberrations at Sunday mass, declaring them "against nature" and condemning them in the strongest terms. Robert knew that the Lord damned those who opened the door to such thoughts, punishing them with exclusion from paradise and letting them burn in hell.

The night after the thunderstorm, he had dreamed about William. He was naked beside him, and they were touching each other. Aroused and deeply ashamed, Robert had woken up in terror. For fear that William would notice, he had run outside to cool himself off with ice-cold water from the spring. It was the Saracen's fault; it was the sight of him that had inflamed Robert, opening a door inside him that now he could not shut. He found himself imagining things he would never have thought himself capable of; provocative, deeply shameful images flashed through his head. The Saracen was desirable, but William was so much more than that. He couldn't even wrestle with him without getting excited. Never again would he touch him except when their work demanded it.

Robert covered his face with his hands. He was a disgusting monster, and he deserved to burn in hell until the end of time. In fact, the Saracen was probably the devil's messenger. Robert ran through the forest, bewailing his terrible fate, praying and begging for forgiveness. He swore not to bring down guilt upon himself but knew he wouldn't succeed. The flame sparked within him by the sight of the Saracen was still glowing. Robert forced himself not to stoke it further with thoughts of William. He knew he was born to suffer all his life, and beyond it in death, and felt eternal shame for it.

He did not go back to the mews until after dark.

"Where have you been?" William snapped. "I thought you wanted to hear what the Saracen had to say about hoods."

Robert did not answer.

"What's the matter, Robert?"

"I'm damned," murmured Robert as he got into his bed and rolled up in his blanket.

Butterflies in his stomach and a feeling of weakness were now his constant companions, becoming almost unbearable whenever he caught William's eye, touched his hand by chance, or stood too close to him while they were working. He got a lump in his throat, and he struggled to breathe.

And yet he managed to hide his feelings for William, even though at night, in his dreams, he would throw himself at his friend's feet and declare his love.

November 1192

For the last few weeks, Odon had been going to the whore-house on Rose Lane almost every day. Since his father's death, he had enough money for such amusements.

He had been with Carla for the first time in August. Unlike the other whores, she never said a word about the pitiful dimensions of his manhood. She hadn't even smiled at it. Instead of mocking him, she proved her desire for him every time he visited her, and her passion helped him rise above his own inadequacies. She writhed beneath his hands, moaning with pleasure when he entered her as no other woman ever had. Since that first day, he had found himself unable to do without her lustful embrace and gentle touch. He was attracted to her as if she were a real lover, rather than one that could be bought.

If he could not go to her immediately, that familiar helpless rage would rise up in him, but it would last only as long as it took for Carla's door to close behind him. As soon as they were alone together, she would throw her arms around his neck and seduce him with her desire, leaving no room for doubt about his skill as a lover. She filled him with such pride that he felt he would never again be able to do without her love.

It was Odon's third visit that week, but he could hardly wait to have Carla in his arms. She made him happy. For some time he had been bringing her little gifts: a flower, a pomegranate, a colorful ribbon for her fine hair, a small piece of soap. She received these things with childlike joy, placing an affectionate, almost chaste, kiss on his cheek. Lying with Carla was different. It was playful, tender, and unusually affectionate compared to Odon's previous conquests. With her he didn't need to prove himself. And yet he tried. He wanted her to enjoy the act of love with him. He knew how much she liked it when he stroked the small of her back or gently caressed her breasts and teased her nipples with his lips before he entered her. Since his second visit, he had paid for a whole night whenever he came to see her. Sometimes he brought meat and wine, and they would sit at the tiny table in her room, eating, drinking, and laughing like old friends. Tenderly, he would caress the back of her knee or the hollow of her throat and gently bite her neck until she shivered. He loved feeling Carla's aroused response to the things he did. He needed her, and he wanted her to feel the same for him.

Only once had he been with one of the other whores. He had been angry because Carla had not immediately taken him to her room. But rather than paying back Carla, he had only punished himself. He had gone to the other whore without tenderness of any kind and forced his own rhythm on her while she lay indifferently under him, staring up at the ceiling in boredom. It had felt bad and false, as it had before he knew Carla. It had pained him to get up from an indifferent whore when he could have found relief with Carla and let her go, rosy cheeked and fired with lust, after a final intimate embrace. After his night with the other whore, he rode home bad tempered and resentful and vowed never to go to Rose Lane again. But the very next evening he sunk into Carla's arms and enjoyed her tenderness all the more. Hearing her pleasurable whimpering, he knew he was not just any old customer, but her true lover.

Now, nearing the whorehouse, Odon walked faster. He was greeted like a friend when he entered. The servant gave a two-fingered whistle, summoning the whores who were not at that moment servicing customers. Odon frowned. It was no secret that he had not gone with anyone but Carla for a long time. Normally, therefore, he was simply invited in and shown through. As the girls came out of their rooms, the owner took Odon's arm and led him aside.

"You're a bit early today. Carla's still with a customer," she explained, smiling ingratiatingly. "If you don't want to wait, choose another girl. I'm sure a bit of a change will do you good."

A mighty roaring sound filled Odon's head, so loud that he pressed both hands to his temples. Now, at this very moment, another man was with Carla, sweating, snorting, lusting. With a bigger member, perhaps. In fact, certainly. The idea was unbearable. Odon had to go to Carla and throw out her customer. He stormed past the bewildered-looking servant like an enraged boar. But the door opened just before he reached Carla's room, and a man came out, adjusting his clothing and wiping his ragged beard. Carla appeared behind him, her hair disheveled and her cheeks lightly flushed.

Had the stranger made her whimper, or had she just tolerated him? Furious with jealousy, Odon thrust the man aside and pushed Carla back into the room. He closed the door behind him with a mighty kick. He took Carla in his arms, pulled her close to him, and buried his face in her neck in search of her scent. He breathed in deeply. The smell of strange sweat caught in his throat. She smelled of the other man. Odon could hardly breathe. Carla belonged to him and him alone. No one else should possess her, only him!

"You're trembling," she said anxiously, feeling his forehead to see if he was feverish. "You're not getting ill, are you?"

"I can't bear it. I won't let these fellows touch you anymore. You belong to me," he spluttered.

"The old woman doesn't see it that way. More and more customers are asking for me. I'm making her rich, thanks to you, too, my sweetheart," said Carla teasingly, turning away abruptly.

The agony of jealousy was almost enough to drive Odon mad.

"She'd never let me go," continued Carla over her shoulder, even though Odon had not said a word about taking her away with him. "Not even you can do anything about it."

"Oh yes, I can," he retorted.

"What do you mean?" She turned to face him. A spark of hope seemed to glint in her eyes.

"I'm going to take you away from here."

"Surely you don't think the old woman will let me go, just like that?" Carla burst out laughing.

"What do you take me for?" Odon shouted. "Do you think I'm going to let some old innkeeper woman tell me what to do?"

Carla shrugged and shook her head in silence. Odon did not see the tiny smile that flickered across her face.

He pulled her to him. "You won't have to sell yourself anymore. I'll take care of you from now on."

February 1193

William awoke, terrified and confused. Trembling, he stayed in his bed and looked into the darkness. His heart raced, his ears roared like a mountain stream, and his hands were moist with perspiration.

Frozen with fear, he listened to the night's blackness, probing with all of his senses the grave-like silence that surrounded him. He thought he could smell the damp earth into which he had laid to rest his beloved, and he feared he would be overwhelmed by this ever-tightening crushing sensation.

"Enid, my poor Enid," he whispered. "It must be so cold in your grave."

Sometimes he would go for weeks without dreaming about her, and then it would be every night. The dreadful images appeared so clearly before his eyes, it was as if they were branded on his soul. Would he ever be rid of them, or would he have to suffer them forever?

William threw back his blanket and got up. With trembling fingers, he combed back his hair, which was hanging down in damp strands before his face. A feeble ray of moonlight penetrated the wooden shutter, reminding him where he was.

Cautiously feeling his way, he worked his way over to the shutter and opened it far enough to let in some of the pale light from the narrow crescent illuminating the night. The clear, cold air smelled of imminent snow. His breath swirled in small clouds. Soon he was so cold he could not feel his feet, but the cold did not begin to bother him until goose bumps covered his whole body.

"I'll avenge you," he whispered. His voice was raw and shaky, but he was determined to find Enid's murderer and punish him. The thought of revenge had always been with him, even though his days were quite full enough from his work in the mews.

He carried the little plaque with him at all times, and he showed it to every stranger he met. In this way, perhaps, he could find out whose it was, and then he would be able to pursue the monsters who had ravaged Enid. But so far he still had no answers.

He crept back to his bed and covered himself. He thought about Saint Edmundsbury. He had been wanting to visit for some time, and he decided to do so as soon as he could. It took a while for the woolen blanket to warm his frozen bones.

Robert woke him roughly the following morning. "Wake up, lazybones! Old de Ferrers has sent a messenger to tell us to get the falcons ready for a long journey."

"Where to?" asked William as he dressed.

"No idea. All I know is that we're leaving the day after tomorrow."

William looked at him in surprise, muttered something under his breath, and pulled on his boots.

Starting a journey in an icy wind with driving flecks of snow was not ideal, and William had tried in vain to persuade his master to wait a day or two for better weather. When he had taken his leave of David, the boy had looked at him as if he was being abandoned. Despite William's insistence that he would soon be back, David had howled. Now, William was riding silently beside Robert, wrapped up in a fur-lined wool cloak and feeling guilty.

They made slow progress, not least because of the falcons, which were stowed beneath their cloaks for protection. But the worst affliction was the cold. It burned on their skin and crept mercilessly into their joints. Neither the thought of a warm fire and something hot to eat nor the steaming mulled wine they made and gulped down eagerly during their stops lessened the cold. The day seemed to stretch before them endlessly, and the bleak winter landscape offered little in the way of distraction. There were hardly any animals to watch, apart from a few birds and squirrels. Most creatures had burrowed underground, occasionally emerging from their hiding places in search of food.

On their first night on the road, which they had since learned was to take them southwest, to the county of Devon, the men had set up camp in a sparse alder forest and built a roaring fire at de Ferrers's command.

William had put the falcons on a branch not far from the fire, and now he distanced himself from the others in order to relieve himself. He left the forest road and followed a narrow path that led up a low hill. William knew the tracks of all animals, and he did not need to look closely at the prints in the frozen earth to know which ones had walked this path before him. He had also noticed the scratches on the alder trunks right away, an unmistakable sign that badgers lived nearby. William knew that they liked to use the barks of trees to sharpen their claws and clean off crusted dirt. William stood still and passed his water. He had often observed badgers with Enid, so he knew that a black-and-white-striped head would peep out from one of these burrows before long, and that a broad gray back with short, powerful legs and feet with long, strong claws would follow. Immobile, William waited for the first badger to appear.

Judging by its size, it was a full-grown male. Snuffling busily, he hurried through the tufts of sparse yellow winter grass, sniffing here and there. He suddenly dove into one of the many holes spread out over the hillside, only to reappear from another. Soon another badger appeared from one of the holes, snuffling curiously. It sped off but soon returned, dragging a woolly object for its sleeping place. William could tell from the swollen belly of the slightly smaller creature that it was a female heavy with two or three young.

A simple badger had such a good life, William thought fondly. He had a wife, his own home, and soon children, too.

"A man without sons is to be pitied with all one's heart," Jean used to say.

"I shall have sons," cried William defiantly into the gathering darkness before tramping back to the others.

The wind had died down, but nightfall made the cold even more biting. They had blankets for all, but even those who had secured themselves a place by the fire did not sleep well.

They got up the next morning and continued on their way, stiff in their joints, tired, frozen through, and peevish.

How must soldiers feel when their masters ordered them into the field in weather like this, wondered William, shivering. When it was bitterly cold, did they go to their deaths with greater indifference? Did they fight in order not to freeze, or in order to go home sooner?

Every mile they put behind them felt like ten to William. At the same time, though, the closer they came to the southwest, the more tolerable the weather became. The cold let up, and it stayed dry. On the last day of their journey, the sun even appeared. It did not really warm them yet, but it gave hope for the approaching spring.

Soon, the first tender violet blossoms were nodding to them from the side of the road. They seemed to compete for the strange travelers' favor with the sunny yellow of early blooming coltsfoot.

After a long ride across the lonely north of Devon, they at last reached Barnstaple. The cruciform shell of the castle keep sat mighty and proud on its position high above the town. The most important castle in north Devon was the property of Henry de

Tracey, who owned extensive and fertile lands and was one of the most powerful barons in the southwest of England.

"How wonderful that you have done me this honor, old friend." De Tracey greeted William's master with a friendly smile. He waited until Sir Walkelin had dismounted before embracing him.

A young girl stood beside their host. Judging by her fine clothes, William guessed she was de Tracey's daughter. She had twisted her abundant nut-colored hair into a single heavy plait that reached all the way to her narrow hips. Her soft, smooth skin was of a highborn pallor; her nose was dainty and turned slightly upward toward the heavens. But it was her incredible sea-blue eyes that most impressed William. He stared at the girl as if struck by lightning. He could hardly breathe, his chest had become so tight. His heart began to pound as if he had been sprinting, and his hands were moist and cold. When the girl smiled at him, he felt like the happiest man alive. At a stroke, he was so sick with love that he could not swallow a single morsel at the banquet de Tracey held in honor of his guests.

Angels' laughter, William thought, could not be more beautiful than that of this young girl. He found out that her name was Maud; he savored the name like a sweet fruit, tasting it slowly on his tongue. Pages and squires constantly surrounded her, buzzing around like bees on a flower, taking care of her every need. Several knights, both young and old, knelt at her feet. Anyone who had experienced anything told tales of his heroic deeds, making sure to trump all previous speakers with colorful words about his own daring. De Tracey clearly disliked the free and easy way the men courted Maud's favor, so after the meal he sent his daughter to her room. Once she had stepped haughtily out of the hall to sulk, a measure of peace was restored. Robert and William left the falcons in the hall, as their master had ordered, and made their way to the quarters that had been assigned to them.

"Her eyes shine like stars," said William passionately, pointing upward. "And when she smiles, it warms my heart, as if it were already spring."

"I really don't know what you see in her," Robert sighed. "How can you be so blind? Can't you see what a conceited goose she is? She's leading you all by the nose."

"Oh, you're just jealous!"

Robert blushed and flung open the door to the servants' quarters. "Jealous? Nonsense. What of?"

"Maybe it's that she hasn't cast an eye on *you*," he replied spitefully, then immediately wished he had bitten his tongue. Robert was certainly embarrassed enough without his tactless remark, for Maud had not even looked at him. "I'm sorry," William murmured, ashamed. He turned away and pretended to be busy locking the door.

"You've nothing to be sorry about, William. She means nothing to me. But *you* do. When I see you becoming obsessed with something hopeless…"

"There's true friendship," William said, directing an angry frown toward Robert. "Point out to me that I'm a worthless pauper and that a girl like Maud is unattainable. As if I didn't know that myself!"

William moved through the cramped and cluttered room, dropped onto his bed, looked for his bundle, and took off his right shoe. Earlier, he had landed on a sharp stone when dismounting his horse. His foot was still in pain. Carefully, he started unwinding the bandage he had been wearing since the beginning of the journey. In winter, when it was very cold, the cracked skin on his foot was often so sensitive that the slightest scratch would bleed. He had learned to manage well with his twisted foot, and he scarcely hobbled at all anymore, but it was still a nuisance. Once he had unwound two of the bandages, William could see that the remaining layers were stuck together with dried blood. Although he tried to remove the bandage with care, part of the wound came open again with a sharp pain. William gritted his teeth and rummaged among his things for the pot of vegetable fat.

"Here it is," cried Robert with exaggerated cheerfulness, catching the little clay pot before it could roll off William's bed. "Is it really painful?" he asked, trying to make peace. He opened the pot and held it out so William could use the ointment.

"It burns," William replied, spreading a hazelnut-size ball onto the injury. He did not feel ashamed in front of Robert, though he did in front of the other boys and men, who would always make fun of his foot. He'd endured so much crassness, so many stupid jokes, and he had no desire to have to assert himself in this new group, too.

Robert knew very well what he was thinking, and he moved aside a little so that the others would not be able to see William's foot.

William knew this was Robert's way of apologizing, and he smiled at him gratefully as he massaged his foot.

"My master's going to marry her in the spring," they heard one of the younger squires boasting. "And then I'll see her every day!"

"And while you're pining, your master will be the buck that mounts her," one of the other squires roared gleefully, slapping his thigh with hilarity.

Robert and William just looked at one another. What a disagreeable fellow. Couldn't he just leave the boy alone? Both of them smiled. As so often was the case, they did not need words to know that they were of one mind.

William did not dream about Enid that night, but about Maud, whose glowing silk-soft skin was driving him wild. He woke up in the morning not only in turmoil but also feeling guilty. Torn this way and that, he tried to convince himself that he couldn't mourn Enid forever. After all, he was young and had his whole life in front of him. Nevertheless, he felt like a miserable traitor.

A little later, as he wandered through the castle like an infatuated tomcat in the hope of meeting the pretty Maud, he saw a large group of riders arriving. Although he had not seen him for an eternity, William recognized one of them immediately. Odon! Just the way he sat on his horse—as if he was superior to all others—was unmistakable. Cruelly and unexpectedly, the smell of the dungeon came back to William. Mad Leonard rattling his chains and his own feeling of hopelessness: they were suddenly as real to him again as if he were still sitting in the cell at Thorne. William could feel the sickness rising. He closed his eyes and took two deep breaths.

"You've done nothing wrong; he can't do you any harm anymore," he told himself quietly, trying to bolster his courage. He turned on his heel and hurriedly limped back to the servants' quarters, where he found Robert.

"I was just looking for you," said Robert happily. "We're to get ready to go hawking."

William made no reply.

"Goodness, you look terrible, as if you'd run into the devil incarnate."

William remained silent.

"Will, what's the matter?"

"Odon's here," William whispered hoarsely.

Robert scratched his head. "It might be best to tell old de Ferrers that you had some trouble with him, before Odon does."

"No. He won't go to de Ferrers. And neither will I."

"As you wish." Robert shrugged.

"I've done nothing to be ashamed of, so I won't run away from him anymore."

William limped away; his foot was still hellishly painful.

When they got back to the castle after the hunt, the banquet table had been set. The cooks would have to pluck and draw whatever the falcons had caught during that day's hunt before preparing it for the next day, or the one after that. As usual, William and Robert sat on one side of the long table with the other falconers.

As was customary, the lord of the castle sat at the center of the other side of the table, with his back to the wall. By his side, where Lady de Tracey would have belonged if she was not dead, sat Sir Walkelin, the guest of honor. He had led an elite troop of soldiers that made a significant contribution to King Richard's victory in the battle of Arsuf. De Ferrers was among the closest confidants of the king, whose return was still awaited.

William frowned, seeing that Odon was allowed to sit next to Maud, who was on her father's other side. What in the world did that lout, of all people, hope to gain? When the meat was carried in, William understood. The young man serving Odon was the one who had bragged that his master was going to marry de Tracey's daughter.

The idea that Odon would have this enchanting creature as his wife caused a burning pain in William's stomach. His thoughts black as crows, he kept looking over at her. When Maud started making eyes at Odon, William tore off a piece of the fine bread before him, kneaded it into a ball, and took a grim bite. Didn't Odon have anything better to do than kiss Maud's hand? He was holding it to his mouth and nibbling on it like a chicken leg.

Nothing and nobody could distract William from the two of them—not the loud laughter and conversations around him, not even the music of the minstrels hired by de Tracey. William just kept watching Odon and Maud, though he could hardly bear to see them so close to each other. Her laughter cut him to the quick. William's throat felt rough and dry. Odon kissed Maud's hand as naturally as if he had done it all his life; he whispered sweet nothings in her ear and put his arm around her waist in a familiar manner. When she blushed, threw her head back, and laughed throatily, her eyes sparkling with seductive charm, William could no longer stand it and rushed out of the noisy hall.

Outside, it was quieter, though a few servants and maids were sitting around the fire and feasting, too. The cool night air tempered William's overheated mind. He paced restlessly.

"What's the matter now?" he heard Robert ask suddenly. He had noticed his friend's agitation and followed him outside.

"Did you see how shamelessly she was making eyes at that scoundrel?" said William, enraged. He kicked a stone and sent it flying across the courtyard.

"Well, Will, it looks as if she's going to marry him."

"Why must it be Odon, of all people?"

"Forget her, Will. She's not for you."

"I can't. You don't know what it's like when your heart tells you to love someone you'll never have. How could you understand my suffering?"

Robert swallowed hard and said nothing.

"I can't sit there and watch any longer. I'm going to bed," William growled.

"Nonsense. You're going to pull yourself together and come back inside with me," Robert said, taking his arm and pulling him back into the hall.

The meal had finished, and pipers and drummers were striking up the dance. The guests, especially those who had drunk their fill of de Tracey's fine wines, were enjoying themselves tremendously. William saw that Odon and Maud were no longer sitting at their places, and he was taken by surprise when he heard Odon's menacing voice.

"What are you doing here, William? I didn't think you'd dare show yourself in front of me ever again." Odon glared angrily. "You're lucky my aunt decided to drop that matter with you and the priest. If it had been up to me…" Odon drew his thumb across his throat.

William was innocent, and yet he was supposed to feel grateful that the lady of Thorne was no longer pursuing him. Nothing William had seen, not even the fact that Odon was guilty, counted in front of any judge in the world, not against the word of Lord Elmswick. It had not escaped William's attention that Odon had inherited his father's title.

"Aren't you de Ferrers's falconer?" said Maud, joining the conversation with an alluring smile. She seemed displeased neither of the young men was paying her any attention.

"Yes, mistress." William bowed. She knew who he was! His body filled with warmth and happiness, as if the girl had set light to his heart. He felt his ears burning and worried that he would turn bright red.

"De Ferrers's falconer?" Odon roared in disbelief. "Too great an honor for someone like you, even if you are a knight's bastard."

"Shall we call him Falconarius the Cripple?" She trilled with laughter. "One of our stable boys limps, too. A warhorse crushed his foot when he was little. Do you think we should have made him a falconer?" she asked Odon in mock innocence and then snorted.

Only a short while before, William had thought her laughter was like an angel's. Now, though, he found it cruel and condescending.

Odon obviously found her contempt amusing, and he looked triumphantly at William. "My dear Maud, aren't you being a bit unkind? Can't you see how he's pining for you, the poor thing? It breaks his heart that I'm going to get you and not him." Odon roared with laughter.

"Well, he'll soon find a girl he can marry. For someone like him, a wife doesn't need to be of as high a station as I am, or as beautiful and clever. In his hut at night, he can't see who he's mounting anyway."

However uncommon her beauty, her soul was obviously common enough. William turned away in disappointment. The flame in his breast had been abruptly extinguished; it was as if Maud had tipped a bucket of water over it. The look in her sea-blue eyes was so cold and disdainful, and her cruel mockery so humiliating. Her laughter just sounded dirty. There was nothing angelic about her now. How right Robert had been, whereas William had been blinded by love.

Odon and Maud went away, and William stumbled to his place. He sat down beside Robert and put his head in his hands. "I'm tired," he whispered.

"Perhaps you're right. We should go to bed."

In silence, they made their way back to their room.

"She's not worth wasting a single thought," said Robert gently as they lay on their straw mattresses.

"I know," William murmured, and yet the memory of Maud's mockery and disdain kept him awake for a long time that night. He tossed from side to side. Robert was already asleep, and the other men who had been allocated to their room had gone to sleep, too. Maud and Odon deserved each other, thought William bitterly, getting up quietly. He had to get out from this stuffy, overcrowded accommodation. He stepped carefully over Robert and two more snoring men and crept outside.

William shivered in the clear and frosty night. He had not brought his cloak with him. Dressed only in his shirt, he would not be able to stay outdoors for long. He looked searchingly up into the firmament and started. Where he had expected to see twinkling stars, the sky was glowing red. The night was not yet over, and it would not be dawn for a long time yet. It looked almost as if something was on fire in the distance, and yet…William shook his head. The light was very different from anything he had seen in the sky before. It was of such a peculiar, almost godly beauty that he could not take his eyes off it. Even when he heard the cry of the

watchman, who had noticed the glow, he still could not stop looking at it. Soon more men came running up, pointing at the sky.

"It's a sign," one of them shouted. "A sign from God!"

William felt every hair on his body standing on end. What
kind of a sign could it be? Perhaps the bloodred sky presaged some
awful misfortune? William crossed himself, and the other men
did the same. Some even fell to their knees in terror and began to
mutter the Lord's Prayer.

Whatever kind of sign it was, it was far too cold to stand
around any longer. If he did not want to catch his death, he had
to return to his room and warm himself up. After a last look at
the strange light, he went back and folded himself up in his wool
blanket. He closed his eyes, and he could still see the light as if it
shone deep inside him.

The following day, the disturbing glow was on everyone's lips.
The news spread through the castle like wildfire. Those who had
seen it described it to the others in moralizing terms; those who
had missed it kicked themselves. Robert and the other young men
became irritated because William just shrugged when they asked
him why he had not woken them up.

Evil presentiments and gruesome speculations about the mysterious glow circulated, casting a pall over the boisterous mood
that had prevailed before.

Only a few days after the remarkable apparition in the sky, a
messenger dashed into the courtyard and hurried to de Tracey.
Wide-eyed and gasping, he reported that King Richard had been
taken prisoner on his way back from the Holy Land.

A disbelieving murmur ran through those present. A
few crossed themselves in fear; others spoke excitedly among
themselves.

"The glow in the sky," someone cried.

"A sign from the Lord," another wailed.

The messenger could not give any details of Richard's imprisonment, except that Leopold of Austria had captured him and was holding him in one of his castles.

De Tracey gave orders that the messenger be given food and drink and a place to sleep that night, so that he could ride back out at daybreak and further spread the news.

Speculation about what would happen now turned into a heated argument. De Ferrers called for cool heads. To reassure them, he insisted that no one would dare to harm a hair of the English king's head during his imprisonment. They should worry more about Prince John, who was extremely ambitious and had been making every effort to seize the throne during Richard's absence. The lords who had gathered at de Tracey's decided it would be prudent to return to their estates and await whatever might come to pass.

Oakham, October 1193

During the night, their best hunting bitch had been whelping, and now she was in a wooden box filled with straw surrounded by a dozen healthy puppies.

Robert had been sitting with her since late the previous evening, and he was by her side for the dawn birth. He cut the cord for two of the first five puppies, since the bitch had been unable to do it herself, and laid them in front of her so that she could sniff their scent and lick them dry. When there was a pause in the delivery, he felt her belly and could tell that more puppies were waiting to see the light of day. He softly encouraged the exhausted bitch not to give up until the last puppy arrived.

At daybreak, David woke up and went to the kennels. He loved the dogs more than anything else, and he looked in on them every day. He was overjoyed that the puppies had finally been born. He knelt beside the box to look at them, his eyes full of devotion, but did not touch them. Blind as tiny moles, they squirmed about clumsily in search of their mother's teats.

Much moved, Robert looked at them and stroked the bitch's head affectionately. "You did very well. William will be pleased when he gets back from the village." The bitch looked at him trustingly with her round eyes, wagging her tail weakly.

Hounds were important helpers during the hawking session. This was why William insisted that Robert train them himself, a task Robert was all too happy to take on since he still preferred working with dogs over working with falcons. Although he could now claim to be a good falconer, he had not developed a connection like William's, whose understanding of falcons was extraordinary, far beyond that of most people.

Robert sighed at the thought of his friend. His unchaste desire to be physically close to William was flaring up more and more often, causing him much distress. He knew it was a sin and felt genuinely ashamed, and yet he was helpless against it. It was wrong to think of William in this way, and he himself was no better than that miserable worm lurking in the apple offered by the serpent to Eve. Because Robert knew this, he was all the more grateful for his friend, and he wanted to be devoted to him for his whole life.

Hoofbeats in the courtyard roused Robert from his disturbing reverie. He stood up, composed himself, and went outside.

"Sir Odon," he said, bowing humbly upon seeing this unexpected visitor. "What can I do for you?"

"I'm on my way to Sir Walkelin's. My horse stumbled and hurt himself, and I'm thirsty," growled Odon.

The mews was at least a mile away from de Ferrers's hall. Did Odon really have to make a stop here? Concealing his displeasure, Robert went to the spring and fetched a bucket of fresh water. Odon dismounted his horse and approached Robert. He snatched the wooden dipper out of Robert's hand and drank without a word of thanks.

Robert gave the visibly exhausted horse a bucket of water, too, taking the opportunity to check the injured ankle. It was grazed and badly swollen. He tried to comfort the noble beast by stroking its neck. It will need a couple of days' rest and a dressing to recover, he thought, but he did not say anything. Odon surely knew what he was doing. When Odon went to mount the horse again, the exhausted creature drew back.

"Stubborn as a mule, this nag, but I'll cure him of that," roared Odon angrily. It took him two attempts to get back in the saddle. He rode away without saying farewell.

Robert watched him go for a short while and then headed back to the kennels. When he entered, he found David standing with his back to the half-open door, gasping for air as if someone had him by the throat. Immediately, Robert counted the puppies. None of the young were missing, and they all seemed to be in perfect health.

"David, whatever's the matter?"

The boy pointed outside agitatedly and made some noises that sounded more animal than human, and yet they demonstrated how badly he wished he could express himself.

"En," David stammered. "En!" With a terrifying grimace, he tried to make himself understood to Robert. Tears ran down his cheeks as he punched himself in the face and belly, kicked at the air, and fell to the ground.

At first, Robert thought poor David must be possessed by the devil and tried to calm him down. But the boy kept calling for En. William had told Robert about Enid, including the gruesome way she and her child had been killed. David had obviously witnessed the terrible deed and wanted to tell Robert about it now. Robert could feel the poor boy's fear in his own soul. He was overcome with cold horror. If he understood David's wild gestures correctly and could believe them, Odon, or a man who looked like him, had been among the murderers.

David stared toward the place where he had seen Odon riding off, and he kept pointing in that direction. Then he hugged himself and began swaying from side to side, humming a desperate-sounding children's song.

Robert went up to the unfortunate boy and held him tight. "Don't be afraid, David. I'll protect you and make sure no one harms you, all right? I promise. But William mustn't hear of this, do you understand? It would worry him terribly."

When William came back from Oakham that evening, David had already gone to bed. He slept with his knees to his chin and the blanket pulled over his head. Every now and again he groaned to himself.

Robert knew his friend was still thinking about avenging Enid's death, but he knew, too, that William was not a match for a knight like Odon. When it came to lures and slingshots, he knew what he was doing, but he did not know how to handle a sword or a lance. If he heard that Odon might have been involved in the attack on Enid, he would throw himself blindly at him at the first available opportunity. Since Odon was stronger and knew all the fighting arts, he would thus seal his own death.

At the thought of losing William, Robert's heart twisted painfully. Never would he allow that. He had to protect his friend, and that meant not mentioning a word about David's damning behavior. He looked over at the sleeping boy, anxiously hoping that William would not notice David's fear.

"Odon arrived today," said William quietly.

"Really?" Robert said, pretending to be surprised. "What has our master done to deserve that honor?"

"He wasn't the only important visitor," said William with a sarcastic smile. "There was a whole crowd of lords, even Marshal and the Earl of Arundel came. I think Sir Walkelin summoned them. They were taking counsel with each other about the king. I didn't catch everything, only that old de Ferrers offered himself as a hostage. They obviously can't put the whole ransom together all at once."

"With the riches of all the lords, as well as the church?" Robert shook his head in disbelief. "I wonder how much they're asking."

"It must be a huge sum. Just think: every nobleman has had to hand over a quarter of his income, and even the monasteries and abbeys have had to pay. And yet it's obviously not enough. But they've reached an agreement with the emperor. Richard will be released in exchange for a down payment on the ransom and the princely number of two hundred noble hostages. It seems Queen

Eleanor herself will go and fetch her son from the emperor. Rumor has it that John and the French king were threatening Richard's throne."

"Well, you heard quite a lot," said Robert in amazement. He was glad that William was too preoccupied with the news to notice David's restless sleeping.

"I spoke to Marshal briefly," William went on. "He said being a hostage was not as terrible as it sounds. In fact, it is a great honor. Apparently even one of the king of Navarre's sons is willing to take Richard's place. Besides, he says, nobles who sacrifice themselves for their king are not held in chains or in damp cells. They will be treated like guests, though they have to defray their own costs as well as those of their servants, and obviously that's expensive. The plan is that the families of all the noble hostages will move heaven and earth to ensure that everyone in the land pays their feudal levies so that the prisoners can be released as quickly as possible."

Despite the reassurances, William's concern over the situation was writ large on his face. And then his expression suddenly softened. "Marshal told me about Athanor. I knew it was the first sword my mother made on her own, but not that he always carries it. He showed me," he announced, his cheeks flushed with pride.

This touching sight made Robert feel as if he were carrying a red-hot stone in his guts. Every fiber of his being was run through with his attraction to William, and it grieved him. If he was to lose his friend, he would never get over the loss. He had to find a way to prevent David from ever catching sight of that villain Odon again.

"I haven't seen my mother for such a long time! It's been more than eight years since I left Saint Edmundsbury," William murmured.

"Perhaps it's time you went and visited her. You've talked about it often enough," suggested Robert. After a long pause he continued. "You could take David with you. Who knows what might happen here while Sir Walkelin and Henry are away. Melva isn't as hale and hearty as she was. She can't shake off that cough. I'm sure David would be better taken care of, for the moment at least, with your family."

"Do you really think so?" He shrugged. "Perhaps you're right. Would you like to come with us to Saint Edmundsbury, if Sir Walkelin gives us a few days off?"

"I'd like nothing better in the world than to meet your family," Robert replied truthfully.

William nodded with satisfaction.

Just two days later, their request was granted. Fortunately, the two older falconers' assistants were accustomed to getting along without the head falconer for a few days at a time. Nevertheless, William continued to give instructions until the moment before their departure.

"Good heavens, Will, you can't leave them alone for one moment," Robert teased him with a grin.

"But this time all the animals are staying behind, and we're not going away because it's our duty to do so," William explained, clearly troubled by a guilty conscience. "What happens if one of the falcons falls ill?"

Robert just sighed. He had heard that Odon was not leaving Oakham until the day after they did, so he was anxious. Just as long as Odon did not come into the mews while David was still there.

"I'll ride with you for a while and then head a few miles north for one or two days," he told William as casually as he could as they checked the horses' harnesses. It was just too good an opportunity to miss; Robert wanted to use it to make some inquiries about Odon.

"Does that mean you don't want to come to Saint Edmundsbury after all?" asked William, visibly disappointed.

"Of course I will. It's just that there's something I need to do first," Robert reassured him, nodding vigorously. "An affair of the heart, if you know what I mean."

"Woe betide you if you don't tell me about it," William threatened with a laugh.

William told Robert how to find Saint Edmundsbury.

As they parted, William waved and said, "Come and join me soon, you old heartbreaker."

Without knowing what he was hoping to discover, Robert rode to Elmswick and kept his ears open.

Evidently, the young lord did not enjoy great popularity. Robert learned that the common people feared Odon and his men. He obviously still preferred to pick on those who could not defend themselves. Having a title and power had not changed him one whit.

Apart from Odon's familiar bad traits, Robert did not come across anything new. Just as he was beginning to think he would have to leave empty-handed, fate came to his aid.

In one of the inns, he noticed a particular knight—one of Odon's companions, he gathered from the braggart's talk. Although the red-cheeked man, whose name was Bevis, was obviously drunk, Robert offered him a tankard of ale and tried to question him. He cursed his own master in the hope that Bevis would do the same, and he boasted of fictitious amorous adventures with women in order to loosen the man's tongue.

Bevis spoke of heroic deeds and told tedious tales of being a soldier—nothing that had anything to do with Enid. So Robert claimed his master had slain a goblin who was about to steal a bag of gold from him, and suddenly Bevis, gesturing expansively, began to talk of a horrible witch in the forest. When he noticed that everyone was listening, he reveled in their attention and reported that his master, Sir Odon, and another man had been there, but that only he had been brave enough to kill the terrifying woman when she tried to bewitch them with a gruesome song. The chubby knight boasted of this grisly deed; he clearly considered himself a hero for it.

Robert could hardly contain himself. The red-cheeked Bevis was a nobody; he had seen that immediately. He was convinced

Bevis was only claiming the grisly deed as his own in order to show off. The real murderer, of course, must have been Odon. Robert took a deep breath. How fortunate that he had convinced William to bring David away from Oakham. If he was to be named as the only witness against Odon, there would be no chance of success against any judge in the land. Odon's services to the king were too valuable for a simpleminded youth to accuse him of anything.

The following day, Robert turned northeast to follow William to Saint Edmundsbury. After a few miles he arrived at a very pretty little market town. A delicious smell of roasting meat wafted over to him from one of the stalls. A loud rumbling from his stomach reminded him that he had eaten hardly anything the day before and nothing at all so far that day. Robert dismounted his horse, took his place in the line of customers, and looked around him. The town was swarming with people, some carrying heavy baskets or bundles to market, others pushing or pulling wheelbarrows. The street was filled with carts loaded with barrels, flagons, and baskets. Pigs rooted in the dirt, cats raced about the houses, chasing mice, and children played in the quieter corners.

Robert watched a young, dainty fellow clumsily trying to load a small but heavy barrel onto a wheelbarrow. Amused, Robert was considering helping the man when a knight on horseback swept by so close that the man lost his balance and fell into the filth. Robert recognized the rider immediately. It was Odon!

Without so much as looking back at the poor fellow, Odon just rode on.

"You're next." A women tapped Robert's shoulder from behind. He turned around, looked at her as if she were a ghost, and shook his head. No, he had to follow Odon and see where he was riding in such a hurry.

☾☾

William felt strangely apprehensive as he rode into the smithy yard after so many years. Two new buildings had been added, a stable and a dwelling house; otherwise, not much had changed since his departure.

The yard had been swept clean. In front of the house, the last few fragrant herbs swayed in the light breeze. A dog ran up to them, hackles bristling, and barked furiously. William sighed with disappointment. He knew, of course, that Graybeard must have died long ago, but his absence was unexpectedly painful.

"All right now, that's enough!" He heard a woman's irritated voice and then saw Rose hurrying out, a little less light on her feet than she used to be. Her hair was beginning to go gray, her hips had thickened somewhat, and she looked worn-out.

"How can I—" she began before stopping short. "Jesus, Mary, and Joseph! William?" She looked at him more closely as he dismounted. Then she spread her arms wide and fell on him delightedly. "My God, William, how you've grown. You're a man, a real man," she observed, holding his face with both hands. They smelled of flour and spices, as they always had, as if she had just been making pies.

For a moment, William felt like a child again, as if he had never gone away. "It's good to be home again," he sighed. "Are you all well?"

"Yes, my boy. Your mother and Isaac have their hands full, as usual. Isaac's daughters are married. Marie lives close by—she has four children and comes to visit often. I hope you're going to stay awhile, for then you'll see her. God, it's wonderful to have you back. Oh yes, Agnes has three children, too. The youngest was born this spring, and we haven't seen her since then." Rose smoothed her apron. "Let's go to the smithy and find your mother."

"Wait."

Only now did she notice David, who was standing beside the dusty horse, looking a little lost. "Well, well. Who's this that you've brought with you?" she asked kindly. William could tell from the tone of her voice that she knew David was different.

"This is David," he said. "David's sister was my—" William swallowed. He and Enid had not really been married. "Wife. She's dead."

Rose looked at him in silence; her eyes held more compassion and distress than she could have expressed with words. Then she turned to David, stroked his arm, and nodded at him with a smile. "Welcome, David." She took his hand, just as she used to take her sons' hands, and took a deep breath. "Now let's go to the smithy. William's mother will be so surprised."

When William opened the door to the workshop, he felt nerves rising in him. His hands suddenly felt damp and cold, and his pulse raced as it always had. Would his mother be satisfied with what he had achieved, or would she apply the same standards to him as she did to herself and demand more than was possible?

The thick, pungent smoke in the workshop momentarily made William feel faint. Time seemed to have stood still here. The rhythm of hammer on metal—three ringing blows on the iron, then one on the anvil—was still familiar, and all of a sudden he felt at peace. He looked over at Rose and put a finger to his lips to indicate that she should wait by the door with David. Then he walked over to Ellenweore's anvil. She was standing with her back to him, busy with the fire. William picked up some tongs and smiled when one of the older apprentices recognized him. He winked and put a finger to his lips again.

"The round-nosed tongs," Ellenweore ordered one of the assistants, without looking around, and held out her hand.

William put the flat tongs in her hand and gestured to the assistant to stand back.

"For goodness' sake, I said the round-nosed tongs." Ellenweore turned around furiously and stood silently still, as if changed to stone.

"William!" she exclaimed, putting down the piece she had been working on and embracing him. She held him so close he could feel her heart beating. She did not let him go for half an eternity; then she placed her hands on his shoulders and looked at him proudly. Finally, she turned to the others and asked, beaming, "Doesn't my son look wonderful?" Although William now towered over her, she put her arm around him and stroked his curly brown hair affectionately. Suddenly, she laughed in embarrassment. "He's become a man."

William had been expecting a cooler welcome. He used to long to receive the affection from her that he got from Rose, but in vain. For the first time, he felt how much his mother loved him. He could see in her eyes that she had missed him, and he was happier than he had been for a long time.

"Come and say hello to my son," cried Ellenweore with a laugh, waving to everyone to join the circle.

Peter, who had worked in the smithy with Isaac even before Ellenweore, was the first to come and shake William's hand; then came Brad, the former apprentice, and a couple of men William did not know. And then someone else emerged from the background.

"Let us through now," said a commanding and energetic voice.

"Jean," cried William, even though he could not see him.

The crowd of men divided and Isaac, followed by Jean, walked up to him.

"Father." William embraced Isaac.

"Let the boy go now. I want to bid him welcome, too," said Jean, clapping William on the shoulder with mischief sparkling in his eyes. "Not as strong as a smith, but a fine fellow nonetheless."

"Let's go to the house and have a drink," suggested Isaac, nodding at Jean and Peter. He went over to his wife. "He's become a splendid fellow, our William." He put his arm around her and looked at her lovingly. A boy popped up beside Isaac. He looked about as old as William had been when he'd left Saint Edmundsbury. The resemblance to Isaac was great, though the boy had his mother's red hair and freckles.

"Henry?" William could hardly believe how tall his brother had grown.

The boy looked at him defiantly and nodded.

"So you're already working hard and helping in the smithy," William observed, glancing at his leather apron.

"As much as I can," Henry confirmed with a vehement nod.

William could see in his mother's eyes and smile how proud she was of Henry. "It's good that you have at least *one* son who loves smithing," he said quietly.

Ellenweore and Isaac gave their assistants a few instructions and then led the little procession over to the house. Along the way, William introduced David to his mother.

Once they were sitting at the table and had drunk to William's visit, he told them about his work as head falconer with the de Ferrers family at Oakham, explaining that they were Normans and owned lands on the mainland.

"A marvelous country, Normandy," Jean declared, putting on the strong Norman accent he had always been able to mimic and laughing happily.

William relished his time at Saint Edmundsbury. The smithy no longer felt threatening, and everyone made him feel as though he had been sorely missed. Old quarrels were forgotten, and his friendship with Jean was as close as ever. William talked to Isaac, allowed himself to be indulged by Rose as always, and felt more content than he had for a long time. If only Robert would come soon and they could enjoy their time at Saint Edmundsbury together. William had eight days, one for each year he had been away.

❦

Robert had followed Odon to a narrow alleyway, where he had disappeared into a house. For some time, Robert had been waiting, watching the house. A harried-looking woman, round with child, had opened the door and let in Odon. Robert had pressed himself to the wall, so as not to be seen. Had the Almighty led him here so that he could save this poor creature? Was that why he had felt this inner restlessness and known he would not find peace until he rode to Elmswick? Who could the woman be?

Robert knew that Odon had been married to the beautiful Maud de Tracey since the spring. He was obviously not as besotted with her as every other man, including William. It was hard to imagine that he would cheat on her with a woman as ordinary as this one, a woman who was expecting and who was not nearly beautiful enough to rival Maud. But if she was not his lover and the child she carried was not his, what was Odon doing in this house for such a long time?

Robert bit his lip apprehensively. Odon had let the young priest in Thorne drown without the slightest scruple, and he and his friends had probably killed the defenseless Enid for the fun of it. Who knew what he might be doing to the poor woman inside? The familiar feeling of helpless rage at Odon rose up in Robert. "It's always the ones who can't defend themselves," he snarled, making up his mind to intervene.

Just as he was about to make a move, the door opened and Odon stormed out, snorting with fury.

Robert held his breath and looked cautiously around the corner.

Odon did not notice him; he mounted his horse and rode off.

The door had slammed shut behind him. The woman was nowhere to be seen. Robert stood still for a moment, his heart pounding, and then ran across the alley. He knocked on the door and listened anxiously.

It was not long before the young woman opened the door expectantly, as if she had been hoping for Odon to come back. She looked at Robert in surprise and hurriedly wiped the tears from her face.

"May I speak with you for a moment?" he asked politely, relieved that she was alive.

The woman looked at him suspiciously.

"Please, I *must* speak with you." He looked around, then whispered, "It's about Lord Elmswick."

"You've just missed him," she replied coldly and went to shut the door in his face. But he had already placed his foot in the doorway.

"I know. I deliberately waited until he was gone."

"Tell me what you want," she ordered.

"Is everything all right, Carla?" a neighbor asked, casting a threatening glance at Robert. "Or is this fellow bothering you?"

"No, no, it's all right, thanks."

"Will you let me come inside?" asked Robert.

"Very well," she conceded, showing him in.

"I've known Odon a long time," he began. "My father was…" Robert took a deep breath. It was unwise to talk about Logan. He had to win the woman's trust in order to warn her, but he must not give too much away or he would put himself and William in danger.

The young woman looked at him impatiently. Her left cheek was red and swollen. Odon must have struck her.

"He hit you," said Robert sympathetically, pointing at her face.

She raised her hand involuntarily and touched her cheek. "He's never done it before."

"In Thorne, he used to be fond of beating up the weak. Believe me, I know what I'm talking about. I fear you may be in great danger," he said, taking a step toward her. His hands touched her shoulders and she flinched, as if she was afraid of being struck again. Robert's gaze fell upon an overturned chair in the middle of the room. Had there been more than a blow to the side of her head? He picked up the chair and set it down again. "What I have to tell you about Odon is far from pretty. Perhaps you should sit down."

The woman started trembling, and, before taking a seat, she rubbed her thigh as if it hurt. Had she tripped over the chair? Robert moved it toward her.

Carla nodded gratefully and sat down.

Quietly but urgently, Robert told the story of Enid and her child. He weighed his words carefully so as to spare the young woman. At the same time, though, he wanted her to understand very clearly what it was he was warning her against.

"How do you know that Odon had anything to do with it?" she cried in horror.

Robert told her about David, who had been beaten within an inch of his life that day and had recognized Odon a short while ago. He also told her about the knight, one of Odon's men, who had boasted about the death of the forest woman.

"If you want to avoid any further wrong, you mustn't tell Odon about my visit or about David," he warned her when he had finished.

The young woman nodded, closed her eyes, and swayed. Robert suddenly feared she might collapse to the floor. He took the water pouch from his belt and held it to Carla's mouth. "Have a drink."

"He's always taken good care of me," she said pensively after taking some water. "It was the lullaby I was humming that made him so angry." She sobbed and looked at Robert, disbelief in her eyes. "He had never been so beside himself with rage before, not even when I told him I was with child against his wishes."

"I beg you, you must beware of him. Stay away from him if you can." Robert thought of Bevis's tale. "The lullaby—that must be the song Odon's companion claimed Enid was using to bewitch them."

"Perhaps I should give the pigsticker a chance," Carla murmured quietly. It sounded as if she was talking to herself, not Robert. "He has a big purple birthmark on his left cheek. Most people find it repulsive. I don't. I've seen much worse." She stood up with a deep sigh and led Robert to the door. "Thank you for coming."

There was nothing further to add, so Robert bowed in farewell. "May the Lord protect you, you and the child."

Near Saint Edmundsbury, October 1193

William played with the dog in the yard, enjoying the autumn sun. He was the smithy's second dog since Graybeard's death, and he was still young. The other end of the stick William held was firmly clenched between the playful puppy's teeth. William pulled hard. Wagging his tail and growling at the same time, the puppy tugged at the stick, fighting as if he was defending a delicious prey. William thought fondly of Graybeard. The dog had been by his side throughout his childhood. No other dog had ever won his heart so. He knew from Isaac that one morning they had found Graybeard dead in his corner. It comforted him somewhat to know that the old dog had not suffered in his last days. Sighing, he let his four-legged opponent have the stick and was just about to turn away when a man rode into the yard.

"Robert. At last." Overjoyed, William greeted him, holding back the excited dog. "It's about time."

"You were right. Every child does know the way to the sword-smith woman's workshop," exclaimed Robert, impressed, as he got down off his horse.

The dog took advantage of William's looser grip and ran over to Robert, wagging his tail happily.

"Well, aren't you a friendly chap," Robert greeted him, stroking his untidy pelt and slapping his haunch.

"When I arrived he came close to eating me alive, but you're his best friend straightaway. Who says dogs are loyal?" he grumbled with a smile and embraced Robert. "I'm glad you're here at last, you old heartbreaker. Come, let me introduce you to my family. Give me the reins. We can have one of the apprentices, or my brother, take care of your horse."

"You look in fine form," said Robert.

"That's what my mother says," laughed William. "But it's no wonder I feel good here. I wouldn't have thought it myself. And you should see David. He's really blossomed. Everyone's kind to him. He's allowed to help Rose in the garden and in the kitchen, and he really appreciates it. By the way, she's the best cook I know. Have a sniff. That smell is coming from the bake house."

Robert was accepted like an old friend. Everyone had heard a lot about him, and they were curious. William had told them stories about Thorne, about Logan, Odon, Nesta, and Sibylle, but above all he had talked about Robert and how happy he was to be able to work with him again.

"What Jean and Rose are to you, that's what Robert and David mean to me," he had explained to his mother.

What Jean liked about Robert was that the dog had accepted him immediately; Rose treasured his compliments about her cooking. When Robert started questioning Ellenweore about smithing, and listening to her with growing enthusiasm, he won her over completely, too.

Only Isaac, surprisingly, was more guarded. "Robert is…" he began, when he was alone with William. "He's unusually devoted to you, have you never noticed? I don't like the way he looks at you."

"He's a good person, Isaac, the best and truest friend a man could ask for," William insisted.

"And I'm sure he wants only the best for you, but—" Isaac stopped.

"What do you mean, 'but'? What do you have against him?"

"I wonder if his motives are pure." As he said this, Isaac did not look at William.

"Oh, Father. *He* was the one who helped me get the position with the de Ferrerses, not the other way around. Robert would never cheat me or use me. You're doing him an injustice."

"He's hiding something from you, I'm sure of it," Isaac insisted grimly.

"Then he must have his reasons. I trust him completely," declared William confidently.

"Even if it's something unrighteous?"

"You've never doubted me, Father, so trust me now, too, please. Robert would never do anything to harm me, believe me."

Isaac nodded, though he did not look convinced. "Be that as it may. There's always a place for you here. You are always welcome, whatever happens. But I insist you bring a good woman with you soon, and a couple of well-behaved children."

"As soon as I can, Father, I promise." William laughed. "As if you didn't have enough grandchildren from your daughters already." Then he started telling Isaac in detail about his work as a falconer. "Being head falconer is quite an honor, you know. The falconer is a real confidant to his master, and he has a certain amount of influence. But like the cupbearer he also has great responsibility, for hawks are valuable property. In many families, the men have been falconers for generations—they marry across falconer families only and pass their knowledge down from father to son. But it's a good way for a bastard son to rise, too. I don't know my father, but I'm the bastard son of a knight, and I can dare to hope, even if I can't rely on my father's help, but only on my feeling for animals. Standing at my master's side, I meet the mightiest barons in the land, and I can earn their respect. In this way, I hope, I will win the recognition of the king one day. But I want all the other barons to see what a good falconer I am. Everywhere in England, I want people to marvel at my falcons and to talk about their courage and prowess as hunters."

"You're quite your mother's son, ambitious and full of passion." Isaac clapped his stepson on the shoulder with a laugh. "You'll succeed in everything you undertake, just like her, I'm sure of it."

The time to say farewell came far too soon. The eight days he would spend with his family had seemed long when he arrived, but now they had passed much too quickly. He had not been able to see Agnes and her family, but Marie and her children had looked in at the smithy. Her two oldest daughters, five and four years old, had hardly left William's side. And for the first time since Enid's death, when he held Marie's youngest boy in his arms, something like fatherly love rose up in him without causing pain.

Raymond and Alan, Rose's two older sons, worked with their father in the smithy, while Jeanne, her youngest daughter, had inherited her mother's talents and helped her with the housekeeping. Her bilberry muffins were without equal.

"You're a lucky devil, William. If I had a family like yours..." Robert said quietly when they all gathered in the yard to see them off.

"So you would have stayed here and become a smith, is that right?" William snapped, so harshly that Robert looked at him in surprise.

"For God's sake, no. That's not what I meant. But I would visit them as often as I could, even though it's a long way from Oakham. I wish my father and Nesta were still alive," he murmured sadly.

William cleared his throat with embarrassment and cursed his thoughtless tongue.

Rose hugged them both tearfully, pressing William to her breast for a particularly long time. "Don't worry about David, we'll take care of him. He's a lovely boy. He reminds Jean of Madeleine, who suffered with him when he was a boy—may God rest her soul."

"I've already said good-bye to him. He seems happy to be staying here," William said, smiling sadly. "I'm truly grateful that you're prepared to take him in, just like that, but I feel like a traitor because I'm letting him down."

"But that's nonsense, William! You're not letting him down. You're leaving him in our care, with your mother and me," Rose rebuked him, looking almost offended.

"Forgive me. You're right," murmured William apologetically. He kissed her on the cheek. "He couldn't be better off anywhere else than he will be here, I know that." He smiled at her, then turned to Jean and Isaac, who shook his hand and wished him luck on his journey.

"You're welcome here anytime, Robert. I pray to the Lord that I won't have to wait so many years before William visits us again, and I hope you'll come with him again," Ellenweore said to Robert. "There's something about you that reminds me of my first master. His name was Llewyn. He was a blond Irishman with a Welsh mother. But you don't really look alike," she said pensively, turning to her son. "You were right to listen to your heart and let your stubborn head prevail. You would have made a terrible smith. I'm very proud of you," she said, looking straight into his eyes. "You're so like your father in many ways. I truly loved him."

"Who is he?" William asked shyly, but the question was lost in the tumult of departure. Or had his mother deliberately ignored it? Why had he not used the opportunity of his stay to question her about his father before? "I'll find out who he is," he muttered, then mounted his horse and rode off with a wave.

Winter 1193−94

The days had grown shorter since the return from Saint Edmundsbury. Winter had marked its arrival with hoarfrost on trees and bushes, morning mists, and damp cold, keeping people inside their houses and huts. But early on this December morning, William and Robert were not the only ones who found themselves at Oakham, bidding farewell to Walkelin de Ferrers, who, with his two squires and the Saracen, was preparing to set off to follow the king's mother. Apparently Queen Eleanor had assembled a substantial fleet at Ipswich, Dunwich, and Oxford. She had ordered it to be armed strongly enough to resist not only winter storms but also attacks from pirates, who might try to capture its immensely valuable freight. One hundred thousand of the required ransom of one hundred and fifty thousand silver marks, as well as the hostages, would at last be handed over in exchange for Richard.

Sir Walkelin and his retinue were also joining the fleet as part of the royal escort. Neighbors and friends had come to bid him farewell, amid great rejoicing. Among the crowds that had come from the village to the castle, however, a humble sniffling could be heard here and there, for he was well liked.

After he left Oakham, things returned to their humdrum routine. There would be no news for the time being, and everyone would have to practice forbearance. The royal ships' route took them along the French coast and was by no means free from danger, and the onward journey overland would be just as challenging, especially protecting the ransom from capture. Efforts were redoubled the day after Sir Walkelin's departure, so that the remaining fifty thousand silver marks could be earned as quickly as possible and contribute to the lord's early release.

Henry, Sir Walkelin's eldest son, decided not to travel to see to his father's lands in Normandy until the following spring. He spent the winter hunting in England and got to know and appreciate William and his falcons much better.

In March, news of Richard's newly won freedom finally reached Oakham. Almost exactly a year after the glow in the sky at Candlemas, the Holy Roman Emperor, Henry VI of Germany, the last to hold Richard prisoner, released him in exchange for the money and hostages. First, though, Richard had to swear fealty to him and promise him an annual tribute of five thousand silver pounds.

Prince John, who had taken advantage of his brother's absence to bring as many fiefdoms as possible under his control and to sow unrest wherever he could, found himself in an awkward position after the king's release. In his efforts to seize the throne, he had practiced treachery with all the means at his disposal. It was only thanks to the resistance of many loyal barons that his plans had been thwarted. Now that Richard was free, John had reason to fear his brother's righteous anger, so he fled.

The news spread like wildfire. Richard had landed at Sandwich shortly after the feast of Saint Gregory and hastened to the tomb of Saint Thomas à Becket at Canterbury to pray. After that, he traveled to London and went to Saint Paul's alongside his mother. The whole city, led by FitzAilwyn, had come out to meet him, welcoming him with great rejoicing, despite his announcement—even before his Crusade began—that he would sell London to fill his war chest, if he could find a buyer.

But not even the magnificent celebrations arranged in his honor were enough to keep Richard in London for long. A short time later, he rode north. He prayed for God's help in the abbey at Saint Edmundsbury, one of the most important in his kingdom, and then went on to Huntingdon, where Marshal had ridden to welcome him.

When Henry de Ferrers heard that the king was now on his way to Nottingham, where Prince John was taking a stand against him, he recognized it as a fresh opportunity to serve his king and joined Richard's army. While the king's most loyal subjects besieged Marlborough, which John held, Richard set about conquering Nottingham and Tickhill.

John had amply equipped both fortresses with weapons and food so that they would be able to withstand a long siege, but Richard took them without lifting a sword. The defenders had not believed that the king would ever return. They trembled with fear when he appeared before the gates of Nottingham, completely unexpectedly, and their resistance crumbled amid much wringing of hands. They surrendered without a fight and threw themselves upon Richard's royal mercy. Tickhill, too, fell into his hands without resistance.

Within two short weeks, the king had overcome every single rebel who had dared to stand against him. He let it be known everywhere that his brother, Prince John, had until the tenth of May to present himself at the royal court or be banished forever from England as a traitor.

At Easter, Richard held court at Northampton, with all due pomp, and then further demonstrated his power by having himself crowned king for a second time in a splendid ceremony staged by his mother at Winchester. But it did not matter how much joy and love his subjects showed him. Richard did not grace them with his presence in England for long. He soon made his way to Portsmouth in order to sail back to Barfleur. When he heard that Henry de Ferrers wanted to visit his lands in Ferrières, he offered him and his men a place on a ship in his fleet.

William and Robert were extremely proud and excited to hear that de Ferrers wanted to take the two of them and three of his best falcons with him, as well as a few armed men and his squire. He was probably hoping to go hunting with the king, for he and every other baron knew that Richard was very keen on hawking and had even done it in the East. William was all the more surprised, therefore, at de Ferrers's harsh reaction to the idea of fashioning a hood like the ones used in the Orient.

"Out of the question. I have seen the terrible things the unbelievers do to Christians. Even if some of those heathens are real experts and great lovers of hawking, it doesn't reconcile me to them one bit, unlike our king. You will therefore treat my animals as is customary in England!" he hissed, frowning at William. "You've never been on a crusade. How do you know about hoods at all?"

When he's in a rage he looks even more like his father, thought William in astonishment. He wondered whether his resemblance to the mysterious knight who was his father was as strong.

"The Saracen your father brought home, sir," Robert answered for William. "He told us about them."

"I might have known he would try to bring the East into our house," de Ferrers muttered angrily. "I have never understood why my father spared his life and brought him back to England. As far as I'm concerned, he's still a godless heathen, even if he's been baptized. So go and seel the birds and make yourselves ready for the journey. We'll set off at the crack of dawn tomorrow. We can't keep the king waiting."

They reached Portsmouth in April, two days ahead of the king. Originally, the busy little harbor had been granted to Jean de Gisors, a Norman, and many of the ships there once belonged to him. Among his holdings was Brocheland Manor, where Richard installed himself when he arrived. De Gisors had joined the rebellion in Normandy the previous year, and thus he had lost to the king not only his ships but also his lands on both sides of the English Channel. Richard ordered his army to march into Portsmouth and assembled a respectable fleet. Before his departure, he gave the town its royal charter, so that nothing would halt the ambitious development of the port.

Richard was in a hurry to reach the mainland. He was keen to take revenge on Philip II, king of France. He therefore drove the preparations for departure with all his might. But the weather changed, thwarting his plans. First, a strong onshore wind prevailed, driving the ships onto the coast and making it impossible to cast off. This was followed by days of storms, with variable winds that seemed to toy with the royal fleet. And finally there was a powerful storm that scourged the coast with unceasing rain and made the sea foam like a deadly potion. It was impossible even to dream of crossing the Channel.

William and Robert spent most of the wait either in one of the overcrowded inns or with the falcons. They could not let the creatures out of their sight for fear they would be stolen. One of them had to stay with the birds at all times, while the other made sure there was enough food for them or wandered through the narrow streets whenever the rain let up. The air in the taverns was close and humid with the sodden clothing of those who came in from the outside. De Ferrers visited the king from time to time, while his men spent their time playing dice and telling tales of their adventures in the East.

When at last the storm came to an end, the sea was smooth and brilliant like a gleaming, polished sword. The sky was blue as a field of cornflowers, and the few fluffy white clouds looked like islands of yarrow. Unfortunately it was impossible to set sail in such a dead calm.

Finally, after two weeks of waiting, the wind stood fair.

When de Ferrers reached the harbor with his men at first light, they met William Marshal.

"A fine day for a good crossing." Marshal clapped the young de Ferrers on the shoulder. "I'll see you in Barfleur."

De Ferrers nodded.

"Will you be going on to Lisieux with the king?"

"Of course," declared de Ferrers. "And then we'll continue southeast, to Ferrières."

"Good, then we'll have a chance to see each other," said Marshal, pleased. He nodded at William, who was standing beside his master. "Your first trip to the mainland?"

"Yes, sir." Tired and frozen, he was hopping from one foot to the other and breathing on his clammy hands in an effort to warm them. The night had been damp, though it had not rained again.

"You're sure to like it. Your mother liked Normandy," Marshal said pensively.

"Oh, sir, my mother asked me to give you her greetings," said William impulsively. During his stay at Saint Edmundsbury, he had told her of his encounters with Marshal, beaming with pleasure.

"When did you see her?"

William noticed, with some surprise, that the pulse in Marshal's throat was suddenly beating quickly. "A little while ago, sir. I was at Saint Edmundsbury in the autumn." The thought of home immediately made William feel a little warmer.

"Was she well?" Marshal asked.

"Very well, sir. She was very well. The whole family was fine."

"That's wonderful!" Marshal nodded with satisfaction and cleared his throat as if he had a tickle. "I knew it was the right decision," he murmured.

"We must make haste, my lord. The king can hardly wait to reach Barfleur," a young knight broke in.

"You're right to remind me of it, John. I'm on my way," replied Marshal. Then he clapped William on the shoulder. "Take care of yourself, my boy." He turned to de Ferrers. "Godspeed, my friend."

William bowed. When he looked up again, Marshal had already left and even de Ferrers had turned away.

"He seems to have taken a real liking to you," said Robert. "I could almost envy you, *my boy*," he teased William with a grin.

William changed the subject. "The captain will become disagreeable if we don't get ourselves onto the ship soon."

"Oh dear, the thought of not having good old Mother Earth beneath my feet makes me feel rather unwell," Robert complained. "But there's no turning back now. Let's just hope the sea doesn't swallow us up." He crossed himself with a sigh. William's initial eager anticipation was overtaken by a dull foreboding, which lodged itself in his stomach.

By the time they were finally on board, the sun was rising. One glance over the rail was enough to make William's knees weak, and shortly after they had cast off he was hanging among the sheets, writhing and retching, vomiting the contents of his guts into the sea.

"Not even the meadows of Normandy can possibly be as green as your face right now, and they're supposed to be the greenest on the mainland," Robert joked, though he himself was paler than usual. Once they were out in open water, the wind freshened considerably, and by the afternoon he was feeling no better than William. He too was bent double, emptying his stomach in the same painful and humiliating way as his friend.

They were not the only ones; a few squires and some of the younger knights were seasick, too. They leaned over the buckets placed there for them by the smirking sailors, suffering pitiably. The experienced knights, among them de Ferrers, and of course the sailors, had felt such sickness many times before, and they were highly amused because they were not affected. The wind whipped the sea into towering waves, some of which broke on the deck with a great crash and soaked the travelers to the skin, but all the ships made the crossing without loss.

When at last they were safely moored in the harbor, the sun was rising again in the east, spreading its soft light on the bleak chalk cliffs of the coast. Now that land was within reach, William could examine the town more closely. Barfleur was two or three times the size of Portsmouth. Most of the houses were of stone. They glowed in the dawn light as if glad for the king's visit. A young Norman squire had told William and Robert that Barfleur was the most important port connecting England and Normandy, and that it had an excellent shipyard. He even claimed that the very ship William the Conqueror had used to sail to England had been built there, and one of the sailors, himself from Barfleur, had proudly confirmed it.

As the ships docked, men, women, and children streamed toward them from all sides. The word that the royal fleet was approaching must have spread swiftly.

"It's behind us, and we're still alive," cried Robert, interrupting William's thoughts.

As William nodded, a fresh wave of sickness overcame him.

Robert pointed at a pretty church in the distance. The road toward it was filled with a dense crowd. "Look, the king is already there." Richard and his retinue were on their way, as was customary for travelers, to thank the Lord for their safe passage. Before their journey, too, they had all, including William and Robert, prayed for the protection of Saint Thomas in the church dedicated to him at Portsmouth.

Relieved to have solid ground beneath his feet again, William stepped onto the swaying gangplank and walked unsteadily down it. Gratefully, he placed one foot and then the other on the ground. He turned uneasily and looked back at their ship. No, God knew he was not born to be a sailor; that much was certain.

When they arrived in Lisieux a few days later, de Ferrers and his men stayed at the king's side. He had accepted an offer of hospitality from a member of his retinue, Archdeacon Jean d'Alençon. It was the archdeacon, too, who brought a contrite Prince John before his king not long after. Everyone wondered what would happen to the disloyal brother, and the astonishing news that Richard had forgiven him and was threatening to bring down retribution on those who had counseled him poorly made the rounds all the more swiftly. Richard's leniency was surprising, and behind it many saw the softening influence of his mother, who, as she grew older, was promoting peace.

William and Robert were fetching their master's falcons from a high perch in the hall, where they rested with some of the other guests' birds and two of the king's finest, when Marshal came up to them accompanied by a nine- or ten-year-old girl with long brown hair.

"Oh, William, there you are. I've been looking for you. I've promised this young lady that you'll show her the falcons."

"I want to know all about them," the girl said forcefully, her English tinged with a slightly Norman accent. She smiled charmingly at William and Robert.

"Mademoiselle." William bowed.

"My name is Marguerite."

"A beautiful name," said William, smiling at her.

"I can't abide it. A flower. I would have preferred Alix, like my mother, but there's nothing to be done about it now." She laughed mischievously. "If you're William, you must be Robert, is that right?"

"*Oc*," they answered unanimously in Occitan, the king's mother tongue, although they did not really speak it properly. They bowed, grinning.

"Oh, please speak English with me. My uncle John says I must practice." She smiled broadly, showing a pair of oversize front teeth.

"As you wish, Mistress Marguerite." William bowed even more deeply and winked at her.

"Well, I can see you understand each other, which is excellent," remarked Marshal contentedly. "Marguerite is besotted with falcons. Take her under your wing for a while. She's worn me out with all her questions."

"If you had been a little more willing to explain things, I wouldn't have had to ask so many questions," she retorted acidly.

"What a charming child," William said, trying to conceal an amused smirk.

"I'm not a child anymore," Marguerite protested, and her brown eyes shone with fire.

"She is John's ward, and he's very fond of her," Marshal explained, not heeding her assertion. "And when she's not tormenting you with her questions or climbing trees, she really is delightful company. I leave her in your care, William. Be very careful—she has a lot of strange ideas in her head."

Marguerite looked at him reproachfully, then smiled winningly. Marshal withdrew with a nod.

"Would you like to hold one of the falcons on your fist before I feed it, mistress?" asked William, feeling compassion for her. If she was a ward, her parents must be dead. Perhaps her father had been particularly close to the prince, and that was why she was John's ward and not the king's.

"Can't I feed it?" she asked, her cheeks glowing with excitement as she held her head to one side and looked pleadingly at William. "Please?"

"How could I resist such a request, mistress? Your wish is my command. I am your devoted servant."

Robert, who had been standing there in silence until now, grinned from ear to ear. "William, you old heartbreaker. You can't turn a young lady's head the moment you step onto Norman soil," he joked, pretending to be shocked.

"And why not?" asked Marguerite defiantly, sparkling with such mischief that Robert burst out laughing.

William, who joined in his laughter, was soon wiping tears from his eyes. He placed one of the falcons on her fist and explained how they should be handled, what she needed to watch out for when they were being carried, and what they liked to eat. He answered all her questions patiently. More than once he was reminded of the wonderful afternoon he had spent with Marshal and Princess. Did Sir William still remember it?

Marguerite fed the birds without fear of their sharp beaks, and she never tired of asking questions about them, so she was sad and disappointed when de Ferrers told William, early in the afternoon, that they would be turning their backs on Lisieux early the following morning and heading for Ferrières.

"Oh, what a pity! I've never learned as much in one day as I have today," she said regretfully and curtsied to William in farewell. "I hope we shall see each other again soon."

Ferrières, 1195

They had been in Ferrières for a good twelve months when news of the death of Leopold, Duke of Austria, reached them early in the new year.

It was Leopold who had first taken Richard prisoner, and the report was greeted with an outpouring of jubilation. That the duke had died a pointless death was a matter of particular satisfaction for Sir Walkelin's followers; they were still waiting for their lord, who had handed himself over as a hostage for Richard. Leopold, so the messenger reported, fell from his horse during a staged attack on a snow castle during a tournament. He broke his leg, and when the wound became infected it had to be amputated, but the putrefaction had already spread. Since he was still under excommunication for his imprisonment of Richard, he did not even have the right to a church burial—which most Englishmen thought only appropriate. The messenger also reported rumors that the duke's son was considering returning the hostages that were in his custody, with the aim of ending the church's sanction.

And indeed it was only a few weeks later that Sir Walkelin entered Ferrières, having had a difficult journey. His family was very relieved, and his serfs and household servants were also happy to see their master back and in good health.

The king had summoned Sir Walkelin to thank him for his faithful service, so he told Henry to stay at Ferrières that March while he made his way there with his squires, the Saracen, a few knights, and William and Robert.

On this visit, William and Robert saw the king only from a distance. Their master's audience was but brief, and soon they were on their way back to England again, so that Sir Walkelin could take charge of his affairs again.

As was to be expected, the homeward crossing was no better for William and Robert than the crossing more than a year before, and they were right glad when they finally stepped on English soil. Groaning, they swore a mutual oath never to travel to the mainland again.

Oakham, August 1195

A few months after their return, more than half the village fell ill. Fever, chills, vomiting, and loose bowels confined victims to their pallets.

"In Jesus's name, you're burning up," exclaimed Robert with concern when he went to wake William one morning.

Usually, William awoke before Robert. On this morning, however, he remained on his mattress, groaning and delirious, face flushed and eyes feverish. Memories of his sister's sudden death, memories Robert thought he had forgotten long ago, made him panic. Out of his mind with worry, he ran around the hut, not knowing what he was looking for. He stopped and took a deep breath.

"Leg compresses," he muttered.

Although they had not saved Nesta, they could do William no harm. Besides, they were the only cure for fever he knew. He rushed off in search of cold water and in the courtyard almost knocked over Melva's oldest daughter. She was dragging herself along, barely able to stay on her feet. Suddenly, she collapsed. Robert lifted her up and carried her to her mother's hut. She and two assistants were also sick. Jane, Melva's youngest, was the only one in good health.

Robert put the eldest daughter down and ran to the spring. He collected water and hurried back to the room he shared with William in the main building of the falconry. He wound the cool damp bandages around his friend's legs, wrapped some dry ones around those, and cooled his burning forehead with some wet cloths. But the fever continued to rise unabated.

Many had fallen sick at the castle, too; all normal duties were set aside. Anyone who was well was busy taking care of the sick or burying the first victims.

William vomited violently several times, spouted confused nonsense about dying, and passed watery stools—all without noticing. While he was unconscious, Robert washed him with a piece of linen, rinsing it repeatedly in cold water. He made a bed of clean straw for him, cooled his forehead some more, and fed him cup after cup of the herbal infusion he had made at Jane's suggestion. He took William's hand, as he had held Nesta's before she died, and prayed silently.

Fear for his friend caught in his throat and constricted his chest. He sat at William's bedside day and night, ate only to keep up his strength, and permitted himself neither weakness nor sleep. But exhaustion got the better of him, and he did nod off every now and again. Whenever his head dropped, Robert would wake up terrified, leap up, and run around so as not to fall asleep again. He had to be there for William. But since the hounds and falcons could not be allowed to starve, and the younger assistant could not manage everything on his own, Robert looked after the animals, too. They could not find the strength to hunt, though, so they slaughtered a goat and then a sheep, both belonging to de Ferrers, and used them to feed the animals. They left the falcons in the darkened mews, merely clearing their droppings and feeding them regularly.

Many people in the village and surrounding cottages died. Even Melva passed away after a few days. The sick assistants and Melva's oldest daughter recovered, but Jane, the younger daughter, fell ill and died within a few days.

William could not keep anything down and was losing weight frighteningly quickly, but Robert did not give up hope. He washed William's bony legs, his shriveled sex, and his sagging behind without revulsion, affectionately laid him on his pallet, and prayed to God for mercy. Robert spoke quietly to him, swore to fight for his life, described how wonderful it would be to show their falcons to the king one day, and, weeping softly one night, confessed his love unheard.

The following morning, the skin on William's face at last seemed a little less waxy. He became pinker during the day, and by the afternoon he was quite himself again. He ate and drank like a sparrow, murmured a few words of thanks, and fell asleep again.

Robert stayed by his bedside. He observed the twitching of William's eyelids with the watchful eyes of Argus, worried when he did not move for a while, rested his head on his friend's chest to hear his heartbeat and feel his breathing, and was infinitely relieved as soon as he felt certain William was still alive.

"You look terrible," breathed William the next day, his voice trembling, his face twisted in a subdued smile.

Robert started with fright. It was some time before he realized that William had really spoken to him.

"Good heavens, Will, you should see what *you* look like!"

Walkelin de Ferrers had been among the sick, as had his daughter, Isabella, but fortunately they both survived. In addition to several villagers who had fallen victim to the illness, the lord of Oakham had to mourn the death of his youngest page, an eight-year-old boy of high birth and gentle disposition. Once nobody lay sick anymore, fear of the epidemic receded and life resumed its normal rhythm.

Brittany, 1196

don had answered the king's call the previous year. As lord of Elmswick he owed Richard military service, so now, like many English lords, he was leading a troop of knights and hired mercenaries from Flanders to join the fight.

In his tent, lost in thought, Odon prepared for the coming battle. The Bretons were a stubborn and courageous people; they were not fighting for money or some foreign king, but for their own freedom and independence. Every man who could more or less stand upright and hold a weapon in his hand was ready to fight. It would not be easy to carry out Richard's order to punish these unruly Bretons.

Odon took a deep breath. It felt good to be the leader of such a battle-hardened troop, with no one to dispute his position. Bevis and Milo had not risen as far as he had, and now they were serving under his command. Odon drew his sword and admired himself in the gleaming blade. Is this what a coward looks like? No, he thought, grinning at his slightly distorted reflection. Every day, he gave proof of his resolve. Odon slid his sword back into its sheath, left his tent, and mounted his horse.

"Are you ready, men?" he asked the soldiers, who had been waiting for him impatiently. They answered by stamping their feet and hurling insults at the enemy, arousing Odon's passion. "The Bretons are a devious people. They think they can ambush us in their dark forests, setting traps as if we are wild animals. But we'll be on our guard. They are traitors, cowardly and deceitful, but we're fighting for a righteous cause," he shouted to his soldiers, riding past them as he'd learned by watching William Marshal. He did not really like Marshal, because he seemed to know that Odon was not the bravest, but he did admire his ability always to make the right decision and to keep a cool head during battle.

"We must break the will of this rebellious tribe," Odon thundered. "They will whimper for mercy, but treachery knows no pity and must be punished. Burn down their villages, one by one. Let their fields go up in flames so that their masters suffer from hunger as much as their subjects. They will soon be begging for the king's aid and his crops. They will forget their demands for independence and rue the day they ever rose up against the king. Slaughter armed men without remorse! Leave women and children alone—hunger will bring them to their senses soon enough or kill them off. God save us and King Richard!" Odon spurred on his horse, rode to the front of his troop with his head held high, and gave the signal to set off.

The bloodletting and the burning of villages and hamlets went on for many days. Everywhere, men armed with pitchforks, axes, and flails were slaughtered by knights and soldiers on horseback. Anyone with a weapon in his hand, even if it was just a stick, was struck down, whether he was six years old or sixty. Even the many women who stood in their way were killed. The men poured through the villages like a destructive wave. Wherever they went, they left misery, pain, blood, and fire in their wake. In a desperate attempt to halt them, wailing women and howling children threw themselves in front of their horses and were trampled to death unheeded. The more time passed, the more bloodthirsty Odon and his soldiers became. As long as they were sitting on their horses, they felt invincible. Every day they murdered more men and beasts and burned down more houses, huts, and fields, cutting a bloody swath of destruction across the land.

At night, Odon kept dreaming of Carla. A full year before he left England, she had borne him a strong, healthy boy, and he thought of him more often than he thought of the son and heir borne to him a few months later by the beautiful but insufferable Maud. The boys were at least two years old by now, if they were still alive.

The thought of Carla, and the cold, dark January day on which he had seen her for the last time, tormented him constantly. He had entered the house that day without knocking. It had seemed strangely empty, as if Carla had packed up her possessions.

Odon heard a child wailing and could not help feeling a little pride. He rushed up the narrow staircase in the happy expectation of holding Carla in his arms at last. He was almost with her when suddenly he heard her singing. Pale and trembling, he stopped at the threshold and stared into the small room. That lullaby. Carla was rocking a rush basket suspended from the beam and staring lovingly at her child. It was the most peaceful, most beautiful sight Odon had ever seen, and at the same time the most horrifying.

When Carla noticed him, she fell silent. "You shouldn't have come," she said tonelessly.

"This is still my house. And my son, no?"

"Your house," she confirmed, "but *my* son." Carla left the basket swinging and took a step toward Odon. "We're leaving this place today."

"Where will you go? You have nothing—you're nobody," Odon protested helplessly.

"I'm going to marry the pigsticker."

"You can't do that."

"Who's going to prevent me? You don't own me. I don't belong to you or anyone else. Even the pigsticker's a free man."

"And the child?"

"He'll raise him as if he was his own."

"I won't allow it!"

"And what are you going to do about it? Slit my belly open, like the woman in the forest? Or does that only give you pleasure when there's still a child inside?"

Odon stood there openmouthed, staring at her. How could she know about that? His mouth felt dry. He swallowed. "I—I didn't kill her," he said defensively, unwittingly confessing to having known the woman in the forest. "It was Bevis. If I had tried to stop them, I would have ceased to be their leader. They would have killed the woman anyway."

"She was helpless, and you were armed," Carla replied coldly.

"The other two were armed, too," Odon said in his defense as he confronted the profound contempt in Carla's eyes.

"You let a woman and her child die out of cowardice?" She looked at him in disbelief. Her voice was no more than a disgusted whisper. "Where was your honor as a knight when they cut out the child from her womb? Was she singing that lullaby out of desperation? Is that why you struck me?" Carla began singing the lullaby again.

Odon's helpless desperation turned into cowardly fury. "Shut your mouth. She wasn't a human being—she was a witch!" When Carla just looked at him without betraying any emotion, Odon broke down. "You can't leave me, Carla!"

"I'm marrying the pigsticker. It's all arranged. I'd rather sell him my body than sell you my soul, you devil."

Without saying another word, Odon turned and left. He had not seen Carla or the boy since. He did not even know with what name she had baptized him. Nevertheless, that child meant more to him than the heir that Maud had borne him, for Maud, unlike Carla, had always treated him with disdain and mockery.

Maud was never pleased with him. She hated Elmswick and grumbled constantly about everything. The king's summons had been a welcome reason to escape his wife.

Whenever he dreamed of Carla, Odon would wake up in a bad mood and try in vain to banish all thoughts of her, their son, and that accursed woman in the forest. On those days, he would surrender utterly to the intoxication of killing, which was always available and seemed to prove he was no coward. Why, he kept asking himself, hadn't he just denied ever knowing the woman in the forest? How could Carla have known what happened that day? Had someone witnessed the scene? Or had that mute youth, the one he thought he'd beaten to death, survived?

Oakham, August 1198

The young Henry de Ferrers, who had forbidden William to use hoods, had remained on the mainland for the past three years. William had taken advantage of his absence to try out a hood when manning one of the new falcons, so that he could demonstrate it to his master, old Walkelin.

The Saracen visited him in the mews from time to time and told him what he knew about the use of hoods. As a servant of a high-ranking master, he had not had falcons of his own and had not become particularly familiar with them. But he advised William and Robert as well as he could. He encouraged them to persevere when they were tempted to give up because the hoods did not fit properly, and he tried to remember exactly how they were made. But William figured out how to make the hoods all by himself.

Arrow was a magnificent creature and William's pride and joy. Not only did he allow himself to be hooded easily, but his bold flying and exceptional reliability enthralled everyone who saw the bird.

"I am convinced that a falcon that has been manned with a hood learns to trust people more quickly," William told his master one day. "But a hood isn't just good for training—it's also good for journeys or for the ride to a hunt. It's invaluable, because the bird stays calm and doesn't get frightened by unexpected movements." William's eagerness was boundless, and Sir Walkelin gave him and Robert leave to tame another falcon using a hood. After Arrow they "made" Storm, a tempestuous tiercel, to the hood, and they were more than satisfied with the result. Old de Ferrers was also extremely impressed.

"You called for me, my lord," exclaimed William as he ran into the hall one day and bowed before Sir Walkelin.

"Get ready for a journey. You and Robert are to accompany me to Ferrières again. We will depart from Ipswich in a few days, and we'll take Arrow and Storm with us." De Ferrers grinned at the sight of William's face turning pale. "Still afraid of the sea, after such a long time?"

"Just that awful sickness," he said with an attempt at grim humor. "Ipswich? Doesn't the crossing from there take even longer than from Portsmouth?"

De Ferrers roared with laughter. "Yes, my poor William, that's right, but there's nothing to be done now, so just come to terms with it. Perhaps you can get some advice in the port. There are supposed to be some plants that help against seasickness." De Ferrers laughed again when he saw William's despairing expression. "You may go now," he said, dismissing him and shaking his head with amusement.

"And I swore I would never set foot on a ship again," snorted William when he told Robert about the journey that awaited them.

"We'll get through this together," his friend said encouragingly, and he did manage to calm down William a little.

If nothing else, William probably owed Robert his life, for it was certainly thanks to his friend that he had not died during the terrible epidemic. Even if William would have done the same thing for him, as Robert claimed, he still felt in his friend's debt. "You're right," William finally replied, pretending to be firmly convinced.

When they departed a week later, though, his courage had left him.

"I feel weak in my stomach," he sighed as they approached Ipswich. His mother had once left for Normandy from here, too.

She had been robbed on that occasion, but she had not been nauseated, as she had once proudly told him. "We should try to find something for seasickness; otherwise I don't know that I'll be able to survive the passage again."

Ipswich harbor was swarming with people. On all sides there were peddlers offering all manner of items both useful and useless, like things one might need at sea or on the onward journey, good-luck charms, provisions, herbal medicines, leather bags, wooden spoons, knives. William asked around and got some advice from experienced travelers. Most recommended the little galangal cakes that were being sold by a wrinkled old crone near their ship.

"You should eat some before the journey begins. They're spicy and a bit different in taste, but apparently they help," William said, chewing, when he returned and offered his friend one.

"Not for me, thanks," Robert said, looking at the cake suspiciously and waving it away.

On the open sea, however, the galangal cakes revealed themselves to be quite helpful against seasickness. William was not spared the sensation of illness, but at least he did not feed the fishes with the contents of his stomach this time.

Robert, on the other hand, felt truly awful. He leaned over the rail as he had the first time. William tried to persuade him to try some galangal cake, but Robert stubbornly refused. Once they finally had solid ground underfoot, though, his sickness was forgotten.

William eagerly inhaled the fresh air. He enjoyed the ride through the green forests and bountiful meadows. The sky was a soft, fragrant blue, the air was warm and pleasant, and the rest of the journey almost felt like an outing.

When they arrived at Ferrières, Henry de Ferrers welcomed them with open arms. He greeted his father with exuberant joy, but he shot an irritated glance at William when he saw the hoods on his father's falcons.

"I see you have not only sowed but also reaped the first fruits," he hissed spitefully at the Saracen.

Sir Walkelin deliberately ignored his son's words; the Saracen just shrugged and smiled.

"Prince John and Marshal are going to honor us with a visit in a few days," Henry told his father proudly while they were still in the courtyard. "A messenger brought the news today."

"Well, a little distraction from the life of a soldier is bound to do them good. I hear they have fought much and exceptionally successfully." Walkelin nodded pensively. "We should arrange some hawking for them. If I know our prince well, it would be a welcome change."

"A wonderful idea, my lord." William beamed at his master. He knew from his previous stay at Ferrières, which had lasted more than a year, how pleasant the life could be. The people were friendly and the hunting grounds rich. That they could now look forward to a hunt with the king's brother was a truly special piece of news.

"I'll prepare Arrow and Storm so they'll be in top condition and attract the prince's attention," William promised.

"Well, I certainly hope we can make a bit of an impression with them. Feeding the prince and his retinue—even if it's only for a few days—will cost a fortune, so the visit had better be worth it and John should leave with a favorable recollection of it."

"I'm sure he will, my lord."

"We'll take the best possible care of the prince, Father," Henry said reassuringly. "The soldiers can pitch their tents out on the west field—the grass is short enough. And I'll have servants brought in from the village to look after them all. You and Robert," he went on, turning to William, "you take care of the hunt. You can put up the falconers and their animals in the mews. You know your way around, and Alain—you remember him, William?"

"Certainly. I trained him myself, a good falconer."

"Well, Alain and our hunt assistants will be under your control. Together, you must choose the most suitable terrain for this hunt. Is that all right with you, Father?"

"Marvelous," Sir Walkelin agreed, dismissing William and Robert with a friendly nod.

Four days later, Prince John and Marshal arrived, accompanied by at least three dozen impressive knights and a few nobly dressed ladies and damsels, as well as a swirling mass of squires, pages, servants, cooks, washerwomen, scribes, huntsmen, falconers, a minstrel, and a large number of foot soldiers.

Although Sir Walkelin had prepared, the endless stream still shocked him. He looked at William in bewilderment. Even when they had accompanied Richard to Lisieux four years before, the numbers had not been so high. Sir Walkelin groaned, "This is going to cost us a fortune." But when John and Marshal were standing before him, he put on his most amiable face and pretended to be completely calm.

A young lady with long brown hair rode beside the prince. Her rather austere beauty caught William's attention immediately. There was something familiar about her, as if he had seen her before, but however hard he racked his brains he could not work out where and when it might have been.

"You can close your mouth now, William," said a familiar voice behind him.

"Sir William." William's pensive expression brightened immediately. Marshal approached him with a smile as his page led away his horse. William bowed. "Welcome to Ferrières, sir."

"Four years really are an eternity in such a young life," said Marshal, looking meaningfully at the young woman. William could hardly take his eyes off her. A young squire was helping her dismount. "She's turned out well, hasn't she?"

"Is that Mistress Marguerite?" William asked hesitantly.

Marshal nodded in confirmation.

William felt the blood rushing to his ears. They must be red as beetroots, he thought with shame.

"Girls become ladies, too. Come and greet her."

But Marguerite had already cried, "William," and was running toward him, slightly faster than a young lady should. "How lovely to see you here."

Touched by her warm greeting, William bowed. His face burned as if it had been out in the blazing sun all day. "The pleasure is entirely mine." He hardly dared look at her.

"Uncle John, may I introduce you to William, the falconer I told you about?"

William was taken aback, and before he could prepare himself, she was pulling him over to the prince and tugging at his sleeve.

William's ears became even redder. "Welcome, sir, er...my lord," he stammered, uncertain of the correct form of address for a prince. He bowed as quickly as he could.

"Well, well, so this is the young man I've been hearing about all these years. 'William told me this, William said that,'" uttered the prince, teasing the girl with a smile.

"Don't make fun, Uncle. Even Marshal thinks highly of William, don't you, Sir William?" she said, looking for support. Marshal smiled in confirmation. "Uncle John, may I go to the mews and have a look at the falcons?"

Prince John sighed. "I dare say you won't leave me in peace otherwise. William, would you be so kind as to take care of her?"

"It will be an honor, sir." And a great pleasure, he would have liked to add, but he bit his tongue.

"And I can come on the hunt tomorrow, can't I?" Marguerite begged.

John nodded graciously. "Now go away and leave me in peace."

Marguerite was hopping about with excitement beside William, just as she had the first time he had met her.

William signaled to the falconers accompanying John and Marshal that they should go with Robert. He had Arrow and Storm on his fist and was to take them the short distance back to the mews.

William offered Marguerite his arm. As they walked, she asked him about the hoods, which had struck her immediately, even from a distance. William was only too glad to answer.

"I thought long and hard about what the Saracen told me before I decided to try to make a hood myself."

"I couldn't see what they were made of," Marguerite broke in.

"Leather. They're made of leather." William smiled at her. "I got a cobbler to show me how to sew it, and then I bought a piece of hide so I could try it myself. The Saracen's instructions were quite thorough, but I didn't have any experience or skill in leather-work. What was more, neither I nor Robert had ever held a hood in our hands. I didn't know what was important. So I decided to start with a hood for a peregrine that had already been manned. The Saracen claimed birds accepted hoods quickly and wore them willingly, but the falcon I chose struggled as soon as I tried to put the hood on its head and still wasn't used to it weeks later."

"And then? What did you do next?"

"I made a new hood. But the falcon still resisted when I tried to put it over its head. The poor bird hated wearing it and behaved like a freshly seeled falcon every time, trying to tear it off. I tried it with the other falcons, but they wouldn't accept it, either. After a few months, I was desperate, on the verge of giving up."

"What happened? What made you go on?"

"I understood why the birds hated the hood so much."

"How?"

"Two damp spots on the inside. I had noticed them, you under-stand, but I hadn't paid enough attention. It wasn't until I gave it a bit more thought, looking at the hoods over and over again, that I asked myself where the spots were coming from. That's all."

"And then?"

"You ask just as many impatient questions as you always did," William said, laughing. "Your poor uncle."

"Oh, all Uncle John thinks about are boring things like politics and war, so I rarely ask him anything," retorted Marguerite, a little sourly. "But I think I can make a guess about the damp spots. They came from the falcon's eyes."

"That's right. The hoods were rubbing against their eyes. That was why the falcons hated them." Marguerite's understanding impressed William. She had obviously learned a great deal since their first meeting.

"And how did you solve the problem?"

"I remembered a detail of the Saracen's description that I had paid no attention to until then and modified the hoods so the leather was raised on both sides of the head. That way the hood doesn't touch the falcon's eyes and doesn't rub."

"That must mean you have to make a special hood for every type of falcon, since they vary in size," said Marguerite thoughtfully.

"That's right, too," William confirmed admiringly. Marguerite understood things better than most boys her age. She was clever and beautiful—and unattainable.

Soon they arrived at the falconry, where Alain and the assistants were waiting for them. They showed the prince's falconers, and those of his followers, where they could house their birds and where they would find quarters for themselves. One assistant mocked the hooded falcons, earning an angry glare from Marguerite.

"You would be wise to hold your tongue. I know the king has a high regard for these Eastern hoods," she declared, "and I'm sure my uncle will like them, too."

The man who received this rebuke was about to answer back, but he was prevented by a severe glance from one of the older falconers. William knew he belonged to the de Hauville family.

Robert ordered one of the assistants to fill the shallow baths with water for the falcons who would hunt the next day, so they could cool down. Now it was his turn to greet Marguerite, which he did with accomplished courtesy.

She followed William into the mews, carefully examined de Ferrers's birds and their hoods, and then led William to one of the falcons that just had been brought in. "This is my uncle's favorite," she said. "A beautiful creature, isn't it?"

"Wonderful," said William, but he was looking at Marguerite, not the falcon. It was not until John's falconer came in to fetch the bird from its perch that he pulled himself together and forced himself not to stare at Marguerite. He cleared his throat, which felt dry as dust, and continued the tour until he had to take her back to the castle, savoring every moment he spent in the company of this beautiful young girl.

The following morning, shortly after daybreak, William, Robert, Alain, and the other falconers set off to meet de Ferrers and his guests for the hunt.

William had hardly closed his eyes the night before. He had been too preoccupied with thoughts of Marguerite. Her lively yet infinitely gentle brown eyes had ensnared him and would not let go.

Squires, pages, dog handlers, and hunt assistants swarmed the courtyard, making ready to leave for the hunt. Orders were barked out, harnesses checked, servants sent back and forth, oaths uttered, and helpers mocked.

William searched the crowd for the lovely creature with the long brown hair, but instead of Marguerite he found a blond man on a magnificent white horse. "Oh no, not Odon again," he muttered.

"Why does he have to be here, too?" remarked Robert, having caught sight of him at the same time.

"I must have missed him yesterday," murmured William uneasily. He had so hoped he would never see Odon again. Moving in noble circles, he knew, meant coming across the same people all the time. In Marguerite's case, that was fortunate; he hoped they'd be brought together often in the future. When it came to Odon, however, it was a curse. His evident closeness to Prince John, who seemed on quite intimate terms with him, overshadowed William's pleasure in the hunt. It was not until Marguerite rode up to him, beaming with glee, that he began to feel more confident.

During the hunt, Arrow cut a particularly fine figure. He was in peak condition, brave, agile, and ruthless. From the very start, he flew so magnificently that all eyes were on him. In fewer than half a dozen flights he caught two substantial cranes, which was a remarkably good result.

Prince John's falcon, on the other hand, was not particularly fortunate. When, after several unsuccessful attempts, she tried to bring down a crane, a terrible accident happened. The huge bird defended itself with all its might, eventually seizing the falcon in its dangerous bill. It pulled and hacked at the falcon until she was so badly injured that she tumbled down to earth in a spin. A shocked murmur ran through the crowd of onlookers as she plummeted out of the sky.

John hurried over to help his bird as soon as she hit the ground.

William handed Arrow to one of his helpers and then rode off as if the devil were snapping at his heels. When he reached the fallen falcon, the prince's favorite, he came upon a terrible sight. The bird was flapping her wings helplessly, trying to lift herself, but the injury was too serious. Her right wing was broken; the bone was clearly visible, protruding from the blood-soaked feathers. An open break like this was a death sentence.

Robert, who had rushed over, too, shook his head regretfully, as did Alain and the other falconers surrounding the prince.

John's face was ashen. He looked helplessly from one man to the next, but no one said anything reassuring.

"Make way, make way," cried Odon, pushing himself forward and hardly paying heed to the bird. He looked at the falconers and then turned to John. "If anyone can heal your falcon, it's our good William," he said, grinning duplicitously into the awkward silence and clapping William on the shoulder with a pretense of friendship.

The experienced falconers and William looked at him as if he was quite mad.

"An open break like that doesn't heal. It festers and then kills the bird," John's falconer declared, shaking his head.

"But miracles happen all the time," Odon insisted. "Let William try, my lord."

William felt a wave of heat flow over him. John's bird would die, and no one could prevent it.

Odon rested his gaze on William. It was filled with pure contempt and visceral hatred. One thing was for sure: Odon knew exactly what he was doing.

John looked up at William, his eyes filled with tears. "Do you really think you could help her?"

William gulped with dismay. "No, Your Highness, I don't think so." He lowered his eyes humbly. "But I'll try, if you insist."

"Then try." The prince's voice sounded more pleading than commanding.

"It will take a long time, and even if the break heals, it's unlikely she'll ever fly again," William warned.

"Nevertheless, keep her here and try," John commanded. "I'll speak to your master to make sure he gives you every assistance."

William bowed. "As you wish, my lord." He took the bird in both hands, lifted her up, and carefully carried her away.

"You'll wish you'd rotted to death in our dungeon yet," Odon hissed at him so that no one else could hear.

William paid no attention. Let Odon think he had already broken him. They would find a way to save the bird, even if at that moment it seemed completely hopeless.

"Have you taken leave of your senses?" Robert complained. "The falcon will never recover from this injury—a child could tell you that. What were you thinking when you said you would try? When she dies, which she certainly will, Odon will say it's your fault. You're putting your life at risk."

"And what else, may I ask, could I have done, do you think? Should I have said, 'No, Your Highness, I can't save your bird and I won't even try'? You were there. You know Odon would never have let it rest. He would have accused me of not *wanting* to try. This way at least we stand a chance." William sighed. He had seen Marshal's incredulous expression.

"We?"

"Please, Robert, I'm going to need your help." William put all his powers of persuasion into his expression, and his friend's initial resistance crumbled.

He put his arms around William with a smile. "You know you can count on me. We'll do the best we can to nurse her back to health." His face broke out in a broad grin. "What I wouldn't give to see Odon's face if we succeed. Come, let's strap her up as quickly as we can."

"No, I think we should prevent the wing from moving and splint the break. The wound needs to stay open for a while, or else John's falconer is right, it will get infected and kill the bird."

Robert held up his hands. "You're the herb collector. We'll do whatever you think is best."

Before the prince left Ferrières, he came to the mews one more time to have a look at his falcon and bid William farewell.

"I've arranged everything with de Ferrers. You can take as long as you need to take care of her. All that matters is that she gets better."

"You know I can't promise anything, my lord."

"I know, but I've heard so many good things about you that I am full of hope. I'm sure you'll succeed. And for safety's sake, I'll pray for God's mercy, too."

"We'd better do the same," muttered Robert once Prince John had left. "Perhaps the prayers will help, if nothing else does."

৩৫

Odon crouched behind a large bush and watched the path through the forest. Since the hunt during which John's bird had been injured, he had spent months with the prince, constantly moving. He had endured his moods and battled alongside him. It was hard to win John's respect. Odon breathed in deeply to drive away the oppressive tightness in his chest.

Lately, he had been increasingly preoccupied with the worrying thought that William might have saved John's falcon, contrary to expectation. Fortunately, though, he had thought ahead and given a lad named Guy the task of getting work in the mews and spying for him.

Odon snorted with impatience. The path led directly to the falconry; the boy would have to come along here soon. Odon rubbed his chin complacently and grinned. An idiot like William was no match for him. Even if he did manage to bring the falcon back to health, Odon would be able to prevent him from enjoying the prince's gratitude.

Odon heard Guy approaching and checked that the boy was alone before stepping out from his hiding place.

"Well, Guy, now we'll find out whether you've earned the tidy sum I've promised you," he said harshly, flexing the muscles in his jaw to look more menacing.

At first, the young man was startled by Odon's unexpected appearance, but then he nodded eagerly.

"I want to know everything, every detail, about what has happened in the mews since we left. How is John's falcon? Is she dead?"

"William and Robert have made herbal poultices and watched her day and night," he reported, not without pride. "Nobody would have expected her to recover, but the wing has healed, and the falcon has even done some flying. She probably won't be able to hunt as well as she did, but perhaps she will," he answered, shuffling his feet nervously when he saw Odon turn red with fury.

"God forbid," Odon sputtered angrily.

Guy relaxed a little and smiled with relief when he understood what this knight wanted to hear. "I'm sure she won't be able to hunt properly again."

"It won't do William any good that he's looked after the falcon. You're to take care of that, understood? The last thing I need is for John to feel indebted."

Guy obviously did not understand what Odon expected of him.

He held a purse under Guy's nose and shook it so that the coins inside—large and small—jangled. "This is a small fortune. Think what you could do with it." He moved his head from side to side, as if thinking about how to spend such a princely sum himself. But when Guy approached and eagerly tried to grab the purse, Odon hid it behind his back in a flash. "First, you must hear what it is you have to do." He looked around, so that Guy had to come very close to him to hear his words. He whispered precise instructions in his ear. "Here, with this it will be child's play," Odon ordered, pressing into Guy's hand a small package wrapped in a scrap of linen. "And don't forget, I know where your mother's hut is. Should you try to take the money without fulfilling your side of the bargain, I shall have to pay her a visit she's unlikely to welcome. Do you understand?"

"Yes, sir, you can rely on me. As soon as I've done what you order I'll leave this place. No one will suspect who gave the order. People will think it's a mistake." Guy grinned. "The others all flatter him, but he means nothing to me."

"That's good, Guy. Now go."

When the young assistant was out of sight, Odon rubbed his hands together. "It was really foolish of you to make an enemy of me, William."

❧❦❧

To William's great happiness, Prince John had asked Sir Walkelin to care not only for his falcons but also for Marguerite. He would be unable to offer his ward a proper home while he was waging war. What better solution could there be than to leave his ward with his friend de Ferrers, who had raised two daughters as well as two sons. So Marguerite stayed in Ferrières with Goda, her handmaid.

Goda was not really ugly, just plain, a self-denying old maid of nearly thirty who simply went unnoticed by men. At night, when she thought Marguerite was asleep, she would often beg the Almighty for a husband, weeping heartrending tears and whispering fervent prayers.

Marguerite felt pity for her at these times, but the next day she would round on Goda furiously when she said Marguerite was unlikely to find a husband if she did not behave in a more ladylike way.

"As if behavior were all that matters. Goda is a perfect lady. She can sew, she can sing, and she's an attentive hostess, and yet she's an old maid," said Marguerite heatedly, one morning in the mews.

Robert and William smirked at each other.

"Well now, if you came with a decent dowry, dear Marguerite, and promised to help me with my work, I might be willing to marry you." William sighed dramatically, though of course he would have married her without a penny if it were seemly.

"Only her uncle won't give her away to the first man to happen along, my dear Will," said Robert with a pompous air. "I think you're forgetting that she's the prince's ward and a valuable commodity, a match with which alliances can be sealed and favors repaid. He'll probably marry her off to some long-serving, faithful, but ugly knight with a fat belly, so that the knight can sit back at his ease and ensure his succession. Or else she'll have to capture the heart of one of England's enemies."

William knew his friend's prediction was probably close to the mark, regrettably. Perhaps a young noble would be the one to hold her hand one day. But Marguerite was strikingly beautiful, and she was John's favorite ward. The thought of her belonging to someone else one day almost broke his heart.

"In that case I'd rather join a convent," Marguerite hissed, like an enraged cat. "I refuse to marry some ugly, old fellow."

William just looked at her helplessly as she stalked off angrily. Something indescribable bound him to her. Even Robert, who seemed to have something against every woman William liked, had obviously noticed it.

"She would be right for you, Will," he said with a quiet sigh as he watched her go.

William knew he was right, but Marguerite's future looked just as Robert had described it. That was why every moment he could spend with her in the mews was like a precious gift. With every day he spent near her, she meant more to him. Her easy manner and her laughter, but also her seriousness and curiosity about the ways of falcons, made him inexpressibly happy.

He racked his brains for a long time over how he could please her. At length he suggested to de Ferrers that she be allowed to train a small passager and that he give it to her as a gift afterward. De Ferrers liked the idea immediately, for with Marguerite's falcon he could strengthen not only his own connection to John but also that of his sons. William knew it would be very prudent to earn the prince's favor, for he was now again so close to his brother Richard, who was still without a son, that it was generally believed he would be named as his successor.

At first it had looked as though Arthur was the leading contender. The son of Richard's older brother, Geoffrey, former Duke of Brittany, Arthur had seemed a possible successor as long as John continued to make life difficult for his brother. Now, however, they were united in brotherly love, at least to the extent possible for two men who were so different, and rumor had it that Richard would decide in favor of John.

For all that, William was not particularly interested in making himself popular with John; what interested him was Marguerite. Training her would give him time with her and would let him give her his full attention. The assistants grumbled, of course, because Marguerite was allowed to go wherever she pleased, even though she was not a man, but their complaints made no difference to William. If he had not been the son of a female swordsmith, he might have believed that women were less capable than men. Besides, Marguerite had learned more about falcons in a short time than the assistants, none of whom would ever train a hawk on their own.

As expected, Marguerite threw herself into the task and took it extremely seriously. She was not at all soft and did not even complain when her arm grew weak from carrying the bird. My mother would like her, even though she's a baron's daughter, thought William as he watched her, and the realization cut him to the quick.

Marguerite had often watched when he was handling John's injured falcon; from time to time she had helped out and learned a great deal. William treated the open break in the bird's wing with herbal dressings whose recipes he had learned from Enid.

At first, the falcon scarcely improved, and William felt discouraged, but after a while she began to recover. It took three full months for the break to heal and the wound to close. Thanks to William's attentive, loving care, and to the selection of the finest tidbits to eat, she recovered her strength, which earned him Marguerite's undisguised admiration. When he started flying the falcon again, John had not yet returned to Ferrières. Marguerite's passager was fully trained, so she did not come to the falconry as often as before. In addition, de Ferrers insisted that she be educated as a lady while she was in his household. She received lessons from a priest, and she had to sing, embroider, sew, and learn to keep accounts. Whenever she thought she was unobserved, though, Marguerite would steal away to the mews.

William found the work with John's falcon fascinating, and the better he got to know her, the better he understood why she was John's favorite. She was exceptionally brave and had remained so despite her serious injury; her eagerness for the hunt was as strong as ever.

Marguerite had first trained her young passager with a lure and, after a successful introduction to hunting, had named the bird Sly and left it in William's care.

"Is Lord Elmswick here?" she asked one morning when she came to the mews to look in on Sly.

"No, should he be?" replied William, frowning.

"No, no, it's just that I saw him earlier, talking to Guy over there on the path behind the clover field. He probably rode straight on to Sir Walkelin's. Perhaps he has news of Prince John. He should be coming back soon." Marguerite beamed at William. "My uncle will be amazed how well his falcon has recovered."

It was true; the falcon's recovery bordered on miraculous. Prince John had been away for nearly four months, and William now awaited his return impatiently. The only thing that bothered him was that John's next visit would probably also end Marguerite's stay at Ferrières.

William opened the door to the mews and made a gallant gesture indicating that Marguerite should enter first. Then he followed her in. His eyes probed the darkness in search of John's falcon. She was not on her perch. William rushed forward and found the falcon motionless on the sand.

"She's dead," he croaked, lifting her up carefully. He checked the falcon and could not find any injury.

Tears ran down Marguerite's face. It was a while before she recovered from the shock. At length she looked around the base of the perch, bent down, and picked something up from the ground. She looked at it closely and sniffed at it. "Isn't that a piece of salt pork?"

William looked at her hand in bewilderment. "How did that get here? Haven't I told everyone here a thousand times that you can't give salt meat to falcons?" he shouted. Salt, and therefore cured meat, was pure poison for falcons, and that was one of the first things he taught new assistants. Whom could it have been?

"For heaven's sake, what's going on here?" scolded Robert, who'd heard the shouting and come running.

"Someone has poisoned the prince's falcon with salt meat." Marguerite made her accusation with an assurance that struck William like a blow to the throat. He had thought it might be an accident, but now he realized she was right. There was no other answer.

"What can I tell the prince when he comes back?" stammered William, looking at Robert wide-eyed. "How am I to explain this?" He could not grasp that all his efforts had been rendered futile at a stroke. "The prince will hold me responsible for the death of his falcon. It doesn't matter whether it was caused deliberately by someone else or it was due to a stupid mistake," he told them bitterly. After a while, he added, "Marguerite saw Odon earlier. Perhaps the prince will be here sooner than we think."

"Odon here? That's a remarkable coincidence, don't you think, Will? Where did you see him, Marguerite, here in the mews?" Robert inquired.

"No, behind the clover field. He was talking to Guy."

"I can see Odon behind this outrage, and using a helper so he doesn't get his hands dirty would be just like him, too," exclaimed Robert heatedly. "And killing a falcon is severely punished. A man who is caught can hardly expect to escape with his life. Odon knows that full well."

"I'm going to go and find Guy. If he's got anything to do with this, I'll beat him black and blue," snarled William. He handed the dead bird over to Robert and left the mews, snorting with anger.

In the yard he met Alain, who raised his hand in greeting. William ignored him and sprinted off. But where would he find Guy? In the village or the tavern perhaps? William felt his head clearing as he ran. When he used to run every day to strengthen his foot, the longer he ran, the clearer everything became. He would never find Guy. The youth had appeared, as if from nowhere, after Prince John's departure and asked for work in the falconry. Robert had been suspicious, but William had felt sympathy for the lad when he'd said he had lost his father and mother and was hungry. William had given him a few menial jobs, jobs the apprentices normally did, even though they would have managed fine without Guy. Why oh why had he had to play the Good Samaritan? Now John's falcon was dead and the youth had disappeared for sure.

If Odon isn't behind this, the devil is welcome to take me, William thought angrily as he pondered what to do.

It would be best not to say anything to John about the falcon's recovery. The bird had not survived. Did the prince need to know more than that? John would certainly not believe she had been deliberately poisoned.

Enraged, William kicked a new molehill, sending the earth flying in all directions. Having failed to do what he had set out to do, he went back to the falconry. He found that Robert had already buried the falcon. When he saw that Marguerite had lovingly decorated the spot with crane feathers, William was deeply touched, and his boundless fury evaporated for a moment.

Mastery

Oakham, April 1199
The King Is Dead! Long
Live the King!

The disturbing news spread like wildfire; King Richard had died unexpectedly. They had been back from the mainland only a few weeks when they heard that he had been shot by mistake during the siege of Châlus. He had been struck by arrows many times during the Crusade, but he had always recovered quickly. Therefore, it was said, the king did not take seriously the risk of injury from crossbow bolts and did not protect himself sufficiently. His physicians did not succeed in removing the tip of the bolt from his injured shoulder, so the wound did not heal and started to fester. Knowing that his end was near, Richard called for his mother so that he could settle the succession in her presence. He died in her arms shortly thereafter.

Bowed down with grief at the death of her favorite son but still every inch a queen, Eleanor had buried his body beside the bones of her husband in Fontevraud. Although Richard had absolved the unfortunate archer of all guilt for his imminent death, he was done away with as soon as the king had drawn his last breath, and nobody shed a tear.

Both in England and on the mainland, however, everyone was concerned with the question of the succession. Everywhere, the people were distressed and worried. Although Richard had declared his younger brother heir to the throne, there were fierce disputes over the legality of his decision, and factions began to form. Many loyal subjects of the king wanted to follow Richard's last wish; others thought the rightful heir was Arthur of Brittany, the son of John's dead older brother, who would otherwise have been the rightful heir to the throne. For some time, the Bretons had been fighting for the twelve-year-old Arthur's ascendancy. As soon as the news of Richard's death became known, they had handed over Arthur to the French king in order to secure his support.

Meanwhile, John did not waste any time before heading to Chinon as soon as he heard the news. Once there, he seized the royal treasure and managed to secure the support of important men like Marshal and the archbishop of Canterbury. His claim to the throne looked fairly secure, even if no one knew exactly what would happen next.

As his master falconer, William had become a confidant of old Sir Walkelin's, so he spent enough time in his lord's hall to learn of the situation's difficulty.

"I hope John becomes king. At least he was born in England and speaks our language," said Robert when William told him what was being said in the hall. "Unlike Richard, who never took any interest in England. And as for young Arthur, the Bretons will always come first for him, not the English."

William shrugged doubtfully. Since the incident with the falcon, he feared John, the youngest Plantagenet, and he was afraid that Marguerite would move impossibly far away if he ascended to the throne.

"We'll see," he said darkly. John had given William the opportunity to show him what he could do. Had William succeeded, he could have entertained hopes of joining the court when the prince became king. But the death of the falcon had rendered this prospect null and void. Nothing could be proved against Odon, and he was sure there would never be another opportunity to convince John of his abilities.

"Come, let's get to work. The falcons don't care who is king of England. They won't hunt any worse under one than the other," he said to Robert.

☙❧

Odon paced up and down in his room. Since his father's death, a few things had changed at Elmswick, and the castle had become the place where he felt most at home.

Maud had borne him two sons and was with child again, but still she could not come to terms with life at Elmswick. Despite the various improvements Odon had set in motion before traveling to the mainland, all of which had progressed well during his absence, she still considered the castle beneath her. She grumbled constantly. The hall was too small, the bedchamber drafty, and the wall hangings understated. Even Odon was not up to her expectations.

Sometimes he wondered what he had done to deserve a shrewish wife whom he could never satisfy, having had a father for whom he had never been good enough, either. There were compensations, however, besides the extensive lands she had brought into the marriage. Because of her great beauty, Odon desired Maud with every fiber of his body. Although she showed no genuine fondness for anyone, neither him nor their sons, and was vain and coldhearted, he was nonetheless proud to have her as his wife. The envy he saw in other men's eyes when Maud appeared was too delicious. It allowed him to put her peevishness aside and increased his desire for her.

It was only her mocking expression when she saw him naked that reminded him of other times, and when he felt most hurt he remembered Carla, who had never made fun of him. Since that day in January five years before, he had never again seen her or the son she had borne.

He and Maud had named their first legitimate son and heir Rotrou, after Odon's father, as was customary; the second they had named Henry, after Maud's father. Rotrou was only a few months younger than the son he had with Carla and whose name he still did not know.

Odon wondered what his oldest son might look like. He had not even had a chance to catch a glimpse of the infant child in his cradle. What kind of a boy might he be?

Henry was still small, but he was already quite cheeky, and Rotrou was a rascal, quite to Odon's liking. He was only five years old, but he was already scrapping with the maids' children and was not afraid to threaten the adults, too. He knew very well that he was the son of the lord and that he need fear none of them. Odon's thoughts were still revolving around his sons when there was a knock on the door.

"Forgive me for disturbing you, my lord. A servant from Caldecote would like to speak to you. He refuses to leave and says he has important news he must give you in person. He won't say more." Odon's page looked at his master timidly.

"Take him to the hall," Odon replied brusquely. "I'm on my way."

When Odon came down, the servant had already removed his headgear and was waiting for him. Odon looked curiously at the old man, who was wringing the coif in his hands like a washerwoman.

"What is this news you have, and from whom does it come? Speak up, man," Odon ordered harshly, looking at the man severely. He liked to see the simple folk trembling before him.

"Ah, my lord." The old man bowed humbly several times. "The pigsticker's wife sent me." He sniffed. "She's…she's dying," he stammered. His voice, already shaky, seemed about to forsake him entirely. "And she asked for you to come." He bowed, hunching his shoulders as if expecting to be whipped on the spot.

Odon began to shake like an aspen leaf in the wind and rushed out without saying anything. On his way to the stables, he shouted to his squire that he was riding to Caldecote.

"Alone," he barked when the youth made as if to join him.

He rode the few miles to Caldecote at breakneck speed. He did not know where the pigsticker lived, but he would find his house. If Carla was calling for him after such a long time, things were probably worse than bad with her. Would he reach her in time? Odon drove the horse on pitilessly.

He did not have to ask around much in Caldecote. The people in the very second house knew the pigsticker with the birthmark and told Odon the way. Burning with haste and worry, he got down from his horse in front of the house and hammered on the door until a maid shuffled up and opened it for him. She stared at him, as if turned to a pillar of salt, when she saw what a fine man he was.

Odon pushed her aside. "Take care of my horse," he called out over his shoulder, rushing into the house without paying any further heed to the valuable creature.

Carla was thin and pale. Her cheeks were sunken, her eyes ringed with dark shadows. She was dying. Only her gently rising and falling chest told Odon that she was still alive.

The smell in the room was sour. It reminded him of the unpleasant exhalation of rot and disintegration that had surrounded his father as he battled against death. This time, however, it did not arouse disgust in him but pure terror. He had lost Carla long ago, but Odon now feared for her life as if it were his own. She was the only person who had ever meant anything to him. Despite his horror of sickness and disease, he approached her bed.

She opened her feverishly glittering eyes and smiled with gratitude. "Please take your son." She coughed breathlessly. "I don't want him to grow up here without me. The pigsticker has a son of his own, and he won't want to support my boy after I'm dead.

When he comes back from playing dice at the tavern, it would be better if the boy weren't here."

"You're not going to die, Carla. I'll go and fetch the physician." He was about to leave when Carla held him back.

"He won't come to the house of a simple pigsticker, Odon."

"I'll persuade him. Trust me."

"No, please stay here. I'm dying. Don't leave me alone." A tear ran down her cheek.

"But I won't let you go," protested Odon.

"It's too late. The Lord is already calling me." Carla took a couple of wheezing breaths. "A bastard can become something worthwhile, something better than a pigsticker. Accept your responsibility, Odon. Your son is a good boy."

"I shall acknowledge him and take him in, I promise." Odon stayed at Carla's bedside for a long time, choking back his emotions and holding her hand as she told him, haltingly, about the boy and his early years. At Odon's behest, she also told him about the man who had informed her of the death of the woman in the forest.

Odon asked what the stranger looked like, and when she said he was from Thorne he knew it had been Robert. Why did he stick his nose in and meddle with things that weren't his? He would pay.

As if she could read his thoughts, Carla clung tightly to his hand, sat up effortfully, and pleaded with him, the exertion making her breath noisy. "You mustn't be angry with him. He just wanted to warn me, because he was afraid you would harm me, too. I was with child. It honors him that he wanted to protect me. So let him come to no harm, do you hear me?"

Odon feared she might exhaust herself, so he promised not to do anything to Robert. Tenderly, he pushed Carla back down on her bed, forcing himself to smile at her gently to calm her down, although his soul was still bent on revenge.

Carla paused for breath, then asked him in a low voice to tell the maid to bring her son to her.

When the boy was standing in front of her, she lifted herself up again; her elbow was trembling where it supported her weight. Carla took Odon's hand and placed it on the boy's head. "This is your son. His name is Adam, and I beg you, take care of him." Then she took the boy's hand and placed it on Odon's belt. "Adam, this is Sir Odon of Elmswick, your father. Go with him and obey him always." She sank back in the bed and turned her head to one side. She exhaled noisily and died.

Odon stood stock-still by her bed. Gray and shrunken, she was suddenly as strange to him as if he had never known her. He crossed himself and turned away without a word. As he strode out of the room, the child kept hold of his belt, looked at him wide-eyed, and scampered after him. The boy clearly did not understand that his life had just changed dramatically.

Odon sat the boy on his horse in silence. The maid, who had also heard Carla's last words, rubbed her red eyes dry, caressed the child's foot now that he was high up on the horse, gave him a last wave, and then went back into the house.

Odon swung up behind his son and rode off. After a little while, the boy began to ask questions. He wanted to know when they would go back to his mother and whether it was true that his father lived in a castle. He called Odon "Father" as if he had never known anything else.

At first, Odon was unpleasantly affected by this and wondered whether taking the boy had been a mistake. Who would take care of him and make a man of him? A son he could be proud of, for once? He could put him in a monastery. But that would mean sending him away for a long time, and he didn't like that idea at all. He decided to let Adam grow up with his half brother Rotrou. It was not unusual at all for bastards to be raised alongside legitimate children, and it was the best way to give the boy a reasonable education. Maud would not be enthusiastic, but he would insist on it, and he would ensure that she obeyed. He had nothing more to fear aside from her refusing him her bed for a while.

As he lifted Adam down from the horse at Elmswick, he noticed how much he resembled Carla, and he was gripped by an unexpected wave of affection for him.

"This is my son Adam. He's going to live under my roof from now on," he told everyone in the house by way of introduction. He felt prouder than he ever had before.

Maud complained, as she always did when she did not like something. She threatened, she screamed, and she shouted. But when she saw that Odon was meeting her outbursts of rage with complete indifference, she calmed down.

"He will learn to read, write, and count with Rotrou. And he will also ride, fight, and do battle like him," Odon declared firmly. "You had better get used to the idea that I have another son."

"As long as your lady love's bastard doesn't sleep in our room," Maud hissed. "I wouldn't get a moment's sleep."

Odon accepted this condition and told Adam to sleep in the hall with the knights and servants.

Elmswick, Late May 1199

While Adam gradually settled in, Odon waited to hear who would be king of England. He prayed to the Lord with all his heart that it would be John, for if Arthur ascended the throne and came to hear how cruelly Odon had rampaged in Brittany, it would cost him dearly.

It was at Ascensiontide, Odon found out later, only two days after landing at Shoreham with a few allies, that John Lackland, youngest son of King Henry II, was crowned king of England at Westminster. John's mother, Eleanor, sat at his side for the occasion instead of his wife. People on all sides remarked how alert she still was for her age. Beautiful despite her long gray hair, she still sat lightly and elegantly in the saddle, and as always she was dressed in the finest clothes and noblest jewels.

But John was in a hurry and did not stay at Westminster for long. Immediately after his coronation, he gathered as many men around him as he could and then traveled the length and breadth of England. He visited the abbey at Saint Edmundsbury, journeyed from one important castle to the next, participated in hunts with and without hawks, and tried to ensure the support of as many barons as he could. He had to persuade former enemies, some of whom had mistrusted him for many years, to become loyal subjects and support him.

Odon, too, associated himself with the king. He left no stone unturned in his efforts to make himself indispensable, and so it came about that John finally invited Odon to follow him to the mainland. Overjoyed that the king had noticed him at all, and done him this great honor besides, Odon returned home for a short while to settle his affairs and bid farewell to his wife and sons, whom he would not see for quite some time.

Oakham, June 1199

John came to Oakham, too, accompanied by some of the most important men in the land. De Ferrers, who had known him as a boy and knew how determined and difficult the young king was, welcomed him with full honors. He bowed deeply, dismissed his knights and servants, and invited the king into his hall with an expansive gesture.

William had watched the royal party arrive from afar. He squinted, looking for Marguerite. It did not take long to find her.

Nearly half a year had passed since Marguerite had left Ferrières at John's side—more than five months, during which William had thought of nothing but her and of her expressive eyes, in which tears had glistened as she'd breathed a featherlight kiss on his cheek when they had said good-bye. The days, weeks, and months that had passed since then had felt endless. Life in her absence seemed dull and colorless. He had experienced the journey back to England that February as if in a fog. He had not even noticed the first green shoots of spring at Oakham. Even hunting and working with the falcons had gladdened his heart less than usual.

Now that Marguerite was here, though, he noticed how gloriously the flowers were blooming around him. Their many-colored heads nodded gaily in the light summer breeze. The sky looked bluer than it had before, the sun felt warmer, and the fields seemed more luxuriant.

Marguerite was even more beautiful than he remembered. I shall tell her what I feel, thought William. This time, I'm not going to let her leave without her knowing how things stand with me—whether it's seemly or not.

William looked over at the king, whose expression—a little condescending, masterful, commanding attention—made his still-fresh resolve crumble like a handful of earth. Never, thought William, never will I see forgiveness in his eyes. Not after what happened to his falcon.

Although John had not punished William, and no word of reproach passed his lips, there had been blame and displeasure in his eyes. William had tried to explain, but he did not know what he could say in his own defense. How could he make John understand what had happened? After all, he could not name any witnesses to a deliberate act of poisoning, and it was only his suspicion that pointed to Odon's involvement.

William sighed. Nothing had changed since then. He would have to make the best of things as he found them, now and forever. John would now always consider him a mediocre falconer who could not be trusted with duties beyond the ordinary.

The king was instantly forgotten when William saw one of the younger barons helping Marguerite dismount her horse. William's gaze flicked quickly from him to her and back again. Marguerite was giggling. The sound was bright and harmonious but did not make William happy. On the contrary, it stabbed his heart like a sharp hunting knife. The young man was laughing now. He bowed chivalrously, offered Marguerite his arm, and led her to the hall. William sighed again. If he did not think of something quickly, he might not even get the opportunity to exchange a few words with her. Even if he was invited to the hall to join the banquet that was being prepared for the king, he would sit too far down the table to be able to speak to her.

William took a deep breath of the warm June air. He was so thirsty for her closeness that it hurt. He wanted to make her laugh, to lose himself in her eyes. He had to come up with something, so that he could see her alone for a short while. As he thought about the possibilities, he made his way back to the falconry.

Early that afternoon some riders came to the falconry. William put down the bird he had on his fist and was about to go out when a young assistant came running in.

"The king," he gasped, flushed. He looked wide-eyed at William. "He wants to speak to you."

William was inevitably reminded of the day King Henry had come to the smithy. He had run into the workshop to let his mother know in exactly the same manner as the lad who had just come in. How long ago that was. It seemed like another life.

"I'm coming," he said calmly. His mother had hoped the king was going to order a sword from her. He, on the other hand, could expect nothing from John.

When William came into the courtyard, his heart unexpectedly started racing. Marguerite had come, too. She was so beautiful it took his breath away. He forced himself to close his mouth, which had fallen open in admiration, and to look away from her. He hurried to King John.

"A warm welcome to Oakham, sire." He bowed long and deep. This time he knew the correct form of address, for "sire" was reserved for kings alone. William stayed down for a moment.

"One of my falcons is sick. Marguerite has been pestering me for two days. She thinks I should leave the falcon with you." John frowned and scratched his nose. "She keeps telling me that the falcon I entrusted to you at Ferrières had been cured. Though I must admit I can't believe anyone killed her on purpose. Who would do something so terrible to such a magnificent creature? Besides, the smallest child knows a crime like that is punishable with the gallows."

William looked down. There was no point in accusing Odon. Guy was dead. He had been found murdered in the woods shortly after the discovery of the poisoned falcon, and nothing, absolutely nothing, appeared to support William's suspicion.

The king looked ill-tempered. "I fear Pilgrim would not survive the journeys I intend to make. I have spoken to Walkelin. Even he advises me to leave him here. He spoke of you in nothing but the highest terms and offered your services to care for him until I return, though that may be some time."

William felt the blood rushing through his body to his head. Once there, it heated his cheeks so fiercely they began to burn. Here it was, the second chance he had not dared to hope for.

"Can you tell me what seems to be troubling him, sire?" he asked politely.

"His mutes are as green as young leaves, and he's visibly weak," said John with a troubled look. He snapped his fingers, and a young man hurried in with the bird.

William took the peregrine onto his fist and stroked his breast gently. As if to prove John right, the bird promptly cast an evil-smelling green mute. William shook his head thoughtfully and looked into the bird's eyes. They were almond shaped and dull instead of round and shiny.

"It doesn't look good," he murmured. He felt the weakness that had struck the falcon as if it had struck his very flesh.

"Pilgrim's a good bird. It would cause me pain to lose him."

"Robert," William shouted, looking around for his friend.

"I'm coming," he heard from the mews.

When William turned around, Marguerite gave him a tiny smile that warmed his heart.

Robert hurried in, bringing one of de Ferrers's hunt assistants. They bowed to the king first, then turned to William.

"Take the bird off me and take her inside," he instructed Robert. Then he nodded to the assistant. "I don't need you now. Go back to your work." Then he spoke to the king. "Pilgrim needs rest, sire, good nourishment, and some herbal medicines that I will prepare for him. I promise to do what I can to make him better soon."

"Well, I should hope so," said John with a deep crease in his forehead. At length he nodded graciously and turned his horse.

William glanced hurriedly at Marguerite. He could not let her go again, just like that.

"Excuse me, sire, will you be doing my master the honor of staying at Oakham today?" he asked quickly, bowing once again.

"But of course. I wouldn't miss the culinary delights that good Walkelin has promised me any more than I would miss the pleasure of being able to rest my head on a feather pillow."

"Would you permit me, then, to show our new falcons to your niece, if she wishes?" William added with a pounding heart. He had plucked up all his courage and was all the more grateful when Marguerite nodded immediately.

"Oh yes, Uncle. Please let me stay here for a little while," she begged, giving John one of her most charming smiles. "I would so like to discuss falcons with William for a while longer." She fluttered her eyelashes, which not only drove William to distraction but also, apparently, had the desired effect on John.

"I'm sure your father would have been very proud of you if he could have lived to see how much you love falcons." He smiled at Marguerite. "So yes, by all means." And then, to William, "Bring her to the hall by sunset, no later."

"May I?" asked William, offering to help her down from her horse.

She giggled and squirmed when he gripped her by the waist. "I'm so ticklish," she gasped.

William relaxed a little. So that was why she had laughed with the young baron. As Marguerite turned to face him, her soft brown hair brushed against his cheek, and when she met his eyes, her long penetrating look seemed to drill into him like a lance. He felt a tremendous pressure in his chest, like a huge stone.

"Thank you," she whispered, and again William felt that awful, humiliating blush.

"It is I who must thank you, mistress. For speaking up for me to the king," he said quickly. The heat in his ears told him they must be glowing like the setting sun again. Would Marguerite ever see him when he wasn't blushing?

"I'm so happy to be here," she sighed.

"Would you like…er…shall I show you our newest falcon?" he stammered, then instantly became angry with himself. His question was utterly superfluous.

"How are Arrow and Storm? Did they stay at Ferrières?" asked Marguerite as they walked to the falcons' stall together.

"No, they're both here and in fine form," replied William happily. He told her proudly about the two falcons' latest exploits in the hunt.

Marguerite greeted the two birds like old friends. She approached them respectfully and stroked them gently. She fired question after question at William, just as he was used to from her. She did not chatter as much as she once did, to be sure—she was obviously trying to become a perfect lady—but that did not seem to come easily to her.

William breathed in her scent of herbs and attar of roses. He was finding it difficult to follow her words, for her nearness to him was making him feel faint.

"Oh, please, let's not sit down! We've been riding for so long that my behind hurts," exclaimed Marguerite when William offered her a stool, and then she blushed, too.

How delightful she was when she forgot to rein in her liveliness. William found her even more beautiful when her behavior was unforced, and even more desirable.

"All right, if that's how you feel, a little turn will do you good. Let's go for a walk," he suggested, holding open the door and letting her go first.

Sticking close together, they ran across the big field toward the edge of the forest. Their fingers brushed against each other as if by accident; the contact almost made William burst with desire for Marguerite, and he moved away a little, as if he feared he could no longer hold himself in check.

The trees were coming into leaf, and the pale foliage made the forest seem bright and welcoming. The sun warmed them a little, but it was nothing compared to the fire William could feel burning deep inside him. While he was thinking about Marguerite, she suddenly ran off. He watched her go, frightened.

"Catch me if you can, William!" she cried, full of high spirits and laughing teasingly.

William stood rooted to the spot. Marguerite was surprisingly quick, and soon she had a considerable lead. He was overcome with a terrible fear.

"Wait," he cried, terrified, and set off in pursuit.

Marguerite ran as fast as she could, but William caught up with her. Just as he was about to grab her, she looked at him, missed a broken branch that was lying on the ground, and stumbled. William tried to catch her, but he lost his balance, too. Marguerite fell, pulling him down with her.

The thick layer of leaves on the forest floor was as soft as a king's bed. William was lying on top of Marguerite, and at first her expression was fearful.

"Did you hurt yourself?" he asked anxiously, but he neglected to get up.

Marguerite shook her head. "I don't think so." Her eyes were wide-open and her lips were slightly apart, as if all she was waiting for was to be kissed.

William spotted a tear in the corner of her eye and gently wiped it away. "I..." he began, but instead of continuing he leaned down and kissed her tenderly. He took a deep breath of her intoxicatingly sweet scent and suppressed the thought that he was not entitled to it. Just one kiss, he said to himself, one kiss that can be mine alone, that I'll remember forever, that will unite us forever—even if it costs me my life because the king has me hanged for it.

His lips touched hers very cautiously, for fear she might reject him angrily. But Marguerite let it happen. When she opened her mouth a little, William's tongue gently sought out hers. At first, she returned his kisses hesitantly, then with more enthusiasm, and soon she was breathing as hard as he was.

"I wish I could stay with you here forever," she breathed. Her eyes were sparkling, and her cheeks glowed with warmth.

"We would train falcons and have lots of children," he whispered, and Marguerite shivered as his lips touched her ear. She looked at him invitingly, and he felt brave enough to kiss her neck, very gently and yet passionately.

Marguerite sighed almost inaudibly. She closed her eyes as William's tongue flicked playfully over her neck. He could feel the wild beating of her heart beneath her tender skin. She tasted fresh as the sea and light as the wind, of love and eternity. Emboldened by the fact that she had not rejected him, he covered her cheeks, forehead, and eyes with kisses light as air, then returned to her mouth and found complete abandonment there. William's arousal verged on the immeasurable. As if of their own accord, his hands glided downward, pausing on her slim hips, which he could feel through the cloth of her gown, and worked their way toward her belly, whose softness aroused a wish to protect her for the rest of his life.

"I'll always love you," he whispered.

Marguerite moaned softly as his hand slid upward over her ribs, exploring gently, till it reached her small firm breasts. William longed to experience the softness of her skin, but Marguerite coughed and pushed him away, albeit halfheartedly. "The sun will go down soon. I have to go back," she cried breathlessly.

"Please stay, I can't let you leave." William pulled her to him and kissed her again.

"But I must!" Marguerite looked at him with tears in her eyes, pulled away from him, and tried to stand up. "Ouch, my foot!" She felt her ankle, looking so charmingly helpless that William reached out and stroked her hair.

"Let me see," he said, cautiously removing her shoe and moving her foot. "Does that hurt?"

At first she shook her head, but when he turned her foot a little, she took a sharp breath through her teeth and smiled bravely when he looked at her with concern.

"Sorry." He looked into her eyes and felt he would lose himself in them. "At least it's not broken. It will heal quickly with an herbal compress. We'd better go back to the falconry. Put your arm around my neck. I'll hold you up. I'll bandage you up, and then we'll get your horse before your uncle tears off my head because I didn't bring you back on time."

Marguerite nodded and limped back to the falconry without protest.

William relished every moment and wished the distance could be even greater, so that he could be with her longer. Although she did not complain, he offered to carry her, but Marguerite refused, maintaining the attitude that befitted her station. But after only a few steps, she was clinging to him more tightly. She had never been as close to him as this afternoon, and he had never been so afraid to see her leave. He glanced at her out of the corner of his eye. He would keep this picture in his memory forever. He would never forget the pale scar on her forehead; he had been kissing it just moments before and knew that Marguerite had acquired it when she fell out of her favorite tree years ago.

When they reached the falconry, he treated her foot, placed a gentle kiss on her ankle, and simply smiled when she chided him uneasily.

They rode back to de Ferrers's hall side by side in silence. William did not dare look at her again. If he gave in to his desire to feel her soft lips against his again, or to hold her in his arms, he would not be able to let her go. Did she feel the same?

Marguerite did not wait for him to help her down from her horse. She slipped smoothly down to the ground and walked toward the hall. Unable to touch her one last time, he caught up with her. She was hobbling a little. It's the same foot as mine, he thought, smiling sadly at the thought of what they must look like, the two of them walking alongside each other with the same swaying gait.

"Ah, there you are, my child," said John, looking at her inquiringly as she walked toward him. "Why are you limping?"

"I was careless and twisted my ankle," Marguerite explained, showing her foot. "It still hurts quite a bit," she said, not looking at the king or William.

Could the king tell that something else had happened that afternoon? William's heart raced so fast that his ribs hurt.

"Here, take this for looking after my falcon," said the king, holding out a silver coin.

"What's so funny?" asked John unpleasantly when he saw William's sudden grin.

"Forgive me, sire. I didn't mean to be disrespectful, but I was suddenly reminded of Your Majesty's father."

"My father?"

William nodded and bowed again. "He gave me an almost identical silver coin once, as a reward for finding his gyrfalcon. I refused it."

"You did what?"

"I told him I would rather become a falconer."

"You said that to his face, just like that?" The king shook his head in disbelief. It was obvious he could scarcely imagine that William had dared to be so brazen, and he was visibly impressed when William nodded. "Then you were either foolish or very brave. My father was famous for his rages. I feared him my whole life, even though I was his clear favorite."

"He let me get away with it." William smiled uncertainly and took a deep breath as he decided to give in to a foolish idea. He simply had to risk everything, cost what it may, so he plucked up his courage and cleared his throat. "That's why I dare to hope for your consideration, sire. Because I should like to ask you to grant me something." A chill went through him at the thought of what he was about to do. "I'd like to ask you for Marguerite's hand."

William saw that Marguerite had heard, and he saw her flush. Was she glad? Or maybe she was angry?

The king gasped, and William was afraid a tremendous rage would follow, but instead John roared with laughter. The nearby barons stopped talking and looked curiously over at them. Some of them started whispering, and the king suddenly looked at William quite seriously. "I must disappoint you," he said severely, his voice low. "For the moment you will have to be satisfied with the coin." Without another word, he stood up, offered Marguerite his arm, and asked her to accompany him. He walked past William without so much as a glance.

Hadn't King Henry said almost exactly the same thing that day all those years ago? For one irrational moment, he allowed himself to imagine how it would feel to be married to Marguerite, to be able to kiss her whenever he felt like it and on whatever part of her body he chose. He looked around, red faced, but fortunately the other barons had followed the king and were not paying him any attention. Only Marguerite looked back at him briefly, but he did not rightly know how to interpret her look.

With a heavy heart, he went to his allotted place at the lower table and sank onto the bench beside Robert.

During the meal, Marguerite kept her eyes locked on the white tablecloth spread out in front of her.

William could not take his eyes off her; he kept hoping she would eventually look at him. He stared at her as if in a trance, and he ate less than a sparrow. Marguerite, too, managed only a few crumbs. Was she angry that he had asked the king for her hand? William dared to hope she was eating so little because she was hungry for him and not meat and gravy. His love for her filled him so completely that there was no room in his body for food.

William sighed as he remembered the afternoon, Marguerite's soft skin, and her supple body, which had trembled at his cautious touch. It was said that the king had many wards, but he was obviously particularly fond of Marguerite, for she spent more time near him than any of the others. The children of nobles who lost their parents before they were old enough to inherit inevitably became royal wards. This worked to the king's advantage because he could supervise the running of their lands and, at the same time, rake in the income that derived from them. Moreover, the king had the right, provided no marriage had already been arranged, to marry off his wards as he saw fit, which meant they could be used as attractive lures for an alliance. Who knew what the king had in mind for Marguerite? Perhaps William would never see her again, never be alone with her again.

When Robert addressed him, breaking into his troubled thoughts, William started. "What did you say to the king to make him suddenly punish you with his indifference?" he asked with an anxious glance toward the king.

"Please forgive me. I'm tired. I'm going to bed," William murmured. Then he stood up and left the hall without further explanation.

It had happened with Richard ten years before, and so it was again; the English scarcely had time to fete their king. Barely three weeks after he had stepped on English soil, John set off for the mainland once again. William watched as the king and his retinue readied themselves for departure at daybreak. He was standing near the great hall, behind a mighty oak tree. He had hardly slept the night before and had gotten up long before dawn. He was now keeping watch, sadly hoping to see Marguerite one last time before she disappeared from his life, perhaps forever.

When at last she came out of the hall and mounted her horse, she seemed downcast. Or was she not thinking about him at all? When her eyes cast about as if searching for him, his heart skipped a beat. He stepped out from behind the oak and shyly waved at her, but Marguerite did not see him. Or perhaps she was ignoring him? She turned her horse around and rode off. The wind tussled her long dark hair. William closed his eyes and almost felt it brushing his face, as it had when he had helped Marguerite down from her horse the day before. He struggled for breath, but his throat and chest were so tight he thought he would suffocate.

When at last he opened his eyes, Marguerite was gone.

Saint Edmundsbury,
November 1199

For the first time in a long while, William was spending Martinmas at Saint Edmundsbury.

Ellenweore embraced him warmly, gripped her son's shoulders, and looked at him proudly. "You've really made something of yourself," she said, pushing her red locks back under her bonnet. Her hair was less glossy than it had once been because of the gray strands running through it. She's not getting any younger, thought William. She must be nearly fifty, perhaps even older.

"Where's your friend Robert?" she asked.

"He couldn't come. De Ferrers insisted that one of us be available for hunting. And since Robert doesn't have any family, he wanted me to go. He sends you all his warmest greetings." William kissed his mother's cheek. "That kiss is from him. He says he would give anything to have had a mother like you. He lost his when he was young and doesn't remember her at all."

Ellenweore shook her head and rubbed her temple with her forefinger, as she was wont to do. "Come inside. The others will be so happy to see you."

The farmers around the smithy had brought in the harvest, threshed the grain, and filled their sacks with corn so that it could be stored over the winter. The barns were full to the rafters, and people were in the mood to celebrate after all their hard work. On Saint Martin's Day, masses were said in every church

in England, and the faithful thanked the Lord for a bountiful
harvest and prayed for a mild winter.

After mass in the little village church, William, Jean, Isaac,
and the other men set off for Saint Edmundsbury to celebrate.
They entered the town through the southern gate and headed
toward the market square. Here, the town worthies were perform-
ing the story of Saint Martin, earning tumultuous applause as they
did every year. More and more people seemed to come to the town
every year. The huge abbey of Saint Edmundsbury was known
beyond the borders of England and attracted large crowds of pilgrims, who wandered through the streets after mass and thronged
the taverns, where there was music, dancing, and fun.

William and his companions were looking for diversion, too,
and they straggled from tavern to tavern. They drank and laughed,
putting aside everyday cares and enjoying the happiness of the
moment.

They did not get home until the evening. Rose had prepared a
delicious feast, which consisted of a crisp roast goose with roasted
chestnuts, a highly spiced sauce, and, in honor of the day, whiter
bread than usual. The apprentices and journeymen sat down at
the table with their master and mistress and drank Rose's home-
brewed beer.

William's visit especially thrilled David. He sat beside him,
smiling with delight and silently shoveling his food into his mouth
with shining eyes. Eventually, he stood up and staggered out into
the pitch-black night to relieve himself.

"The amount of beer he's drunk! He'll be pissing like a horse,"
laughed one of the journeymen; another started coarsely miming
the act, and David was soon forgotten. Not even William noticed
that he did not come back, for he too had devoted more attention
to beer than was good for him. Rose was not only a wonderful
cook; she also brewed a splendid, full-flavored ale that sent one's
senses spinning. After a few drained tankards, William was too

drunk to think clearly. He missed Marguerite terribly, so he tried to drown his sorrow and banish all thoughts of her by dancing halfheartedly with the new maid. He sat her on his lap and paid no heed to his mother's disapproving glance.

The more they ate and drank, the more tired they all became, and they were soon nodding off. One of the smiths simply slid down to the floor, two journeymen curled up together on the bench, and most of the others fell asleep where they sat, resting their heads on the table. At some point, William fell asleep, too.

He woke up the next morning with a furry tongue and aching head that reminded him of the days when he had drunk too much beer too often. "Never again," he swore to himself, as he had done so many times before; he knew very well that this resolution would not last either. As soon as his head did not ache anymore, such oaths would fall by the wayside. Beer was part of life, as air was part of breathing. Except that one couldn't get too much air, whereas an excess of beer often had evil effects. William stood up, yawning, and stretched pleasurably.

"You look terrible." Isaac grinned. He was astonishingly alert, even though he had drunk quite a lot, too. "Where's David, by the way?" he asked casually, passing William a tankard of beer.

He sniffed it quickly and grimaced with distaste. His stomach threatened to heave at the mere smell.

"You'd better drink something. It'll soon clear your head-ache," Isaac advised him, pointing at the tankard. "One's enough. Stronger than you think, Rose's brew."

William obeyed reluctantly, then remembered Isaac's question. "Where *is* David?" he repeated croakily, putting his tankard down and looking around.

"I thought he was here with you." Isaac looked under the table and shook his head. "But he isn't."

"The last time I saw him, he was going out to relieve himself. That was last night. I'll look outside," he cried anxiously, tearing the door open and rushing out of the house.

It was not long before they found him in a bush behind the house.

"David!" cried William, turning over his lifeless body and kneeling down beside him. He slapped his cheeks in a panic and tried to sit him upright. "Help me, Isaac! He's fainted!"

Isaac skillfully grabbed David's legs with his hand and gripped them beneath his one good arm so that they could carry him into the house. "His lips are completely blue with cold. Let's put him by the fire," he suggested, once they were inside. Having heard the commotion, Rose came rushing in.

"What's the matter with him?" She leaned over the lifeless body and felt his forehead. "Good heavens, he's burning up!"

David wheezed and coughed. He groaned softly but did not wake up.

"The ground froze hard during the night. The boy's stiff with cold," Rose observed. "We need to get him in a bed right next to the fire."

"I shouldn't have let him go out alone. It's my fault. I…" William could hardly breathe. "I should have looked after him. Why, Rose? Why am I never there when I'm most needed?" Tears ran down his face.

"The coughing doesn't sound good, but David's never been ill before. I'm sure he'll get better soon."

"You're probably right," said William, hugging her. He knew how much Rose and Jean had taken David into their hearts in the past few years. "I'm sure he'll be fine soon," he said, though his instinct told him otherwise.

A few days after they found him, David fell asleep forever. Nothing had helped, not William's herbal infusions and not

Rose's loving care. David had started to run a high fever and to cough dreadfully. His body was racked with cramps, and he died without ever really coming to. William stayed by his bedside day and night, praying fervently to the Lord to spare him. But it had not helped.

They buried David in the field behind the smithy. Jean dug out his last resting place, for William did not have the strength. He was too deeply oppressed by the memory of the time he had dug the grave for Enid and the child, and all the pain he had felt then returned now.

Rose wept bitterly, and even Jean kept having to wipe the tears from his face. William knew he had been particularly fond of the boy because he reminded him of Madeleine.

Ellenweore had told William about Madeleine. She was a girl from Jean's village. They had fled together when robbers burned down all the houses and killed the other villagers. Madeleine had not been simple, like David, but the horrors she had witnessed had left her confused and dependent. Jean felt guilty because, a few years later, he had been unable to prevent her violent death.

"David is with God now," said Ellenweore, probably hoping to soften William's pain with her words.

"And with Enid and my child," he added in a hoarse voice, but the thought gave him little comfort.

Oakham, Winter 1200

hen the news reached them that King John was on his way to Stamford and wanted to see them all there—Walkelin and Henry de Ferrers, William and the falcons he had been taking care of for the king all summer—William could not contain his excitement.

"I wonder if Marguerite will be there, too?" he mused out loud as he replaced the falcons' jesses.

"I doubt it. He probably left her as a lady-in-waiting to his new wife. I've heard the queen is only a bit younger than Marguerite. Fourteen, apparently." Robert raised his eyebrows. "What do grown men see in such young girls? Most of them just stand around giggling all the time, laughing at stuff no one else finds funny."

"Marguerite's different."

"Of course she is," replied Robert soothingly.

"Maybe she really is with the queen," murmured William, ignoring Robert's shrug.

It was said that John had divorced his first wife because she had not given him any children. But perhaps he had other reasons, thought William. Isabel of Gloucester was not only John's wife but also his cousin. It was common knowledge that a marriage between two such close blood relations was forbidden, though kings frequently ignored the prohibition. For John it would be possible to have the marriage annulled and to marry again without difficulty.

There had been widespread speculation as to which lady he would choose as queen of England. And there had already been discussions with the king of Portugal, whose daughter was old enough to marry. John even sent a delegation south to continue the negotiations, but his eventual choice, more than surprising to many, was Isabelle d'Angoulême. Already promised to her neighbor, Hugh le Brun, a member of the Lusignan family, she had to cancel the betrothal in order to marry John, who by all accounts was consumed with passion for her.

After the wedding in August, the couple returned from the mainland in October and made their way to Westminster, where they were crowned on the eighth day of the month.

If the king has married a woman younger than his favorite ward, it won't be long before he marries off Marguerite, too, William thought despondently. It would probably be best to forget her and never see her again.

When de Ferrers and his men reached Stamford a few days later, the king had already arrived and was waiting for them. Try as he might, William had not been able to forget Marguerite. So he could not help eyeing the crowd of people in the hope of catching sight of her.

"Ah, William, I see you've brought my falcon," cried John joyfully, once he had greeted Walkelin and Henry de Ferrers and waved to William to join them.

He bowed down on one knee before the king and held out his fist with the falcon on it. "He's completely recovered. A magnificent creature, sire."

"Put him on the perch there," John commanded, smiling at William and pointing at the stand beside him.

He did as the king asked and then, after a questioning glance at Sir Walkelin, who responded with a tired nod, turned to the king again.

"Forgive me, sire, but my master has brought you another falcon as a wedding gift." William bowed briefly toward de Ferrers.

Then he signaled to Robert, who like him was kneeling before the king. A gorgeous female gyrfalcon stood on his fist. William took her and presented her to the king.

John stood up and looked at her intently.

"Magnificent," he cried. "Beautiful markings and a noble posture. You have my thanks, Walkelin, a splendid beast!" He turned to William. "Did you train her?"

"Yes, sire."

"Well, in that case I'm going to put both birds to the test tomorrow. I'm keen to see how they perform. Tomorrow we're going hawking," he announced with satisfaction, dismissing William and Robert with a courteous nod.

William spent the rest of the evening keeping watch for Marguerite. Over and over again he thought he saw her, only to be disappointed when he found he was wrong.

By the time the benches and tables were being brought in and the banquet was beginning, William had given up hope. He sat down beside Robert, bored, ate without much appetite, and did not take any pleasure in the music or conversations with other falconers, which normally meant so much to him.

Stamford was famous for its large population of herons, and the king hoped to bag a few with his falcons. At his command, the falconers and their assistants set off to prepare the hunt.

Once they had reached the most promising area—close to the herons' breeding grounds—William tested the direction of the wind. To ensure that the king's falcons would perform optimally, he chose a position downwind from the heron colony and had his helpers put up solid shelters to protect the hunting party, the falcons, and the horses from the wind. William was very conscious of the great honor of his position. The king wanted to test him, and he would not fail. He knew precisely what needed to be done and was far too busy with the preparations to worry.

They still had a great deal to do before the hunt began that afternoon. He would meticulously ensure that nothing went wrong. As for what the falcons did during the hunt, that was in God's hands.

During all this, William had the falcons tethered to the ground with pegs so that they would not tire out, and he ordered a servant to guard them from attacks by other animals.

When the king and his retinue finally arrived, William sent one of his assistants to a previously selected lookout post. As arranged, the young man placed himself in an elevated position downwind from the herons but upwind from the hunting party, so that everyone could see him and he could spot the herons as they flew toward them.

William and Robert rode off with the falcons on their fists until they were a few hundred paces away from the hunting party and closer to the heron colony, taking care to remain upwind. When the young assistant at last spotted a heron flying toward them, he dismounted his horse and pointed its head in the direction of the approaching quarry.

Upon this signal, the whole party started to move. They rushed over, looking tensely into the sky and, as soon as they could make out the heron, tried to get to the best vantage point from which to follow the drama. At the same time, they all did their best to avoid scaring the bird with unnecessary noise.

Meanwhile, William and Robert had managed to approach their quarry without causing it to change direction. William let it fly overhead and did not remove his falcon's hood until the heron had flown on a few hundred paces. Now that he knew how to use hoods and had learned their advantages, William no longer practiced seeling.

Robert brought out Pilgrim from under his cloak, as the bird was not used to a hood. On William's command, they both cast their falcons into the air. Although at first both birds stayed low and flew in different directions, not gaining on their quarry at all, the heron appeared to realize that they were after it. It stretched out its neck and regurgitated a fish from its crop. This made its body lighter and helped it to fly better. With all its strength, it now tried to reach the heron colony or at least a nearby grove of trees.

The falcons promptly began to climb. The heron, finding itself unable to gain on the falcons, seemed to know that they were only a danger if they came from above, so it began to spiral upward, too, higher and higher in the air. Since it could not both climb and fly into the wind, however, eventually it had to turn and fly toward the falcons.

The start William and Robert had originally given it now gave the advantage to the falcons. The three birds, which had started out flying in different directions, were now heading toward each other at incredible speed, and the excitement of the onlookers reached fever pitch. Every now and then the heron let out an alarming squawk, all the time trying to climb higher, using the wind to escape its pursuers.

Suddenly, one of the falcons caught up and attacked. The heron tried to escape by abruptly swerving away. The maneuver was successful, and the falcon, now more than twenty yards below, no longer represented a danger—for the moment at least. Meanwhile, though, the other falcon was swooping down toward it.

The onlookers held their breath. The first falcon had missed its target, but the second had spent the intervening time climbing again and now launched its own attack. The attacks alternated in this way, more or less equally, until one of the falcons seized the heron by its neck and the other one joined in immediately.

The three birds fell out of the sky like a single body, but before they reached the ground, one of the falcons let go. The other one did the same, in order not to hit the ground hard. Once the heron had fallen to earth, it tried to fly away, but the falcons immediately started tearing at it.

William and Robert had followed the hunt at a gallop, so that they could be on the spot when the falcons brought down their prey. They were in such a hurry that they sprang straight out of their saddles. Holding out a pigeon, Robert tempted the first falcon to release the prey, while William cautiously approached the heron and tried to grab it by the neck. Once he had done so, he too offered the other falcon a pigeon, which it consumed while still standing on the heron. Once the falcons had gorged themselves, William hooded his and Robert put Pilgrim back under his cover. Then they made their way back to the agreed meeting point. They handed the captured heron over to the king with a deep bow.

"I've seldom seen such excellently trained falcons," John complimented William, clapping him on the shoulder. "In the future you'll be looking after more than one of my birds." Turning to old de Ferrers, he said, "Walkelin, you've no choice but to let me have him."

Walkelin de Ferrers bowed. "As you wish, sire."

But Henry de Ferrers's cheek was twitching. It was not hard to guess that he was hardly delighted with this turn of events. The de Ferrerses had been faithful servants to the Plantagenets for decades, and it was doubtless a great honor that the king was appropriating their falconer for his own use. On the other hand, not having William in their falconry anymore would be a bitter loss.

"Yes, I think I should marry him off," John remarked pensively. He frowned and put his finger to his lips.

William's heart skipped a beat. Was the king really going to allow him to wed Marguerite? No, that was impossible, wasn't it?

"Let me think who comes to mind," John murmured, but he did not seem to need to think for long. "Yes, I know. Richard de Hauville's fief would be perfect. The falconry's been derelict for years, true, but a man like William will soon put that to rights. He'd have enough space for the falcons there and could raise more for me, too. The surrounding area is excellent for hunting: I know it from my youth. Yes, it's a great sorrow to me that the falconry went to ruin when de Hauville died."

William was crestfallen. The king had not so much as looked at him during all this. He had spoken to old de Ferrers as if it affected only him. But now he turned to William, his face expressionless, and looked challengingly into his eyes.

"A young and fertile wife who will bear you children, a pretty holding with cattle, three villages, a large forest, a falconry with plentiful pasture and farmland. That's what you wanted, isn't it, William?" He leaned forward and whispered, "For a knight's bastard with your talents, an estate like that is eminently suitable, I think."

"I shall be forever indebted to you, sire," William stammered, bowing. He would get as a wife not Marguerite but Richard de Hauville's daughter, a stranger. William had never met Richard, but the de Hauvilles were a well-respected family and had produced many great falconers. It was therefore an honor to marry into it. What would they say about it when they heard? he wondered, a little worried.

Suddenly, though, a number of thoughts tumbled into William's head. How did John know he was a bastard? His heart started racing. Did the king know his father's name? If so, how? For a moment he considered asking, but he did not have the courage. Besides, he had Isaac. Wasn't he his real father? William knew how much Isaac wanted a grandchild. I'm going to be a husband, he thought, and Isaac will soon be a grandfather.

When he thought about the marriage, more questions assailed him. Who was the wife John intended for him? What was she like? William turned to the king, but he had since directed his attention to some other men and was no longer heeding him.

"God, I feel sick." William said to Robert after they had parted with the king. "It won't be long before I do what the heron did."

"Oh no, please don't," Robert laughed, but he looked pale and did not seem happy at all.

William rubbed his stomach nervously. He didn't know whether to be unhappy or glad about his forthcoming marriage. For the past few weeks, the thought that his beloved Marguerite would get married one day, and that he would lose her, had never been far from his mind. But he had not really given any thought to his own future. He would probably never see Marguerite again; if he did, it would be on the arm of some powerful baron to whom she had been given as wife. So why shouldn't he get married, too? The longer William thought about it, the more sensible the idea seemed, and the prospect of hunting only with royal falcons in the future, caring for them, and raising new birds for the king began to intrigue him. If he approached things with sufficient skill, soon every baron would be talking about his falcons.

"Just think what opportunities would be open to me as a land-holder," William said to Robert, and the thought made him feel weak with excitement. "Arise, Sir So-and-So. Heavens, Robert. What an adventure stands before me. And it's unexpected, fascinating, exciting," he gasped.

With this promised marriage he would rise higher than he had ever dared hope, higher than his mother. He knew, of course, that bastard sons had a good chance of rising at court, but normally their fathers exerted influence on their behalf. But he had done it alone, through his abilities alone. The thought that he would soon be a lord, albeit of lowly rank, seemed increasingly sensible. Why shouldn't the son of a smith rise to the rank of royal falconer?

William had sat in silence beside Robert during their meal, so deep in his thoughts that he did not notice the furrow in Robert's forehead until they were leaving the great hall together. "You ought to be happy for me," he said.

"So you're going to marry her," Robert confirmed harshly. His voice rang with disappointment. "I didn't think you would be so easily bought."

"You know as well as I do that I can't refuse this marriage," William said, looking at his friend in shock. "And why should I, anyway? I've earned it, and besides it's an excellent opportunity."

"To rise into the higher ranks, yes, I know, but aren't you forgetting someone?" Robert demanded petulantly. "Someone who used to be important to you?"

"I shall never be able to love the woman the king has allocated to me as much as Marguerite. I know that," said William. He knew he was doing his future wife an injustice, but it could not be otherwise. "But I shall respect her, and have Marguerite as the only one in my heart forever."

"All you think about is women! I'm talking about *me*! What about me? You become Sir So-and-So. Fine. And me? Well, who knows? De Ferrers might even make me his new falcon master once you're gone."

"You're jealous! I wouldn't have been surprised to hear that from anyone else, but I didn't expect it from you," William exclaimed angrily, shaking his head. "Surely you don't begrudge me marriage and a title?"

"You no sooner find out you're going to be a lord than you immediately doubt my friendship. You're already like them, even though you're not one of them yet. Don't you understand? I don't want you to go," Robert screamed before walking away.

"What's got into you?" William muttered in disbelief.

The next morning, while William was busy seeing to the king's falcons, de Ferrers and his men left the castle. William did not find out until they were already gone, and he was disappointed to be left behind. Robert had not even bid him farewell.

When the king himself set off a few days later, William took his place in the royal procession alongside the other falconers and mulled things over. Robert wasn't jealous of the forthcoming marriage; he just didn't want to lose his friend. William was angry with himself for not talking to him again. Robert was his best friend, and already he missed him. How was he going to set up a new falconry without him? Who would train the hounds they would need for hunting if not Robert? A future without him was unthinkable. William realized he had to do something.

He spurred on his horse and sped up until he caught up with the king. "My lord, would you grant me a request?"

"I give you a rich wife and you have further wishes?" said John peevishly. But then he laughed. "Go on, William, tell me what's on your mind."

"Robert is a good falconer, and he has a gift for handling hounds," William began hoarsely.

"And?"

"He would be a great help to me when I'm setting up the falconry."

"I understand. But what am *I* supposed to do about it? If you pay him properly, I'm sure he'll be glad to serve you. And if he's a true friend to you, as I suspect he is, he won't hesitate to follow you even if you can't offer him as much as another master. I'm sure de Ferrers will be very reluctant to let him go, but your friend is a free man. He can decide for himself what he wants to do."

"Then will you permit me to go and fetch him?"

"Return to us at Sevenoaks, southeast of London, within the week. I can't allow you more time."

"Thank you, sire. Thank you. I'll see you at Sevenoaks."

When William arrived at Oakham three days later, the de Ferrerses were surprised but welcomed him with open arms.

"Shouldn't you be with the king?"

"He gave me permission to leave for a few days. I beg you, Sir Walkelin, don't be angry with me. I've come because I'd like to persuade Robert to help me set up my new falconry. I know you value him as highly as I do. That's why I've come to you first to ask for your approval."

"First you and now him." Sir Walkelin turned away and poured himself a cup of wine. He did not offer any to William. "Robert is a damned fine man."

"I know, my lord, and he is profoundly loyal to you, as I always have been, too. He wouldn't leave if he thought you would be angry. But we've worked together for so long—" William broke off. Sir Walkelin had volunteered to be a hostage for King Richard. He knew what friendship and loyalty meant.

"Since you left, he's been neglecting his work. That being so, I can't make him my master falconer. I'll have to place someone else over him, and he won't like that. As far as I'm concerned, he can go with you." Sir Walkelin coughed, supporting himself on the edge of the table.

"Are you all right?"

"Why should I be all right? I'm old and worn-out. My back hurts after every ride, and whenever it rains—which, unfortunately, is often around here—my old joints give me trouble. I won't be doing much hunting anymore. Henry will have to find himself new falconers. Now go. Go to Robert. I'm sure he'll accept your offer all too willingly."

"Thank you, my lord. May God bless you and reward you for your kindness." William bowed and set off down the familiar path to the falconry.

"Leave me alone, *my lord*," Robert exclaimed when William asked Robert to join him. "My place is here."

"But I need your help to set up the falconry. Apparently it's in a dreadful state. The king has given me only a few days. We're supposed to rejoin him at Sevenoaks. Just think about the exciting challenges ahead for us!" William smiled encouragingly at Robert.

"I'm sorry, William. I can't leave here."

"But Sir Walkelin has agreed. Please."

Robert shook his head defiantly. "Go now."

It took William three long days to reach Sevenoaks, and he arrived at almost the same time as the king. The royal party had shrunk noticeably. Several of the barons had returned to their estates for some days, and only a few men remained with the king. A downcast William reported to the king, and when the latter asked where Robert was, he tried in vain to hold back the bitterness he felt. Why did Robert have to be so pigheaded?

The king paid no heed to William's dark mood. He accepted the hospitality of this place, with its neat houses and welcoming people, for one night and then granted its charter as a city, which made it somewhat less dependent on the archbishop of Canterbury. The following day, he casually informed William that the house and lands that would be his after his wedding were only a short day's journey away.

William did not know what to think. He could no longer feel glad about his new life, now that not even Robert would have a place in it. How would it all work out?

At daybreak, John gave the order to depart. They were just about to leave Sevenoaks when Robert arrived in haste.

"It looks as if I've arrived just in time," he said, laughing sheepishly, and asked whether he could join them.

The king nodded, and a great weight was lifted from William's heart. With Robert's help, he would be able to fulfill all the new duties of his future life more easily. Although he took pride in being a royal falconer, the realization that Marguerite would never be his was becoming all the clearer and increasingly unbearable. If, by giving up Richard de Hauville's daughter and her lands, he might have been able to win Marguerite's hand, he would have sacrificed his new prosperity without regrets. He would prefer to live poor and unnoticed with Marguerite than ennobled without her. But that option was not available.

He rode beside Robert in silence. The mist that had surrounded them in Sevenoaks had burned off, and the sun now bathed the bleak winter landscape in soft light, encouraging nostalgic thoughts. King John was in a hurry, though, and by dint of some hard riding they reached their destination before sunset.

During their last pause for rest, one of the knights had set off early and ridden ahead to warn of the king's arrival. Thus it was that a good-looking man in his forties, with broad shoulders, an alert expression, and an equally alert mind, came out of the house to greet the king as they arrived.

"Sire, what a pleasure! It is a great honor to welcome you again, this time as king." He bowed deeply.

"It seems an eternity since last I was here. I didn't spend many days here, but they were all the happier for that." The king looked at the man amiably. "This manor, and Richard's daughter, are very dear to my heart. I have therefore chosen an extremely capable—though quite young—man as its future lord. He will continue Richard's work and rebuild the falconry." He put his hand on William's shoulder. "This is William FitzEllen, son of the finest swordsmith in the land." He tapped his sword belt in confirmation; his latest weapon from Ellenweore hung from it.

William blushed. His mother had made swords for King Richard; that John too bore one of her swords by his side at all times filled him with tremendous pride.

"Above all, though, he is an outstanding falconer," John went on. "The steward has always rendered good service. You should rely on him in the future, too, as far as the manor house is concerned."

"My lord," the steward greeted William with a graceful bow. "Welcome to Roford."

He cleared his throat. "What did you say the manor is called?" he asked, flustered.

"Roford Manor, my lord."

"Roford," William repeated, almost tenderly. "It sounds like Orford, doesn't it? Orford is a port in East Anglia. My mother was born there."

"Well, that must be a sign from heaven meaning God is with you and with this marriage," John jovially teased him. "It looks as if you have not only my blessing for this wedding but also the Almighty's. What more could you ask?" John turned to the steward again. "Is everything ready?"

"Yes, sire."

"Then let the ceremony take place tomorrow," said the king to William. "Brief and not too solemn, but you're not the only man who wants to hold his bride in his arms as soon as he can. I haven't seen my dear Isabelle for a long time, and I'm anxious to get back to her. I'm sure she's waiting impatiently for me." He winked conspiratorially at William. "She's insatiable in love, and I treasure it in her."

"If I may, sire, I will have a bath drawn for you and the groom," the steward suggested.

"A shave would not be a bad thing. It can't do him any harm to look a bit more presentable when he comes into his bride's presence." The king laughed, turning to William. "We'll be setting off again immediately after the wedding. My queen is waiting for me south of the Thames. So if you'd like to look around your lands for a while first, I'm sure you have time before there's enough hot water for our bath."

"Everything around belongs to Roford, sir, whichever direction you ride. Would you like me to come with you for a while?" The steward looked at him expectantly.

"That won't be necessary, thank you. I won't be riding any more today. I just want to stretch my legs a little."

Robert offered to accompany him, but William declined. "Leave me alone for a moment. I need some time to collect myself."

"Ah, yes," added the king almost as an afterthought. "If you see Marguerite, send her to me."

"Marguerite?" At the sound of the name, William's heart began to pound.

"Yes, she'll have arrived by now." He glanced at the steward, who confirmed with a nod. "She's going to keep the queen company while I take care of government affairs," the king explained, turning back to the steward. "I'd like to have a look at the books in the meantime."

Stunned, William walked off. Did the king have to meet Marguerite here, of all places, and now? Why did he torment him so? Did he enjoy seeing others suffer? John probably didn't even suspect how the thought of marrying someone other than Marguerite afflicted him. William took a deep breath. He felt terrible. Perhaps he should refuse the marriage? No, that was impossible. He knew he had to fall in with the king's wishes; there was no choice. "So all this will be mine," he whispered, looking around.

The manor house and the village were behind him. In a field not far from the edge of the forest, two foxes rubbed their noses together. "They want to get married," he murmured pensively, sighing from the bottom of his heart. How happy the foxes were. They were free, and they could choose with whom they coupled.

"They look as if they like each other," said a familiar voice from behind him.

"Marguerite!" William's jaw dropped. Was it possible that she had grown even lovelier?

"How do you like the land? It will be yours soon."

Her voice seemed to reach him from afar; he was so bewitched by her sparkling eyes. He fought the temptation to clasp her in his arms and never let go again. Then he shook his head sadly. "I know I should be happy about this bond, but I can't. My heart is already plighted, even if there's no hope of my love being returned."

Tears appeared in the corners of Marguerite's eyes, and he raised his hand to wipe them away. But then he dropped it and stared at the ground. If he touched her now, he would never let her go again, never mind marry some other woman.

"I wish I could. I'm sorry," he stammered.

When he looked up again, Marguerite was running off. Had she understood that he meant her? Surely she knew he loved only her. Why else would he have asked the king for her hand? Even if she felt as he did, it wouldn't alter anything. John had come to a decision and wouldn't change his mind. William came within a hairbreadth of chasing Marguerite, seizing her, kissing and caressing her, but he couldn't even put one foot in front of the other. The king would marry him to the daughter of a de Hauville tomorrow, thus making him a member of the most illustrious family of falconers in the land. That was a great honor, he reminded himself, so he had to behave honorably.

He took a deep breath, stood up straight, and decided to go back. The bath they were drawing for him was bound to do him good. He had to forget Marguerite, once and for all. Once he was Lord Roford, a great deal of work would await him. The falconry, the villages, the forest—he would have to take care of it all. Perhaps there wouldn't be time to mourn Marguerite.

Bathed, his face shaved smooth, William felt a little better, but in the strange clothes John had sent him he felt as if he had slipped into someone else's life. Soon he would no longer be a commoner. Not that he would no longer be accountable to anyone—there was always a feudal lord who stood one step higher. Even King John had sworn an oath of fealty to King Philip of France in return for his lands on the mainland and therefore owed him service. But as lord of a manor, William would have power over many people: peasants, laborers, servants, huntsmen, artisans. They and their families would be dependent on him. While in the tub, he had already begun to consider the steps he would take in Roford.

The River Eden flowed past the village on its way east. Was it capable of driving a mill? A mill could not only grind flour but also drive the hammers for a smithy, or even make felt.

"Are you ready?" Robert's question roused him from his reverie. "The king is waiting for us at the table."

William nodded with a heavy heart.

"Shall we go then...my lord?" Robert went on, smiling mischievously.

"Let's go," said William. He would soon have to get used to being called "my lord." But right then he could not manage more than a wry smile.

Marguerite had made her apologies and did not join them for the meal. William was thankful. It would have been too difficult for him to chatter with her about trivialities while he was longing to hold and kiss her and swear eternal love.

John, in high spirits, drank thirstily of the wine on offer and grew more and more expansive; William just sat there in silence, chewing his meat as if it were a piece of shoe leather.

William did not tell Robert about the meeting with Marguerite until the following morning.

"You really do love her, don't you?"

William nodded mutely.

When they entered the intimate hall of the manor house, John was talking animatedly with the steward.

"Ah, the groom." He welcomed him joyfully when William approached. "Isn't he handsome?" He looked around. "Is the bride ready, too?"

"She's ready, sire, but she's weeping bitter tears," the steward told him.

"Can anyone understand women?" growled John. "First they say yes, and then they say no. They're always changing their minds. I'll tell you this right now, William, only a liar would claim it is easy to be a good husband. I know whereof I speak. I wasn't married once before for nothing."

"Sire, if she doesn't wish it, perhaps we shouldn't," William stammered.

"What foolishness is this?" exclaimed the king, his face turning red.

"Forgive me, sire. I didn't mean to anger you."

"Spare me and come along now. I do not intend to spend tonight here as well. Let her come to the church," demanded the king, leading the way.

William followed him with his head bowed. Robert hurried after him, too.

Out of the corner of his eye, William saw Marguerite approach her uncle. He looked down. It was too painful to look at her. The torment clutched at his throat and stopped him from thinking clearly. His head felt empty and dull.

The priest was standing at the door of the church, waiting for the bride and groom. William stood in front of him and waited to be led to the bride. He looked around cautiously, but he could not see her anywhere. She was probably intending to make a grand entrance. It was not until the king led Marguerite toward him and she took up a position beside him that he understood that Richard de Hauville's daughter was none other than Marguerite.

But his bride was not laughing. She was not even smiling, and she did not seem to be reeling with happiness, as he was. A tear ran down her cheek. Why was she weeping? Didn't she want him?

"I'm sorry," he said uncertainly.

Marguerite just sniffed. Perhaps she had been hoping for a better match? Much as he wanted her for his wife, the thought of possessing her against her will was abhorrent to him. But he didn't want to give her up, either. Perhaps he would be able to convince her if they spent more time together. It was a fact that marriages among people of their rank were normally arranged for practical reasons, not for love—though love did occasionally come later as a gift from God.

And so he accepted the marriage with a clear, almost hard-sounding, "Yes."

When it came to Marguerite, however, only a faint sob passed her lips. Upon an emphatic nod from the king, the priest took this as acceptance.

Once the blessing had been spoken, William gently kissed his new bride on the cheek. He did not dare kiss her on the mouth; he did not want to push her.

"We can leave, sire," Marguerite said impassively, not looking at John. "I'm sure the queen is waiting impatiently for you."

"And you're yearning to be alone with your husband, it seems to me. For tonight is your wedding night," the king said teasingly. He burst out laughing when she blushed, turned away in embarrassment, and stalked off proudly.

William decided to avoid her for the time being, so as not to provoke her any more. He would give her time, though he was disappointed. He had assumed, after the kisses they had exchanged the previous year, that she loved him, too.

☙❧

Robert felt a twinge of jealousy, but he could not help feeling sorry for William. It was impossible to ignore how Marguerite's rejection made his friend suffer. To see William so desperate hurt him more than his own sorrow. Marguerite was the only one who could make William happy, and until that moment in front of the church, Robert had believed she longed for nothing more than to be his wife. Now, however, as they rode to the king's hunting lodge, she was several lengths ahead of William and did not even glance at him.

Robert spurred on his horse to catch up with her and asked what had happened to make her spurn William.

"I thought he loved me," she blurted out. She looked frightened, as if she had said something shocking. "I wanted to die when he confessed that his heart was plighted to another." The tears glittering in her eyes made her look like a child, and Robert was moved.

"I can't believe it," he retorted. Why would William have said something so stupid? He loved Marguerite; Robert was absolutely sure of it. He nodded at the unhappy bride and reined in his horse until he was back alongside William.

"I always thought you loved her," he said, bewildered.

"And I do," replied William in a voice that came from the heart and rang with sincerity. "But I hate the thought of marrying her when she doesn't return my love."

"So why did you tell her your heart belonged to another?" Robert looked at him questioningly.

"I didn't know she was the bride."

"Then you'd better explain yourself as soon as you can, my friend. She was weeping because she thought you didn't want her." Robert smiled at him encouragingly even though he felt raw inside. "Come on, she's waiting."

"Do you really think so?"

"I'm sure of it."

Plagued by sadness aroused by his friend's joy, Robert watched William spur on his horse and hurry toward Marguerite. "You deserve to be happy, my friend."

☙❧

When they arrived at the hunting lodge, the young queen rushed out to meet them.

"John, my beloved royal husband. I've missed you, all alone in my bed," she said seductively and loud enough that his followers heard, too.

Marguerite giggled with embarrassment. They had cleared up the misunderstanding, so she gave William a private but no less flirtatious glance that made his heart race.

"Marguerite, how lovely to see you here. I've missed you so," Isabelle said joyfully.

"My lady, may I introduce my husband, William?" said Marguerite once he had dismounted.

"Your husband?" Isabelle's eyebrows rose. She giggled and looked curiously at William.

"My lady." He bowed deeply before the queen. By the time he looked up again, she had already linked arms with the king and Marguerite and pulled them both away.

"Did you ever allow yourself to dream you could be so happy and come so far?" asked Robert.

William shook his head.

"Let's go into the hall," Robert suggested. "There's bound to be something to eat there, and I'm ravenous."

As they entered the smoke-filled hall, William accidentally jostled a broad-shouldered knight, but his mumbled apology almost stuck in his throat.

"Can't you look where you're going?" snarled Odon. When he saw who had bumped into him, he went on. "What are you doing here?"

Before William had a chance to answer, the king called him.

"William, come here. You have a place of honor at my table today." John bared his teeth in a smile, and he suddenly looked so like his father that William was reminded of old King Henry.

What would he have said to the idea that William would be sitting at the royal table today?

"I simply can't give up the company of your charming wife just like that. I've become too accustomed to her and her constant questions over the years," he said, provoking Marguerite with a wink and roaring with laughter when she put her hands on her hips in protest.

Odon stared at William, openmouthed and speechless.

"Come, Lord Roford," Robert said to his friend, with a mocking grin directed at Odon. "The king awaits you." Then he turned back to Odon and, quietly triumphant, said, "It didn't do you any good to poison that falcon. William became a royal falconer anyway. From now on you'd better keep your distance."

Odon seemed ready to boil over at Robert's impudence, but not a word passed his lips.

"Robert," said William, who had heard his friend's words. He waved Robert over. "Come now." It did not please William to see Robert and Odon pitted against each other. If there was to be an argument, Robert would get the worst of it, just as he had before. It was better to stay out of the way of a man like Odon. A fight was worthwhile only if one could win it.

Countless meat and fish courses were brought forth during dinner, all with delicious sauces, but William could hardly swallow a single bite. Whenever he looked at Marguerite, his stomach turned over. This wonderful woman was his. He rubbed his hands together, but they remained ice-cold; he could not even warm them up on his cup of hot mulled wine.

The king insisted that William and Marguerite stay with him for Christmastide; he even had a separate room prepared for them so that they could spend their wedding night together in privacy. While the table was being cleared and everyone headed off to sleep, John winked at him conspiratorially and wished him a good night.

❦

With nowhere else to sleep but on the hard floor of the hall, Odon stared into the darkness in a rage and gritted his teeth so hard his jaw began to ache. William did not deserve the position of royal falconer, with lands and a wife that were simply not right for a commoner. Why was the fellow so lucky? Odon trembled with fury until one of the maids pressed close to him.

"If you're cold, my lord, I know something that will help." She came even closer, threw her arms around his body, and slipped her hand into the opening of his shirt.

Odon gave in to his sudden arousal, rolled over on top of her, and pushed her shift up without even looking to see who she was. It did not matter. William was up there in a clean room with his wife, enjoying his wedding night, while he had to make do with the filthy floor of the hall. What use was it to him that his wife was more beautiful than William's? Odon hated Maud, though he still desired her body as much as ever. But William evidently loved his wife, and she seemed quite besotted with him, too. Jealousy and hatred merely increased Odon's arousal.

Once he had satisfied his lust, he stood up, relieved himself into the fireplace, and returned to the floor. When the girl tried to snuggle up to him, he shouted at her to find somewhere else to sleep. Then he rolled up in his blanket.

"You won't be beaming with happiness for long, you two," he murmured and soon fell asleep.

ᘐᘑ

When William awoke, the first light of day was piercing the wooden shutters. Naked beside him, Marguerite was still asleep. William looked at her, his heart beating hard. She bore no resemblance to Enid, neither in her appearance nor in her character.

A pained smile flitted across his face. Enid. He felt that his time with her belonged to a different life. He had said farewell to her long ago, but she had not really left him until last night. Now only Marguerite mattered.

William's gaze moved longingly over her breasts, which were concealed by the linen sheet. She began to stretch among the bedclothes, and he became pleasurably aroused again. He leaned over his sleeping wife.

"You're so beautiful," he whispered in her ear, closing his eyes and savoring the scent of her nudity. He ran his fingers through her sleep-tousled hair.

Marguerite turned over, pursed her lips, and threw her arms around his neck. "Just in case I didn't get a son by you last night, I think we should try again," she said and began nibbling his ear.

As they lay together, the house began to stir. Steps and voices could be heard in front of their room, but they did not allow themselves to be distracted. They clung tightly to each other for quite some time. It was not until the king himself banged on their door with his fist and told them to come downstairs that they sprang up, giggling like naughty children, and got dressed.

William pulled Marguerite toward him once more. "I'm so glad Robert cleared up our stupid misunderstanding."

"That's enough. The king's waiting for us," Marguerite rebuked him severely, kissing him passionately on the mouth one last time. She looked into his eyes breathlessly. "I can never thank John enough for giving me to you as a wife. So now come," she ordered. She unlocked the door, took William by the hand, and pulled him out of the room and down the stairs.

The king was deep in conversation with several knights. William and Marguerite joined Robert, who was standing by the fireplace with some other men.

"Look at that girl over there, the one making eyes at Odon," Robert remarked quietly, pointing at a tired-looking woman hovering around Odon. She had matted hair and what teeth she still possessed were rotten. "He seems to have found a new love. Poor

Maud!" He sneered, earning a disapproving shake of the head from William. "All right. I'll be quiet." Robert looked down and sighed softly.

Odon kept looking over at them, but whenever his glance met William's, he turned away. It was not until midday, when they happened to find themselves standing next to each other, that Odon murmured spitefully, "I suggest you never leave Robert alone with her." Odon's mouth was right against William's ear. His breath smelled of ale. "It's always your best friend with whom your wife betrays you. That's why I don't have any best friends." He nodded at Marguerite and grinned lewdly. "Just look how absorbed in his conversation she is, how intimate they look."

Marguerite and Robert did indeed have their heads close together, and they were whispering and laughing.

"What are you talking about? Do you really think I don't trust them?"

Rather than answering, Odon merely shrugged and turned away.

William shook his head. Where does he get the idea I might believe such nonsense? he thought, trying to ignore the unpleasant sensation creeping up his neck.

Roford Manor, January 1201

After spending Christmas with the king and queen, William, Marguerite, and Robert returned to Roford Manor. William still had to get accustomed to being a landowner. The fear of not fulfilling his responsibilities weighed heavily on him. There were so many people over whom he now held sway. He knew too little about what was expected of him and feared plunging himself and those he loved into misfortune because the tasks and duties of a landowner were so unfamiliar.

Fortunately, Marguerite proved to be a thoroughly capable collaborator. She could read and write, and she was very good with figures. Unlike William, she had been well prepared for her position and knew exactly what was expected.

First she had the steward go through the books with her, asking him to report on revenues and outgoings, crop yields, and livestock husbandry. William just stood by, marveling, listening, and paying careful attention. Marguerite explained that it was part of the steward's duties to supervise income and expenditure, and, with the priest, to enter them in the books every evening.

Still, she checked the sums now and then so that the steward did not feel he could do as he wished. A steward had important responsibilities, and there was no harm in him knowing that his masters had a perfect understanding of what he did. He had to plan the menus and food stores with the cook, ensure there were enough provisions in the cellars to last through the winter, and check they were not consumed too quickly.

Marguerite grasped the advantages of the estate as quickly as she understood the difficulties they had experienced in previous years. The fields and cattle brought in decent profits, but the forest was underused. William knew the falconry would bring in extra income, not least because the king would pay generously for the care of his birds.

William was delighted that he could leave the supervision of the household to Marguerite and of the lands to the steward, for a great deal of work still awaited him and Robert.

To begin with, he had to rebuild the derelict falconry, which was close to the manor house. While the house itself had been constantly improved and even extended, the falconry had been neglected for years. The roof needed repair, and the high rail and the perches were no longer usable and had to be replaced. Even the walls of the mews required mending; a few rotten planks that let the wind whistle through needed to be replaced, along with the door fittings and some dangling shutters.

Once he was thoroughly familiar with the condition of the mews, he told Marguerite of his displeasure at its neglect, and she explained why no one had set foot there for so long.

"My father was a falconer, body and soul, like all the de Hauvilles," she said.

"I saw Richard hunt once, at Thorne, when I was still a boy— and didn't know anything about you yet." He smiled at his beloved. "Since a passion for falcons is already in the de Hauville family's blood, all we need now is a pack of sons who feel the same," he said as he drew her to him.

Somewhat reluctantly, she pulled away from him. "My father fell into disfavor with King Henry. I don't know exactly what happened. I was too small, but even I noticed that he changed suddenly. The king had his falcons taken away, and the other falconers left with them. My father withdrew into himself. He fell silent and hardly ever laughed. Not long afterward, he fell off his horse while out on an ordinary ride. He died the same night."

Marguerite's eyes, normally so bright, darkened. "My mother sort of froze. A rich neighbor who'd been eyeing her for some time began to visit her regularly, almost immediately after my father was buried. He helped her and quickly took over the administration of the estate. Soon he asked for her hand in marriage. The steward hated him, and my mother was still in mourning. She put off his advances, but he didn't give up. One day, he pressed his suit one more time and she asked him to leave and not to return. His pride was hurt, and in revenge—perhaps also out of greed—from that day on he had our villages attacked and our fields and barns burned. Within a very short time—despite the steward's best efforts—Roford Manor was close to ruin. My mother wasn't strong enough for this man. She was afraid of further attacks and didn't know how she would help her people survive the winter without her husband. She believed she was to blame for the people's misfortune. Shortly before Christmas she threw herself off the roof of the falconry."

Marguerite's voice had grown quieter and quieter as she told the story. Tears ran down her face. "It took her nearly two days to die," she went on as William stroked her hand comfortingly. "She was in great pain and knew she was going to die. So she called for the priest and sent a message to Prince John, asking him to accept me as his ward. My uncle came as quickly as he could, but she was dead and buried by the time he arrived. He punished the neighbor himself, single-handed. Oh William, if she had only asked for his help sooner, she wouldn't have had to commit the sin of throwing her life away. The steward took good care of Roford, but the falconry has been dormant ever since. My greatest wish is that you will rebuild it. Roford should be a home our children can be proud of." Her eyes were misted with tears.

"It will be," William replied, taking her in his arms. He dried her tears and kissed her. "I promise we will have a wonderful life, with many children and the finest falcons. It won't be long before Roford's falcons will be famous throughout England."

William averted his eyes, carefully examining the low perch he had installed in the hall. Until the falconry was ready, the king's birds would perch here. He stood up and kissed Marguerite on the forehead. "We need timber for the work on the mews."

"You can take what you need from the forest. We don't use enough as it is. There's enough good wood there." She wiped her eyes dry and tried to smile.

"I still don't know enough about Roford to be a good lord and master. I should ask the steward to ride out with me tomorrow and explain it all. Perhaps you would come with me?"

Marguerite nodded bravely. "Then let's look in on Tonley, too, shall we? I would love you to meet my milk-sister. I haven't been able to visit Godith since we've been back. Tonley belongs to Roford and is only a few miles away. I often went to the village as a child, because my wet nurse was from there." Marguerite suddenly looked less sad. "I've heard Godith is the most beautiful girl in the village. I hope she doesn't turn your head."

"How can you think I have eyes for anyone but you?" William protested indignantly.

They were up with the lark the next morning and set off immediately. They rode along the border of the estate, first to the east, then north. The steward told William everything he knew about the land. He spoke of crop rotation and the characteristics of the soil, and about the people who tilled the fields, how they organized their work, and when they had more to do than usual. Then he explained what sort of yields could be expected from arable farming, what measures could be taken to increase revenues from the forest, and where higher profits could be earned.

William listened carefully, asking questions from time to time, and soon realized that the estate was bigger than he had thought. They discussed the work that was needed at the falconry, and William found out that John had left a bag of silver for this purpose. They rode alongside each other at a leisurely pace. The steward was giving him a detailed explanation of the administration of the fief when Marguerite began shifting about uneasily in her saddle.

"It's scarcely half a mile from here to Tonley," she reminded him impatiently after William asked yet another question. "You're not going to see all of Roford today anyway, so why don't you discuss all this later while we're eating?"

"Why don't you go on ahead? We'll follow soon," William suggested, laughing.

"Very well, but do hurry up," she urged them both, then rode off in haste, much relieved.

William watched her go, shaking his head with a laugh. "I think we'd better postpone our conversation and not keep her waiting long. Women as delightful as she quickly grow impatient."

"As you wish, my lord. I am always at your disposal."

"My lord" was the right form of address, but it was still strange to William.

☙❧

Marguerite could hardly wait to throw her arms around her milk-sister. How long was it since she and Godith had spent all their time together, climbing trees like the boys and playing tricks on Godith's mother? Ten years must have passed, perhaps twelve, though to Marguerite it seemed an eternity.

Marguerite relaxed the reins and looked around. Hardly anything in the village had changed. She rode slowly past the bare winter gardens and thatched cottages. A crowd of people gathered on the village green aroused her curiosity. She tried to see what was happening but could not discern why the villagers had gathered. When she heard shrill screams of pain she pulled the reins and dug her heels into her horse's flanks.

A ring of horrified villagers surrounded two people. A man—Marguerite assumed it was the village reeve—was whipping a young woman. As each stroke came whistling down on the poor girl's shredded smock, the onlookers screamed with terror.

"You see, all of you, this is what happens when you don't respect Lord Roford's wishes," roared the reeve, lashing the whip again.

The villagers huddled together like frightened lambs. None of them seemed bold enough to hold back the reeve.

Marguerite clearly heard the man claim he was acting in the name of Lord Roford and gasped with rage. William would never have ordered such a punishment, no matter what the woman might be guilty of.

She slipped down from her horse and walked up to the reeve, a powerfully built man, standing with his back to her. The woman being whipped had fainted and fallen to the ground. As he raised his hand again to strike her, Marguerite snatched the whip so decisively that he spun around in shock. He looked ready to grab her by the throat, but she stood her ground.

By now, William and the steward had arrived, too. They dismounted and lined up behind Marguerite but did not intervene.

When the reeve realized who was standing before him, his manner changed abruptly. He became subservient, offering a few confused statements in his defense.

"How dare you beat this poor woman nigh to death in my husband's name," Marguerite shouted. "If she's done something wrong, she should be brought before a judge or us. How many lashes has she had from you?"

He did not answer.

Marguerite asked again, more harshly, "How many?"

"He threatened her with twenty. She's already had twelve. Please, my lady, she won't survive more," a worried-looking man answered instead. He glanced anxiously at the young woman, who was whimpering softly.

"You're Ralph Redbeard, aren't you?"

"You remember me, my lady?"

Marguerite smiled. "Your flaming-red beard gave you away. I was terrified of you when I was little." The anger receded from her face. "Your daughter?"

"Yes, my lady. My youngest. I beg you, have mercy."

"Take her home. I'll come later to see to her."

As Ralph Redbeard picked up his daughter, Marguerite looked at William. He gave her an encouraging smile and nodded his agreement. The crowd was perceptibly relieved, but there was still fear and anger in the air. They were probably all wondering whether the lady would let the reeve leave unpunished. Some of the villagers were looking at him with hate-filled eyes, and the ring around him grew tighter and tighter.

Shaking with terror, the man fell to his knees before Marguerite, looking first at her, then at William and the steward, then back to her again. But neither of the men stirred.

"You practically tore the cloth off that poor girl's back with your blows. I'd love to punish you myself, but I'm only a weak woman, and we certainly want the job done properly," she told him. She threw the whip to the surprised steward. "You must have known the kind of mischief the reeve was up to here. So you can punish him."

"But, my lady. My lord," cried the reeve, looking anxiously back and forth between the two of them. When he saw the furious spark in her eyes, he held his tongue.

The force of the first blow caught him by surprise. He cried out, arching his back. By the third blow he was whining like a dog and begging for mercy.

"Did she beg for mercy?" asked Marguerite.

The reeve nodded, terrified.

Marguerite said nothing, but she gave the steward a sign and he let fly again.

"That will do," William told the steward after a dozen lashes. He went over to Marguerite and put his arm around her.

The reeve lay on the ground, whimpering.

Although she had not punished him herself, fat beads of sweat stood on Marguerite's forehead.

The steward had not held back; one almost might have felt sorry for the reeve. But the expression of relief and satisfaction on the villagers' faces showed he did not deserve compassion.

Marguerite stood up straight and showed no sign of weakness. Nonetheless, she was grateful that William was beside her. He had given her freedom when she needed it.

Now, however, he spoke firmly. "This man has been reeve in this village long enough," he told the steward.

The men, women, and children looked alternately at their lord and lady, in fearful expectation.

"We'll take him away with us. Bind him," Marguerite ordered the steward. "I'd like to go and see the girl now."

As they were leaving the green, a young woman ran up to them. "That was wonderful," she said, her eyes shining. "Mother would have been so proud if she could have seen it. Welcome home, my lady." She curtsied gracefully.

"Godith?"

The young woman nodded.

Marguerite threw her arms around her neck and kissed her cheek. "It's so good to see you," she exclaimed, taking a step back so that she could see her milk-sister better. "I'd heard you were the prettiest girl in the village. And it was no exaggeration. You have your mother's eyes. How is she?"

"Mum left us a long time ago. Her last child cost her her life. She was too old to be a mother again. The child was bottom downward in her womb and got stuck. She was in terrible pain, but no one could help her. The Lord took them both." Godith pushed her straight straw-blonde hair behind her ear and smiled, though it was obvious from her eyes that she missed her mother dreadfully. "Didn't you want to go to Ralph's house?"

Marguerite nodded, linked arms with her old friend, and led her away. "Do you remember how we used to tremble in front of him?"

Godith nodded, grinning. "He's my father-in-law now."

"You married one of his sons? Which one? Thomas? Or what was his name?"

"Matthew. Thomas is certainly the handsomer of the two, but Matthew is the more reliable. I didn't realize it myself at first, but two weeks after his wedding, Thomas was already on the lookout for another sweetheart, making eyes at all the girls. My Matthew's different. He's a good man, loving and hardworking."

Godith glanced at William and grinned inquisitively. "Our new lord is good-looking. Apparently you've not done badly yourself, my lady."

"I love him more than anything." Marguerite stopped for a moment, because the world was suddenly spinning around her.

"You're going to give him a son soon," said Godith, laughing softly. "In the autumn, when the leaves are dry and many-colored."

"How do you...?"

"I just know. You feel sick in the morning, don't you?"

"Only yesterday and this morning. That's all."

"I've had two children already. Thomas was born at Christmas two years ago, Marguerite last summer. If you're lucky, you'll feel better in a couple of weeks."

"Your daughter's name is Marguerite?"

Godith blushed slightly. "I've always envied your lovely name."

"And I could never bear it," Marguerite squeezed her arm. "I'm glad you've named your little one after me."

Godith beamed. "We're here." She stopped in front of Red-beard's house.

"I just want to look in on your sister-in-law for a bit." Marguerite took both Godith's hands in hers. "I'm delighted that things are going well for you. If you ever need help, you won't hesitate to come to me, will you?"

"Thank you, my lady. It will do Roford good to have a lord and lady again. People prefer to work for people they know, rather than a king who's far away. I hope to see you again soon."

Marguerite stood there for a moment, thinking. She put her hand on her stomach and tried to listen to her insides. Was Godith right to say she was with child? How wonderful it would be to have a little son or daughter. But Godith was bound to be wrong. Her milk-sister was hardly older than she was; she wasn't some wise old woman. How could she know? Marguerite shook her head. It was too soon to rejoice about a child, or even to tell William. Just as she was making up her mind to go into the house, William arrived.

"Are you all right?" he asked anxiously. He let her go ahead when she assured him she was fine.

The young woman was on her pallet, whimpering.

Marguerite went up to her, took her hand, and stroked it gently. "My husband should have a look at her wounds. He understands these things better than I do," she explained to Redbeard's wife, but the latter still looked at him suspiciously as he approached her daughter's bed.

ᏮᎧᎧ

So this is how it feels to be feared because one is a nobleman, thought William as he looked at the young woman's ravaged back.

His mother had never made any secret of the fact that she did not think much of the noblemen, though she did her very best to forge perfect swords for them. Most barons did not use their power for the people who depended on them; instead, they used it against them. Who could blame the young woman's mother for not trusting William? She did not know him and had no way of knowing that he had been born a commoner like her.

The lash marks glistened blue on the young woman's skin. Blood oozed from the open welts.

"I'll send someone over later with a pot of herbal ointment. You can put some on the wounds so they heal better."

During his time with Enid, William had perfected the blend for the ointment he used on his foot, and since then had maintained a regular supply. It burned a little on open wounds, but it helped marvelously.

Ralph Redbeard wrung his hands and turned to Marguerite. "He would have beaten her to death. You saved her life, my lady. I am indebted to you from the bottom of my heart."

"What did your daughter do to earn this punishment?" asked William.

"Only what decency required her to do," her father growled angrily.

"Decency?" Marguerite wanted to know more.

"Since his wife died, the reeve has been chasing everyone's daughters. He's got two girls of marriageable age with child already. Who knows how many married women are carrying his offspring and keeping it quiet?" His face was so red it almost matched his beard. "And if a girl resists, well, you've seen what happens."

"You're a big man, and you're not the only one in the village. Why hasn't anyone stood up to him?" Marguerite asked.

"The reeve has many relatives around here. Including the steward."

"Does the steward harass all of you, too?" asked William. He had thought the man honest.

"No, he's always been fair," Redbeard assured him sincerely. "But his wife is the reeve's sister. 'Blood is thicker than water,' he always said in that threatening way of his. There are nine brothers, all of them older than the steward's wife. They've got her under their thumb, and they stick together come what may. Everyone here knows it. So we've all held our tongues and hoped that God would come to our aid one day soon."

William nodded. "It's over—I promise you. I suggest we go out to the others now. I'm sure they want to know what's going to happen."

Sure enough, when they emerged from the cottage, the villagers were standing in front of the church, whispering curiously.

"What man in the village is reliable, trustworthy, and conscientious?" William said in a thunderous voice so that everyone could hear him. "Who would make a good reeve?"

The villagers hesitated. They obviously did not dare to say what they thought. But one old man was brave enough to speak out.

"Redbeard is a good man. He is honorable and has his heart in the right place."

The villagers nodded in agreement.

"Well, let's try him out," said William, turning to Ralph. "Report to the steward tomorrow and he'll introduce you to your new position."

"Does he have children to care for?" asked Marguerite, glancing at their prisoner, who was standing beside the steward with slumped shoulders and bound hands.

"A daughter, my lady. A good girl," replied Ralph, looking worried. "She hasn't had it easy since her mother died. What's to become of her?"

"Bring her to me immediately," answered Marguerite.

Redbeard looked at her in surprise, and the villagers whispered excitedly.

A shy little girl of about ten, looking shamefaced, was pushed hesitantly toward Marguerite. "Her name is Alice."

"Until we've decided what to do with her father, I'll take her with me," declared Marguerite, before leaning down to the girl. "Fear not, Alice. Nothing will happen to you."

The steward pulled her up onto his horse and they rode off.

Alice looked back at her father only once; he was firmly tied to a rope and had to run along behind them.

That evening, William and Marguerite discussed with the steward what penalty they should impose on the reeve, and they decided to banish him. Everyone in Roford needed to understand that William was a good lord who would not tolerate such injustice. Alice, who was not answerable for her father's shameful behavior, was given the choice whether to go with him or stay at the manor as a maid.

"He needs me," the child said diffidently. "He wouldn't last long without me. I've taken care of him since my mother died. I can't leave him alone."

Marguerite found it hard to let her go, but William insisted, even though he felt sorry for the girl, too.

"You gave her the choice instead of deciding what was best for her. Now you can only let her go."

ᏬᏩ

From that day on, even as they carried out their duties as Lord and Lady Roford, William and Marguerite were closer than ever. Every evening, as they sat in front of the fire, exhausted, they would tell each other about the difficulties they had encountered that day and ask each other for advice.

William knew he still had a lot to learn, and Marguerite was an excellent counselor. Although he had not been born to his present position, as she had been, and had not been brought up to it, the behavior of the villagers had demonstrated to him that he was not one of them, either. He was a lord now, but he could not call on any family ties, not even his father, for neither his mother nor King John had ever given away the secret of his birth. He had not been granted the education necessary for becoming a lord. He had not learned to fight with a lance or a sword; he could not write, read, or do sums. So he had a great deal to learn before he would be able to hold his own among the other lords. At all costs, William wanted to avoid looking like an upstart.

He had the village priest come and help him do battle with letters, and he asked a young knight to make him familiar with weaponry.

The steward, whom he had mistrusted after the incident with the reeve, proved himself honorable and true. But it was Marguerite, more than anyone else, who turned out to be his indispensable teacher on the way to being a lord.

During the years she had spent at court as John's ward, she had met many important knights, barons, and churchmen. And since then she had constantly questioned John about everything and everyone. She was very well-informed about the complex web of baronial fiefdoms and families.

Marguerite knew who was promised to whom, which families were close, and which ones hated one another and why. She had listened attentively when John talked over things with his men, and she knew which towns and estates were particularly important for this or that title or even for the crown. Moreover, she had an unerring instinct about which barons could be carefully cultivated and which were better avoided, which were chronically devious and which could potentially be trusted.

"Our king does not understand who wishes him well," she explained to William one evening as part of a commentary on certain important connections between influential and less important families. "Unfortunately, he rather likes surrounding himself with men like your good friend Odon and doesn't realize that they stay close to him only for their own reasons and would betray him at the drop of a hat if it was worth enough to them. He doesn't believe that many lords flatter him and tell him what he wants to hear in order to win his favor. There are many men like Odon in his inner circle. They know how to exploit every situation to their own advantage and have no scruples about bringing misfortune down on others. That's what makes them so dangerous. Odon was always trying to poison John's mind against you. He did it well, I must admit. He kept making small insinuations about you, sowing doubt. As long as I was at court, I could spoil his little game. But now I'm no longer beside John, and Odon and other envious men can do us harm."

She put her hand to her stomach and grimaced for a moment, as if in pain.

"What is it?" William knelt down beside her. "The child?"

He was all too familiar with the dangers of childbirth. Since Marguerite had told him that she was with child, he had been tormented by dreams in which he saw Enid and his son as he had found them.

"It's nothing. Godith told me it often pulls a little as the belly grows. I'm fine."

William nodded, but his fear would not be put aside. He had to protect Marguerite and their child.

He hardly went hawking these days, and he neglected the training of the falcons because he did not want to leave his beloved wife alone. But he missed the work and became more and more insufferable as a result. He would quarrel with Marguerite for no reason, only to go to her later filled with remorse, seeking comfort

in her arms. On several occasions, he tried to tell her about Enid—
but how? With what words? If he himself couldn't live with the
fear, how could he burden her with it?

"You've worked very hard these last few months. You haven't
spared yourself for one moment," he said, worried. "You should
rest more."

"But I feel wonderful. What would you say to my visiting the
queen? She has a lot of influence on John. I'm sure it would be helpful to know she was on our side."

"Absolutely not. You're not traveling, not in your condition,"
William insisted. The thought of not having Marguerite constantly
by his side was almost unbearable, especially now. If he hadn't left
Enid alone, she wouldn't have been murdered.

"But it's months away," retorted Marguerite, argumentative as
a child that felt misunderstood.

"I won't have it, and that's that," he shouted before striding out
of the hall. She wouldn't understand, but he didn't care. All that
mattered was that she should stay with him so that he could rush
to her aid whenever she needed him.

Once out in the courtyard, he reached into the purse he kept
on his belt at all times and took out the enamel plaque. "I must stay
near her. Nothing must happen to her," he whispered, almost as if
swearing an oath, and stroked the slightly irregular surface of the
enamel.

That night, when Marguerite came into the room and lay
down beside him, he had known her so fervently it almost made
her afraid. When he noticed, he felt ashamed, mumbled something that might have been an apology, withdrew from her, and
turned his back on her.

For the first time in years, he shed tears for his dead son, but he
did not tell Marguerite why he was weeping.

Robert sighed. Once again, William had spent the entire day in silence. He thought he knew what was going through his friend's mind, for more than once he had seen William look at the enamel plaque and seen his expression become distant. So he was not surprised, one day, when he came upon a puffy-eyed Marguerite sitting alone in the hall, with her embroidery frame in her lap, sobbing softly.

"Is there anything I can do for you, my lady?" he asked diffidently, kneeling before her.

Marguerite sniffed and shook her head.

"It's William that's making you suffer, isn't it?"

At that very moment, William came out of the couple's bedchamber, stormed across the hall, and disappeared into the courtyard without a word of greeting.

"Did you see his expression? He's become so grim," Marguerite protested. "Anyone would think he didn't want me, or the child. I don't understand." She wiped her face in a movement that was almost childlike.

"There is a sad story in William's past," Robert began. "I think that's what lies behind his mood, especially now, when you're expecting a child." He did not know whether it was right to talk to Marguerite about this. But then he started telling her what he knew about Enid's death. "He buried them both himself, with his own hands," he concluded.

Marguerite, whose eyes had widened with horror as she listened, started sobbing again, even though Robert had spared her the grisly details. "Oh, my poor William. Now I understand what has been tormenting him, and why he won't let me travel to see Isabelle. He's afraid for me and the child."

"There is something else you should perhaps know. I think Odon had something to do with Enid's death. William has no idea, and I think he's better off not knowing. We'll probably never know exactly what happened, and maybe it's better that way. So let him have a little time. When the child is born, I'm quite certain his mood will improve."

Marguerite nodded pensively. "Thank you, Robert. You're a true friend."

ᎧᏩ

Instead of returning to the mews, Robert took a horse and rode north. Marguerite and William were in love. They were made for each other, and yet their love caused him more pain than he could bear. He knew how William felt about her and could not blame him for it. Marguerite was worthy of love. She possessed not only outward beauty but also inner beauty; she was clever and cultured, friendly, sympathetic, and just.

Although the thought that he would never be able to have William for himself almost drove him mad, Robert wanted nothing more than William's happiness, even if it meant pain for himself.

The more he thought about William, the harder his heart beat. He's so handsome, thought Robert, and he noticed that he was becoming aroused. His feelings for William were false, unnatural, and forbidden, he knew, but at the same time they were so exquisitely pleasurable he could not see anything wrong with loving him. From time to time, however, his lustful thoughts made working with his friend nearly impossible. Whenever his desire got out of hand, he would slip away and ride the few miles to Guildford.

When Robert reached this lively town, he went to a place he knew well, where men who felt as he did met in secret. Driven by lust, he wandered around the latrines, enjoying the sensation of being examined and desired. Lascivious words reached his ears and brought his blood to a boil. Blushing guiltily, he admired all of the men until a tall one with strong arms and a prominent chin gestured that he was interested.

Robert burned with desire. All he could think about was finding relief. So he nodded and allowed the man to push him into a
dark corner. Two more men, still flushed with sin, crept past with
their heads bowed in shame. Their lust had been slaked, and now
they belonged to the devil. Robert knew God would punish them
for the sin of sodomy, the same as him. But he did not care; only
his desire mattered. Whatever resistance he might have once put
up had vanished.

Robert could hardly breathe when the stranger passionately shoved him against the wooden wall. The man lecherously
pressed against Robert from behind, and his sweaty stench
mixed with that of the latrine. Robert felt his smock being lifted
up and shuddered. Guilt and fear blended with the rapture
unlocked by this exquisite recklessness. Robert breathed faster
as the stranger began to pant with pleasure, enjoying the force
of his movements.

When it was over, and Robert's lust was satisfied, he rushed
away, filled with shame and remorse. He adjusted his clothes and
ran to the nearest church as fast as his feet could carry him.

Once again he had given in to this unspeakable sin, even
though he had sworn many times that he would never do it again.
He threw himself to the ground in abject humiliation, weeping
and praying fervently. His guilt tormented him more each time,
but he kept returning to that place, obeying his disgusting urges.
Robert wept with despair. He knew that bishops and other lords of
the church, even kings, fell prey to sins of this kind, but even that
gave him no comfort.

ᘓᘒ

Odon ran his fingers through his lank hair, his face twisted in a
triumphant leer. By pure chance, he had noticed Robert on his way
across the market square. He had changed direction and fought

his way through the crowd so as not to lose sight of him and followed Robert all the way to the latrines.

He's a criminal sodomite, Odon gloated to himself. Isn't that good news!

When Robert emerged from behind the latrines, flushed with his exertions, Odon clenched his fists. "You'd have done better not to say anything to my Carla," he snarled. He was about to pounce when Adam ran up to him.

"Father, will you buy me a pony? I've seen one in the market. Tell him, Roland." He pulled at the tunic of the young knight accompanying him. "Tell him. The pony's brown and has lovely soft eyes. Please, Father."

Odon saw Robert disappear into the church. He looked uncertainly at Roland.

"The pony is no longer young. It's calm and obedient, just right for a boy of his age," Roland murmured approvingly.

Odon peered over Roland's shoulder. Robert would not stay in the church forever, but with Roland and the boy also here, he would not be able to follow Robert.

The young knight whispered the price of the pony in Odon's ear.

"Very well, then." Odon sighed, took out his purse, and counted the sum into the knight's hand. "I have something to attend to. Wait for me at the south gate once you've bought the pony, and take my horse with you."

"Thank you, Father, thank you." Adam was hopping from one foot to the other in his excitement.

Odon watched them go, making sure they really did go back to the market.

Someone like Robert deserves to be punished, Odon thought bitterly. To his regret, the unmentionable vice was increasingly tolerated. Sinners were hardly persecuted at all anymore since the rumor spread that King Richard had publicly admitted to it, twice.

There was probably no point, therefore, in denouncing Robert to the magistrate. Odon stroked his chin. Suddenly, he remembered the looks Robert had bestowed upon William when he'd thought no one was watching. Odon had been unable to make sense of them at the time, but now it all fell into place.

Robert did not come out of the church for a long time.

"I know what you've been doing," Odon murmured in his ear from behind. At first he had intended to grab Robert by his smock, but the thought of getting too close to him was repulsive.

Robert whirled around as if the devil had him by the tail. "What do you mean, Sir Odon?" he asked, acting unconcerned, but his trembling voice betrayed the fear coursing through his limbs.

"You should never have turned my Carla against me."

Robert relaxed a little. "I don't know what you mean, Sir Odon," he said. He was about to turn away when Odon punched him in the shoulder and knocked him to the ground.

"I don't think you should act so superior, you miserable sodomite!"

All the color drained out of Robert's face. His cheeks were suddenly white as snow, his lips bloodless, his eyes wide as they looked at Odon in disbelief.

Odon spat on the ground in disgust.

"I saw you. In the latrines. How do you think your friend William would like it if he found out what you get up to there?" Odon stroked his smooth chin again. "I'm wondering whether I should tell William myself, so that I can see his disgusted expression, his disappointment, and his rage, or…" Odon grinned from ear to ear but did not finish the sentence.

"Or what?" Robert broke in.

"Or whether you would prefer to disappear from his life on your own free will. Send him word that you don't want anything more to do with him, and I'm rid of you forever. A small price to pay for a big sin, don't you think? And in case you're thinking of letting him onto your secret, I advise against it. Unless of course you want to heap even more guilt on yourself."

"What do you mean?"

"Well, it would certainly be hard for William to lose another wife. Things happen so easily. I hear the good Marguerite often goes out riding, all by herself." Odon grinned spitefully. "All alone in the forest, and in her condition. As you know, that's been the undoing of many a woman."

"You're a swine, Odon."

"Hold your tongue, sodomite. Loud talk doesn't make you a hero." Odon gripped Robert by his surcoat, though it made him feel sick to have Robert so near. "If you don't disappear from William's life this very day, you'll have his wife on your conscience. And believe me, it won't be hard for me to throw suspicion your way. William will believe you followed her, and he'll strangle you with his bare hands."

☙❧

"Robert," William called again. "Robert, where are you?"

"He's gone, my lord," answered the young assistant William had hired only a few weeks earlier. "Is there anything I can do for you?"

"Gone? Where?" asked William. "We were going to start training the new passager." More and more recently, Robert had been disappearing for half a day at a time without telling anyone where he was going. Did he have a secret lover?

"I don't know, but he said to tell you he's not coming back," the assistant said timidly. "He packed up his things and left."

William ran out and looked around. Perhaps Robert was still nearby. He ran to the stables in a panic; Robert's horse was not there. "When did Robert leave?" he asked the stable boy breathlessly.

"A good while after the bells rang midday, my lord. He came in from Guildford, fetched his bundle, and left straightaway."

William ran to the manor house and called Marguerite. "Did Robert come to see you before he left?"

When she walked solemnly toward him with her head down, he knew she had spoken with Robert. She looked up with tear-filled eyes. "I don't understand. He was cold and abrupt with me, but I'm sure it pained him to be so. He didn't explain—he just said he had no choice. William, you have to ride after him and bring him back."

William felt an icy blast in his heart, remembering the remark Odon had made shortly after his wedding. Images of Robert and Marguerite whispering or laughing together thrust themselves into his mind. A stab of jealousy pierced his chest and left him gasping. He remembered the day he'd seen Robert kneeling before Marguerite in the great hall. She had burst into tears. Had he been declaring his love?

Nonsense! Didn't Robert always have some romance? Hadn't he kept disappearing for half a day at a time without saying where he was going? But what if he was secretly meeting Marguerite?

"William," Marguerite interrupted his grim thoughts. "What's the matter? Why haven't you gone off to look for him?" She laid her hand on William's arm, but he pulled away.

"He left word that he wasn't coming back. Robert is a free man; he must know what he's doing. I can't force him to stay." Having said this, he turned and left. As soon as he was far enough away, though, he whispered, close to tears, "Why, Robert? What have you done that you steal away like a thief?"

October 1201

A month after Robert's unexpected disappearance, Marguerite brought a fine healthy boy into the world. He had a charming mop of red hair and was the spitting image of Ellenweore.

"He just doesn't have her green eyes," observed William, sounding almost disappointed.

"Oh, my love, infants' eyes are always blue to begin with," Marguerite said reassuringly. "You can't see what color they really are until later. So don't give up hope just yet."

William lovingly kissed the tiny boy's small but prominent nose. "I miss Robert," he murmured, cradling the child in his arms. "I would have so liked to introduce him to Richard." They had named the boy after Marguerite's father, though the custom was to choose the name of the firstborn son from the father's side. Since they did not know anything about William's father, and since they were maintaining Richard de Hauville's legacy, William had suggested Richard.

Naturally, William spoiled both mother and child for the next few weeks. He had apples and grapes brought to Marguerite in bed, ordered honey cakes to build up her strength, and carried little Richard around with him every day, at first only in the bedchamber, and then as far as the hall; eventually, he showed him to everyone in the manor. He was proud of his son.

Marguerite breast-fed the child, though she could have afforded a wet nurse. The boy flourished, and his young mother soon recovered from the effort of childbirth and resumed her duties around the manor.

"Will you please let Richard sleep," she scolded William as he tried to take the boy out of his cradle. "What about kissing me instead of him?" She laughed and spread her arms.

William put his arms around her waist.

Pregnancy had softened Marguerite's body and made her even more beautiful. His hands slid down her back and onto her delightful behind. A roguish smile crept across his lips. He remembered very clearly what it felt like when he discovered the charming flaw there. It must have been two or three days after their wedding. Marguerite was standing in front of him, naked. His hand had slipped slowly down her back, and then he had turned her around so that he could feast on the sight of her small, firm buttocks. At first he thought she was just standing a little crooked, but the cleft that ought to divide the rump into equal halves had a definite leftward kink at the top. He had traced it with his index finger, and Marguerite had immediately tried to turn around.

"No, stay there," he exclaimed. "It's charming."

"But mother said no one should…"

"Shh," he replied, covering the spot with tender kisses that sent shudders of ecstasy up Marguerite's spine.

William could feel his desire surging afresh as he remembered. He kissed her and murmured, "You're the most beautiful woman in the world."

At that moment he could not help understanding Robert. Marguerite was so beautiful that one could not really blame him for falling in love with her. For the first time since Robert's departure, William thought he understood why his friend had decided to leave. It must have simply been too painful to love Marguerite and see her every day without being able to possess her. Perhaps it was right that Robert had distanced himself from both of them. Having no outlet for his love must have been as terrible for him as the constant awareness that he was betraying his best friend with every longing stare at his wife. William nodded almost imperceptibly. One thing was certain: he himself wouldn't have behaved differently.

"The steward can carry out his duties without you for a while. Why don't we go to Saint Edmundsbury soon?" Marguerite said, breaking into his thoughts and kissing his cheek gently. "I can hardly wait to meet your family and introduce the little one to them. What about you? Richard is five months old, and the weather is mild enough for us to travel easily."

William suddenly noticed how homesick he felt. It wasn't only Robert he missed; it was Jean and Isaac, as well as Rose and his mother.

"All right," he said as Marguerite looked at him pleadingly. "Why not?"

"I wonder if Robert will ever come back," she said suddenly, her voice troubled, almost wistful.

"I suppose you miss him," he replied testily, letting her go.

"Of course I do. Don't you?" Marguerite looked at him in astonishment.

"Certainly," William muttered, thrown off balance. The idea that anything more than friendship bound Robert and Marguerite was absurd. Robert might have loved Marguerite, but the other way around?

"So what are you waiting for? Why don't you start looking for him. Maybe he went back to Oakham. We could stay with de Ferrers on our way to Saint Edmundsbury," Marguerite suggested. Fresh suspicion rose up in William. Why did she keep asking about Robert? After their wedding, Odon had used his insinuations to open the door to mistrust in William's heart, and now he couldn't close it, try as he might. The suspicion that Odon might possibly have spoken the truth had struck home like an arrow and poisoned his thoughts.

"No, we won't do that. That's enough. Don't talk about him anymore," he commanded harshly, leaving her standing there. He strode away and did not return to their bedchamber until Marguerite was already asleep.

He undressed, lay down beside her, and blew out the candle. He stared into the darkness for a long time before finally falling asleep. Images of the dungeon at Thorne mingled in his mind with memories of Robert. He tossed and turned in bed and awoke bathed in sweat. He lay there, greatly distressed, and thought about loyalty and friendship. Losing Robert affected him more deeply than he cared to admit and heightened his fear of losing Marguerite.

The sun rose, and the first rays pierced the slits in the shutters, bathing the room in soft light.

Marguerite woke up and stretched. "Sleep well?" she asked, kissing William's cheek. "Ugh, you're scratchy!" She rubbed his fresh stubble and laughed.

William took her in his arms and held her tightly, as if by doing so he could prevent her from slipping away from him, and all of a sudden everything that had been burdening his soul for so long came pouring out.

"He was my son, too," sobbed William, once he had finished telling the story of Enid's death and their child's gruesome end. "He was so tiny, much smaller than Richard was when he was born, so sweet and innocent." William clung to Marguerite like a drowning man. "There's nothing I fear more than losing you and Richard."

"I know, my love." She rocked him in her arms like a child, kissing him tenderly. She whispered in his ear, "Let's set off for Saint Edmundsbury soon. The change will do you good, and so will being near the people you love."

Near Saint Edmundsbury, March 1202

William had insisted they wear ordinary clothes so that they could travel without a retinue and avoid the risk of being attacked. The mild weather allowed them to make good progress, and William felt more at ease the closer they got to Saint Edmundsbury. No longer burdened by the pressure to become a smith, he could think of nothing lovelier than returning home. He could hardly wait, and he was full of pride about being able to show his mother, and especially Isaac, their long-awaited grandchild.

William enjoyed the ride through newly awakening nature. He held his son close to his body, keeping him warm and safe. "You'll see, little one, Rose smells of flour and delicious pies," he whispered, kissing the child's tiny, cold nose.

A few days later as they rode into the smithy yard, William's heart began to race furiously. He paused for a moment and took in the tranquil setting, trying to preserve it in his memory. He slipped down off his horse; dismounting with a child on his arm was no harder than dismounting with a hawk on his fist. Once Marguerite had likewise dismounted, he handed the child to her, tied up the horses, and led her to the smithy.

But what was this? The workshop was silent. Something was wrong. He opened the heavy wooden door and stepped inside. There was no fire in any of the forges and no smith at any of the anvils. Fear crept over William.

Marguerite had come into the smithy behind him and was looking at him questioningly when he turned around.

"Something must have happened." He left her there and ran over to the house.

They were all gathered in Ellenweore and Isaac's room; Rose and Jean, Peter and the other smiths, the assistants, and all their children were silently crowded in. Ellenweore sat on the edge of the pallet on which the gray and hollowed-out Isaac was laid out.

Someone had wound a garland of roses around his remaining hand.

When William came in and saw his mother's red-rimmed eyes, he guessed he had arrived too late. "Is he dead?"

"He was very ill, my lamb," Rose told him gently, spreading her arms to embrace him.

William wept like a child, breathing in her familiar scent. He could hear Ellenweore sobbing. It pained him to think that his mother was suffering. William untangled himself from Rose, went to Ellenweore, and embraced her. Tenderly, he kissed her now-gray hair. Although she was still very strong, she had aged more in the past two years than he had expected.

Isaac looked strangely unfamiliar. "Father," said William, laboring to get the word out. He leaned down and kissed Isaac's colorless, cold cheek. He fell to his knees by the pallet, pressed his head into the bedclothes, and wept heartrending tears. "I brought you your grandson," he sobbed, "and my wife. Look how beautiful she is!" It was as if William thought he could bring Isaac back to life with his words.

After a long while, he stood up, went out of the room, and brought in Marguerite.

"This is Marguerite," he said by way of introduction, and Marguerite curtsied deeply, as if she were not the daughter of a baron and her mother-in-law were not just a swordsmith.

Ellenweore stood up and looked deeply into her eyes, as if she could see into her daughter-in-law's soul. Then she saw the child, and a tear rolled down her cheek.

"He looks like you," William said softly.

Ellenweore embraced her son, stroked Marguerite's hair, and reached out for her grandson's little hand.

The smiths and assistants, Jean, Rose, and the children all left the small room one by one. They shook Ellenweore and William by the hand and murmured their condolences.

Henry walked past William with tear-filled eyes and gave him a hostile look. "You've come just in time, haven't you? But the smithy is mine, do you hear? He was *my* father!"

"Isaac was a fine man," said William through gritted teeth. "You'll be a worthy successor to him. I'm not here to dispute your inheritance."

Henry nodded sheepishly and left.

William asked to be left alone with Isaac for a moment and left Marguerite in Ellenweore's care. He sat down beside his stepfather's deathbed and prayed.

"You would have been the best grandfather a child could ask for," he whispered after a silent prayer, suppressing a sob. "The boy's name is Richard Isaac, after Marguerite's father and mine." He crossed himself, stood up, and went out to join the others.

Isaac was buried the same day, next to poor David and not far from the shed where William had hidden the king's falcon all those years ago. The memory of that day made him sob again. Isaac had always been on William's side. Even if he was old enough now and did not need anyone to speak for him, he still missed Isaac's fatherly advice.

Once the grave had been covered with the last shovelful of earth, William and Ellenweore stayed behind while the others went back to the house.

William cleared his throat. "Henry will be old enough to take over the smithy soon."

Ellenweore nodded. "He's doing well. Still, I hope he'll be glad to have me beside him for a few years yet. The day will come when I'm too old for hard work." She stroked her son's arm comfortingly. "Don't worry, William, you'll inherit the smithy at Orford eventually."

William was still looking down at the dark earth covering Isaac's grave. "I know, Mother." He already owned enough land, and he did not need the smithy, but he did love Orford.

"I'm so proud of you, William. Isaac would have been very happy to see you with a wife and child. You stole his heart from the very beginning, and he loved you as he loved Henry."

"I know, Mother," William replied soothingly. "Come, let us join the others in the house." He offered her his arm and led her away.

"Do you still want to know who your real father was?" Ellenweore asked quietly and almost fearfully.

William hesitated for a moment. All these years he had hoped she would tell him, but now it didn't seem important. "No, Mother. Isaac was the only father I ever had. Nothing else matters."

"Indeed," she said, visibly relieved.

Back at the house, they joined the others at the big table. Rose and her helpers had prepared a variety of meats, cakes, and sauces, as was customary, and now they all ate together.

After a few tankards of ale, the mood became more relaxed, and Peter told the story of when Ellenweore first entered Isaac's smithy. Everyone laughed when they heard that Isaac had believed a woman's place was at the hearth, not the forge.

"Isaac wasn't always right, and he soon saw his mistake. Fortunately. Whether it was because your mother was a good smith or a bad cook, we'll never know," Jean joked. This earned him a furious look from Ellenweore, which he returned with a fat kiss on the cheek. "You're the finest woman smith in the kingdom. You know how much we all admire you, even our young baron here. Isn't that right, my lord?"

"My lord?" Ellenweore looked at her son with a frown.

William cleared his throat with embarrassment.

"Yes, dear. William explained it to me earlier. He's a proper lord now. This young lady here hasn't just given him a healthy son—she also brought a fine piece of land into the marriage, complete with a falconry, where he tends the king's hawks. And on top of all that, it seems to me, the lucky fellow also gets a heart full of love from her."

Ellenweore looked at Marguerite, who flushed with embarrassment, and then at William. "A lady," she murmured, and William feared she might reject Marguerite for that reason, but Ellenweore smiled at her kindly. "A lady she may be, but I can see she's above all a good girl. I could see it in her eyes immediately," she said, touching her daughter-in-law's arm.

In her eyes. Like with falcons, thought William, touched by his mother's words.

"And she can clean vegetables, too," laughed Ellenweore. Then she turned serious again. "I'm glad you brought her here and grateful that I can hold your son in my arms." Ellenweore took a deep breath, wiping away a tear. "If only Isaac had lived to do the same. He always said you would bring him a grandchild one day."

William put his arm around his mother and drew her to him.

Rose sniffled, stood up, and put the child in Ellenweore's arms. She had been rocking him the whole time. "I'd better get the next pie out of the oven."

Ellenweore rocked the boy, tickled his throat, and kissed his cheek lightly. "Ugh, his swaddling cloth is full," she protested. "So that's why you handed him over, is it, Rose?" She held her nose, and when everyone laughed, she joined them.

Leaving Saint Edmundsbury a few days later was particularly hard for William this time. His mother seemed overworked. The day after Isaac died, she was back in the smithy.

William wondered about her health. Would she save her strength, or would she overreach herself? How many more times would he be able to sit at table with her and talk? Would his son be able to visit Saint Edmundsbury often enough to remember Ellenweore?

Isaac's death left a big gap, so they tried to persuade William to stay for a while. But he refused.

"We need to get back to Roford. I have to take care of the falcons," he told his mother while they were alone together in the workshop, cleaning Isaac's tools.

"What happened to Robert? Did he stay in Oakham, or did he go with you?" she asked. She obviously had not noticed that Robert's name had gone unmentioned during their stay.

"He worked for me, yes, but he went away."

"It felt to me as though you couldn't ask for a better friend. What happened?"

"I don't know. He left. One day he was there—the next day he wasn't," murmured William. He explained that he suspected Robert of being in love with Marguerite and believed that Robert had disappeared for that reason. He had never spoken so intimately with his mother before.

"I was afraid of losing her. That's why I didn't go after him," he said finally, filled with shame.

"Love sometimes leads us down strange paths, and it punishes the unhappy lover most cruelly." She touched William's arm with her rough, powerful hand. It had liver spots he had never noticed before.

William nodded uncomfortably, scratching the ground with his foot as he used to when he was a boy. Perhaps it was true that Robert was suffering the most. But what if Marguerite was pining for him, too? The old jealousy started gnawing at his heart again.

Ellenweore was sorting Isaac's tools and placing them in their holders on the wall. "Hopeless love is painful. It can drive people to do bad things. You can't understand that. You've got the woman you love, after all. Have you ever asked yourself what kind of sacrifice you would have been willing to make if the king had married her off to someone else? Sometimes a particular love is impossible." She thought for a moment. "But even if it's against all the rules, if it simply cannot be, for whatever reason, it's never a bad thing as long as it comes from the heart, is pure, and is ready to relinquish everything."

William was puzzled by her words.

Ellenweore blew off some iron filings from one of Isaac's files, rubbed the handle with a piece of leather, and hung it in its place. "You once told me that David and Robert were as dear to you as Jean and Rose are to me." She paused, looking as if she was remembering something. "They disappointed me badly once, too, but I wouldn't have let them go for all the world. I was unbelievably proud, but my love for them was greater."

William felt he had been found out. Was he arrogant? Too proud to forgive?

"Look for him and talk to him," Ellenweore counseled him, breaking into his thoughts. She stroked his hair, just as Isaac used to.

When Marguerite came into the smithy looking for him, William was glad that he did not have to talk about Robert any longer. Between him and Isaac, he had lost two of the most important people in his life in quick succession.

"We'll stop at Oakham on the way back. I hope to find Robert there and have a chance to speak to him," William said to Marguerite as casually as he could while they were saddling the horses before their departure.

"Good," she said with the appearance of indifference, but a tiny smile of satisfaction played on her lips.

They said their farewells to Ellenweore, Jean, and Rose.

"Come and visit us soon," said Marguerite, embracing them one by one.

William seconded her invitation, and Jean immediately threatened to turn up in a month or two.

"Nothing could make us happier," Marguerite assured him, beaming.

Ellenweore kissed and tickled her grandson one last time. William was surprised at her tenderness. Had she been so affectionate with him when he was an infant? He embraced her, closing his eyes and trying to implant in his memory her scent of charcoal and iron.

They waved to the smiths and assistants, who had gathered outside, and set off.

During the ride to Oakham, William remained stubbornly silent. Walkelin de Ferrers had died the previous year. It felt strange to be returning to Oakham Castle without him there. William reflected, questioned himself, covertly eyed Marguerite, and came to the conclusion that only death was final. He would ask Robert to come back—that is, if he found him.

Marguerite, radiant with happiness on this glorious spring day, looked at him and blew him a kiss. She loved him; William was sure of it now. Robert posed no threat there, even if he did desire Marguerite. Had he not proved, by going away, that he could be trusted?

When they reached Oakham, William found, to his relief, that Robert had indeed gone back there. Henry de Ferrers was on the mainland with the king, so only the steward was at the castle. William talked to him, then asked Marguerite to wait for him while he went to the falconry alone. The path awakened memories of the many good years he had spent here and strengthened his wish to get Robert back.

William could not find him in the mews, so he started looking outside. He took the path leading to the big field where they used to train the falcons to the lure, and he passed the copse of oaks. Suddenly, he noticed two men running after each other. Despite the distance, he recognized Robert and one of the stable boys. Robert was looking around like a man with a guilty conscience.

William became curious and followed them discreetly; he hid behind a bush and watched them. Despite the dense undergrowth, he could see both men clearly.

Robert was standing by a tree with his face against the trunk, like a child playing hide-and-seek. The stable boy had followed him, and he looked around anxiously before pressing himself against Robert. William saw him whisper something in Robert's ear. What happened next was so incredible that William thought he would choke.

Robert lifted up his smock to his chest and offered his exposed rear to the stable boy. It shone like the full moon, and the stable boy seemed to like the look of it. He rapidly bared himself, too, and, filled with lust, thrust into Robert.

William closed his eyes in disgust. He felt faint. His stomach burned with acid.

"How could you, Robert?" he cried in dismay, once he had run far enough away. He vomited, then spat on the ground. He thought of the time he was so close to death. Robert had cared for him and washed his naked body. Had his friend touched him in an impure way? William felt defiled, cursed, and helpless, and he kicked furiously at a pile of rotting leaves. A hedgehog that had been hiding inside scampered out and fled to the nearest bush.

When Robert came into the falconry a short while later, William was waiting for him in the mews.

"William," cried Robert in surprise, taking a step toward him. "How wonderful to see you."

"Why?" William asked aggressively. "Why do you do that?"

"What do you mean?" Robert asked, taking another step toward his friend. He went to touch his arm, but William pushed him away brusquely.

"Don't you dare touch me. A man like you who sins against nature will bring down the wrath of God upon his head and deserves neither my friendship nor my forbearance." William drew back.

"Please, Will," Robert pleaded in dismay. "I've never wished anything bad for you. You were never supposed to find out. That's why I left."

"You're a traitor." William spat. "A godforsaken sodomite, a sinner, a transgressor, a criminal." It came pouring out with such force that William shocked himself.

"I've never betrayed you, William. It's love that binds me to you. And friendship."

"Coming from your mouth, even a good word like 'love' sounds sinful. I shudder to think what you did to me when I lay sick and close to death." William felt goose bumps breaking out all over his body. He had always trusted Robert. How could he ever do so again?

"I didn't touch you in any improper way, truly," Robert pleaded. "I washed you, I wiped away your waste, I cared for you until you were well, but I promise you I have never touched you impurely. You're my best friend, the only person who means anything to me. But I always knew I couldn't have you, and I've accepted that."

"You, have me?" William snorted with anger. "The way the boy in the woods had you? It's disgusting, Robert."

"Forgive me. I can't help it."

"Nonsense. Of course you can help it. Go, get yourself a wife, and find the right path. Then I'll forgive you. The blacksmith's daughter has her eye on you. Why don't you court her?" William stared at him, baffled. The girl was a beauty; all the men were after her, but Robert did not give her so much as a second glance.

Robert shook his head. "I've tried, believe me. I went to the woods with her, and she tried to seduce me—she didn't care that we weren't married—but I couldn't do it."

"What do you mean, you couldn't do it? You could have married her if your conscience told you it was wrong otherwise."

"I couldn't, William." Robert pointed at his crotch. "It wouldn't work. My flesh wasn't willing. When it comes to women, I don't know what to do. I don't like them. The softness of their bodies repels me."

William couldn't believe what he was hearing. "Very well, not her then, but someone else," he said angrily. "You certainly liked Marguerite."

"Oh no, Will. I love Marguerite like a sister, no more. I love only you. I feel so much desire for you that it hurts. Ever since Thorne," he added under his breath.

William snorted. It wasn't Marguerite that Robert loved; it was *William*. That couldn't be. "I came to ask you to come back to Roford," he said expressionlessly.

"Really?" asked Robert, touched but unsure.

"But under the circumstances," William went on unshakably, "we have nothing more to say to each other. Marguerite and I will journey on today. Without you."

"William, I beg you, let me come with you."

"So that you can corrupt my son, too?" As he uttered the words, William knew he was doing Robert an injustice, but at that moment fear and disappointment were stronger than friendship and compassion.

Robert stared at him, wide-eyed. "No, William. I would never do that! You have a son? May I see him? Please, I swear I would never touch him."

"You will not accompany us. My decision is final, and don't you dare follow me to the hall," replied William with a slight tremor in his voice. He left the mews. The light outside was blinding, but it offered a good excuse for the tears that were running down his cheek.

Not far from the hall, Marguerite ran up the path toward him with the child on her arm.

"For God's sake, dearest, what happened? You look as if you've seen the devil himself."

"Robert won't be coming with us," William said through gritted teeth, taking Marguerite by the arm and pulling her away.

"Why not? What's the matter?"

"Not now. I'll explain some other time. Please." William stormed off, sniffling. How could he make her understand what he didn't understand himself? At the beginning of the day, he had rejoiced at the thought that Robert would be coming back, but now he just felt dull and empty. He would miss Robert, yet he couldn't find a way to see beyond his anger. He had known him for so long. How could it have escaped him that his friend was a sodomite, accursed and condemned to continue to suffer long after his earthly life was over?

They departed for Roford that very day, and on the way back they stopped at Smithfield. William had decided to visit the market there again; though after the events at Oakham he did so only halfheartedly. Marguerite was exhausted after their journey, so he arranged accommodation for her and the child in an inn and wandered toward the marketplace on his own.

Memories of his first visit to Smithfield came flooding back, forcing out all thoughts of Robert. He thought about Tanner, FitzEldred, and FitzOwen, and a wave of sadness came over him. When he was close to the square where he had met the two merchants for the first time, a gyrfalcon being sold by one of the bird dealers caught his attention.

The falcon was almost snow-white, with a few pitch-black flecks on her breast and back, and had an aura like few birds that William had ever seen. He went closer and looked more carefully. She was unusually large, even for a female gyrfalcon. Her posture, beak, legs, and feet were as perfect as her markings and the condition of her plumage. William rubbed his hands together. They were moist with excitement, and his fingertips were tingling. This was a still quite young gyrfalcon from the north, perhaps Iceland.

William shook his head and turned away as if uninterested, though he found it difficult to take his eyes off the bird. A little farther on, he stopped and pretended to look at another trader's wares. There was certainly no need to ask the price of such a noble beast; a bird like that was sure to be exorbitantly expensive.

While William looked around at the other stalls, the image of the falcon would not leave him alone. What would King John say to a bird like that? William knew how keen he was to own the most beautiful falcon in the land, and a white gyrfalcon was something rather special, even for the king. As far as William knew, he had only one such bird. It was to him that William owed his marriage to Marguerite and, as a result, her lands and the title of Lord Roford. How he would love to give him such an extraordinary gift as a token of his gratitude.

William strolled on, but the bird did not leave his thoughts. I'll regret it for the rest of my life if I don't at least ask the price, thought William. It was not until he was standing in front of the dealer's stall that he realized his feet had taken him there on their own accord.

He looked at the dealer's other birds and then took another close look at the gyrfalcon. Her eyes had been seeled. William sighed. Would it become customary one day to use hoods for manning? His experiences with the hoods had all been positive.

"When did you catch her?" he asked the dealer as casually as he could.

"Not quite a month ago, noble sir," the man replied, puffing out his chest. "North of York. She found her way to England all by herself, the little beauty. Damned rare, something like that. And as you can see, she's already been seeled."

"So she's still completely wild and hasn't been trained at all."

"Well, for someone who knows what he's doing…" the dealer answered ingratiatingly, bowing slightly.

"Oh, I know very well what I'm doing, and I tell you she'll be very hard to train."

"She's still young and has the experience of hunting that falconers value so highly," the dealer insisted self-confidently.

"What you mean is that she's tasted freedom long enough to want it back. It's certainly risky buying a bird like this. You can't even see her eyes. She might be blind for all I know." William turned away as if to leave the stall.

"God forbid, sir. I saw her round, shining eyes before I had them sewn shut."

"A man who doesn't really understand seeling can cause a serious injury." William did his best to look doubtful, shaking his head in apparent mistrust.

"Well, I warrant you wouldn't know what to do with such a magnificent bird anyway. Gyrfalcons should be flown only by kings, after all," said the dealer, now visibly affronted, yet there was a hint of pride in his voice.

"One more reason to give me a good price. You won't find many buyers here." William looked around and pointed at the simple peasants who had gathered around the stall to gawp. "Tell me, how much do you want for the bird? But think carefully. Set the mark too high, and I'll do an about-face and won't be back. You know you're going to have difficulty selling her at this market. Not that there aren't enough rich men in London, but a white gyrfalcon isn't for them, as you pointed out."

"Well, there are royal falconers here," the dealer boasted, feigning indifference and waving his hand airily.

"Indeed? I know most of them and I haven't seen a single one. But if you think..." William turned away, trying to look utterly unconcerned.

"Wait, sir!"

"So how high is your price?" asked William, still walking.

The dealer named a figure that took William's breath away. The bystanders shook their heads in disbelief. Some of them went away, making contemptuous remarks; others stayed where they were, just so they could see whether William would buy the bird for such an outrageously high price.

"You are a miserable cheat!" cried William, enraged, turning to face him again. "For a falcon that hasn't been manned or trained, you demand the kind of price she might fetch if she were made of pure silver! You should be ashamed of yourself. I ought to call the officers." William pretended to be ill-tempered. Even if he could haggle the man down to half the price he had named, the falcon would still cost as much as three very good horses. Nevertheless, he mentally counted the coins in his purse.

"She's the finest falcon I've ever put up for sale, and she's worth every penny," the dealer protested.

"He's trying to cheat a baron," William heard somebody say, and the circle of onlookers nodded in agreement.

"You heard that. If you won't meet me halfway, you'll have to man and train the falcon yourself before you'll be able to sell her. And as I'm sure you know, that requires patience and time, not to mention experience. Only the finest feed will do for a bird like this. Otherwise, sooner or later, she'll fly off. Training her will require at least one assistant, preferably two. But even if you manned her yourself, she wouldn't be worth half what you're asking." William was exaggerating wildly, but that was all part of haggling. "But be

my guest. If you feel up to it and want to wait that long for a sale."
William shrugged his shoulders to feign boredom and made as if
to leave again.

Despite the noble bird he was selling, the dealer was rather
poorly dressed. The man had probably fallen victim to dice, like so
many, or perhaps he was a drinker. If he did not sell fast enough, he
threw away more money than the animals brought in.

"Wait, noble sir! I'll meet you halfway, so you can see I'm a fair
man." The price he now named was lower, but it was still a long
way off what William was prepared or, more to the point, able
to pay. He knew that a gyrfalcon that had been trained to hunt
cranes, herons, or kites could cost as much as fifteen or twenty
good horses. So what would a white gyrfalcon like this one be
worth? It really would be a gift worthy of a king. Besides, he was
enjoying the challenge. So he came straight back with a price of
his own, barely half what the dealer had first asked. In order to
add weight to his bid, William took out his purse and showed
that he had the necessary funds. "That's all I have—as you can see.
So take the money and seal the bargain, or else go on waiting for
someone else who will pay more for a bird he can't fly for himself."

Grumbling, the dealer scratched his bristly eyebrows, which
made him resemble an owl. He postured a little, mumbled something that sounded like a curse, hesitated, and then finally pulled
himself together. "Very well. I see you know how to handle a bird
like this," he grunted.

When William returned to their room at the inn with the falcon
and saw Marguerite, his conscience pricked him. It was such a
touching sight, her sitting there on an unsteady stool with the
child in her arms, giving him her full attention. William sighed.
He had promised Marguerite cloth for new clothes, and now they
would not be able to buy it.

She looked up at him, and his eyes shifted downward guiltily. She did not deserve to be disappointed.

"What a magnificent bird," Marguerite whispered reverently. "For the king?"

William nodded glumly.

"I've been wanting to thank him for a long time for bringing us together," said Marguerite with a gentle smile. "But tell me, dearest, how did you pay for such an expensive creature?"

"She hasn't been manned, she was captured wild, and apparently she's not ready to be trained."

"A challenge, then," laughed Marguerite.

"When you hear what I paid for her," William confessed sheepishly, "you won't be laughing anymore."

"You haven't a penny left, have you?"

William opened his right hand, revealing his last two copper coins.

"For goodness' sake, you look like bad conscience personified."

"It's not enough for the cloth I promised you."

"Oh, William, you should know me better." Marguerite held her head to one side and looked at him archly. She went over to her bag and took out a leather purse that clinked when she shook it. "On long journeys I always carry a few coins. It'll be enough for the cloth."

"Oh, best of all women, you're an angel," William said with relief.

"Well, I'm pretty satisfied with you as a husband, too," she said ironically, putting away the purse. "Once you've trained the falcon and she's ready to be presented to John, he'll reward you more than generously. I'm sure he'll be absolutely delighted and will give you her weight in silver."

"But I didn't buy her to be rewarded," William protested. "I bought her to thank him."

"I know, my love. You're far too good to think of your own advantage," she teased. "Nevertheless, we won't end up out of pocket. John loves me like a daughter, and he must think highly of you, too, or he wouldn't have chosen you as my husband. So why shouldn't he reward you as generously as any of his other barons?"

William shrugged. He could hardly wait to take home the silver falcon, as he now called her, and start training her.

Once they had bought the cloth for Marguerite, they set off for Roford.

When they arrived, William put the falcon in the mews to recover from the journey. The sand and the perches were clean; the birds were resting.

He was about to shout "Robert," so that he could show him the gyrfalcon, but then he remembered. Robert was gone. Forever.

William placed the falcon on a block and fastened her leash to the ring. He would have to train her with Humfrid, the older and more experienced of the two assistants. He stroked the bird's white plumage and thought of John's father, Henry, and his gyrfalcon.

"You're much more beautiful, and much more expensive, than she was," he whispered to her. "What would you think if I named you now, instead of waiting for your first hunt?" He stroked her noble plumage gently. "I think we should call you Blanchpenny. The king's little fugitive brought me luck once, and since you've cost me almost all my silver, it seems a thoroughly appropriate name. Don't you think?"

That evening, as William came out of the mews, he thought he saw Robert at the spring. His heart began pounding furiously. Hadn't he made it clear that he didn't want to see him again? "What are you doing here?" he shouted, striding toward the spring.

"I'm fetching water for the horses, my lord," the man answered, obviously surprised. When he turned around to ask what was wrong, William saw it was not Robert but one of the stable boys.

"Ah, of course. Yes, do go on," William muttered. He turned on his heels and walked over to the manor house. He had to forget Robert!

Within the first few days, William made a hood for Blanchpenny so he could man her. He told Humfrid to remove the seeling threads, then carried the unseeled bird around with her special hood on, feeding her the usual tidbits. Finally, he took her outside, too. In this way, he got her accustomed to him.

It took longer to win the trust of this white female than it had with many other birds, for she was particularly wary. But one day things had moved along far enough for William to start training her with Humfrid's assistance.

He was always helpful and friendly, but neither he nor the other assistants could take Robert's place. William missed him more and more as each day passed, though he would never have admitted it. Humfrid tried hard, and William had never seen him be rough, but Blanchpenny could not bear him and protested loudly whenever he took her on his fist.

William let her fly to the dragged lure over and over again, and it was soon apparent that she was not only beautiful but also graceful and courageous. Occasionally she was too courageous; one day she hurt herself and could no longer grip with her right foot.

"Please, God in heaven, don't do this to me," William pleaded desperately. If Blanchpenny's foot didn't heal, she wouldn't be able to hunt and would no longer be any use as a gift for the king.

Terrified, William applied bandages and herbs, speaking softly to her as he did so.

William had shared with Marguerite his delight in Blanchpenny's hunting, as well as his satisfaction with her progress and, now, his concern for her, but he still carried on imaginary conversations with Robert. Whenever he caught himself doing this, he felt ashamed and cursed himself for a fool.

After a few days, he bent Blanchpenny's claws upward, bit by bit, fervently praying that God might be merciful and let the injury heal so that he could go on training her.

Three weeks passed, during which he missed Robert's calm and support more than ever. There had been no obvious improvement. Blanchpenny's claws were open now, but she still could not grip with her foot.

One morning, while William was sitting down and eating some cheese for breakfast, a wave of pain flowed through him. He gritted his teeth and closed his eyes. For some days, his stomach had started burning after only a few mouthfuls, as if he had swallowed fire. He moaned and pushed the bread away. With the best will in the world, he could not swallow any more. He stood up and nodded to Marguerite, ignoring her concerned look.

"Please excuse me," he murmured and set off for the falconry.

It was concern for Blanchpenny and a guilty conscience about Robert that were making him ill. His stomach felt hard and painful, as if he had swallowed a large rock. He reached for the clay pot on the massive iron shelf and took half a handful of fennel seeds. For some time now he had been chewing them more and more often to combat the pain, and he imagined they gave at least some relief.

When, for the first time since her injury, Blanchpenny stepped onto the glove he used to feed her and reached out for the proffered chick with her right foot, William's stomach pains disappeared instantly.

"Well done, good girl," he praised her, rejoicing inwardly and feeling a sense of release. Now at last he could work with her again. The king was on the mainland, busy with an apparently endless war, and probably would not come back to England anytime soon, yet William could hardly wait to get Blanchpenny trained to the point that he could hand her over whenever he wanted.

Roford Manor, May 1203

A good year had passed since William had witnessed Robert's shameful deeds at Oakham. Marguerite tried several times to prize the details from him, and one day it all came pouring out.

"I wish I had never seen it. Who knows how long he had been practicing these outrages," he groaned in despair. "I was disgusted, but also relieved, and that's what I'm most ashamed of. Odon implied that Robert and you…I didn't want to believe it, but…" He fell silent for shame.

Marguerite said nothing to end his torment. She just looked at him without saying a word. There was disappointment in her eyes, but also something akin to understanding.

"I find what he does repulsive. It's a sin and it's depraved. But even that wasn't the worst. Robert confessed that he wanted me the way a man might want a woman. I find that incomprehensible and disgusting. I can't have him around me anymore, much as I want to." William crumpled. "I miss him terribly and that makes me afraid." He had often wondered, lately, what would have happened if he had never caught Robert. His friend would have come back without confessing his love, and they would have worked together as before. But would his suspicions about Marguerite have been set aside?

William hid away more and more often, though Marguerite tried everything to distract him. Not even in their bedchamber, when she tried to entice him to lie with her, was he really with her in his thoughts. It was only when little Richard ran to him and leaped whooping into his arms that William felt light and unburdened.

In the evening, when he emerged from the falconry and Robert's favorite hound ran up to him, whimpering, disappointment and sadness at his loss rose up in him afresh. The dog had followed him everywhere since Robert left, as if he feared losing William, too.

This particular dog had caused Robert a lot of trouble at first. He had been a sickly whelp, and his survival had come by dint of great effort. Titch, as Robert had named him at birth for his scrawny frame, was neither particularly strong nor a good hunting dog, but he was good-natured and loyal. He patiently tolerated little Richard's clumsy affections, which consisted of grabbing his fur with his tiny hands, and reminded William of Graybeard, whom he also missed terribly.

In recent months, William had developed a deep furrow between his eyebrows. Sometimes, Marguerite would stroke it and whisper, "I don't want you to go on being unhappy. Send a messenger to bring back Robert."

But William could not bring himself to do it.

One evening, William came out of the falconry a little earlier than usual. He was crossing the courtyard when he saw his son crouching on the ground, holding out a kernel of corn to a little sparrow.

"Here, birdie," he called in his clear childish voice, adopting a honeyed, ingratiating tone. Richard would be a good falconer one day.

The boy suddenly looked up and noticed his father. His earnest little face brightened in a big smile. He staggered up to William like a drunken sailor.

Richard always melted William's tenseness. He smiled, spread his arms wide, and leaned forward to pick up the boy. But the next moment the smile died on his lips, and his arms fell to his sides. He stared in disbelief at Marguerite, who had just stepped out of the hall, and at the man standing beside her.

Richard, not noticing that his father was distracted, threw his arms around William's left leg and squeezed it. "Caught you," Richard cried happily, leaning back and beaming at William as the latter looked down at him.

Robert? What's Robert doing here? wondered William. He picked up his son and looked at him as if he were the anchor that would save his life. Affectionately, he ruffled his son's red hair, which reminded him so much of his mother.

"Horsey," the boy ordered, kicking his sturdy little legs as if spurring on a horse.

"All right, climb on," William said. He could not bring himself to look back at Marguerite and Robert. Just as he had when he was a child, he wanted to pretend that what shouldn't be there wouldn't be—if he simply ignored it. He placed the child on his shoulders, turned away, and ran off.

The boy whooped with pleasure, cheerfully digging his heels into William's collarbone so he would go faster. "Hup, horsey. Hup," he cried.

William held Richard's little feet tightly and crossed the courtyard at a run. Please, let him be gone when I get back, he begged God, and when he met up with the head groom, whose face broke into a grin at the sight of father and son, he headed back toward the manor house.

Marguerite was standing in front of the hall, alone. William breathed again. He must have been mistaken. He had probably taken one of the servants for Robert.

"I told Robert he could stay in the falconry tonight," she told him as he tried to go past her. She took her son's hand and kissed it.

"Hup, horsey," cried Richard again, drumming against William's chest with his feet. William walked slowly and carefully into the hall, as if walking in quicksand.

"Horsey. More horsey," Richard shouted angrily.

William whinnied like a horse and pretended to rear up. "Free me of this wild horseman," he ordered the nursemaid with feigned joviality, then swung the child down from his shoulders. "Take the boy into the kitchen and give him something to eat," he told her, pouring himself a cup of wine.

As soon as they had left, he turned frostily to Marguerite. "What is he doing here?"

"You have to clear the air with him, my love."

"Does he think I can forgive him so easily?" William spat.

"No, he doesn't. But you can't avoid him forever."

"I wouldn't be so sure."

"That's exactly what he said." Marguerite smiled. "That, and that you're the most obstinate person he's ever known. But also the most lovable," she added, with a widening of her eyes. "Please, William, you must forgive him."

"Is that why he came here, so that my wife could grovel on his behalf?" William could hear how uncharitable he sounded, and he was ashamed to speak to Marguerite like this, but he could not help himself. He steadied himself against the table.

"Robert has never flouted an order of yours. It was I who sent news to him by messenger. He thought it was your wish that he should come back. He found out only just now that the messenger came from me, not you." Marguerite took William's face in her hands. "I know how much you miss him. Do you think I haven't noticed you're still suffering terribly? Some people have to be forced to find happiness. That's why I wanted him to come."

"Then send him away. He has nothing to do in my house. He'll just corrupt my child with his wicked urges." William drained a whole cup of wine in a single chug.

"What he has done is a sin. There's no doubt about it. But no one, and I mean no one, is proof against error. And pride, William, the kind of pride you are showing toward him, is also an offense against our Lord." Marguerite put her hands on her hips. "Who are you to judge him? You're not a priest—you're his friend, and as such you should stand by him. Take your example from Marshal, since you admire him so much."

"What's he got to do with it?" retorted William, snorting irritably.

"He always stood by King Richard, even though they often disagreed." Marguerite took a step toward William and fixed her eyes on his. "No one ever heard William Marshal say a single bad word about Richard's aberrations. Ever."

"Well, Richard was the king, wasn't he," said William furiously.

"King or no king, friendship means being able to forgive."

"But Robert won't repent and refuses to take a wife," William objected helplessly.

"What difference does that make to you? As long as he leaves you alone?"

"Why is it so important to you that I forgive him? Why, Marguerite?"

"I can no longer just stand by when you're suffering so much," she replied softly, stroking his cheek lovingly. "The pain when you eat—did you really think I wouldn't notice? You're tormenting yourself for no good reason."

"But…"

"Oh, my love, you've always been able to count on Robert, and we have a lot to thank him for. If he hadn't intervened, our marriage would have begun with the stupidest misunderstanding, wouldn't it have? It's time to forgive him."

"But I can't forget what I saw," William protested again.

"You must stop thinking about it. Robert would never harm you; still less would he corrupt your son. I know you're as sure of that, deep in your heart, as I am."

"He will burn in hell!"

"He already is. Having you still angry with him is a kind of hell for him." She wrung her hands until the skin over her knuckles was quite white. "I told him to come back tomorrow. Please, William, for your own sake, forgive him. You haven't been yourself since he left. You're always downcast, you fly into a rage over nothing, and you're often unjust. I understand your pain, so I haven't complained. But it must end now. Robert has made a mistake. He shouldn't have to pay for it forever."

"But he'll do it again," William railed, his desperation plain to see.

"Then you'll have to turn a blind eye. It's his life. He's the one who will have to pay for his aberrations on the Day of Judgment. All you can do is try to help him. You owe him that, because you're his friend."

When they went to bed that night, after a meal taken in silence, Marguerite snuggled up close to William and stroked his naked, almost hairless chest.

"I want to see you as happy as you used to be," she murmured. "I need your strength. Particularly now, since I'm expecting again."

William sat up and looked at her in astonishment. "You're with child?"

Marguerite nodded with a diffident smile, and a marvelous sensation of warmth and security flowed through William.

"That's wonderful! Are you feeling well?" he asked anxiously, stroking her belly tenderly. He thought of Richard and all the happiness his easy laughter brought him. Yes, he wanted many more children with Marguerite! Many sons and daughters.

"Yes, my love. I feel fine." Marguerite laughed and kissed him on the mouth, then looked deeply into his eyes. After a long time, she said quietly, "Let Robert work for you again, even if you can't quite bring yourself to trust him yet. Please, William." Her hand glided down from his chest to his stomach. "I love you," she whispered, still stroking him. Her hand moved into his lap, and he surrendered helplessly to the pleasure of her tender caresses.

Thus Marguerite finally won her victory, and Robert was allowed to stay. At least for a while, as William emphasized.

Robert threw himself into his work at the falconry as if he had never been away. Even the new assistants respected him immediately, obeying him without demurral. Only William still behaved somewhat clumsily.

"The peregrine needs to be readied. I'm going hunting with her today," he said one day. He still could not manage to sound as friendly as he used to, though he could see how Robert suffered at this rejection. "Humfrid is coming," he added. He would never have admitted it, but deep down William was afraid to be alone with Robert, so he preferred to arrange things in such a way that one of the assistants was always present. And yet Robert and he had once been able to be completely relaxed with each other. Like on the day they tussled in the grass and then watched the Saracen and the girl.

William frowned. Robert had not seemed any less aroused than he. So he must have liked the look of the girl. Or had he been attracted to the Saracen's body instead?

"Stop staring at me like that," William roared when he saw Robert looking at him sadly. He knew all too well that he was being unjust.

Robert lowered his eyes guiltily. He never rebuked William, no matter how harshly he behaved toward him.

December 1203

The first hoarfrosts of winter had coated the grass and trees in icy crystals for some days. A thick mist hung close to the ground, and the sun was doing its best to hold off the first big freeze when a messenger arrived at Roford. King John and his queen had returned from the mainland and wanted to spend Christmas at Canterbury. William and Marguerite were expected at court, along with the royal falcons.

"At last we can give him Blanchpenny," said William joyfully, lifting Marguerite in the air and whirling her around, despite her rather plump body.

When he put her down, she laughed, panting breathlessly, her cheeks shining like apples. "Christmas at court will be wonderful, I'm sure. I've been wanting to introduce our son to John and Isabelle for so long."

Marguerite immediately started planning their journey. Two young knights in their service, three foot soldiers, and four hunt assistants would accompany them, along with Robert, a falconry boy, two dog handlers, the nursemaid, a handmaid, two servants, and little Richard, who had turned two that autumn.

William found this large retinue excessive, but Marguerite insisted on it.

"When you appear at court, you must show who you are and what you have. You're a baron now, and you must behave like one. They all look at each other, judging clothes, horses, falcons, retinues. So if you want to have status among them, and it's definitely advisable, you must give the impression of being prosperous and munificent," Marguerite explained confidently. "I'll have a new surcoat made for you quickly."

William shrugged. "As you wish, dearest." He knew he could depend on her experience. Not for nothing had she lived near John for so long; she knew exactly what was customary at court.

For the first time since Robert's return, the thought that Robert would be with him made him feel confident. None of the barons who would be there knew what had disturbed their friendship. Nobody would feel obliged to ask about his absence and bring a guilty blush to William's face. As far as the care of the falcons was concerned, they were an experienced enough partnership not to worry about the difficulties of such a journey. And yet William found himself fearful of all the unfamiliar customs he would encounter during the days at court. Much as he longed to bring Blanchpenny to the king, proximity to royalty made him feel uneasy rather than excited.

After a solid week of hectic preparations, at last they were ready to depart. Since they were accompanied by men on foot, they did not make particularly swift progress. Moreover, William and Marguerite wanted to protect Richard, so they paused to rest more often than usual.

It took them five days to reach Canterbury.

During the day, the sky was clear and sunny, and the air was very mild for the season, but as soon as the sun went down it became bitingly cold, so they sought out inns and monasteries where they could spend the night in warmth and safety.

While most travelers to Canterbury were headed for the marketplace and entered through Westgate, William and his retinue entered through the ancient Roman Worthgate, at the southern end of the town, because the royal castle was situated right inside.

The magnificent accommodation tower was almost as large and imposing as the Tower of London. The bailey, which was surrounded by a formidable stone wall, was crowded with people and animals. Laughter and curses filled their ears, along with loud greetings and the baying of hounds. Strong servants with calloused hands walked by bearing water, hay, and oats for the innumerable guests' horses; shoveled dung; rubbed overheated horses dry; and generally tended the valuable beasts as well as they could. Now and then, as they crisscrossed the bailey, they would slip on the hard, icy ground, and if they didn't catch themselves in time, they would struggle to their feet again, cursing and red faced.

Since there was not sufficient room in the stables for all the horses, some wooden bays had been erected where the animals could be tied up in rows.

William slipped down off his horse, gave Blanchpenny to Robert, and lifted Richard down from his seat in front of Marguerite. He waited patiently for one of his knights to hurry over and help her down from her horse.

Marguerite, who was accustomed to stays at court, had made sure there was a beautiful, brightly colored tent in their baggage. Before they left, she had explained to William that the only people to get accommodation in the hall or in one of the bedchambers would be the ones who were particularly dear and precious to John. Normally, when the king held court at Christmas, there was simply not enough room in the castle for the many visiting knights, soldiers, and servants, and they would have to sleep in tents they brought with them.

William told one of his knights to find the steward and ask where they should pitch their tent. He asked Robert to take care of the accommodation of the falcons. Until his marriage, William had never had to think about arrangements of this kind, but he was a master now, even though he was still getting used to giving orders and having around him young men like this knight, who hoped for nothing more than the chance to defend him or his wife.

William held his son in his left arm and offered Marguerite his right. He led her up a massive external stairway and into the tower.

Richard wriggled and wanted to walk, but a severe look from his father immediately stilled his urge to rebel. He stuck his index finger in his mouth and turned to look over William's shoulder.

A dense mass of guests and servants was going up and down the stairs, making the wood creak and groan worryingly.

"I'm so excited," Marguerite murmured happily. "Christmas at court is wonderful, believe me."

When they came into the great hall, which was decorated all over with ivy, mistletoe, and other greenery and smelled of cinnamon and spiced wine, William felt weak with excitement.

England's mightiest barons, dressed in much more magnificent clothes than his own, with fur-lined cloaks and precious swords, stood around in small clumps, drinking wine and chatting merrily. William knew, from his mother's stories, that most of them had known each other since childhood; many were brought up together as pages and squires before receiving their knighthoods, and most of them were related, either by blood or by marriage.

"Put Richard down. I'll hold his hand, so you can shake hands anytime you need to," Marguerite murmured, and William obeyed. Richard wanted to tear off immediately, but Marguerite was too quick for him. "Don't you dare run away," she whispered, looking severely at her son.

Richard nodded like a good boy and stared at his mother with wide eyes.

Whereas Marguerite was obviously quite at ease, greeting this or that baron with a radiant smile, William was overcome with the familiar feeling of not belonging. Who was going to shake his hand? He had certainly met some of the guests and had been introduced to them as de Ferrers's falconer, but it was unlikely that any of them would remember.

His heart raced, but he led his wife on with his head held high, pushing his way through the crowd until he reached John's throne.

The king, glad to see them, stood up and embraced Marguerite for a long time. He laid a hand on William's arm as he bowed deeply. Some of the barons whispered among themselves, probably asking their neighbors why the king showed William such favor.

Queen Isabelle, too, greeted Marguerite joyfully. She smiled graciously at young Richard and held out her arms to take him. But John beat her to it and raised the boy high in the air.

William held his breath anxiously. Normally, his son screamed with all his might and struggled whenever a stranger picked him up.

John looked intently, but not unkindly, at Richard. Despite the finger in his mouth, the child smiled and used his free hand to feel the sparkling jewels on the king's robe. John grinned with satisfaction and started tickling the boy until he turned away and gurgled with pleasure.

"A fine young fellow," he told the proud parents. "What's his name?"

"Richard," replied Marguerite. "After my father."

"Excellent." John smiled contentedly.

"Guillaume!" The king called Marshal by his Norman name. "Look at this splendid boy!" He lifted up Richard and then handed him back to Marguerite.

"Marguerite, how lovely to see you and your husband here," Marshal said, clapping William on the shoulder.

William flushed. Although he had spent days discussing the ways of the court with Marguerite, he now found he did not know how to address Marshal. He was a baron, too, now, albeit of lesser rank, and had to observe the rules. "The pleasure is entirely ours, Sir William."

"William, just William," Marshal corrected him kindly, showing William that he now considered him his friend and equal.

William heard the whispering start up again and smiled at him shyly. "William," he said quietly.

"Have you brought my falcons, William of Roford?" asked the king with mock severity, obviously unhappy not to be the center of attention.

"Yes, my lord, and not only them," William quickly replied. "I have a present for you, too. Will you permit me to leave for a moment?"

"Make haste! I love presents, and I'm an impatient man," he said, laughing.

This time William did not have to push through the crowd; a path silently opened in front of him. He rushed down the wooden stairs on the outside of the tower and looked for Robert.

"Blanchpenny!" he shouted, long before he reached him. "Give me Blanchpenny!"

Robert untied the leash from the high rail he had set up for the falcons, hurriedly slipped on a glove, and handed Blanchpenny to William. She was wearing a hood so that the journey would be less tiring. William took it off so that he could carry her into the hall unhooded. Very few people knew the uses and advantages of hoods, and William had already been mocked more than once because of his enthusiasm for them. They would probably not catch on until kings had their birds trained with them, recognized their benefits, and publicly endorsed them.

Once Blanchpenny was standing on his fist, he held her jesses firmly in his left hand and gently stroked her breast with the other. He spoke softly to reassure her and walked back to the tower with confident ease.

When he reentered the hall with the magnificent gyrfalcon on his fist, the crowd parted for him again. This time, though, an admiring murmur spread across the room. William walked up to the king. He felt as though he were walking on air. His mother must have felt like this when she gave the sword Runedur to the young King Henry, John's older brother. She had told him the story many times, describing how terribly excited and yet, at the same time, extraordinarily calm she had felt. William desperately hoped he appeared more composed than he felt.

"Sire." He bowed before King John. "This is Blanchpenny."

"Blanchpenny? That was the name of my father's favorite falcon," he said, not without emotion, and approached. He examined the falcon, his eyes wide with delight. It was not hard to see how much he liked what he saw.

"She earned me a coin from your father, which I refused, and I asked him if I could be a falconer instead." William smiled and was surprised to see Marshal smiling, too, as if he already knew the story. "Today, sire, it is my turn to give you something. To thank you for allowing me to marry your ward." William offered John a glove so that he could hold the falcon himself. "I hope you will accept my gift." He bowed deeply.

"Did you train her?" John asked, trying to sound severe, but obviously too delighted for William to feel anxious.

"Yes, sire," he replied without hesitation. "And I promise you she is not just a beauty—she's also a magnificent hunter, indefatigable, swift in flight, courageous, and very agile."

John took the bird onto his fist and showed her to the barons in the hall. "See what a wonderful creature!"

William had spent a good deal of time getting Blanchpenny used to stepping onto the fists of complete strangers without becoming distressed. He had not wanted to make a fool of himself when he handed her over to the king, after all. Now, though, she spread her wings a little.

But John was experienced and knew how to carry her. He held her far enough from his face and spoke friendly words to her before setting her on the high rail beside his throne. There were two other birds there already, and although they were magnificent gyrfalcons themselves, they were no rivals for Blanchpenny. She was the only one with white plumage and unquestionably the finest.

"A splendid creature, sire. Will you take her with you when you travel or will you leave her in William's care?" Marshal inquired, winking at William.

"Well now," John thought aloud, "perhaps I'll do both. We shall see. In any case, the young baron can certainly expect an appropriate reward from me."

"That was kind of you. Thank you," William murmured to Marshal when John had turned away. To continue to care for Blanchpenny would be an extraordinary honor and would probably also entail a generous fee. But that was not the only thing; of all the falcons William had ever manned and trained, Blanchpenny was his favorite—perhaps because she had caused him some anxiety at first and remained timid for so long.

"She really is magnificent. You have earned the recognition you will now receive." Marshal nodded to a man who had just arrived. "Would you excuse me? Duty calls. John has called a hunt for tomorrow. I hope I shall be able to speak with you a little more then, if not sooner."

Marguerite was conversing animatedly with Isabelle, and William began to get bored. He did not have much in common with the other barons; most of them were talking about battles on the mainland and the French king's stratagems. The air in the hall was heavy with wood smoke and the odors of so many people. Once William realized that no one would miss him, he decided to go for a ride and use his slingshot as he had when he was young, to bag a couple of songbirds to feed to the falcons. He was reluctantly reminded of Odon and the stone he had slung at his head to save Robert's honor. Hopefully he would not come across Odon here.

William left the hall, told Robert where he was going, saddled his horse, and rode off. Once outside the city walls, which were ringed by a well-stocked moat, he crossed a field and entered a sparse forest. The dead leaves were ankle deep on the ground and clung to his horse's hooves.

William dismounted and led the horse by the reins. The forest gave off that irresistible fragrance of damp earth he loved so much. He inhaled deeply, closing his eyes with pleasure. After the tumult at the castle, the silence and peace all around felt good.

Suddenly, he heard a noise in the undergrowth. His eyes widened with shock. He drew his hunting knife and listened. Ever since his encounter with the wild boar at Orford that time, he had been cautious. He heard a piteous whimpering, like someone weeping. A child? William was on his guard. Children did not normally wander about alone in the forest. So who was hiding in that thicket? He crept closer to the sound, peered through the bushes, and found a boy sobbing quietly, his body contorted. Blood was dripping from his right leg and sweat covered his face. Suddenly, he turned pale as chalk and fainted.

William examined the leg carefully while the boy was still unconscious. There was much blood, though the wound was not deep. "The lad was lucky," he murmured in relief. He looked around and finally found what he was looking for.

There were several birch trees nearby. Their leaves would have been good for healing the cut, but it was winter and the branches were bare. The white bark was almost as good, though. He went up to one of the trees and started peeling off some bark. It was easier to do this in the spring, when the sap was rising, but with care he managed to remove a piece nearly as big as his palm. He hurried back to the boy. First he had to wake him up. William sprinkled him with water from his pouch, slapped his cheeks, and spoke to him, kindly but firmly. When the boy came to and tried to spring to his feet, William pushed him down gently.

"Stay there. I'll take care of the wound," said William. He closed the cut with smooth birch bark; once moistened and pressed down, it stuck to the skin by itself. The boy was still pale, and his hair was wet with perspiration, but already he looked somewhat more lively.

William asked him what he had been doing. "I was making arrows," he said apologetically, pointing at some sharpened sticks. "My knife slipped."

"Does it still hurt?"

The boy shook his head bravely. "Not at all," he claimed, but it was obvious he was fibbing.

"It's dangerous in the forest. You shouldn't have come here alone."

"But you're alone in the forest," the boy protested.

"And I know how to take care of myself, because I'm more experienced than you are," said William, gently punching the boy's nose. He picked up the blood-smeared knife, rinsed it with water from his pouch, and wiped it dry with some leaves.

The knife was rather big for a boy of his age. William looked at it more closely and noticed an enameled decoration on the handle. His stomach suddenly churned, and his left hand moved of its own accord toward the purse on his belt. But he did not need to look inside to compare the decoration on the knife with the plaque in his purse. William knew they were as alike as two eggs. He turned the knife over and saw that the other side of the handle was decorated with an enamel plaque, too. And yet the leaf looked slightly different, as if a different craftsman had been asked to match a lost original.

William's pulse raced. Whomever the boy had got this knife from—he must be Enid's murderer!

"Where did you get this?" he asked urgently, holding the knife under the boy's nose.

"My father gave it to me a little while ago. I'm nearly eight years old, and I'm to be a page soon. He got it from his father, but not until he became a page himself," the boy explained excitedly, and when he saw how closely William was looking at the enamel symbol, he went on. "It's an elm leaf. My father is Lord Elmswick, you see. I've got a pony, too, even though I'm a bastard."

Odon's son! He's Odon's son! William's head was pounding so hard it was impossible to think clearly. All he felt was rage and impotence. For a moment, he was tempted to put his hands around the boy's neck and squeeze. But the little fellow was looking at him so innocently that William just smiled, albeit thinly.

"A bastard is just as good as a son born in wedlock. I'm a bastard, too, and so was William the Conqueror, the first Norman to sit on the throne of England. Your father told me about him," he heard himself say calmly.

"Is that true?" the boy asked uncertainly, smiling shyly.

William nodded. "What's your name?"

"Adam," replied the boy with a sniffle.

"Is your father here, too?" William's throat was so raw that even clearing it did not help.

"Of course. He has to be. He's the captain of the queen's bodyguard," the little fellow said, filled with pride. "I thought you knew him. You ought to know that."

"I've known him for a very long time, actually, but I didn't know he was serving the queen now." William's voice was shaking. Knowing that Odon was with the queen and therefore very close to Marguerite filled him with hellish dread. "Let's go."

Odon, thought William. Odon is to blame for Enid's death. Why does that not surprise me? His stomach hurt, as if it were filled with sharp stones. He'll pay! "I'll take you back to your father," he said roughly.

They left the forest at a breakneck gallop.

"But you have to show me where I can find him," William said, spurring on his horse to even greater speed.

They had not quite crossed the field in front of the city gates when a rider came toward them. "Adam," he called out. "Adam, where are you hiding?" The man looked around searchingly.

William immediately recognized Odon. He seemed to be in a panic.

"Here I am, Father," the boy answered loudly, throwing up his arms in the air.

"What are you doing with my son?" cried Odon when he saw William.

The realization that Odon cared for his son, like any other father, struck William as completely unexpected, but it did not soften his rage.

"He saved me, Father," Adam reported. "I cut my leg with the knife."

William leaped down from his horse, leaving the boy in the saddle. Odon dismounted, too. He opened his mouth as if to say something, but William did not give him the chance to speak. He pounced on him, grabbed his surcoat, and shook him, beside himself with fury.

Odon, however, was no stable boy. He was a trained fighter with plenty of battlefield experience. He loosened William's hand with a skillful twist of the wrist and punched him hard in the midriff. William staggered and fell back onto the damp earth. A sharp stone poked painfully into his back. Odon came after him and dug a silver spur into his shin. William sprang up, but his back and leg hurt badly, and Odon was quicker. His fists struck William's nose and stomach so accurately that he doubled over. Then Odon kicked him in the kidneys so hard he could hardly breathe.

"No, Father, you mustn't beat him! He helped me!" cried the boy, terrified. "Please don't hurt him."

Odon looked at his son, who was still sitting on William's horse, in disbelief. "What are you whining about? You saw him attack me, didn't you?" he snarled at Adam, dropping his guard for a moment.

William knew he could not let this opportunity pass. He gritted his teeth, straightened up, and punched Odon in the face from below. He was not a trained fighter like his opponent, but rage and desperation gave him strength. He was lucky and caught Odon's chin in such a way that he collapsed as if his legs had been swept from under him. William drew his hunting knife, dragged his adversary upright, and put the blade against his throat.

In the meantime, the boy had climbed down from the horse. "Let my father go," he cried, pummeling William's back with his little fists, but this did not distract William.

"Do you remember the woman in the forest?" he shouted as Odon tried to struggle free. William's nose was throbbing as hard and painfully as his outraged heart. "You killed her and ripped her unborn child from her womb. That was *my* son!" he shouted, beside himself with rage, pressing the knife against Odon's neck. He would kill him, here and now. Finally, he could avenge Enid's death. He had never been able to forgive himself for not being there to help. Now at last he could make it up to her.

"I had nothing to do with it," Odon protested cravenly as the blade dug into his skin.

The child's blows became weaker and finally stopped. He looked expectantly at his father.

"It's no use lying, Odon. Your knife, the one you gave this boy, tells a different story. The plaque with the elm leaf is missing on one side. I found it in my Enid's house the day she died, in her bed."

"But I didn't kill her, it was Bevis and…" Suddenly, Odon burst into mocking laughter. "You didn't know before today and only found out because of the knife? Your friend Robert never said a word? That faithful soul has known for years—I've no idea how. I wonder why he kept it quiet?" He wiped a tear from the corner of his eye. "Perhaps because he dreams of climbing into bed with you at night."

"Be silent for once, you devil, or I'll slit your throat," William threatened, pushing his knife into Odon's neck hard enough to draw blood.

"Please," Adam begged fearfully, touching William's arm. "Please don't kill him."

The sight of the boy pleading for mercy calmed William down. For so many years he had felt sure it was his destiny to avenge the murder of Enid and their child. He had spent many sleepless nights imagining how he would bring her murderer to account, if he could only catch him. Yet now that he had Odon in his power and had only to drag the knife across his throat to carry out his revenge, the thought of spilling blood repelled him. He could hardly breathe. He couldn't let Odon get away with it.

He tightened his arm around Odon's throat. "You killed Enid and my unborn son. For that you *will* pay."

"But I've told you it wasn't me. It was the other two. She lay with me of her own free will. I couldn't have known she was yours. You weren't there, after all." Odon's voice became shrill, sounding like a frightened woman's. "The idiot tried to protect her. Where were you?"

"That needn't concern you," he said through gritted teeth, feeling like he was about to choke. "Just because she was alone and unprotected doesn't give you the right to have your way with her and then kill her. If you're as innocent as you claim, why didn't you help her?"

"Risk my own skin for some savage?" Odon laughed out loud. "She wasn't worth it."

"Father, no," cried Adam in shock.

"Shut your mouth, Adam. This all happened long ago. Things have gone well for our good William here. He's had a better wife for some time, a new son, even a title," he said, with such a degree of condescension that William could hardly control himself. The knife pressed against Odon's skin again, drawing out a trickle of blood.

Fat tears rolled down Adam's cheeks, leaving dirty streaks on his skin. William could not tell whether he was crying with disappointment or fear, but he felt sorry for the boy. He had nothing to do with his father's misdeeds and certainly deserved a better example than Odon. William thought of the village reeve and his daughter, and he suddenly knew what he had to do.

"You took my son from me, so today I shall take yours from you," he announced calmly.

Adam's eyes opened wide.

"If you do anything to him, I'll kill you," Odon threatened hoarsely, trying to free himself from William's grip. He calmed down when William increased the pressure on the knife.

"Oh no, Odon, I'm not like you. I wouldn't touch a hair on an innocent child's head, and I wouldn't allow anyone else to." William breathed in deeply and calmly. In the place where hatred had lurked moments ago, he now felt only emptiness. "I shall take the boy as my page and bring him up to be a decent human being. If you have any feelings for him at all, you will behave like a man of honor yourself in the future." He pushed Odon away like a sack filled with refuse, seized the boy, and set him on his horse before swinging up into the saddle behind him. "I advise you to keep quiet, or the king will find out you had his falcon poisoned."

They returned to the castle together without exchanging a single word about what had happened.

"Come with me," William ordered once they had handed over the horse to a stable boy. They strode off toward his tent.

Robert was feeding the falcons, so William had to wait. He put his finger to his lips, indicating to Adam with a severe look that he should keep quiet.

Once all the falcons had their fill and were securely fastened to their blocks, William went up to Robert and punched him hard in the pit of the stomach.

"What have I done now?" his friend asked, bent double, his face contorted with pain.

"How long have you known?" William demanded.

"Known what?" Robert stammered, rubbing his stomach and groaning.

"That Odon had Enid on his conscience. Why didn't you say anything? How could you keep that secret from me?" William was overcome with despair and close to tears. "Once a traitor, always a traitor. I never should have trusted you."

"But Will, please! I was just afraid for you. I knew you would have attacked him without a thought, but you're just a falconer who knows about lures and such. Whereas Odon is a soldier who knows all the arts of war."

"And yet today I beat him," said William exultantly.

"Jesus! Are you all right?" asked Robert anxiously, grabbing William's arm.

"Yes, of course," William shook his hand off.

"And Odon? You didn't…"

"No, he's well, far too well. I could have killed him, but—" William broke off and shook his head. "I dreamed of this revenge for years, and then I couldn't carry it out."

Robert clapped him on the shoulder with relief. "You were right not to heap guilt upon yourself. His death wouldn't have brought Enid or the child back to life, but an act of revenge would probably cost you yours."

"Still, he owes me a son, and today I took his. Adam," he called, waving to the boy, who was still standing by the tent's entrance. "This is my new page. For the moment he'll stay here with you. I'm making you responsible for him. You will not touch him."

Robert looked at him, surprised and saddened at the same time. "I...you..." he began, but his voice failed him.

"I know the boy is Odon's bastard, but he shouldn't have to pay for his father's sins," William explained. "I shall make sure he becomes a decent human being."

"You can rely on me. Of course, I don't know what a page is supposed to learn since I've never been one, but I can teach you what to do with hounds and falcons. Come, I'll show you two falcons that belong to the king." Robert put his hand on Adam's shoulder kindly and steered him gently toward the rail where John's peregrines sat.

William watched them uneasily, wondering whether Odon would let the matter with Adam rest.

�❧�

When they set off for the hunt the next morning, William rode beside the king, thanks to the white gyrfalcon, and carried on an animated conversation with him. Odon had to be at the queen's side at all times, so he was forced to take up a position near the rear with the ladies. He twisted his reins furiously between his fingers.

William's gift to the king had been on everyone's lips since the day before. Everyone, truly everyone, praised the noble creature's beauty and William's open generosity. The lords were curious to see whether the falcon was good at hunting, too; some had even placed bets.

For Odon, it was already beyond irritating that William had received Marguerite as his wife, but it was almost unbearable that now William had the king's particular favor again thanks to his absurdly costly gift. The worst, though, was that William had revealed to everyone the identity of the boy who would be accompanying him from now on.

Several knights had already congratulated Odon for having his bastard taken on as William's page and praised his daring choice. Odon kept his feelings to himself, nodding in apparent agreement even though he was consumed with rage. He could have done without today's hunt, since he still understood little about falcons. But he understood them well enough to know how to do them harm. Logan had always impressed on him that cured meat was like poison to them. He had acted cautiously enough to avoid being found out, so he was all the more surprised to discover that William knew and might report the matter to the king if he did not remain silent. Did William have a secret witness?

Who could it be? Guy, the lad he had recruited to kill the bird, wouldn't be bothering anyone. Showing considerable forethought, instead of paying him, he had killed him as a precaution. Had someone found the body? Odon snorted. He had made sure no one saw him. William couldn't know anything, Odon thought. Perhaps he was just suspicious. Nevertheless, Odon decided to stay on his guard until he could ensure that William fell into disfavor with the king. He had no idea how he was going to go about this yet, but it was just a question of time.

The long procession of barons, falconers, dog handlers, hunt assistants, and their accompanying ladies who wanted to join in the hunt with their little merlins soon reached a broad plain with fields, marshes, and small ponds, where winged prey had been sighted earlier.

Odon stretched up in his saddle and looked at Robert. Adam was laughing. He seemed to be enjoying himself. The boy looked so like Carla! It pained him to lose her son to William, for he was fonder of Adam than of Rotrou. His son by marriage looked exactly like him, but from Maud he had inherited precisely the characteristics Odon most disliked. He looked around again, searching for Adam. His eyes met Robert's, and his nostrils flared. Woe betide you if you come near my son, you accursed sodomite, he thought, staring at Robert. But Robert just smiled and laid his hand on Adam's shoulder in a friendly manner.

Odon clutched the reins tightly. Why had William left the boy in the care of this man, of all men? Odon sniffed contemptuously. Robert obviously didn't take him seriously as an adversary. "Don't be too sure you're safe," he muttered. Did William know about his fine friend's unnatural behavior and Odon's threat? Perhaps he thought it was just slanderous lies. One thing was certain: Robert knew who Adam's father was and would probably take his revenge on the boy for the injustice he had suffered at Odon's hands.

Odon clenched his fists angrily. He certainly wouldn't have spared William's son if he'd had him in his clutches.

He broke off for a moment; then an evil grin spread across his face.

❦

The hunt turned out to be a great triumph for William. Not only was Blanchpenny beautiful and therefore exceptionally valuable; she had also flown marvelously.

Delighted with the hunt, John was in an excellent mood and promised to reward William with further lands and titles. Moreover, he announced that William would be accompanying him on his travels until the molting season so that he could take care of Blanchpenny. As soon as she started to molt her first feathers, however, William and Robert were to head back to Roford with her and the other falcons so that they could house them properly and capture, man, and train more falcons.

"May I speak to you briefly?" William asked Marshal, blushing. Earlier, while they were on their way back to the castle, he had decided to ask his advice. Now that they had handed over their horses to the stable boy, there was finally an opportunity to speak to Marshal in private.

"Of course, my boy. Go ahead." Marshal nodded amiably.

"I need the advice of an experienced man." William took a deep breath. "My stepfather, whom I greatly respected, is no longer with us, and I don't know where to turn," he began as they walked toward the accommodation tower.

"You want to talk to me about Robert, don't you?" Marshal broke in.

"How did you know?"

"Look, William. I'm not blind. Carefully observing the people around me is a skill I have used and developed in all my years at court. I urge you to practice it yourself. On many occasions it has helped me to stay one step ahead of dangerous men and situations. Now, as to Robert, even a blind man can see that there isn't the same understanding between you that there once was. What happened? What made you so angry with him?"

"Is my disappointment so obvious?" William looked around to make sure no one was eavesdropping and then whispered, "I caught Robert committing the sin of sodomy in the forest."

"I see," said Marshal.

William waited awhile for him to continue, but in vain. "Richard was your friend, wasn't he?" he asked cautiously.

"At first he was just my king. Although I fought against him and alongside his father, I have him to thank for my marriage, which was not only a good match, but has also been very happy. With time, yes, he did indeed become my friend."

"I hear he twice confessed to the unmentionable vice."

"Well, my boy, Richard had many failings, you know. As do we all. But his good characteristics outweighed them. God makes us account for our sins on Judgment Day—that's what the church teaches us." He crossed himself, and William did likewise. "Richard needed me, and like a true friend I never let him down.

Like many of us, he attracted blame on more than one occasion. He kept postponing his marriage to the French princess, even though it harmed him and the realm. Whether it was because he couldn't come to terms with the idea of lying with a woman or for other reasons, I couldn't say." Marshal shrugged. "And I don't care."

"I heard he has a bastard," William said. "So he did. I mean, he must have been attracted to at least one woman."

Marshal stopped—they were quite close to the tower now—and looked at William. "He didn't deny that he was the father, but does that mean he was with that woman? To tell you the truth, I doubt it. At one time, people used to say Richard chased after anything in a long gown. Then they said he took no pleasure in women but did from men." Marshal sighed. "I'm just a man. What right would I have had to be Richard's judge on earth? Only God could see into his heart."

William stood there, his head bowed, and sniffed quietly.

"Anyone who has a true friend in this life, William, someone he can count on, is a happy man. I've tasted betrayal more than once, and I can tell you it leaves a sour taste when you see people you trust turn their backs on you. Friendship only really shows itself in times of need."

"But Robert's betrayal hurts so much," William protested.

"Did he ever try to draw you into sinning with him?"

"God forbid! No!"

"Well, in that case I don't understand why you charge him with betraying you."

"He confessed that he desired me. Can he still feel honorable friendship for me?"

Marshal clapped him on the shoulder. "I know it's hard for you, but I'm sure it's not easy for him. And yet he doesn't hate you. If he were my friend, I would reward his loyalty and forgive him. But it's up to you."

A page came running up and bowed first to Marshal and then to William.

"Sir William, the king desires you to be at his side."

"I'm coming." William nodded. "Will you excuse me?"

"Of course. Go." Marshal smiled reassuringly.

William went with the page and thought about Marshal's words. His instinct told him Marshal was right. As he entered the great hall, he saw how kindly Robert was talking to Adam, even though he knew who the boy was. Robert was a good person and would never turn against him or his family. When he looked up, William smiled at him, for the first time in a long time unable to resist his friend's questioning expression.

Canterbury Castle,
Early January 1204

A cozy fire crackled in Queen Isabelle's bedchamber.

"Richard's bath is ready, my lady." The young handmaid had poured the last bucket of water into the small tub and checked that it was not too hot.

"Are you sure you want to bathe the little one yourself? Shouldn't we call for the nursemaid instead?" the young queen suggested anxiously, but Marguerite dismissed this with a smile.

"You'll see, my lady, he loves hot water. The worst that can happen is that he gets us wet. So if you're worried about your beautiful gown…"

"Oh, you silly goose," cried Isabelle cheerfully. "What do I care about a bit of water? Go on, put him in!" She turned to the maid, who was standing there with the bucket in her hand. "You may go."

Richard, who was wearing a knee-length linen shirt and nothing else, ran across the room, shrieking, when his mother tried to catch him. But Marguerite was too clever for him and cut off his escape. Richard swerved sharply, fell flat on his naked bottom, and stood up again immediately. Howling with laughter, he tried to escape his mother, but she caught him and soon had the wriggling little scamp in her arms.

"I'm going to eat you up, every bit of you," she warned him, putting on a sinister voice and scrabbling at her son's pale neck, tickling him at the same time.

Richard yelped and playfully struggled to get free.

"That's right—now we're going to give you a bath," his mother cried as she placed him in the shallow tub.

"Bath, bath," shouted Richard happily. He stopped wriggling and raised his arms obediently. Marguerite pulled his shirt over his head, cupped some water in her hand and poured it down his downy back.

Richard slapped the surface of the water enthusiastically, laughing with pleasure when it splashed.

Isabelle jumped back and laughed. "Here, put some attar of roses in the water. At least he'll smell like a flower, even if he does splash like a puppy."

"Don't want to smell like a flower," Richard shouted, shaking his head and slapping the water again with all his might.

After only a few moments, the floor around the little tub was soaking wet.

"Soon the people downstairs will be thinking there's a leak," Isabelle said. "In fact it's just a dwarf having a bath in my room."

Richard splashed enthusiastically and played with a small boat that William had carved for him out of an ox bone. He stayed there until his lips began to shine rather blue, and Marguerite decided to take him out of the water.

"No, stay in," Richard protested, wriggling so energetically that she could not put him down on the floor.

Isabelle rushed over with her own linen towels. "Come here, you little frog." She was about to drape the cloth over him when her eyes suddenly narrowed to slits. She threw the towel over the child and turned her back on him abruptly.

"What is it, my lady? Are you all right?" cried Marguerite, frightened.

"Am I all right?" Isabelle turned and approached her with a menacing expression on her face. "The king has yet to give *me* a child," she said aggressively, beating her breast in indignation. "And believe me, I've given him more than enough opportunities."

"Oh, my lady, you're still so young. You'll have a child soon, too." Marguerite relaxed.

"But *I* wanted to be the one to give John his first son! A proper little prince," cried Isabelle furiously, stamping her foot like a child.

"And you will. After all, his first wife didn't bear him any children."

"Indeed she didn't, but what about *you*?" Isabelle screamed. "Do you think I'm blind? The loving way he looks at you all the time should have made me suspicious long ago."

"My lady, if I may, I'm only his ward, and he loves me like a daughter, no more than that," said Marguerite in an effort to pacify her.

It was certainly true that John was always particularly kind to her, but it had been like that since her childhood.

"Indeed? Well, Richard's crooked bottom can't just be a coincidence. His crack is bent to the left, just like John's," Isabelle screamed, leaving the room.

Once the heavy wooden door had shut behind her, Marguerite sat down on the bed. Her hands were trembling, and the blood was coursing through her body with such force she was unable to think clearly. "But my William is his father," she called out.

"Isibel," cried Richard, patting his mother's face with his little hands. They were ice-cold.

"You'll catch your death," murmured Marguerite as she dried him and dressed him absently, lost in thought. The unborn child in her womb wriggled, and Marguerite stopped for a dreamy moment. She smiled. It was the first time she had felt her second child move.

☙❧

While Marguerite and the queen were giving little Richard his bath, William took the opportunity to catch Marshal in front of the great hall.

"You're right, my lord. I've thought long and hard about what friendship means to me. Robert is still important to me, whatever has happened. I suspect he is suffering at least as much as I am, so I'm going to follow your advice and forgive him." William still did not feel comfortable addressing Marshal as simply William.

"It is good that you have decided to be magnanimous." Marshal cleared his throat. "Walk with me a little. I need to go to the stables, and I have something to tell you." He took his sword from his page and strapped it on. "Athanor has saved my life more than once." He nodded to the page. "You may go." When the boy looked at him with incredulity, he waved his hand as if shooing a fly. "Go."

After a short pause, he cleared his throat again. "I was young, a nobody. I had nothing besides my position at court. I was always a soldier through and through. If I had not been able to serve my king, I might have gone hungry, but it's the grief that would have killed me. In those days I was just as devoted to the young Henry as I later was to his father, Richard, and now John, just as a knight should be." Marshal forced out a tormented smile. "But I did love her."

William did not understand whom Marshal was referring to or where his story was going.

"We knew there was no future for us, but that was unimportant. Only the moment counted. For love, William, love doesn't demand prudence—she makes you forget it. When our ways parted, I didn't know she was with child, and when I saw her again she was married. It was terribly painful, even if I could never have made her my wife."

He stared into space, as if he could see his memories there. "Isaac came along while we were talking. Straightaway, I could see that he knew who I was. It was the fear in his eyes that gave him away. He was afraid he would lose both his wife and his son. At that moment, Isaac must have sensed the intimate bond between me and your mother, and observed a certain resemblance between you and me." He pointed at William and himself. "I am sure he loved your mother and you very much, but no more than I did. That day, in her workshop, I saw that her dream of her own smithy had been fulfilled. The two of you had a home I never could have offered. I understood that I had no right to expect anything from her."

William stood and stared at Marshal in disbelief. His face was drained of all color. "Are you trying to tell me…"

"I know this comes as a surprise."

Marshal was his father! The very man he had so often dreamed of, seeing him coming to fetch him. William gasped. They had spent one afternoon together when he was a boy, a single afternoon. It had been the best day in his young life and the beginning of his love of falconry. Still, it was too little time to be close. Isaac had taken care of him all those years and had always been there for him.

It felt as though the ground were falling away beneath his feet.

"Please, William, you must believe me when I say—"

"Isaac is the only father I've ever had," William broke in without looking at him. "That's what I told my mother, too, when we were carrying him to his grave and she asked me if I still wanted to know who my father was. She kept it secret all those years, though I kept begging her to tell me." William laughed despairingly. "It wasn't until Isaac died that I knew *he* was my real father. The man who worked with Jean to make me wooden shoes to straighten my foot a little. And it doesn't matter whether it was any use. What matters is that he did it to help me, not because he was ashamed of my limp." He fell silent for a moment, apparently looking back into the past. "Yes, I remember your shocked expression that day, the first time you came to see us at the smithy. I'm sure you hadn't imagined your son would be like me."

"When I saw you for the first time, I had the strange sensation I'd been transported a long way back to a different time. I could almost smell my wet nurse's scent and hear her voice. Your mother's expression told me you were my son, and I had recognized myself in you. Baudouin immediately saw who you were, too. That's why he didn't understand when I wasn't very friendly to you. He knew of my great love for Ellen and rebuked me for not taking you in my arms."

"I'm sure you didn't expect a cripple for a son," said William resentfully.

"No, William. I didn't expect a son at all. And when I saw you had a limp, I wasn't angry with *you*. I was angry with God and myself, because it wasn't fair that *you* should bear the punishment for my sins."

"Well, as you see, I live with it, and quite well at that," replied William, still somewhat offended, but Marshal was so lost in his thoughts that he did not even appear to hear him.

"We knew we were not destined to walk together for more than a short stretch of our journey on this earth," he continued pensively. "We both had big dreams. They seemed mad, unachievable. So we didn't admit to ourselves that our love might prevent us from realizing them. And believe me, it wasn't easy for your mother or me to stay true to our dreams. Why do you think she left Normandy without telling me I was to be a father?"

"She probably thought it would be a matter of indifference to you," replied William defiantly.

"No, William. It wouldn't have been a matter of indifference, and it never has been since I've known of your existence. You can choose to believe me or not. It's up to you," Marshal said regretfully. "She said nothing because she loved me and knew very well that a shared path was impossible for us. As the young king's tutor, I was penniless. I would never have been able to give her a smithy. For your mother only ever wanted one thing, and that was to be a smith. I knew that, just as she knew that I only ever wanted to serve my king and England."

William knew his mother, knew how she thought, and therefore also knew that Marshal was right. Yet he could not imagine her in Marshal's arms and did not want to.

"Don't think I'm going to call you Father," he blurted suddenly.

"I don't expect you to, my son, but come to me if you need my help, immediately, whether you think I will do something for you or not. Promise me that."

At that moment William had nothing more to say.

☙❧

"She just turned on her heel and left," Marguerite reported, wringing her hands in agitation once they were finally back in their tent after the evening banquet. "And she didn't so much as look at me while we were eating. I understand why she's angry, but she's wrong."

Marguerite looked at William. "You and I know Richard gets his crooked backside from me, but what about her?" Marguerite blushed when William raised his eyebrows and nodded energetically.

"I must admit I often think about that delightful little flaw and how you purr when I kiss you there."

"William," exclaimed Marguerite, keeping her voice down and shaking her head reprovingly. She glanced at the corner where the nursemaid and Richard had withdrawn. They were both fast asleep.

The blazing fire in front of the tent threw shadows onto the cloth walls. They could hear voices outside. Robert, the two knights, the hunt assistant, and Adam were still sitting there, telling one another stories. Soon they would lie down to sleep on the floor of the tent, while William and Marguerite shared a comfortable bed made of straw and animal pelts.

"But I like it," grumbled William, pretending to be hurt.

"Stop it. This is deadly serious. If Isabelle thinks Richard is John's son, it's a disaster."

"You're right, my love, but when we talk about your lovely bottom I find I can't think about anything else."

"You're impossible."

"I'm not." William fell silent for a while. "I'm thinking about it hard. That's what you wanted, isn't it? Perhaps you should think about where *you* got your crooked behind from. I think Joan, John's bastard daughter, would be about your age, wouldn't she? Who knows how many other ladies the young prince might have courted besides your mother?"

"Are you suggesting my mother and John?" Marguerite gasped. "You go too far, William."

"Even a young lady of high rank might find it difficult to turn down a handsome prince." William was trying to get her used to the idea, while at the same time he was thinking about how it had been with his mother and Marshal. "Haven't you ever wondered why your mother chose him as your guardian, of all people? Mightn't it suggest she knew him better?"

"Better, yes. But no, William, I can't believe it. She only ever had good things to say about my father, and besides, I would have known. I mean, I'm sure John would have told me if he was not just my guardian but also my..." She could not bring herself to say the word.

"If he was your father?" asked William. His thoughts were revolving around his earlier conversation with Marshal. Wasn't this a remarkable day? Could such strange coincidences really happen? "Perhaps he doesn't even know. After all, not every night of love produces a child. And if your mother never said anything? Perhaps because she wasn't sure herself? If she was already married, she would at least have known, from your lovely little flaw, whose daughter you really were, and it would have been easy to keep that resemblance to John a secret from her husband. Not many people in the country would be likely to know about that peculiarity of the king's body, after all."

"What should I do now? I can't let the queen go on believing that Richard is John's bastard. But can I go to the king and say, 'Sire, I hear you have a crooked cleft between your buttocks. Since I have exactly the same feature, I believe I must be your daughter.' No, William, with the best will in the world, I can't do it." She laughed despairingly and shook her head.

"Certainly not," he agreed with a grin, trying to imagine how John would probably react. "Perhaps the queen will calm down eventually."

"Pah! Calm down? You men would go to war over such a thing. Believe me, it's no different for women. She won't let it go."

"Or else you could open your heart to Isabelle."

"And bring down the king's displeasure on my head, when he's the last one to hear of it? You don't know how furious he gets if he feels someone has betrayed him. No, William, that won't work either." Marguerite sent up a short prayer to heaven. "Lord, help me to do the right thing."

๑๑

Odon tossed and turned on his bed. He had not been able to rest for days. Every time he closed his eyes, he saw Adam's cheerful face and thought he heard his clear, high laugh. Worried, he opened his eyes again. How long would the boy remain so innocent? Odon had seen him with Robert and William that afternoon and had watched them for a long time.

What offended him most was the sincere admiration the boy showed for the two men. He had saved him from poverty in the pigsticker's home. In fact, he had spent more time with him than with his heir, Rotrou. Even if he had not been driven by the desire to be a good father, but by the fact that Adam reminded him of Carla, and that he therefore needed him, Adam had looked up to him from the very first day as no one else ever had. Filled with devotion, Adam had listened to his father's boasting and applauded proudly when he heard of Odon's heroic deeds in Brittany. He had never been insolent, provoking Odon's rage, nor had he asked awkward questions about his mother or demanded anything. Just like Carla, the boy had simply loved him.

Rotrou, on the other hand, was as cold and calculating as Maud; he made constant demands on his father and yet was never satisfied. He disapproved of everything and made fun of Odon. And when his father tried to chastise him, the boy would hide behind his mother's skirts and eye him gleefully while Maud defended him and his misbehavior. Oh yes, he might have been able to spare Rotrou to be William's page. Odon laughed out loud. William would have broken his accursed teeth on that little rascal, but not Adam.

Odon threw back the blanket and got out of bed. He would not concede Adam to William.

"Don't think you can take my son and get away with it," he hissed, slamming down his fist on the little table in front of him, upending a wooden plate with a few stripped chicken bones. He knocked back the rest of the wine in his cup, wiped his mouth on his sleeve, and rubbed the sweat from his brow, then fell back onto the edge of his bed.

First Robert had taken Carla away, and now William was snatching his eldest, the only person who still meant something to him. He could not possibly allow it. Somehow he had to get rid of Robert and William forever, so cleverly that no one would suspect him.

At the moment, the queen was likely to be his most powerful ally, though she did not suspect it. She was young and unsophisticated, and that would be helpful. A queen should never confide in her bodyguard. However much the man who protected her might pick up from scraps of conversation here and there, it was an unwritten law that she should have respected. But, in her desperation, Isabelle had not obeyed it. She had opened her heart to Odon. He had nodded understandingly, shaking his head furiously from time to time.

"She must have bewitched the king. No man in his right senses would willingly be unfaithful to you, my lady," he declared, although from the first he had wondered what John saw in Isabelle. She was certainly very pretty, but she was not so out of the ordinary that it was worth offending the powerful Lusignan family. "You must keep her away from him," he'd advised the young queen. "Until he explains himself, you should not back down. You're bound to bear him a prince soon, and you don't want the king to divide his attention between his bastard and his heir."

With these words, Odon had looked meaningfully at the young queen and felt very pleased with himself. It would not take many more words to cause her to press her husband to banish this rival of hers from court forever. In this way, William would find himself at a disadvantage, permanently.

Odon would prick William's pride by teasing him about his bastard son, waiting for William to lose his temper and do something careless. Odon grinned. For added security he had another plan, too. William was fond of little Richard, king's bastard though he might be. What could be a more obvious solution than to ensure that he somehow lost the child? And if John really was Richard's father, he certainly wouldn't like it if the boy disappeared. His rage would once again be directed at William.

ᗱᗡᗰ

"Is it true my father killed your son?" Adam asked quietly one evening, looking at William with glistening eyes. "I can't believe it.

He's always been good to me, you know. The pigsticker beat me and fed me on scraps, but he treated his own son like a prince. My father has a son by marriage, too. But he's never favored him."

William did not really know what to say to the boy. The thought of Odon still made him angry, but Adam was obviously suffering, and he felt sorry for him.

"The pigsticker?" Robert's ears pricked up.

"My mother married him just after I was born. Apparently he treated me like a real son at first. But then my mother bore him a boy with a red birthmark on his cheek, and from then on the pigsticker loved only him. When she was on her deathbed, she called for Lord Elmswick and handed me over to him. She was ill, you know, very ill."

"Was your mother's name Carla?" asked Robert. "I thought so," he murmured when the boy nodded. "I met her once, only briefly, but long enough to know she was a good person."

William glanced at him questioningly. What did Robert have to do with Adam's mother? Was she the one who told him about Odon's part in Enid's death?

"I can hardly remember her face—it's all blurry," Adam said, interrupting William's thoughts.

"Everyone we ever loved keeps a place in our hearts forever. If you've been listening to the priest at church like a good boy, you'll know that our earthly shell is fleeting, but that good people meet again in heaven. Until then, you must live a righteous life, so that you can be reunited one day, you and your mother. Don't you think she would be proud if she knew you were at the king's court?" asked William kindly.

"I'm sure she would," Adam said, nodding bravely.

"You are my page, and one day you'll be a squire. If you're honest, clever, and loyal to your king at all times, you'll eventually become a knight and have a good life, both here on earth and in paradise. A deed like your father's, though, doesn't lead to eternal life after his time on earth, but to hell. I let him go because a just God will punish him for his deed."

"So he did kill him?"

"I wasn't there, so I can't say so for sure. But it doesn't matter whether he killed him himself or just stood by, as he claims, because he was too cowardly to help him or my wife. He allowed it to happen, and that makes him as much a murderer as the man who held the knife. Mark my words, my boy. He who allows unrighteousness to pass makes himself as guilty as the wrongdoer himself."

"I'll never be a coward, I promise." The boy's innocent soul was in anguish, and the struggle against it was visible in his eyes.

William put his arm around the boy. "You're a good lad, Adam."

"I will always protect you, your lady, and your son." Adam thrust out his chest and beat his fist on it. "With my life. I give you my word of honor."

William smiled tenderly. He was certain that his decision to take in the boy had been the right one. While he was still reflecting on this, Marguerite came in. Adam rushed out, so she would not see his eyes were filled with tears.

"I can't bear it any longer." Groaning, Marguerite sank into a chair and rubbed her back. "The queen is still miserable. Whenever I walk into the hall, she gives me a nasty look and leaves as soon as she can. It's been like this for three days. She's not just venting her displeasure on me, though, but also on her husband. I hear she won't even let him into her bedchamber. I must talk to her, Will. To her or John. I can't sit and do nothing any longer."

"Better you rest first. You're pale, my dear. I can see that your back has been bothering you for days. The journey must have been too much for you." He kissed her on the cheek. "What would you say if Adam brought you something from the kitchen and you allowed yourself to be waited on for a while?"

"But I have to speak to her eventually," she protested weakly.

"Of course, as soon as you're better. Now lie down for a while."

On William's command, Adam hurried off and came back with roast meat, cheese, and a slightly wrinkled apple, as well as sparkling cider and enough bread for a whole company.

The nursemaid and the knights did not receive their food from the castle kitchens. Maids from Canterbury distributed cabbage, meat and fish pies, eggs, onions, bacon porridge, bread, and beer among the barons' retinues. The men did not eat in the hall or inside their tents but sat together, huddled around the constantly burning fires in front of their tents.

Once Marguerite and the child had been taken care of, William and Robert went silently to the hall to join the king's banquet again. There were only two days to go before Epiphany, when Christmastide would finally come to an end.

"I'm glad you get on so well with Adam," William remarked spontaneously.

"He's a good boy," he replied at length. "And he's plucky, unlike his father."

"I've always been able to rely on you." For the first time in a long while, there was not a hint of reproach in William's voice.

"Nothing's changed there, William."

"Good," he said, satisfied. It was bad enough that he had to worry about Marguerite. She was taking the trouble with the queen too much to heart. At first, William had hoped Isabelle would voice her suspicions to her husband and that she would accept his explanation—whatever that might be. But in vain. Either she had not said anything or his answer had made matters worse. William sighed. Women seemed to think and behave differently from men. Their ways of waging war were more subtle and brutal. Whereas a man with any pride would strike a rival down, women banned their straying husbands from their beds. This dubious tactic would gradually wear down the king, to be sure, but it would also, thanks to his bad mood, spoil the festive period for all their guests.

"You don't look very well," said Odon from behind William and Robert just before they reached the hall. He grinned smugly. "The queen is crying her eyes out and hardly eating. And you don't look any better. It's understandable. It must feel terrible to raise only bastards in your house. I wouldn't want to be in your shoes. Truly humiliating. And another one on the way soon. Or perhaps you think the child your wife is carrying is actually yours this time?" Odon laughed condescendingly. "It's not a bad position to be in, keeper of a royal bastard, but it must be painful to have other men's delightful children swarming around you when you haven't produced any offspring of your own. I mean, Adam and Richard are both wonderful sons, but they're not yours!"

While William looked at him, aghast, Robert clenched his fists. "You talk too much," he said to Odon.

"Leave it, Robert." William held him back.

Odon clapped William on the shoulder and pretended to feel for him. "The king's right to your wife is older than yours, but you'll get over it. After all, he could have made a better match than you for the girl if it weren't for his bastard. So you were lucky," Odon asserted with a sneer.

For a brief moment William regretted not having slit his throat in the forest.

"One day I'm going to smash that asinine face of his. How can he suggest that about Marguerite and the king?" growled Robert once they were far enough away from Odon. "Or is there some truth to the rumor?"

"No." William turned to him in shock. "I should have told you about Isabelle's suspicions. It's a stupid mistake, that's all. Richard is my son. I don't have the slightest doubt about it."

"Of course not, that's what I said."

Although William had always known that Richard was his son, he was still beset by a guilty conscience because it was not long ago that he had suspected Marguerite of being Robert's lover. He knew, from his own painful experience, how jealousy could gnaw at one's heart, and how destructive the terrible feeling of being betrayed could be. Hatred, envy, and resentment consumed their victims from within, making them pitiable and weak, just as the perpetual desire for revenge blinded its victims to the beauty of life.

ෆ෧ා

Odon rubbed his hands with satisfaction. The first part of his plan had been set in motion. He had got the young queen so worked up that she had sworn revenge. So now he could concentrate on the second part.

"Follow me," he murmured to the young maid, waving to her.

"Right now?" she asked, blushing as she put her hand under her bonnet to push back a stray hair. Her hands were red and chapped from her work. Everything about her was ordinary. That was why she was perfect for his purpose. Her complexion was doughy, her nose a little too wide, her lips narrow, and her eyes too close together. She was indistinguishable from any other girl, except for one thing: she was desperately in love with Odon and determined to do anything for him.

Most maids did not get their hopes up when a knight took them to bed. It was a simple give-and-take, nothing more. A little affection and relief in exchange for a warm, soft bed and a hearty meal. But this girl had fallen for Odon. He had seen it in her eyes long before he'd bedded her for the first time.

Odon did not look for beauty—his wife had that in abundance. He sought admiration and complete submission. A girl like this would want to come back, not for the warm fur blankets on his bed, but for him. Odon had known immediately that he could exploit her devotion to carry out his plan.

"They'll beat me if I'm caught," she breathed.

Odon knew what she liked, so he held her neck and whispered in her ear, "I need you." He felt her shiver as her resistance melted away. Not the way you think, he thought arrogantly, but for something that will cost you your head if you're caught. He grinned enticingly, took her by the hand, and pulled her away.

In a dark corner where no one could see them, he took her in his arms and kissed her until he could feel her knees trembling.

"You have to do something for me," he said. "It's very important."

The maid, whose name he could not even remember even though she had told him twice, groaned softly as he began to squeeze her breasts.

He interspersed his whispered instructions every now and then with tiny kisses on the spot he knew made her particularly amenable.

"But—" she protested.

"I thought you loved me," he said reproachfully, making as if to push her arms away from him.

"Oh, I do, I do," she exclaimed heatedly. "I'll do it, exactly as you say."

Odon pressed her to him, grinning triumphantly over her shoulder.

☙❧

"Your Majesty, may I speak with you in private for a moment?" William bowed. During the banquet he had decided to go to the king in Marguerite's place, in order to clear up this unpleasant matter once and for all. It had not escaped him that John kept glancing resentfully at Isabelle and had finally flown into a rage because she, for her part, had completely ignored him.

"Not now," snarled the king. He was standing with his back to William and staring into the fire that bathed his room in a soft light.

"Please, sire. It's extremely important."

"Important," said John contemptuously. "Important for whom? For me, for England, or for you?" He turned and looked at William with his deep black eyes.

"For you, for England, and to a certain extent for me," William admitted.

"I thought so," John growled. "Make haste, or I'll change my mind."

William had carefully prepared what he should say to the king, but suddenly it was all gone. He cleared his throat.

"Well?"

"Would you like to know why the queen is angry with you?"

"What do you know about it? Come on, out with it."

William cleared his throat again. "Your lady thinks you are the father of my son." He bowed his head humbly.

"She thinks *what*? I'm Richard's father? Who put such nonsense in her head? Marguerite was my ward, nothing more. I've never touched her!"

"Well, it seems you and little Richard have something in common. Your lady saw it and drew the conclusion that you must be the boy's father."

"But you don't believe that, do you?" The king looked questioningly at William.

"No, sire."

"Why not? Because you love your lady? Because I said I'd never touched her?"

"That, too, but there's another reason."

The king nodded encouragingly.

"Marguerite has the same feature as Richard and, apparently, you."

The king went pale suddenly. "What do you know, exactly?"

William flushed. "Not much, I must admit. I only know that the queen thinks my son is yours because his bottom is a little crooked, instead of being divided into two equal halves." Marguerite had been right. What he was doing was unthinkable. Accusing the king of having a crooked backside. It would not be surprising if John had him tarred and feathered.

While William was still thinking about what John might do to him because of his effrontery, the king began to laugh. Quietly at first, then louder and louder. "You know what this means, don't you?"

"I think so, sire."

"Alix de Hauville was my first love," said the king, sighing nostalgically. "She never admitted that Marguerite was my daughter, but she must have known." He shook his head pensively, then smiled roguishly. "Well, if that's the way things are, I hope my sweet Isabelle will grant me a place in her bed again when I tell her Richard isn't my son but my grandson, and that his mother is my daughter. Since Alix died long ago and can't be a rival anymore, I think the queen will forgive me. Thank you for coming to me, William. You shall come to the feast tonight as usual. It's the last night we celebrate the birth of Christ." The king clapped William on the shoulder. "Go now, and don't say a word to anyone, do you hear me?"

Standing outside the king's door, William found he was almost disappointed. Why had he thought the king would be glad to find out that Marguerite was his daughter? The news seemed to have left him cold. Apparently he was glad to have an explanation for Isabelle and that was all. He had not said a word about Marguerite. Another father whose child meant little to him.

ⓢⓖⓢ

"My lord! Your lady, quickly!" It was Adam, running up to William as he crossed the courtyard on his way from the king. "She's not well!"

"Oh God, please no," cried William, chasing after him immediately.

When he rushed into the tent, the young queen was standing helplessly beside the unconscious Marguerite and looking at her fearfully. "I'm sorry," she stammered. "I didn't mean it." She rushed out of the tent.

"What happened?" William looked at Marguerite's handmaid and carefully raised his beloved.

"The queen was shouting and screaming at her," the frightened girl reported. She was not yet twelve and far too inexperienced to be of any real service to her mistress, but Marguerite had insisted on bringing her into the household because she was the daughter of an important de Hauville. "And then my lady fell into a faint. I tried to catch her, but it was too late. I'm sorry, my lord." She burst into tears.

"It's all right," said William to calm the girl down. He carried Marguerite to her bed. "Bring me some water and a towel," he ordered, and the handmaid ran off to get what he needed.

William sat down on the bed beside Marguerite. When the terrified girl brought him the water, he nodded, dipped the towel in it, wrung it out, and dabbed Marguerite's face with it. "How are you, dearest?" he asked gently when she came to.

"What happened?"

"Nothing, my dear."

Marguerite sat up. "Yes, it did. The queen, she was so angry." Tears were running down Marguerite's face. William knew they were tears of despair. She simply could not bear injustice.

"What's wrong?" he asked, still worried. "Are you feeling better now?"

"Oh, I feel wonderful! The queen thinks I'm her rival, so she hates me, and all I did was babble." Marguerite closed her eyes and turned her head away. "I'm such a fool."

William stroked her head gently. "It will be all right, my love, I promise you. The king said I shouldn't tell anyone, but I'm sure he didn't mean you."

"You've spoken to him?" Marguerite turned to face him.

"Yes, I told him everything. He's going to talk to Isabelle, and he wants to see us both at the feast tonight. Until then, you need to look after yourself." Turning to the young handmaid, he said, "Go and fetch a midwife. I'd feel better if someone came to see her."

☙❦

Odon had heard why Adam had called William, and he was quietly jubilant. The queen had been in a foul mood when he went to see her that morning, furious and ready to attack, as one might expect of a jealous wife.

He himself had advised her to confront Marguerite, even though he knew this would not help; rather, it would inflame her further. But that was the whole point.

Odon hummed a tune one of the troubadours from Aquitaine had performed many times lately. Had the queen actually attacked her rival? Perhaps there had been a fight, and Marguerite had accidentally fallen? If her labor pains began now, and she lost the child, William would be bound to lose his temper and fall out with the king and queen. Odon looked up to heaven. What a wonderful day!

His plan seemed to have worked in every respect. He was thoroughly pleased with himself. If fate was kind to him for a little longer, he would soon be able to reap the fruits of his labors and see William and his followers thrown out of court.

The truth was that he had never forgotten the affair with William and the slingshot. Odon could still hear his companions' mockery. He'd fallen like a tree, he whom they had all feared until that day. From then on he'd had to fight for respect. Until then,

Robert had never fought back, no matter how much Odon humili-
ated him. To everyone's amusement, he had even burst into tears
occasionally when Odon abused him. Odon had earned the respect
of his companions by means of his bullying. But once William,
who was smaller, younger, and physically inferior, had stood up to
him and encouraged Robert to do the same, his position as leader
of his little band came into question.

Odon snorted angrily. The woman in the forest had been like
William. She herself was to blame for what happened. Why did
she put up a fight? Why did she try to put off the men with her
ghastly song? If she had just kept her mouth shut, nothing would
have happened to her, Odon thought contemptuously. But no, she
had to sing. How foolish to beg him for help, him of all people. As
if he would have risked looking like a coward for her sake.

"You accursed cripple, I'll finish you off," he snarled. He still
had a trump card up his sleeve, and he was going to play that, too,
in order to be sure that nothing else would go wrong.

❧❧

"And tell Emma that Richard shouldn't stay up so late. He's still too
young to sit by the fire and listen to the men's gruesome stories."
Marguerite looked around anxiously. "I don't understand why
they're not back yet. It will be dark soon. You must scold them
if they come in any later." Marguerite smiled at her young handmaid. Emma, the nursemaid, was a reliable person. Richard was in
safe hands with her. So she did not need to worry, and yet she had
an uneasy feeling. She tried to suppress it by twisting and turning.
"Well?"

"You look lovely, my lady." The girl's whole face was beaming.

"I can only second that, fair as a princess," William peeped
into the tent, then came in and kissed Marguerite on the tip of her
nose.

"I feel wonderful, too," she murmured. "Since I heard that the queen wasn't going to be angry with me anymore, I feel on top of the world." She smiled. "The midwife said fainting in my condition is perfectly normal. So you don't need to worry, do you hear?"

"Good, now we can go at last. The king is waiting for us, my lady," said William archly, offering her his arm.

"I'd be honored, my lord."

As they were walking toward the hall, they saw Odon gripping Adam by the arm.

William was about to intervene, but Marguerite held him back. "Leave him alone. He won't do anything to the boy. It's good for him to see that nothing bad is happening to Adam in our house."

"That's the only bad thing about being married to a clever woman—you have to accept that she's always right." He kissed her hand and led her up the stairs to the accommodation tower.

❧❦❧

The boy had not given him so much as a glance. He had even tried to steal past without greeting him. Odon was outraged.

"One moment, young man." He grabbed Adam's arm and held him back. "Perhaps you overlooked your father?" He looked him fiercely in the eye, trying to look menacing, but the boy's expression made him feel unusually gentle.

Adam looked down and shook his head without a word.

"Are they treating you decently?" asked Odon, hoping to break the ice between them. "If you don't want to stay with them—"

"I do." Adam immediately lifted his head.

Odon did not want to show his disappointment. He patted his son's shoulder. But the boy shrank back, as if his touch was unwelcome.

"Why?" asked Adam, almost inaudibly, looking down again.

"Why what?" Odon barked.

"Why did you let it happen?"

"It's not my fault. You said yourself that I had no choice. Your fine young lord was going to kill me if I didn't let you go with him."

"I meant the woman and the child. Why did you let them be killed?"

"Come, come, you're not going to cry about that, are you?" Odon rebuked him. "You're my son, and you must behave as such."

"But I don't want to be your son anymore," he cried petulantly. He tore loose and ran off.

Baffled, Odon watched him go. "You'll pay for this, William. Setting my own son against me." He turned and strode off toward the tower to fetch the queen from her room and lead her down to the hall.

As usual, most of the guests had already gathered there, having taken their places on benches at the tables. The hall was filled with whispered conversations and laughter. The king had arranged for jugglers, minstrels, and pipers to entertain his guests with jokes and comic songs.

Odon frowned when he saw John approach his wife, greet her with a warm smile, offer her his hand, and lead her to her place. They looked more in love than ever. An uneasy feeling crept over Odon. What could have happened? Odon tried to keep a cool head. Queen Isabelle had probably prevailed in the end, ensuring that the king would banish Marguerite and William from the court. He studied the crowd of people in the hall and noted with satisfaction that neither of them were to be seen. And Robert was not sitting on one of the benches either.

None of them suspected that Odon had another unpleasant surprise in store for them. When the suspicion for this particular piece of villainy fell on Robert, he would get his just deserts at last—and so would William—and Odon hoped it would finally cost him his neck. Odon's whole body roared and throbbed with ecstasy. Although it was still rather cold in the hall, he felt more comfortable than he had felt in a long time.

"May I hand you over to your page and sit down?" he asked the queen as he pushed her chair in toward the table. He bowed when she indicated that he could leave her.

Odon's place at the royal table had been at the same level as William and Marguerite's lately, with the result that he was always sitting opposite them. This time, though, it was some other baron, a *real* one, that was sitting down there. Odon grinned at him broadly, raised his cup, and drank to his health. This was going to be a truly enjoyable evening.

What a pity he hadn't brought Maud. Her beauty would have been on everyone's lips, and countless men would have envied him. Odon took a swig of wine. It ran down his throat easily. Perhaps it was better that he hadn't brought Maud, after all, he reflected. If the king had once lusted after Marguerite, how his heart would have been inflamed by the much fairer Maud! No, her presence would just have made things difficult.

He turned contentedly to the page standing behind him and had his cup refilled. In the future he would make sure the king did not meet Maud. Just in case.

Now that William no longer seemed to enjoy the king's favor and represented no danger, he would get Adam back and train him to be a proper knight. Perhaps he would ask Marshal. Odon nodded with satisfaction when a large platter of carved meat was placed before the king, and his page set about finding a choice piece for his master. It couldn't be long before he received something he could get his teeth into. His stomach was already growling.

He watched tensely as the king and queen were served. He saw them whisper to each other, and then the king raised his hand. The hubbub in the hall immediately went down a notch. The few who had not noticed that John was going to say something were called to order by their neighbors, and after a few moments there was not a whisper or a rustle to be heard. Odon leaned forward a little, the better to hear the king.

☙❧

"Come, Richard, we need to go. It will be dark soon." Emma reached out her hand to drag the boy away.

"No," he protested throatily, and when he saw the nursemaid's stern look he went on, a little more tamely. "Please."

Batting his eyes had already had the desired effect twice that day, but this time Emma was firm. "No, Richard, we have to go. Your mother is already going to be displeased that we've stayed out this late." She beat the dust off Richard's smock and smiled cheerfully. "We can come back tomorrow."

"Promise?" the child asked, tilting his head to one side. He had spent half the afternoon playing by the brook, throwing leaves into the water and watching them be swept away. He had clapped with pleasure when Emma had skipped flat stones over the surface of the water, and finally he had started scratching at the hard earth by the bank with a twig.

"Yes, I promise, Richard, but now we must make haste. Come."

The little boy reached up and trustingly slipped his hand into hers. But after only a few steps he tore loose, full of high spirits, and ran on ahead as fast as his little legs would carry him.

Emma followed him quickly enough, never letting him get more than two or three steps ahead of her. It was not far from here to the tents. There was just a narrow band of fields between the tent site and the sparse woodland from which they would soon emerge.

Suddenly, a young maid was standing on the path in front of them, as if she had sprung out of the earth. She spread her arms and called out, "Come, I'll catch you and make you fly like a bird!"

"Come here, Richard!" Emma said loudly. She did not know this maid. "Richard," she said again, this time a little more firmly, but the boy was already throwing himself into the strange girl's arms with a joyous laugh.

Emma was by his side immediately. "We have to go!" she told him firmly, trying to get hold of the boy.

"Don't touch him," the stranger hissed softly but threateningly. "His father wants me to take him with me. He loves me, you see. So let us pass." She tried to push past Emma, but Emma did not make it easy for her.

Richard had become like a son to her. She had spent night and day with him since he was only a few days old. Who did this shameless person think she was? Claiming his father had sent her? Sir William would never have given orders to someone like her to take the child anywhere! Determined, Emma pulled the boy away from the maid, but the stranger would not let go. She clung firmly to Richard's little legs, and he started to cry.

"It's your fault he's howling," the maid complained. She let go of the boy's legs, grabbed Emma's hair instead, and pulled hard.

The nursemaid set Richard on her right hip and tried to free herself with her left hand. She managed to tear herself away and run toward the edge of the forest.

When she glanced back hurriedly to see whether the maid was following, she had disappeared. Just as unexpectedly as she had appeared.

But Emma went on running as fast as she could. The field was not far now.

Suddenly her breast was burning, or was it her shoulder?

"You're not taking the boy away from me again," the maid murmured in her ear.

Emma's neck was icy-cold; she felt sick, and everything began to spin around her. With all her remaining strength, she tried to clasp the child to her. Richard screamed and struggled. Then everything went black.

❦

"Friends, vassals, allies," the king said solemnly, setting the feast in motion with his jewel-encrusted golden goblet raised high. "As you know, we have been gathered here for several days to celebrate the birth of our Lord Jesus Christ—until tomorrow, which is Epiphany."

Approving murmurs could be heard.

"But there is another happy event we should be celebrating."

Jesus, the queen is with child, thought Odon in surprise, looking at her curiously. So that was what she had been telling her husband. Perhaps William would appear at court again, after all.

"You all know that I have one married daughter already, for you all know Joan. Today, though, I found out that I am the father of another child."

An excited whisper ran across the room.

Odon looked up in astonishment. So it wasn't the queen! It must be about Richard. It couldn't be anyone else. Obviously, the queen had directly accused her husband and demanded that Marguerite and William no longer sit and dine at the royal table. Odon stroked his chest with satisfaction and raised his cup. Everything was going according to plan.

The king raised his hand again for silence. "I would like to present my daughter and her husband."

Odon gulped. His daughter?

The king waved, and Marguerite, followed by William, approached him through a side door near the royal table.

"Alix de Hauville, my daughter's mother, was a beautiful and clever woman. And since she was also a loving wife with a generous heart, she did not reveal to her childless husband that it was I, not he, who was the father of her daughter. She even kept it secret from me. Therefore, I embrace Marguerite, whom I used to consider my ward, for the first time as my daughter." He pressed her to him and kissed her on the forehead.

"How can you be sure you're not being tricked, sire?" Odon said, jumping out of his seat, swaying slightly. Wine on an empty stomach did him no favors.

The king frowned, then smiled roguishly. "Well, my dear Odon of Elmswick, let us put it this way. My body has a feature that only a few of my playmates and my wet nurse know about." The king laughed loudly and looked fondly at Marguerite. "Since Marguerite and her son both possess the same charming feature, I don't doubt that she is my daughter and he my grandson."

Odon sank back onto the bench. Little Richard wasn't John's son, but William's. The thought hammered at his brain. He needed more time to take it all in. William wasn't a husband selected by the king for his discarded lover, and he wasn't a cuckold forced to bring up another man's bastard. He was the king's son-in-law. Odon drained another cup of wine, immediately demanded a refill, and drained that in a single gulp, too.

"Well, where is my grandson?" asked John, looking about. "Have him brought to me so that I can show him to everyone."

Odon sighed with relief. Everything would turn out well, after all. He was curious to see how William would explain the child's disappearance. Odon grinned maliciously, took another drink, and stood up again.

"What a pity you found out about your daughter so late and married her off to someone unworthy of her," he said to the king, slurring his words. He ignored the indignant murmur around him. This was William's deathblow.

"I see the wine is doing your talking for you," replied the king sharply. "But you care about me and the welfare of my kingdom, and that honors you, even though you must know that of all my wards, Marguerite was always my favorite. For that reason I did not choose just any husband for her. William's being an outstanding falconer and a faithful subject made the choice easier, but the decisive reason was his excellent ancestry."

"The son of a woman swordsmith," Odon jeered. "Some ancestry, something for Sir William to be really proud of." A few men were laughing with Odon. "I'm sure you could have picked a better son-in-law."

"Well, my dear Lord Elmswick, even if the mare is quite ordinary, an extraordinary stallion can be the beginning of an outstanding breed. And it's not only true for horses. William is the son of our dear friend and faithful counselor William Marshal," the king announced, nodding at Marshal with a smile.

This was greeted with murmurs of astonishment.

Odon saw Marshal turn pale. He obviously had not known that the king was aware of his paternity. Odon snorted. Good God, that, too? Wasn't it bad enough that William was the king's son-in-law? Did he have to have the mightiest baron in the land for his father, too? Odon wiped his forehead: sweat was pouring down his temples. Why did William, of all people, have to have so much luck?

"Come, my child, sit down at my table, with your husband, in the place that belongs to you." The king indicated the seat next to him. Marshal, who had been sitting there, immediately shifted two places farther over. The men beside him left the top table without complaint and took their places. For them all to sit down, it was necessary for everyone on this side to shift over, including Odon, who now found himself farther from the king than before, thanks to William.

Odon's chin quivered with rage.

When Robert was offered a place quite close to Odon, but higher up the table, and sat down with a mocking glance, Odon tasted bitter gall in his mouth.

Ever since he had been at court, he had been trying to attract Marshal's attention and win his respect. He was the bravest and most famous knight in the land. He had served four kings. He was old and dignified but still an excellent warrior, a man who oozed physical power. In short, he was someone who was universally admired. If the fourth son of a more or less insignificant baron had been able to climb so high, shouldn't it be possible for Odon, the only issue of the Elmswicks? Over the last few years, Odon had talked himself into believing that he could go as far as Marshal, even though he had never been successful in jousting.

Odon reached out a trembling hand for his wine cup, grabbed it, and knocked it over. The red grape liquor flowed across the table and dripped onto the surcoat of the man sitting opposite.

"For God's sake, Elmswick, can't you look what you're doing? If wine fuddles your brain, maybe you should hold back."

"Go to hell!" said Odon indistinctly. He snapped his fingers and told a page to right his cup and refill it.

"And now, let us have a toast to my beautiful daughter, my splendid son-in-law, and my delightful grandson," John's voice rang out. And then, impatiently, "Why isn't he here?" He looked around irritably, then nodded to the lutenists and pipers. "What are you waiting for? Start playing!"

❧❧

"I wonder how the king knows," Marshal murmured in William's ear. "Did you…?"

"No, I didn't."

"Your mother wanted me to keep it a secret, and I honored her wish. Apart from Baudouin and, just today, you, no one knew—at least I thought so, and I'd put my hand in the fire for Baudouin. He doesn't particularly admire John."

William risked a brief glance at Marshal's face. He looked genuinely distressed.

"Before my wedding, the king told me I was entitled to this match because I was the bastard son of a knight, but he didn't mention any names," William whispered. "I have no idea how he knew. I've heard he has spies everywhere." Adam, who was standing behind him, placed a piece of roast meat on his trencher.

William nodded his thanks, smiling to himself when he heard one of the other pages whisper, "You should have picked out a better piece of meat for your master. If he's as strict as mine, he'll beat you black and blue later for not serving him well."

"He isn't," Adam told him, his voice resonant with conviction. "He's a good man, and the best master anyone could ask for." He bowed to William. "Forgive me, my lord. I swear I'll do better in the future."

William simply nodded. It was good that Adam was amenable to words of criticism, because in fact he had no intention of chastising his pages, as most masters did. Logan had never struck the boys and had still managed to make them industrious hard workers. The falconer had been exceptionally strict, sometimes even unfair, but never violent.

"You must also make sure I get enough wine to drink," he reminded Adam, who immediately filled William's silver goblet.

"I will learn, my lord."

"First, though, learn to keep silent at the table," William said gently but with enough severity that not a single word passed Adam's lips for the rest of the feast.

William went on eating, nodding at a baron here and there and feeling their curious looks like needles. They kept putting their heads together, whispering and laughing. He suspected they were looking for similarities, perhaps even differences, between him and Marshal, and working out how they could use this new state of affairs to their advantage. One or two glanced disdainfully at Odon, for he had behaved not only badly but also foolishly, and he could hardly expect further signs of favor from the king.

The longer it took for the king's page to return, the more worried William became. "Why isn't Richard here yet?" he whispered to Marguerite. The lines over her eyes told him she was also concerned.

"Shall I go and look for him?" whispered Adam without being asked. "Perhaps they woke him up and he started screaming."

William should have reprimanded him for his impertinence, but at that moment he was grateful for the boy's suggestion. "Ask Robert to go with you. I think it's more likely that Richard got away from the nursemaid and is wandering around among the tents. She probably can't find him. It wouldn't be the first time." William sighed and reassured Marguerite, who was looking at him anxiously. "We'll stay at the table until Robert and Adam come back with our little fugitive. There's no need for the king to worry about his grandson."

He looked over at Odon and noticed how pleased with himself he seemed. It did not seem like him to accept the recent announcement with such equanimity. It must be a source of great resentment that William and Marguerite were part of the king's family now. Why was he grinning?

ↁⱺↁ

Robert and Adam found the king's page in the courtyard.

"I can't find him anywhere, and the handmaid won't stop howling," he said tensely.

"Stay out of the king's way for a while yet. We'll find him," Robert reassured the boy.

Once at the tent, he asked where Richard might be. "Emma wanted to take him to the little patch of forest over there beyond the field," said the young handmaid, sobbing. "The forest isn't big enough to be dangerous, that's what Emma said, but I'm worried even so. She was going to be back before it got dark." She used a corner of her apron to wipe her eyes. "Perhaps I should have told Sir William a long time ago, but I thought they would be back any moment."

"Maybe something happened to them." Adam looked genuinely worried about little Richard.

Robert ruffled his hair. "We'll set off on horseback and see what we find."

Adam nodded vigorously. "Maybe Emma's hurt, or even Richard."

"God save us, don't say such things or they might come true." Robert seized two horses and a pair of flaming torches and asked one of the hunt assistants to join them. He set Adam in front of him and told him to be quiet and keep a good lookout. No one could say what dangers lurked in the forest. "So keep your eyes peeled and your ears open, even if it's pitch-dark and you're a bit afraid."

"I'm not afraid of the dark."

"Good." Robert smiled, patting him on the back.

They crossed the field and entered the heart of the forest. The only sounds that broke the night's silence were the muted thumping of their horses' hooves and a single hoot from a screech owl.

"Shouldn't we call out for them? If they've lost their way or are hurt, we'll never find them otherwise," suggested Adam.

"No," said Robert. "I can't believe they lost their way. Emma is reliable and would never put Richard in danger. They've been attacked. I'd wager my life on it, and if I'm right, we need the element of surprise."

"There, did you hear that?" Adam whispered, but the darkness seemed to swallow his voice.

"Silence," said Robert angrily, tugging his reins and listening. "It's nothing."

"Yes, I'm quite sure I heard something. There, in that bush."
Adam slipped down off the horse.

"Wait for me. You won't see anything without a torch."

Suddenly, Robert heard the groaning, too. "I'm coming!" he
called out softly, waving the torch about and listening. He could
see a branch moving. "Come, over here," he said to Adam and the
assistant.

They found the nursemaid in the undergrowth.

"Emma." Robert helped her sit up. "Emma, where's Richard?"

"I'm sorry," she groaned. "I tried to protect him."

"She's bleeding." Adam's eyes were wide with shock. "Someone
must have stabbed her."

Robert looked at the hand he had used to support Emma. It
was covered with blood.

"Don't worry about me," insisted Emma, tears running down
her face. "You must find my little Richard. She took him away.
You must get him back, you hear? She claimed Richard's father
had sent her, but I knew she was lying. Someone like her...I think
they went deeper into the forest. Richard, my Richard, get him
back!"

Robert spent a moment thinking what he should do. He could
not take the nursemaid with him, but it was too dangerous to leave
her alone in the forest. Adam was too young to care for her. He
would not be able to protect himself or the injured girl against a
wild animal. So Robert told the hunt assistant to take Emma back
to the tent, where she could be cared for, and then come back with
reinforcements. In the meantime, he and Adam would continue
the search.

Because the night was so dark, their progress was slow. Robert
waved the torch from side to side in order to see, and they strayed
off the path.

Suddenly, he stopped. "That looks like a hut over there, doesn't it?"

"It could be the old hunting lodge. One of the king's hunt assistants told me about it. Some of the knights use it for trysts," Adam said, sounding older than his years. "I heard my father has been here, too."

Robert looked at him in surprise. "We'll look and see whether she's hiding here with Richard, but be quiet. They may not be alone." He put his finger to his lips and they dismounted. Cautiously, they crept up to the hut.

"Maybe we can surprise them in their sleep," Adam whispered. "Everything seems dark."

Knightly blood flows in his veins, thought Robert, with a certain amount of disapproval. Sometimes he was unable to forget that Adam was Odon's son. But Adam is a good lad, not like his father, he corrected himself.

"We'll try going in. I have my hunting knife, and I know how to handle it, but you're unarmed. We need to think this through." Robert thought for a moment. "I'll take the torch. If you can, try to take Richard. I'll deal with the woman. Let's hope she's alone. As soon as you've got Richard, run out. Hide, but don't go far."

Robert tested the door quietly, to see if it would open. It was unlocked and opened with a creak. Cautiously, they stepped into the hut.

The torch illuminated the interior with an unsteady light, throwing long flickering shadows across the wooden walls. The maid was asleep and had not stirred. Richard was sleeping, too, his breathing regular.

Robert was relieved to see that nothing had happened to the boy. William would not have been able to bear losing this son, too. There was no one else in the hut, so they should be able to manage.

On Robert's signal, Adam crept over to the maid's bed. She was lying in such a way that he could not reach Richard, so Robert had to wake her.

"Hey, you there," he thundered, frightening himself as the sheer loudness of his words shattered the silence. "Who are you, and what are you doing here?" He held the torch in front of her face in such a way that she could not recognize him, and he dragged her out of the bed.

"Be quiet," she hissed reproachfully. "You'll wake my child."

Adam picked up the sleeping Richard, and the maid noticed, grabbed the child's leg, and refused to let go. The commotion caused Richard to wake up, and he started screaming. He struggled fiercely, trying to get loose. "Obert," he cried, reaching out his arms as soon as he recognized the familiar face.

"Adam, hold him tight," warned Robert, trying to scare the woman by moving the torch close to her face. But she still would not let go of Richard.

The child was kicking and squirming more and more violently, and he scratched at her face until she let go.

"You little devil," she screamed at Richard, making to slap him, but she never managed it.

Robert punched her in the face, giving Adam the chance to run outside with Richard.

The maid staggered, holding her nose and wailing. "I'll tell him you hit me," she whined, crouching in a corner and weeping.

Robert removed the leather strap he wore on his left wrist and used it to tie her up.

"Who will you tell? Who told you to seize the child? What's his name? Tell me!"

The maid did not reply.

꘎꘎꘎

While the table was being cleared, the mightiest barons in the land, friends and confidants of Marshal, came to them. They greeted William and Marguerite more warmly than before, clapped Marshal jovially on the shoulder, and congratulated him on his son's excellent match—and on his grandson, who would bind him even more closely to the king.

"Don't you want to introduce the boy to everyone?" Odon chipped in, his words slurred. "Where is the boy? I want to pay him my respects."

On the other side of the hall, one of the hunt assistants ran in and gave William a sign.

"What's happening? Where's my grandson?" the king asked angrily.

"I've sent Robert out to look for him, sire. He's probably run off again, the little adventurer. Excuse me a moment." William signaled to the assistant to come over.

"Richard's nursemaid has been stabbed, and the boy has been taken away," the assistant whispered agitatedly, loud enough for the men around William to hear. "Robert told me to ride straight back to the forest. But I thought it better to inform you first so you could get some extra men ready," he stammered, noticing that the king was staring at him.

William was about to rush off, but John held him back. He gave a sign, and several knights surrounded him. Even before the king could give his instructions, Robert and Adam came into the hall. They were not alone.

"Richard!" Marguerite rushed to Adam and took her son from the boy. "Is he all right?" she asked anxiously, kissing and hugging the child. She looked her son in the eye and checked his body.

Robert held the maid.

Odon stood motionless beside the other barons, pale and silent.

"This woman stabbed Emma and took the boy into the forest," Robert told William, bowing to the king. "Get down on your knees in front of the king," he ordered, shoving the maid to the ground.

"Why did you do that?" asked the king with seeming calm. Only the swollen vein in his neck showed his anger.

"His father told me to. My own true beloved," she replied, smiling confidently.

"William!" The king turned to his newfound son-in-law and looked at him angrily. "Why did you do that?"

The king's knights formed a circle around William.

"I did nothing of the sort," he stammered in astonishment. "I've never seen this woman in my life."

Marguerite looked at him skeptically.

Out of the corner of his eye, William noticed Odon grinning with glee.

"Not him," said the maid, waving her hand grandly. "He's not the boy's father, and he's certainly not my beloved."

"So who is?" asked the king severely.

"Another lord, a better-looking one." She looked at William disdainfully.

"And does this lord have a name?"

Odon was almost invisible behind the other barons.

The maid shrugged her shoulders and looked at the floor.

A child's voice suddenly rose from the throng. "Excuse me, sire."

"And who are you?" John asked.

"My name is Adam, sire, Adam of Caldecote. I'm one of Lord Elmswick's sons."

"I see, *one* of his sons." The king seemed to understand perfectly. "What do you want, Adam?"

"I promised never to be a coward, sire." Adam looked at the ground, fidgeting, and then looked up. "So I'll tell you what I know."

William saw tears in the boy's eyes. Adam had promised *him* never to be a coward, and suddenly he felt sorry for the brave little fellow. Whatever he was going to confess—he seemed to find it hard.

"I've seen my father with her," Adam announced with a sob, his voice constricted. "*He's* her beloved."

"Elmswick!" roared the king, and an angry murmur ran through the crowd. After a moment or two, Odon stepped forward.

"Is this your lord?" John asked the maid, pointing at Odon. "Look carefully before you speak."

She did not look up. "I mustn't say anything. He'll hurt me," she whispered.

"If you don't want to be tortured, you'll look at him and tell me whether he's the man," the king demanded.

The maid looked up and nodded. "He told me I should raise the child. That I was better for him than her," she said, pointing at Marguerite. "He knows what's good for the boy, since he's his father."

"Your ignorance will cost you your life," roared the king. "Odon isn't his father, but I am his grandfather!" He turned away. "Lock her up. She'll hang for this." Then he approached Odon with a menacing air. "Whereas you, Elmswick, are not ignorant but underhanded. For someone like you, death at the end of a rope is far too soft a punishment. Why did you have my grandson seized?"

"I didn't know," Odon claimed desperately. "I just wanted to teach William a lesson. I wouldn't have done anything to the boy. Please believe me, sire!"

The king took a deep breath. He appeared to be exercising all the restraint in the world. "You are of noble birth, and your father was a loyal servant to the crown. Therefore, I believe you when you say you didn't know Richard was my grandson and will show mercy." His words, though mild, still sounded menacing.

Odon did not seem to notice. He relaxed visibly and was obviously relieved.

But William could not believe what he was hearing. Was the king really going to let this traitor get away with it, just because he came from a good family?

"I give you thanks, sire," said Odon, falling down on his knees before the king.

William's nostrils flared. He had to hold back from protesting aloud. Then the king's voice rang out again.

"Your title shall be forfeited, and you shall leave your manor. Should any lord ever grant you safe harbor, he too will lose his lands. Since no blame attaches to your wife, however, I grant her permission to leave you and go back to her father's house, with your children, so that he may take them into his care. No harm will come to him from me."

Everyone heard the king's words. Some of the barons stepped back so as not to stand too close to Odon.

"Without a title or a manor, you are a nobody from now on," King John continued, looking at Odon with contempt. "No baron will employ you, if his title is dear to him, and yet you will have to feed yourself by your own labor. Henceforth, you will spend your days as a day laborer or a beggar. And on the day that news of your death reaches me, I shall arrange a feast in celebration, to thank God." John bowed slightly. "Now get out of my sight!"

William cleared his throat with relief, and when Marshal cleared his throat, too, one of the lords said, with a laugh, "Like father, like son" and ordered his page to give both men something to drink.

William looked at his father with interest. Did they have something else in common? A bodily feature, perhaps, like the one that linked Marguerite, Richard, and John?

"My lords, please forgive me if I withdraw with my son," Marguerite said apologetically, gesturing modestly to point out her condition and the exhausted child on her arm. She curtsied in front of John and nodded at the lords with a friendly smile, then gathered herself to leave.

"Allow me to excuse myself, too," said William hurriedly. He sensed that Marguerite was angry, and he wondered why. Had she not understood that he had nothing to do with the taking of Richard? He bowed deeply to the king, searching his face for permission to leave.

John nodded graciously, and William hurried after Marguerite. He stroked his son's back affectionately and then held out his arms to take the child from Marguerite, for he was far too heavy for her.

William waved to Adam to come over, and Robert came, too. He handed William a torch and took one himself. Then he went ahead with Adam.

Marguerite did not say a word on the way to the tent. It was not until they had drawn the curtain over the entrance to the tent, and Richard had joyfully said "Emma," that she turned furiously on William, eyes blazing. He put down the boy next to the bed where the nursemaid was resting.

"Comfort Emma, so she gets well quickly," she said softly, smiling. The boy cuddled up to the nursemaid, stuck his thumb in his mouth, and fell asleep almost immediately. She went up to William and rebuked him in an angry whisper. "What happened today is simply too much. Odon arranges for our son to be taken from us, and you, you lie to me!"

"But I—"

"Don't try to talk your way out of it," she interrupted, snorting with fury.

"I'm not," said William, provoked. "I don't even know what you're talking about."

"So you don't know what I'm talking about." Marguerite fought for breath; her voice was close to cracking. "I mean the news of your origins. Why did I have to find out from the king instead of you? I kept you informed about the situation with my uncle right from the start. But you? You didn't look as if this evening was the first you heard about being Marshal's son. Or am I wrong?"

"No, I—"

"I thought so. It's humiliating that I'm the last one to know. What other lies have you told me? Did Odon have other reasons to take Richard from us?"

"No, believe me! I've never lied to you," William protested indignantly. "I didn't know myself until—"

"Not saying anything is just as reprehensible as saying something false. You told me Isaac was your father."

"For God's sake, let me speak," William shouted, immediately regretting his loss of temper.

Marguerite's jaw dropped. She looked at him in disbelief.

"I only found out myself some days ago. I always knew that Isaac was my stepfather but until recently all I knew about my father was that I owed my existence to a knight. My mother wouldn't tell me more, and when Isaac died I couldn't bring myself to ask her the truth. I knew it would upset her. So Isaac was my father until Marshal confided in me."

"I still don't understand why you didn't tell me. Where was your trust? Why did you keep it secret from me?"

"I don't know." William shrugged and looked miserably at Marguerite. "You were so preoccupied with Isabelle's accusations, and I was ashamed and hurt. Marshal had known for a long time that he was my father. So many questions bothered me. Why did he keep it secret from me for so long? Was I a matter of complete indifference to him? Why didn't he ever try to see me? But I was tremendously proud to be the son of the most famous knight in the land, and I had to get things clear in my own mind. You know that I've always admired him. When I was a boy, I dreamed that my real father would come and get me. But he let me down. He told me it was what my mother wanted, and he had no choice. I needed to think it over."

"And?" Marguerite asked sharply.

"His being my father has brought me nothing but good, for without it I would never have got you." William attempted a winning smile and stepped closer to her. But Marguerite's eyebrows were still furrowed with fury. In truth, her anger had nothing to do with him. It was from the fear of losing her son, a fear that still sat deep in her bones, and he knew it all too well.

He took her in his arms and kissed her. "Richard is fine," he whispered reassuringly in her ear. "Odon will never be able to harm us again."

Before they went to bed, William went to see Robert to thank him. "I can rely on you. I never should have doubted it." He embraced him. "I need you, not just as a falconer, but above all as a friend."

"You can always count on me, Will, you know that."

William nodded, then turned his attention to Adam, who was sitting by the fire not far away and immediately jumped up.

"You're a good boy, and today you proved to me that you meant it when you promised never to be a coward. I'm very proud of you."

"Even if it's my fault that my father has to live in poverty now?" "It's his fault, Adam, not yours. *He* did all these terrible things, and now he's being punished for them. *You* were concerned with justice. Perhaps he'll think things over and become a better person, so that at least he doesn't end up burning in hell."

"You're bound to send me away now," Adam whispered, close to tears.

"Why would I do that?"

"My father isn't a lord anymore," said Adam in a small voice.

"You're a good page, and you'll be a fine, loyal squire." He patted Adam's shoulder kindly. "Go to sleep now, and don't worry."

"Thank you, my lord."

"Thank *you*, Adam."

"Our son is a brave boy, just like his father and grandfather," Marguerite remarked when William joined her in bed. It was her way of saying she was no longer angry with him.

"I love you," he murmured, kissing her.

"I'm homesick for Roford," she confessed quietly, passionately returning his kiss.

And a Few Closing Remarks...

Over the years, I have carefully, and with great enjoyment, researched the historical facts of this period, but turning real events and hearsay into interesting stories is a fascinating challenge. I hope I have succeeded in ensnaring you, the reader, with my novel, for that would be the greatest reward. If you are wondering which of the events I have described are fiction and which history, perhaps the following notes will make things clearer, though of course they cannot include every historical detail.

De arti venandi cum avibus (On the Art of Hunting with Birds) is the definitive reference book on falconry in the Middle Ages. It was written around 1250 by Friedrich II, Holy Roman Emperor of the German Nation. Because of this work, Friedrich is thought to be the man who introduced the hood to Europe.

William, and his pioneering use of the hood in medieval England, is therefore definitely imaginary. Nonetheless, Friedrich was probably not the only hawking enthusiast to learn about and adopt hoods during the Crusades. Records show that Richard the Lionheart indulged his passion for falconry in the East and observed Arab falconers and their birds with delight.

The kind of rise William experiences in the novel was certainly not the norm, but it was absolutely possible. At least one of King John's falconers is known to have risen to the position of royal falconer without any family connections (see Robin S. Oggins, *The Kings and Their Hawks* [New Haven, CT: Yale University Press, 2004], 44).

Marguerite and her parents are imaginary characters, too. One could call them cuckoos in the nest, for the de Hauvilles actually were one of the greatest and most successful falconing families of the twelfth and thirteenth centuries. And it should be noted that a marriage was a common and completely accepted way for the king to reward good service. This applied to falconers just as much as to knights.

Like his ancestors and descendants, John was an avowed hawking enthusiast who owned a large number of birds. Some were presented to him as gifts or in support of requests for favors, some he bought himself, and others were acquired by his falconers. In fact, in the year 1205, it was decreed that any falcon entering an English port had to be inspected by Henry and Hugh de Hauville before they could be sold elsewhere. The king's falconries were spread throughout the country, so he could hunt at any time, wherever he found himself, without having to carry his falcons on his constant travels.

The hunting scenes from the *Traité de Fauconnerie* (German translation, Dr. Peter N. Klüh, *Schlegel/Verster van Wulverhorst* [Darmstadt: Verlag Peter N. Klüh, 1999]) were the perfect basis for the description of hunting with birds of prey.

The records do not show whether William Marshal (first Earl of Pembroke, also known as Guillaume le Maréchal or the Marshal) had any love affairs before his marriage, and they do not give any indication of how many "bastards" he may have fathered. Who knows, perhaps there was a great love in his life, like the one I have created for him with Ellenweore. I am sure of one thing, though: Marshal would have been fond of this far-from-ordinary woman and her charming, obstinate son.

I would like to stress that the book in your hands is a novel and not a history book. Nevertheless, the political and historical background of the time is very important. It is worth remembering that the level of people's knowledge of current affairs depended very much on their social standing. Only the most important news (as well as a great many rumors) spread far enough by word of mouth to reach the common people. For this reason, as in my first novel (*The Copper Sign*), I have described only as much history as the main character would have known. Although a falconer would have had a better view behind the scenes than a swordsmith, William does not know as much as a baron whose family might have served the king for generations.

William Marshal, however, a scion of the lesser nobility and perhaps the most famous knight of his time, served four kings during his breathtaking career and rose to be regent of England. He certainly would have had a quite different insight. Look forward, therefore, to my next novel, for the charismatic Marshal finally comes to the fore as the main character in the third part of the trilogy.

As far as the language of twelfth-century England and Normandy is concerned, it was subject—just as ours is today—to constant change. It was influenced by the Norman French of the aristocracy, by the Latin of the Church, and by the Anglo-Saxon of the common people. New words entered the language from those encountered by knights, servants, and laborers during the Crusades (Arabic, Persian, and so on). I therefore decided to use a readable English, avoiding modern words and expressions, without using a pseudo-medieval language.

William Marshal's wedding did take place in London, as did the attacks on the Jews on the day of Richard's coronation. A contemporary witness, William FitzStephen (*ca.* 1174–83), was my inspiration for the description of the outskirts of London (see Henry Thomas Riley, ed., *Liber custumarum*, Rolls Series, no. 12, vol. 2 [1860], 2–15, London Records Office). Even the glow in the sky is mentioned in some sources. As a rule of thumb, it can be said that events concerning historical figures are more or less backed up by evidence. This does not mean that I have not allowed myself a little poetic license. Henry de Tracey, for example, really was one of the most powerful barons in the southwest of England and is one of the historical figures in the novel, but I invented his daughter Maud, who married the fictitious Odon, and the meeting of the barons at de Tracey's house.

It is the nature of the historical sources that they include gaps and contradictions. Carefully, but with great pleasure, I have evened them out by using my imagination.

On the subject of homosexuality, it is important to note that this word was unknown in the Middle Ages, as was its modern definition in terms of a sexual preference. So-called sodomites were held responsible for all kinds of catastrophes; they were condemned, at least partly, because it was believed their behavior was a passing phase to which they succumbed through sinfulness and obduracy.

Opinions are divided as to whether Richard the Lionheart was homosexual. This may be because of the ambiguous sources of the twelfth century, or perhaps because his time, in which attitudes to homosexuality were much less explicit than they are today, gave rise to many different interpretations.

But as no one knows that for sure and many of Richard's admirers, even today, think the idea is unacceptable, fearing this could affect their hero's image, the question that arises is, Does it really matter whether Richard the Lionheart in fact preferred men or women, or perhaps liked both?

I hope one thing at least: that no one can seriously condemn Robert for his love for William.

Acknowledgments

Many years ago, while I was doing my research, I met Dr. Peter N. Klüh, and he very quickly passed on to me his fascination with falconry. Dr. Klüh is a veterinarian and falconer, but above all he is a publisher of books and magazines about falconry. Though chronically short of time, he nevertheless tackled my texts with painstaking attention to detail and checked them meticulously, for which I am extremely grateful. For his support in the creation of this novel and his suggestions as to how to approach the subject of falconry, I thank him from the bottom of my heart.

I would also like to express my gratitude to the falconer Dieter Koschorrek, who has managed the falconry on the Grosser Feldberg, near Frankfurt, for some forty years. He gave me the opportunity to expand my book knowledge through exposure to the birds themselves. Just holding a falcon on my fist and feeding it was a remarkable experience; the falconer's explanations, and the chance to see the birds from up close, were a source of inspiration.

Prof. Dr. Helga Meise has enriched me, both as a person and as a writer, with marvelous conversations about literature and critical examinations of my novel.

I thank Dr. Michael Schmidt, a Frankfurt orthopedist, for advice on club feet and their treatment, and Mrs. Ulrike Schön for her commitment as a test reader and severe, though always positive, critic.

My agent, Bastian Schlück, deserves particular thanks for always being by my side with friendly and professional advice.

I thank my translator, Aubrey Botsford, and my editors, Gabriella Fort-Page and Buzz Poole, for their constructive collaboration, and the talented illustrator Franz Vohwinkel for the wonderful drawings that decorate this book.

Last but not least, an especially affectionate thank-you to my parents, my children, and my friend Françoise Chateau-Dégât for their understanding and loving support.

About the Author

Photograph © 2011 Ilona Dreve

Born in 1964, Katia Fox grew up in Germany and southern France, and started her career as an interpreter and translator. After the birth of her third child, she turned her attention to the English Middle Ages and started to research blacksmithing. That research inspired *The Copper Sign*, the first installment in her captivating trilogy set in medieval England. She lives with two of her three children, splitting her time between Provence and a small town near Frankfurt. She also visits England as often as possible to continue her research. *The Silver Falcon* is her second novel.

About the Translator

Aubrey Botsford has previously translated novels by Yasmina Khadra and Enrico Remmert. He lives in London.